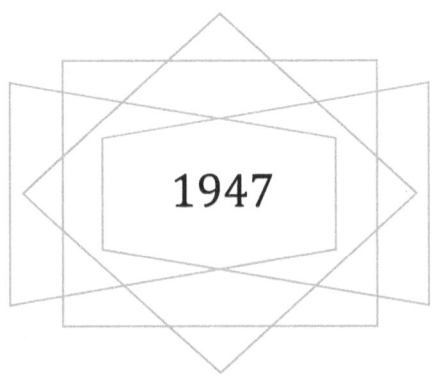

1947

PROLOGUE

The raspy ring of the phone startled Meg from her book. She was a bit annoyed since she was deep into the story, hearing the voices she had invented for the characters, seeing the scenery the author had described so vividly that she could feel the sun warm her skin, smell the grass and flowers that surrounded the characters, even though she was inside her own house, curled up in her favorite chair with an afghan wrapped around her shoulders.

The phone rang a second time and Meg sighed, shut the book with her fingers between the pages saving her spot. She uncurled herself, slipped her shoes back on and walked to the kitchen.

The phone had already rung twice more by the time she took it off the hook.

"Hell...," she was interrupted before she could finish.

"Mom."

She recognized the impatience in his voice. His father had the same tenor when he was nervous and excited at the same time.

"What is it Bruce?"

She knew better than to try to dilly-dally with politeness and pleasantries.

"I found an old file of Dad's on my desk...there are photos of a ...well, not to be gruesome and insensitive, but there are pieces of a body."

Her heart had sunk and bounced up into her throat before he had finished talking. She had to swallow a few times in order to moisten her mouth and throat.

"Mom?"

"I'm still here."

"I was just wondering about...there are two people with the last name of Rubidoux named in the file."

She faltered a little and tried to slow her breathing.

"One was named Sylvestre and the other Judah...Juma...Yuma..."

"Juneau, his name was Juneau."

"That's it, like at the cemetery. So, it's true?"

"We've never spent much time with your father's family."

Skirting around the thing she did not want to answer or know, her son's questions felt as if they were coming at her more rapidly.

"The file says they were suspected of murder."

There it was.

Megan took a deep breath and tried to quietly exhale.

"Mom, is this the same case Daddy was working on that night in the par...Mom, I have to go."

Always in a hurry.

"We'll talk later and Bruce?"

"Yes Mom."

"Be safe."

"I love you."

"I love you too. Bye."

The phone clicked on the other end before she could finish saying good-bye.

Slowly, she placed the phone in its cradle and then tried to set herself down in one of the kitchen chairs, but slumped down instead.

The feeling of where her finger was squeezed in the book was beginning to hurt as deep indentations were showing.

Her mind raced back and forth in time through memories trying to find answers. She stood up, dropped the book on the kitchen table letting her finger slide out from in between the pages and walked to the closet in her bedroom, opened the door, retrieved a step stool and set it down so she could step up.

She felt as though it might as well have been a twenty foot tall ladder.

Blindly, she reached back on the shelf to the corner she couldn't see. Her fingers found the box and pulled it sideways so that she could grab it better.

She took a deep breath and exhaled intimidated...no, afraid of the contents.

Once she grabbed it she stepped down, marched into the kitchen and sat it down. She took a small step back, still within arm's length and lightly ran her hand over the top.

The lid taunted her to lift it, but then she remembered what lay on top.

She had only held that once.

She stared at the box longer, wondering why she had kept everything and realized she didn't know. She had just filled the contents, put the lid on, took it to the closet and shoved it far back into the darkness, like a cancer that had been contained and was now about to metastasize.

A pocket of air was stuck in her throat and she swallowed it as she closed her eyes and let her hand glide off the lid.

She took in another breath and let out a final sigh as she slowly turned and walked out of the kitchen.

TOM
MARCH 1928

1.

AN UNWELCOMED FIND

Sylvestre's head bounced off the passenger window of the Durant. He wrapped his arms around himself when he noticed how cold the inside of the Chevrolet had become. The sound of the engine let him know that the car was just creeping up to the top of Torrey Pines Road. He peered out the window, but it was too dark to see the edge of the bluffs.

Suddenly, his head hit the roof of the car as Juneau drove over another bump. Sylvestre's bladder started to strain. He knew he couldn't last much longer over the bumpy road.

"Pull over," he told his younger brother Juneau.

"You've got to be kidding. We pulled over less than an hour ago."

"It's all the beer I drank."

"That's not my fault."

Sylvestre glared at him.

"Alright, but can you at least wait until we get up to the flats? If we stop now we might end up having to push the car."

Sylvestre nodded and gritted his teeth and kept crossing his legs and grabbing his crotch until the car felt like it had leveled off.

Juneau stopped the car and watched his brother fall out as he opened his door. He hoped that the breeze coming up from the ocean and cliffs might sober him up a bit.

As he took in a deep breath he was thankful it didn't smell like the sweat and dirt he'd smelled all weekend

Juneau was also thankful their mother had insisted he learn how to play the fiddle so he never did participate in the debaucheries to the extent Sylvestre did. Sylvestre picked himself up and dusted himself off. He looked into the car and grinned.

"Oops."

Juneau hoped he wouldn't have to pick his brother up as he heard him fall into the back of the car.

They were returning from a weekend of ranching at their cousin's. Like most San Diego ranches, there was always a large feast at the end of the weekend to share with friends and family. Most of the friends were family through one extension or another. Guests provided the music through pianos, fiddles, basses, guitars and trumpets. All learned through second-hand instruments that made parents cringe when played.

Those that became good enough were given instruments bought at second-hand stores or even stolen. Juneau had been blessed. His mother and father saved up enough money to buy him a new fiddle when he attended enough functions. It was frivolous, but they knew their other seven children would never be as talented.

Juneau started thinking about the feast and all the food. It amazed him, that there could be so much food when they were all so poor. The family hardly ever went into the city, near the waterfront. They had their own homes near the water further up the coast. They just didn't want to associate with "the others", though people in the city were familiar with the ranchero families and were polite to them. It was just more comfortable amongst their kind. A few cousins had ventured and made it in the city, but they were hardly seen or spoken about. It was as if they had vanished.

There had been stacks of homemade tortillas and tubs of salsa. Some which made Juneau's eyes and nose water from the spiciness. Plates of chili rellenos lined one of the tables, followed by beans and Spanish rice. He had already scouted out the ice cream machine and cheered on the kids who were turning the crank. It hadn't been that long ago that he and Sylvetre were turning that crank. He could still remember spooning the leftover ice cream off the wooden spatulas and having the sticky sweet dessert run down his face and arms.

Sometimes he stayed away from the endless pounds of steak that had been grilling over a spit and bar-b-que all day, remembering that these creatures had at one time been his playmates.

The car suddenly rocked, startling Juneau from his dreams. He looked over and saw Sylvestre desperately trying to open the door. He just stared at him, not sure of what had happened. Sylvestre kept pulling frantically on the door handle, until Juneau thought for sure the handle would come off the door. Finally the door gave way, throwing Sylvestre backwards onto the ground. Juneau couldn't see him, but could hear him retching. Sylvestre jumped up, vomit down his front, trying to get into the car. Juneau was trying to keep his distance from the odor, but Sylvestre was trying to grab at his shirt. He put his face right up to Juneau's, the sourness beginning to make Juneau sick himself. He slapped at Sylvestre's arms and finally broke them loose and pushed Sylvestre back. He realized his brother was gibbering, and not in any language he was familiar with.

"Get a hold of yourself," he yelled at Sylvestre who was now out of the car and on the ground again. He swore this would be the last time he would let his brother mix mescal and beer and then drive with him. "Pink elephants," he thought.

"B-b-b-ody," Sylvestre stammered.

Juneau slowly leaned toward him, not sure of what he had just heard.

"A b-body...pieces...girl...cut up...bur... sack...hanging from a tree!"

Tom Rubidoux's eyes felt like sandpaper. He rubbed them and leaned back in his chair and looked at the picture of his wife, leaned forward and picked it up. He knew he was going to be in trouble. He had promised he would be home in an hour seven hours before. Now, the sun was already rising through the valley making the office a hazy grey. He brushed the picture lightly and set it back down then reached the phone. He jiggled the handset a few times until the operator picked up.

"Plymouth 254."

"Just a second, please."

"Thank you."

"Connecting you now."

The phone rang four times before Meg picked up. There was nothing but sleepy breathing on the other end. He thought about what to say, but couldn't come up with anything crafty.

"Hi."

There was nothing at the other end.

"It's me."

"I know who it is. Tell me college boy, didn't they teach you an hour only has 60 minutes in it."

"I missed that day."

"Hmmm."

"I lost track of time."

"Well, if anyone could find it, you can Detective."

"Very funny."

"Tom, you know how you get when you're this exhausted. You can't work like this."

"I know...I just...I told Cory I would finish the reports and I just lost track of time."

"Finishing his reports?"

"Our reports. He had date."

"Corey had a date?"

"Yes, he had a date."

"With whom," she asked, with the "who" drifting off.

"I don't know, some girl."

"Well, I figured that."

There was more breathing as Tom just listened to her.

"It's Corey," she finally continued, "how many dates has he been on since you've known him?"

"I can see why you would ask when you put it that way."

"You didn't ask, did you?"

"No, I didn't," he said smiling.

"You know Detective, for as many cases that you have solved you are horrible when it comes to the personal lives of those who are close to you."

"I would have been a journalist or writer if I wanted to do that," he quipped.

She sighed, "Are you going to make it home?"

"I'm sorry, no...I'm making a lot of progress on this case."

"I'll swing a clean shirt and tie by and some lunch after the kids leave for school."

He could hear her smiling.

"I love you."

"I know you do. You know, you're the only husband who says that. I'll see you in a 240 minute hour."

He smiled as she hung up and then cleared his throat as he heard the operator still listening on the other end.

When she hung up he smirked then hung up the phone and got up from his desk. There were only a few beat officers around he greeted them as he walked to the bedroom to splash some water on his face. He was drying himself when he heard his name.

"Chief Moran is on the line."

"Thanks."

He looped his suspenders back over his shoulders as he walked back to his desk.

"This is Detective Rubidoux."

"Rubidoux," he sounded a bit surprised, "get yourself up the 101 - Torrey Pines Road."

"Sir?"

"There's been a murder. A girl's been chopped to bits and hung in a bag by the road."

"Yes sir."

"Take care of the two witnesses who found her."

"Yes sir."

"Tom,"

"Yes sir"

"I believe the witnesses are your cousins."

The jostling of the car was enough to keep Tom awake. His car wasn't accustomed to the constant bouncing and swaying caused by the poorly paved road. Torrey Pines Road had been a recent addition to road maps and the recently formed 101 highway. There were several other police cars and he pulled up behind them. He stepped out of the car, tried to stretch out his back and then reached back in to grab his jacket. He changed his mind and threw it back. The marine layer was already beginning to burn off and he wanted to make sure his cousins saw his gun and holster. He didn't want them cracking jokes, although, under the circumstances, they probably wouldn't be. At least he was sure about Juneau, it was Sylvestre he wasn't too sure about...until he saw them. Off to the side, on the running board of their car, Juneau and Sylvestre sat. Sylvestre had an obvious stain down the front of his shirt. Tom knew where they had been the night before. He didn't attend many of those family functions anymore even though his sister always called to invite him, hoping for his presence. Juneau saw him as he walked towards the group of officers and kept watching him as he stopped at the group.

"Who's in charge here," Tom asked the group of men.

"I am," one off the officers spoke up. "You are," he said as Tom showed him his badge on his belt.

"No, it's fine. I'll need some information and the use of some of your men and facilities."

He surveyed the scene. There were a couple of men standing over a lump of burlap a few yards away.

"Is that the victim," he said nodding towards the pile of burlap.

"Yes sir."

They walked towards two of the officers.

"They found the body," one of them said pointing towards Juneau and Sylvestre.

"Yes sir. The one with the puke down his shirt was out taking a dump or piss and stumbled into this tree."

They stopped at the burlap sack. Tom knelt down and scanned the area. He looked at the long rope.

"It was hanging from the tree," he said more as a statement than a question. He noticed all the blood pooled at the bottom of the sack and the big pool that the sack was sitting in.

"Yes sir."

Tom took a stick from the ground and pried the opening. He moved around so he could take a look in.

"One of them took the bag down and opened it?"

"Yes sir. The one with the puke..."

"The one with the puke down his front," Tom said cutting the officer off.

"Yes sir."

Sylvestre.

"How do we know he took the bag down and looked inside?"

"He told us."

"Which 'he'?"

"The one with the..."

"...the puke down his front. Thank you, Officer."

Even as kids Sylvestre's curiosity was always getting him in trouble.

Tom looked around and stood back, running his hand through his hair. It didn't stay and flopped back down over his brow. He looked up at the tree and branch. Then he looked around on the ground and back at one of the officers.

"It was a full moon last night?"

"Yes it was sir. Why do you ask?"

"Why would he have taken the bag down and opened it? It wouldn't have been seen if it was dark."

"Maybe he wasn't taking it down. Maybe he was putting it up," another officer speculated.

Tom nodded his head once, agreeing that the probability of that was good, but not so much when Juneau was added in the calculation, which was something he couldn't share with the officers.

"Let's say for right now he was taking it down. He had to be able to see the bag," Tom said, "and if I saw a bag with a big dark stain hanging from a tree, and I was drunk...because I'm assuming he was drunk...my curiosity would have gotten the better of me too."

"I'd say he *was* drunk," the officer who greeted him said. "He smells like he'd had a wild time, but this whole thing sobered him up."

Tom knelt down again and peeled the edges of the bag to take a better look. The bag had hardened a little as the blood had dried.

Tom could hear the buzzing of flies even before the edges cracked as he pulled the bag open.

"If someone could see the bag to pull it down, maybe someone saw something else." The sole of a foot was the first thing Tom saw. He peered around, trying to disturb as little as possible. He heard the officers around him start to wretch.

"If you're going to throw up, do it in the road away from here."

He refocused his attention on the body. The smell of decomposition, more puke, blood and excrement had been contained in the bag but was now releasing like a fog. His eyes started to water and he quickly tried breathing from his mouth, but the odor was so foul that it started to attach itself to his tongue and taste buds. He concentrated even harder because he didn't want the officers see him weaken. Then he saw the head with matted hair and make-up smeared along the side of the face. The eyes were half open. He looked closer and saw what he needed to.

"Her breasts are intact."

"What the hell does that have to do with anything?"

"It means he was trying to hide the body or he cared about her. He...or she...wasn't some sort of sex fiend."

He stood up and took his pen out of his shirt pocket and a small notebook out of his back pocket. He started to write, picked the pen up and looked at the nib. Then he shook the pen and tried writing again, but there was no ink.

"Need a pen sir?"

"Yes, thank you."

He took the officer's pen and wrote his notes. He nodded to the officer taking photos.

"Let's get photos taken...before we ruin everything," he said sarcastically. "Let's start with this," he said opening the bag so the officer could focus the lens on the contents. The officer hesitated.

"Come on," Tom said impatiently.

"I'm sorry Sir; I've just never seen anything like this before."

"Take a deep breath, focus on a small part and click."

The officer did as he was told and took the photo. Tom realized the officer had probably grown up in town and had been too young to have been in the war.

"You have taken photos at a crime scene before though?"

The officer nodded.

"Good," he stood up, "then you know what to do with the rest of the photographs."

The officer nodded again.

"Get the body downtown." He started to walk away. "And the bag of course too."

Sleep deprivation was starting to get to him. He walked towards the two men waiting for him while he kept shaking his pen. The officer started to follow him but stopped when he put his hand out.

"Go help the other officers while I talk to these two."

"Yes sir."

He walked up to them and addressed Juneau first.

"Cousin."

"Tomas."

"Tomas," Sylvestre said in his own stupor.

"I see the family shin dig was a success," He said pointing at Sylvestre's shirt. He looked around his side and could see a bit of the bottom of his pants.

"Jesus Ves, did you sit in it too?"

"It was a rough night."

"Grandma was asking about you...as always," Juneau said innocently, but Tom caught the resentful look Sylvestre gave him.

"Yeah, well, it's hard getting up there."

"Did you know we were here?"

Tom nodded.

"What happened," Tom asked.

"They don't think we did it, do they," Juneau asked.

"No, but why would you ask that?"

"I just...well, you know how they can be," he stammered as his breathing started to speed up.

"I'm not sure what you mean," Tom said honestly.

"You know what he means," Sylvestre snapped accusingly, "or has your Waspy conversion shielded you from your heritage?"

Then Juneau's meaning hit him.

"No, you are considered witnesses," he said, leaving off the 'for now' that he said to himself, but the inference of his tone was caught be Sylvestre and missed by Juneau. It was Juneau he was trying to protect. "I do need you both to tell me everything that happened. I'll start with you Ves. Let's go take a walk."

As his cousins related their story he took notes and asked them if they would go to his station to fill out an official report with a couple of the officers.

"In this shirt? Without anything to eat," Sylvester wanted to know, exasperated.

"Mama will be worried," added Juneau.

"I'll send a couple of the officers back to the house to drop off your car."

"In our car?"

Tom ignored him.

"How are we going to get home," Juneau wanted to know.

"We'll figure something out."

The dust settled back down to the ground after the cars were driven away. Tom watched them go and had been so wrapped up in his mind that he didn't even get out of the path of the cars, so some of the dust settled down on him. The cars drove out of sight as Tom watched them from the middle of the road then he immediately moved his attention over to where the bag had been found. For right now he had to focus on clues and couldn't think of the bag being filled with a body.

He just couldn't – not without becoming ill.

For now, it was just a bag. He walked down the road until he was lined up with the tree where Sylvestre had found the bag and then turned around so he could see the scene that might have been a window to the whole scene that had unfolded earlier. Tom measured his steps across the road away from the tree, wondering if he had been the only one to notice the blood, or lack of, at the crime scene. Carefully he scanned the ground for anything that might look out of place and almost wished it had been damp so that any footsteps would have been encased in the earth. There was only dry dirt and gravel. The area was changing in color as the shadows from the trees and clouds moved over his head, but he didn't notice and kept moving forward. He was in such a deep concentration that he almost ran into the tree that caused the change in color and looked up with a start at the tree.

A car, heading north, went speeding behind him and he turned to look.

Refocusing his attention to the pines that lined the bluff, he turned around to make sure he was still lined up with that other tree. Something triggered in his brain and he started looking at the trees. His gut told him that someone might have seen something, but his rational brain told him that the probability was slim.

Murders in the city were easier to solve. A densely populated area had a ton of witnesses and clues. A murder in the country usually meant heartache for the officer who became wholly involved with the case because a murderer was usually never found.

There was something about this one that Tom felt was different.

He didn't know what yet, but he knew there was something.

As a child, he would deprive himself of lunch, use any money his parents gave him to buy the novels of Arthur Conan Doyle and would take his brothers chores and find other odd jobs to buy the novels. Many times this led to his body meeting with his mother's switch. She was very judicial as to where the switch hit or the marks it left. She felt any child not working was a waste and a source of losing money.

Tom scanned the trees as closely as possible, hunting for any trace of another person. He started to move in closer to one of the trees when he felt something hit the back of his head, causing him to look up. When he reached back with his hand he found that there were several pine needles stuck in his hair and collar. Shrugging his shoulders, he bent down to take a closer look. There was a pile of needles pressed down flatter than the other and there was also a pile moved completely. Tom took his pen and pushed the moved pile until it was a wide circle. There might not have been rain, but the needles had provided a good enough canopy to keep the ground damp. He grinned as he outlined the print of a man's shoe from the air with his pen and investigated the print closer to see what direction the person had moved. He looked around the ground more, looking for more signs. The toe of the visible print was heading north and was deeper than the heel. The person, man, was leaving...in a hurry. Tom noticed there were other needles moved around, indicating the person had been standing at that spot for some time, nervously. It seemed the man didn't know whether to run or stay. By the grooves in the ground closest to a tree, Tom assessed the man had decided to stay...or hide...or even more disturbing – to watch.

He followed the direction of the first print he found. There was another further up. Tom measured out the distance of the steps with his own stride. The distance becoming further with each one he found.

The man had broken into a run.

So did Tom.

He stopped at the gravel where the footsteps became less noticeable. Tom could see where the feet had landed and slid a little while getting traction to move. Then they stopped again - right where the tire tracks dug deep into ground. The car had spun out a little.

Tom heard a car pull up behind him. He ran back towards it waving his arms for the driver not to bring it any further over the clues. The car skidded. The driver didn't open the door.

Tom reached across his waist for his gun. The dust settled and the door opened. Tom started to draw his gun from the shoulder holster when the driver jumped out waving his arm.

"Don't shoot me," the driver yelled.

Tom grinned as he returned the gun to its original position. He turned back around and started to look at the tracks again.

"You know, you really look like shit," Corey Hayes said smirking.

"Thank you," Tom said not breaking his gaze. "What took you so long to get out of the car?"

"I didn't want to get any dust on myself or in my car."

"You're never going to make it with children Corey."

"I'm my only child."

"What brings you up here?"

"Captain Moran was starting to wonder and sent me to look for you. I started to wonder when I saw your car a mile back."

Tom stood up and looked back in the direction he had come from.

"A mile?"

"Yep, I thought you might have fallen off the bluff or something, but then I followed all the clues you left." He looked down at the tracks Tom had been inspecting. "Looks like you found something."

"Yeah, we need to get some plaster up here. I found some footprints back there."

"I know I saw them."

"And then these," he said pointing down.

"You know," Corey started.

"I don't want to hear it. Just do it."

"If the captain asks?"

"We're doing it for records."

"He'll know you're lying."

"Give me a ride back to my car. I have a camera and blanket we can use."

"Meg came by the station. She left you some clean clothes, said to be careful and then gave me a kiss and said to get home as soon as possible. You know I'm going to steal her from you one day."

"Yes, but then you would have my children as well...speaking of which...how was your date last night?"

"It was fine," he answered curtly. Tom studied him for a second.

"Fine, I covered your shift and paperwork for only 'fine'? That's a bit disturbing."

Tom was about to open the door and get in when he noticed Corey was staring at him.

"What?"

"You know I could go down there and get the camera and covers. That way you could stay here to make sure the evidence isn't disturbed."

Tom looked down at himself. His shoes were covered with dust and one of his knees had dirt ground into it. His shirt also had dirt, food and perspiration all over it so that it was no longer a white. He nodded it head in understanding.

"I see. Tell me weren't you shot as a rookie?"

"Yeah."

"What did you do when you bled over your uniform?"

"I beat the guy up for putting a hole in it and then I took it and my undershirt off and leaned over so I wouldn't mess up my pants."

"Just go get the stuff out of my car, bring it back and then drive back down and send one of the boys up."

"You want your clean clothes?"

"Why, when they'll only look like this in another couple of hours," he said pointing down at his current condition. "I'll pick them up at the station...with my kiss."

Juneau and Sylvestre had already been released by the time Tom returned to the station. It was also already dark. He hated days that started and ended before he could ever see his home and family in the light. Now it was two days since he'd been home. He showered and shaved at the station and dressed in the clothes Meg had brought him. He knew he wanted to look decent if he was going to be this late.

He felt bad about not being there for his cousins after he had told them he would return them home, but he had to admit to himself a bit of him had also done it out of selfishness. He liked being with his extended family, but only in small doses. He also knew his aunt would have "made" him sit down and she would have fed him. Tom fondly remembered memories of all his aunts and their cooking. Meg was a good cook, he didn't starve, but she had been raised in a different culture, with different foods. She hadn't been able to master salsa, chili rellenos or tamales. As far as he could remember everything came in a tortilla, including peanut butter and jelly.

That was until he had been moved to the city as a young boy.

He stared at himself in the mirror. There were too many things going on his mind: the murdered girl, his job, his family and the fact that he hadn't finished looking at the trees where he had found the first footsteps.

Those weren't the most nagging of his thoughts though. There was one that was more bothersome and distressful.

Why had she been chopped up and left for someone to find?

2.

A Common Man

Tom opened and shut the door quietly then brought one foot up, untied the laces and removed his shoe and then the other so he wouldn't clomp across the wood and tile floors. Carefully he stepped away knowing there had to be a few toys left out. There were always toys out. He had lost count as to how many times he had sprained an ankle or bruised a body part by tripping on a toy while getting water or going to the bathroom in the middle of the night. The brightness of the moon made it easier to navigate through the halls. First he stopped at his desk, turned on the lamp and set down his briefcase, then took the keys from his pocket and rifled through to his desk key. He slid the key in the keyhole, but the scraping of the metals against each other seemed unusually loud. Tom thought the sound would wake somebody and stopped. He listened, but no one stirred. He opened the drawer, took his gun and holster off and put it in the drawer and then made sure he locked it.

That was their rule as parents. Tom and Megan (more so Megan) were terrified that the boys would stumble across it and try to use it on each other.

Tom had seen first-hand what a firearm could do to an animal...and a man.

He left the office, walked down the hall and stopped at the oldest boys' room. Slowly he cracked the door open and peeked in. He smirked as the two came into view, knowing he could fire his gun and they wouldn't stir. He entered and stopped in between their beds and looked down at them both. Bruce lay on his back with his mouth opened. His snoring would sometimes wake Tom and Meg up. Tom wondered how many bugs the child had eaten over his short life. Louis was asleep on his side with a stranglehold on his teddy bear, German. Bruce had named the toy when Louis was brought home with it from the hospital after he was born. Bruce had just learned how to read. Louis had come home with a tag stating his name. So had the stuffed bear - "Made in Germany." Bruce just hadn't seen the "y".

Tom thought that was the only disadvantage to having children. They wanted to name everything that entered the house. That was fine until he had to go up and down the street yelling the dog's or cat's names. Tom refused to let them name the other two children. Bruce and Louis had begged Tom to let them name Alice or Joe. Tom said he would refuse to let them name them Butterscotch and Licorice.

"How do you think I'll look yelling up and down the street for them? What will the other kids think?"

"Well, Mommy's always saying how much she wants to eat us."

Alice and Joe it was.

Tom peeked in at Alice. He pushed her hair away so he could see her eyes and pout as she slept. He was tempted to poke or nudge her so she would wake up and look up at him. He knew she would get up and throw her arms around his neck and nuzzle into him.

He left her room to finally check on Mighty Joe. Tom wasn't surprised to find the baby's covers kicked off. The boy just didn't like to be restrained - just like his father.

His little fat fingers curled around a corner of his blanket. It was hard to wrestle anything once it got in that grip whether it was a toy, a bottle, food or hair. The dog and cat had learned to stay out of his reach.

It had taken Tom 45 minutes to get to his bedroom door since entering the house.

He walked to the closet and set his shoes down carefully so they didn't make a "thud". Then he walked around to Meg's side of the bed and looked down at her as he removed his tie and unbuttoned his shirt. He couldn't understand how men couldn't love their wives or home lives. Most of the men he knew talked about their wives with disdain and chose words that made it sound like the wives were more possessions or business partners at best. He never heard them talk about them with respect. He believed in the things that Meg believed in and, most of all, he respected her opinion and trusted her, something he knew was not common, but his upbringing had given him a different perspective.

He had seen and heard men in the department go down into the Stingeree, even though it supposedly had been cleared out years before by the mayor's wife and a posse of friends. He visited the area south of Market for other reasons. The women down there were fond of him; mainly because he had grown up behind the bars and he was unattainable.

He felt he would have been just like most of the men he knew if he had stayed in San Diego and not gone back east to college.

The men on the ranches treated their wives like the cattle most of them owned. Women like his grandmother, mother and aunts resigned to only existing to maintain the house, children and kitchen. They never had any desire or knew any desire to do anything else.

That's why the east and Meg had been so fascinating to Tom. The women had ambitions and careers besides school teachers and nannies. No, back East there were women doctors, lawyers, scientists, politicians and writers.

Luckily for Tom, Meg was one of those.

He had first run into her at the university library. He was leaning over the desk of the librarian trying to get the woman to help him. A woman walked right up next to him.

"Hi Susan."

"Oh, hi Meg."

"I had a book held for me yesterday."

"Do you mind," Tom huffed, "I've been waiting for some time."

"No, I don't mind. You haven't returned the books to the selves have you?"

Susan went and looked at a shelf and pulled Meg's book. She walked back and handed it to her.

"Thank you," Meg said gleefully taking the book, smirking at Tom and walking away. Susan then looked back at Tom.

"What about my book," Tom asked exasperated.

"We shelved it. All holds are 24 hours. The policies are posted everywhere," she said pointing at several signs.

"What about her book," he waved in Meg's direction and demanded to know.

"Oh, she knows the policies," Susan said.

"What am I supposed to do," he said, his voice beginning to rise.

"I suggest you go back to where you found the book in the first place."

She turned around and then added, "And please, lower your voice...this is a library."

Tom returned to the shelf where his book had been. It wasn't there. Part of him wasn't surprised, but he looked on the shelves next to that one and the ones above and below. He didn't realize that Meg was watching him from a few feet away. She quickly looked down at the book she had taken off the shelf and added to the one Susan had retrieved for her. The book had been occupying the vacant space Tom was staring at. She flipped back to the cover. 'Crime Scene Investigation' was the lettering embossed across the cover.

She stood up from the table and walked behind him.

"So you're a detective are you," she whispered.

He turned around, "What?"

She waved the book in his face with her finger still saving her place. The sight of the book in her hand angered him. Hadn't she caused him enough inconvenience already?

"Would you be checking that book out," he asked.

She lowered the book and studied him. "You're a very serious boy," she stated and then studied him for a second. "You're not from here."

She smiled at him, waiting for him to answer, but it seemed that she was enjoying his inability to formulate an answer.

"No, you're not from here," she answered herself, satisfied.

"Would you be checking that book out," he repeated in a different tone.

She held it out, but then retracted it from his hand just as he was about to grab it.

"Ah...why were you checking this book out?"

"Why, were you," he asked.

She looked down at the book again. She knew it was strange for her to be looking at such a book. Then she smiled and looked back at Tom.

"Morbid curiosity."

He nodded his head and then reached for it again.

"May I."

She handed it to him.

"You're reason?"

"I'm studying forensic science."

"So you are a detective."

"No, not yet. Thank you...for the book."

He turned and walked out of the aisle.

"You're welcome," she said down the aisle after him, "My name's Megan."

She heard him trip on a chair and fall down.

"Shh," several people yelled.

A few weeks later, Meg was on duty at the hospital she volunteered at on the weekends when she heard the policemen come into the emergency room. She lifted her head and looked for a second and then returned to studying since it didn't look like there was anything out of the ordinary. She looked up again when one of the officers stopped in front of her station.

"Someone from our station has been shot and we need some help," the officer told her.

"You brought him in?"

"It's not that bad. He took one in the leg and one in the ass...sorry, I mean rear."

"Ass is fine," Meg said smiling. She got up from her desk and walked around to the officer's side. "Where is he?"

"In the car."

She followed the officer to the door. The back door of the car was open and she could see the soles of the wounded officer's shoes. Then she saw his legs and saw that he was indeed shot in the ass because he was laying face down. But, he wasn't wearing uniform pants.

"I thought it was an officer that was shot," she asked the officer.

"No, it's someone helping us with crime scene investigations. He's a student from the university. Our suspect was still at the location when we all arrived and decided she just really didn't like the idea of even being a suspect."

Meg got closer and poked her head in the car to look at the man's butt.

"Hi," she said.

"Hello," the man said without turning around. "Will you respect me in the morning," he asked her as she pulled a piece of his torn pants away to take a look at the wound and then the other one in his leg.

"So," the officer continued, "She thought she'd take a few shots at all of us. Mr. Rubidoux took a few for the team."

"I wouldn't have gotten hit if your fat ass hadn't been in such a hurry to get out the door," Megan heard the injured man say.

"Now, that's not a very nice thing to say. Besides, I told you to run," the officer defended.

"Well," Meg said, "it doesn't look that bad. A couple of stitches ought to fix you right up. Let's get you out of the car so a doctor can take a look at you and stitch that up."

The man shimmied back and pulled himself out with Meg's and the officer's help so that he was able to stand while leaning on the car.

"Wait here and I'll go get a wheelchair."

"I really don't have a good opportunity to run in this circumstance," he sassed off and turned around.

"You," Meg said surprised.

"Hello," Tom said. "About that wheel chair?" He felt the blood draining from his face and feigned into the officer who propped him back up.

"Oh, yes."

Flustered she ran into the hospital and grabbed one of the chairs. She stopped half way to the door and ran back towards her desk.

The two men could see all this from outside.

"Where the hell is she going," Tom wanted to know.

"I don't know, but wherever it is she forgot the chair."

Tom looked at the officer.

"You're an idiot. Just drop me!"

"Okay," the officer said letting go.

Tom hit his head on the car as he fell to the ground. Now, not only was he lightheaded, but his head was bleeding too.

"Go get the chair," he yelled at the officer.

Meg came back outside with an intern just as the officer was loading Tom into the wheelchair.

"Sorry, we didn't wait for you," Tom sarcastically said over the officer's shoulder.

"I went to get a doctor. What happened to your head?"

"Nothing," he grumbled.

"Did you put the brake on?"

"What," the officer said. He turned around to see Meg and pushed the chair slightly out of range so that Tom fell to the ground as he dropped him.

"Ow! My butt."

The officer went to help Tom up, but Tom swatted at him.

"Leave me alone! I'll crawl in!"

"You know I can't do that Mr. Rubidoux. My father wouldn't allow it or like it."

Tom sat on the ground as the officer went to retrieve the chair and the intern took a look at the cut on his forehead and other wounds. He looked up at Meg and saw she was trying to keep from laughing.

Tom was lying on his side with a huge bandage and ice bag on his butt and one on his leg. The doctor was finishing the wrap on his forehead. Meg stood patiently by assisting the doctor when he asked. Tom couldn't help but feel that she was still trying not to laugh. He looked at her.

"You find me quite humorous."

"No, but you do bring out my curiosity."

He winced as the doctor tied off the bandage.

"There, we'll keep you over night. We'll try to keep you as comfortable as possible. I know it's going to be tough since there's no comfortable position for you at this point. Let's try to make it so he can sleep on his stomach."

"I hate sleeping on my stomach."

"Then, may I suggest you face the other way the next time you get shot at."

"Will you assist Mr. Rubidoux, Miss Bancroft."

"I'll take care of him Doctor."

"Lovely," Tom said.

"You know, you could pass for one of the men in 'The Spirit of 76.'"

"Thanks," Tom said.

She moved to go help him with the pillows. He became very uncomfortable and squirmed.

"It's all right, I can fix them."

"Stop it. Let me do my job," she said.

She grabbed one of the pillows and he reached out to grab it back. They tugged back and forth for a moment.

"Let go," she demanded.

"No, I can do it myself."

"Mr. Rubidoux, let me help you." She gave the pillow a big tug and it burst under the strain sending feathers everywhere.

"All right," Tom conceded, "you can help me."

Meg returned after feathers had been cleaned up as best as possible.

"Would you like something to eat," she asked bringing in a tray.

"I was told you were done for the day."

"I am. I felt a little bad for your predicament. Peace offering," she said holding forth the tray.

"I don't know. What is it and is it poisoned?"

She lifted the lid, revealing its contents, "Steak and potatoes, a salad and cherry pie."

He tried to sit up and then realized he couldn't. "Could you help me...possibly," he asked sheepishly.

She smiled. "Sure." She moved a chair in front of him and sat down with the tray on her lap. She proceeded to cut up some of the food, then stabbed it with a fork and moved it towards his mouth.

"Open wide," she said and then shoved the fork towards his mouth.

He looked down at the fork and resolved that she really wasn't trying to do him any harm. Begrudgingly, he opened his mouth and she carefully put the fork in his mouth. He carefully closed it and she pulled it out as it lightly dragged against his teeth.

"Mmmm," he said chewing. "I didn't realize how hungry I was." He chewed a few times more and swallowed and thought of something. "Say, this isn't regular hospital food."

"No," she said shaking her head, "We were having it for dinner. More?"

"Please." He took another bite of food. He stared at her, he knew it wasn't polite, but he was fascinated. Her face became flushed, letting Tom know that she could feel him watching her.

"Tell me, really, why you were looking at that book," Tom asked.

She didn't know why, but she was a little embarrassed. "I really was just curious. I read Sherlock Holmes all the time."

"Really, so do I. I think that's why I became interested in investigation. Also, I didn't have the grades to get into medical school, so forensics has become the best compromise of the two."

"I've watched you around campus. You're always with a group, but you never seem to be with anybody."

"Anybody? Are you talking about my fraternity brothers or the girls?"

"Both."

"Forward, aren't you? Well, I don't do well with either," he continued when her face flushed. "Women are my brother's specialty, and I only really count my family as friends. The guys are all right, but I just come from a completely different background. What about you and your chatty clatch and beaus?"

"They've always been part of my life. I love the social scene."

"I know...I've seen you at a few parties."

"I've just never found anyone interesting."

"Or anyone who isn't completely taken aback by your frankness?"

She started to get mad, and then realized he had been paying more attention to her than she had first thought.

"But you're not," she asked.

"Not what? Intimidated? Hindered?"

"Taken aback," she clarified.

"Let's just say...," he thought about his next words carefully, "let's just say I have spent a lot of time around direct and strong women who know what they want. Besides," he added, "I've always liked a challenge."

Their first date was to the library. Meg loved helping Tom study for tests and proof-reading papers for his classes. She knew it would have been hard for her to find someone to offer her a job and her parents disapproved of this interest of hers. Tom honestly didn't care and he seemed to relish the ability to discuss his interests and genuinely appreciate her perspectives.

Tom had never been very graceful. His brothers and cousins didn't know what to make of him. He was shy, quiet and thoughtful. The girls always thought he was good looking and they flirted with him insistently, but he just never had an interest in anyone. To him, women were to be respected, cherished and taken seriously.

He had witnessed more than a young man should what the opposite could do and the tragedies it could bring.

With Meg he had discovered something else. He wondered if his time volunteering with the police had toughened him a little. She fascinated him, and for the first time he wanted to do whatever he needed to change so he could be with her. Meg was someone who would go toe to toe with him and not just tell him what they thought he wanted to hear because they wanted him to do something for them or something from him.

None of the other girls back home were like her.

Dates for them continued with dinner, the nickelodeon, museums and lectures. They would take long walks and talk about everything and the courtship would have would have continued that way if Woodrow Wilson hadn't decided to take the country into war.

Tom let the moment to ask Meg to marry pass by. He had been too scared to ask her, even though he'd had the courage to enlist. Worst of all, Megan had been waiting for him to ask, even before the war had come. When he didn't, she became upset and their parting words to each other were heated. He went to the train station by himself and stepped on alone amidst the other soldiers who were hugging and being hugged by loved ones.

Meg ran to the station when she realized what her stubbornness was about to cost her and Tom.

She missed him by ten minutes.

Tom thought for sure he'd lose her to some other man who stayed behind. He knew his chances of returning and repairing the damages were slight in the infantry. There was a stroke of luck when he arrived in Europe. One of the officers he had worked under had sent a few wires to those in charge on his behalf. He was commissioned to lieutenant of the Military Police.

The battles he did fight in were few, but they didn't take care of the guilt he felt for serving most of the war behind a desk. He saw injured and dead soldiers daily and they only reminded him of those that were sacrificing their lives while he moved behind the scenes taking care of the crimes his fellow soldiers were committing. To compensate, he fought his own war with himself.

He went through his daily routine, taking on more and more to try to forget. Back in the states, Meg waited for word from him...and waited...and waited. First she became angry, then worried. She had heard from a classmate where he was stationed and what his post was, but she was afraid to write. And, why should she? If he really wanted her, he should contact her.

She was being stubborn. He was being ignorant.

It wasn't until he was called to the murder of a young Parisian woman that Tom was finally slapped out of his reluctance.

Even as he slowly approached the woman's body he became clearer on what he was going to get Megan back – how he would apologize and grovel if he had to in order to get her back and make her his wife.

His plans were solidified when he flipped the girl over and that the girl once had the same colored eyes as Megan as well as hair.

Tom had to fight to keep his composure. What if this had been Megan? She would never have known how he really felt. It took all he had to focus on the scene, finish his questioning, filling the paperwork and not to run. But run he did, as soon as he could to the wire office and fired off a quick note to her hoping he wasn't too late.

I've been an ass Stop Wait for me Stop I love you Stop

3.

A Morbid Curiosity

Tom felt something fluttering at his eyes. He tried to move his legs, but they were extremely heavy and there was a tremendous pressure on them. He thought he smelled the strange odor of stale milk mixed with boy and grass.

He felt a tug at his left eyelid as one of the boys was checking on him.

"Are you awake, Daddy?"

Tom smiled and opened both eyes to see he was looking straight into Louis' eyes.

Louis sat back a little on his lap and studied him, looking into one eye and then the other.

"Daddy, are you awake?"

Tom just stared at him. Why was he asleep in the study?

"Good morning Detective," he heard Megan say behind them, "Come on Louis. Come finish your breakfast."

Louis slid off Tom's lap and went scampering out the door. Tom still sat there for a moment and looked at his desk. He had been going through the photos of the crime scene that had been dropped off right before he tried to go to bed. He quickly rifled through them again until Meg stood at the door way.

"I wondered where you had gone to last night," she said.

He looked up.

"What?"

"I felt you looking at me, and then you walked away. I kept waiting for you to come warm up the bed."

He had a couple of the pictures in his hand and waved them.

"They dropped these off. I wanted to take a look. I didn't expect to fall asleep on them."

"Or drool?"

"Drool?"

"Drool."

"I drooled on them?"

"You drooled on them."

He looked at a few of the pictures closer.

"That's why some of them are sticky?"

"That's why some of them are sticky." She smiled, "you were ready to blame one of the kids, weren't you?"

He grinned.

She watched him look at the pile of pictures and sort through them. She could see he was trying to find something that would ignite the fuse that would explode into a solution.

"Do you want to talk about it?"

He looked up. "What?"

"Do you want to talk about it?"

"No, not just yet. Give me some time."

She ran her hands through his hair and then her finger around his ear.

"Don't get too obsessed, Detective."

He looked up at her.

"I get worried when you frown like that. You might burn or short-circuit something in that mind I find so attractive," she smiled at him.

He nodded.

"I just don't want you getting..."

"I'm a police officer."

"I know, I'm just saying..."

"I know what you're saying. I will be careful."

She pulled her hand out of his hair.

"All right," she said before stopping at the door and turning.

"Louis, get back at that table and finish your breakfast," she yelled. Then there was the sound of small feet running down the hall and Alice appeared at the door.

"Hi Daddy."

His heart melted, "Hi Sweetheart."

He could see she wanted to come in, but wasn't sure she should. Meg looked down at her. Tom flipped the photos over so she wouldn't see anything.

"You can come in."

The little girl walked in and climbed up on his lap and put her hands on either side of his face and gave him a kiss on his lips. She pulled her face back and wrinkled her nose.

"Your face is all prickly, Daddy."

He rubbed it.

"Yes, it is. I need to shave."

She started to slide off his lap.

"I have to get ready now. You'll take us?"

"Yes, I'll take you."

"Louis, get ready for school," Megan said after the little boy again.

"Bruce's sticking his spoon in my cereal," Louis protested.

"Bruce, are you dressed yet?" Meg started back down the hall.

Tom looked back down at Alice. "You better hurry along and get dressed too."

"Okay Daddy."

She leaned up to him. He leaned down so she could give him a wet kiss and then finished sliding off his lap and ran out of the room.

"Bruce, Louis, hurry up. Daddy's taking you."

Tom heard the stampede come out of the kitchen and around the corner and caught a glimpse of the blur as they ran by his door. He got up to change his clothes.

The murdered girl would have to wait.

The children were scampering out the door and Tom was walking through when the phone rang. Meg shifted Joe over to her other hip so she could answer the phone. Tom stopped for a second and watched her.

"Hello," she said.

She looked back at Tom.

"No, he's not here. He's dropping the kids off and then he'll be in...um...no, I'm sure he's left already. Yes, I know. He doesn't sleep much. Good-bye."

She hung up the phone.

"Tsk, tsk - teaching our children to lie," Tom asked dryly and rubbing Joe's head.

Meg ignored him.

"That was Corey. The coroner is waiting for you."

"You could have let me talk to him."

"No, I know how it works," she said narrowing her eyes at him, "You get on the phone with him and there's a chance you won't take the kids to school."

"You just don't want to."

"Especially, not like this," she said waving her hand up and down at her attire.

Tom looked at her. It was the first time he realized she was still in her pajamas and her hair was messed up.

The heels of Tom's shoes reverberating off the floor were the only sound he heard walking through the building. It would have been eerie to him if he hadn't been lost in his thoughts. He may have intentionally become lost in his mind remembering how much he dreaded going to the morgue. His family had always been around death whether it was one of the many family members dying from old age or accident or one of the many animals being slaughtered.

As a boy he remembered seeing the bodies lying in wait on ice and there were a few times someone would have to shoo him out of the room when he was inspecting the body out of curiosity. He remembered how waxy they all looked with their lips pulled back over their teeth making it look like they were all snarling.

That curiosity changed when the body was that of his father who had died after being trampled by his horse.

It was then that Tom realized that death could sometimes mean that horrible things could be done to a body...and loved ones.

That and it may have been just looking so close and so long at death and the different aspects and angles of it that made him nauseated. He had to focus on not really looking at what he saw and convince his mind that it was nothing. It might as well have been a picture in a book.

"Are you trying to avoid the obvious," Corey said leaning out the doorway as Tom strolled by the room.

"Huh, oh," Tom said turning around and walking back.

He entered the room and quickly had to regroup himself. He had let himself go for a moment and almost bolted back out the door when he saw the bodies lying on the tables.

"Over here, Tom," Corey said.

Tom maneuvered through the tables and stopped next to Corey. He looked down at the table. He was looking down at the chest and then moved his gaze down to the genitals.

"This isn't our victim. This is a man," he said pointing at the body to Corey. "And, it's all in one piece."

"That must be why you're a detective."

"Over here Sherlock," Dr. Hill, the coroner, said behind him.

Tom turned around and saw the pathetic pile and pieces that had once been a young woman. He thought he had swayed when Corey bumped into him.

"Sorry," Corey said. Tom looked at him and noticed he was ashen. Corey's body convulsed and he threw his hand over his mouth.

"Over there," Hill yelled pointing in the direction of one of the drains on the floor.

Corey spun, bumped into the table with the dead man and stumbled to the drain as his body convulsed again and vomit started oozing from beneath his hand. He fell to his knees over the drain as he wretched again.

Tom looked back at the coroner and they both smirked and shook their heads. Corey started to return to the table but the doctor looked at him.

"Don't be an ass. Grab a pan and pour some water until that mess is cleaned up."

Corey did as he was told - a little irritated that he thought he was being treated like child. He joined Tom and the coroner when he was done. He took his handkerchief out of his pocket and held to his mouth and hung back a little behind Tom. Tom turned and looked at him.

"Not everyone can have a rock hard heart and constitution like you," Corey snapped at Tom.

"Weren't you in the infantry," he asked.

"I went through the whole war with my eyes closed. I actually ran into a tree once."

Tom and Hill just stared at him for a minute and then chose to ignore the comment.

"What have you found," Tom asked.

The coroner was still staring at Corey.

"Hill," Tom said louder to get the coroner's attention.

"Oh," he looked down, "there's a lot of things going on here." He leaned closer to the table where one of the legs was. "Without saying, whoever did this was sick, but take a look at this," he said while he prodded the stump end of the thigh. Tom looked further down the limb at the ankle and noticed it had been broken.

"The ankle was broken when the body was stuffed in the bag," Hill confirmed. "Rigor mortise must have set in making it hard to compact the body. She wasn't a person at that point."

Tom looked up at him.

"This is what I wanted you to look at."

Tom and the coroner leaned down to take a closer look at the leg. The doctor looked up.

"Can you see Corey?"

"I can see perfectly fine."

"But you're standing behind Dux."

"I can see everything I need to."

Hill returned to the body and began to point things out to Tom who was tuning out everything Hill was saying so he could focus on the body and only the gist of what the coroner was saying. The coroner went along and picked up different body parts and moved things so the two detectives could see what he was talking about.

The murderer had begun to dismember the woman before she was dead, but after she had been raped. Some of her teeth had been broken not long after she was dead and part of her ear had been torn away during a struggle. The coroner picked up one of her hands and turned it over so they could see the palm and fingerprints.

"See right here, in the stratum corneum and the stratum tumluncosum," Hill started.

"Are you purposely using big words so we know how much you paid for your education," Corey smarted off. "Could you use words we can understand?"

"He's talking about the fingerprints," Tom translated. "The little swirls and lines on your fingers," he said pointing at his own fingers.

Corey frowned, and then, when Tom and the coroner went back to the woman's fingers, he looked down at his.

"Embedded in her...," Hill looked up, "...finger beds, swirls and lines..."

Corey snorted at being made fun of. Tom grinned without looking up. He saw the body again for what it really was and focused back to the task at hand.

"What is that? You can hardly see it," he said to Hill

"I'm not sure. Here," he said grabbing a magnifying glass, "you can get a better look."

Tom took the glass and looked closer.

"It's some sort of residue. At first I thought it might be ash, but now I'm not so sure. I've been running different tests, but I haven't been able to get a positive chemical response out of anything."

"So, the man - right, we know it was a man - was dirty? Is that what you're saying," Tom asked.

"No," Hill said, "he had some dirt, ink, grease, ash or dust - I don't know - somewhere on him that the woman managed to get on her."

"You know the woman wasn't dirty and wasn't one of our local prostitutes," Corey stated, rather than asked.

Hill smiled.

"No, she wasn't a prostitute. She regularly bathed and didn't seem to have had intercourse that often."

"So, she bathed. That doesn't mean anything," Tom corrected.

"Why the...," Hill stopped in mid-sentence.

Tom looked up at him.

"Why the 'what,'" Tom inquired.

"Nothing," Corey defended, "Just the women we've spoken to down in the old Stingaree - well, a lot of them bathe."

Hill nodded looked down and picked up one of her arms and one of her feet and held them up. He wanted Tom to get a closer look and he wanted to see if he could get under Corey's skin. Corey immediately turned a greyer shade than he already was and Hill saw him swallow hard after convulsing a bit making the coroner grin.

Tom leaned in to look closer. Corey leaned in the opposite direction.

"Uh," Tom said and stood up.

"What," Corey asked impatiently.

Tom turned and looked at him, and shook his head as he turned and looked at the appendages again.

"Looks like a young arm and foot to me," Tom said, then over his shoulder, "don't you agree Corey."

"Yep."

"What is wrong with you? I've never seen you react this badly before," noticing the redness and dampness of Corey's eyes.

"It was probably all the booze from last night."

Tom focused on the parts again.

"What is it that you want me to see?"

"Well, it would help if I pointed to the area I want you to actually look at, but now that you mention it, I'd guess she's in her twenties...was in her twenties."

He turned the arm and foot so that the cut areas were facing Tom.

"It looks like they were gnawed off."

He heard Corey's feet run away from him as Cory wretched in the drain again.

"More like sawed."

"You mean like a tree saw?"

"No..."

"Hack saw?"

"What I mean when I say 'no', I mean no saw."

"Could you please speak English," Corey yelled from over the drain.

"It was a knife blade, but I'm going to have to look at all the cuts a little closer, because…well, I've never seen anything like it. It doesn't look like any boat knife, fishing, ranching or hunting knife…I'm telling you. I don't recognize it. All I know is that it was serrated."

"What did you say," Corey asked, finally coming back to life.

"You're somewhat of an expert on knives, aren't you Hayes," Tom remembered. "You have that big collection and all…"

Corey came closer, but not too close.

"What do you think it looked like again?"

Hill described it again.

Corey shook his head, "I don't recognize the description, but I'll check my collection to see if I might have something similar to give us an idea. You know, it could be foreign."

"That might mean the killer served in the war."

"Or he's foreign," Corey added.

Tom nodded his head, "I suppose you're right." He looked at another table behind the coroner.

"Is that the sack?"

"Um," the coroner looked behind him, "Oh, yeah."

Tom walked around to take a closer look. Hill followed.

"Nasty mess," he said, "hard to imagine that," nodding back towards the girl, "was in this."

Tom was looking at the inside of the bag.

"I am constantly amazed as to what one human being is capable of doing to another."

Tom looked up at him, "I thought you served in the war…"

"My services weren't of use on the line. I was an officer's aid."

"Just what did you aid him with," Tom asked and grinned.

Tom moved his attention back to the sack and wrinkled his nose.

"Is this all…"

"I haven't finished my analyses of everything," Hill said. "As far as I can tell that's her hair, pieces of skin and blood. Some of the dirt it was around or in transferred in through the burlap."

"May I," Tom asked holding up an index finger.

"Sure there's plenty of dust in there for other samples."

Tom ran his finger over some of the dust while Hill continued talking and rubbed it between his finger and thumb and then looked closer.

"This was another reason why I thought it might be a fishing knife."

"Why," Corey said far behind him.

"You're still here," Tom asked without looking up. "I thought you left."

"No, still here. Why did you think it might be a fisherman?"

"A lot of those guys bring home fish in these sacks."

"That would go with my foreigner theory. Maybe it was one of the Portuguese community."

Tom was studying the outside of the sack. There was a logo on the beat up piece of paper that Tom recognized.

"I would agree with you Hayes," the coroner said as he watched Tom, "But I also found this stuck to one of her legs."

He reached to the end of the table and picked up a skinny strip of paper that had long ago been folded in the center. He held it up over his shoulder so both detectives could get a look.

"What is it," Corey asked.

"It appears to be an old matchbook cover," Tom said as he reached out for it. The coroner held it out for him to take.

"I don't recognize the logo," the coroner said.

Tom inspected it more closely and smiled a little. "Let's hope you don't. It all makes a lot more sense."

Hill didn't know what he was talking about.

"She might not have been a prostitute, but there's a good chance she was down in the old Stingeree."

Tom had a captive audience.

"This sack has only ever been used for potatoes. This dust, I bet, is from potatoes."

Corey had finally joined them.

"I don't get it."

"You should," Tom answered.

"Potatoes are used in some forms of bootleg liquor," Hill clarified for Corey.

"The clubs, supplemented good liquor with homemade hooch before and after the raid of 1912," Tom said.

"That's right," Hill added.

"This particular supplier of potatoes has only sold to two men's clubs. One being the Robin's Nest, which has been an empty shell for years, and the other," he said holding up the matchbook, "was The Agate Club."

4.

THE AGATE CLUB

Tom strolled down Fourth Street like he didn't have a care in the world. Walking down to the old Stingeree was like walking into another part of time for him. He had been in the area on other cases, but never ventured in to sneak a peek in case he was seen.

This was business, if his old catechism priest could see him now he would have a legitimate excuse for stepping inside.

His memory flashed back to his youth when his uncle had brought him down to live in the city and to work in the men's club.

Tom, it seemed, had proven to be one too many to feed in a family that was already busting at the seams. He was no use on the ranch. Any time anyone was looking for him to reprimand him for not finishing his chores they would find him in some quiet spot with his nose stuck in a book, usually a murder mystery.

Any time it was mentioned someone had died or had been killed Tom would spout off "how" or "from what". He was the one that always wanted to look at the dead body at wakes or funerals and more than once his hand had to be grabbed before his poked at a corpse.

That alone was lethal in an environment that had a policy that children were to be seen, not heard.

He had felt the lash of his mother's whip or his father's razor strop far too many times to count. His mother finally gave up when she broke her cane across his back as punishment for letting several calves out before branding, which seemed to be more frequent after his father died.

Apparently her brother appreciated his quick wit and mind and offered an alternative because he knew of someone in the city who would take him in.

Tom would go to work with him down in the city and send his earnings home to help support the family. His board and meals would be covered.

She had his bags packed and in the back of the car before he even knew he was leaving. She stood on the porch, blocking his entrance into the house and pointed at the car.

"You're going with Tio."

Tom turned, looked at the car and obeyed.

He didn't know where, for how long...it was probably the only time in his life that a command from his mother actually felt like it was the right thing to do.

He was surprised the look on her face told him that she was shocked he had obeyed her so quickly. He started to get a little anxious that his uncle wouldn't step on the gas enough to drive away before she might realize she'd made a mistake and wanted him back.

Tom knew The Agate Club wasn't the only bordello that had survived the woman's reform raid of 1912, but it was the one that was the most audacious of thumbing its nose up at the crusade. Many of the women of the crusade had no choice – it was either let it stay open or raid it and risk having their husbands caught and their private lives smeared across the front pages of the society registers and news.

Tom grinned when he thought back at the conversation he overheard Judge Charles Miller Frost and one of the businessmen having about their victory over their wives.

"I told her, 'by all means, Beatrice, come on down to the club'," Frost recounted. "I'll either be in the far booth at the right or upstairs, through the double doors on the left."

Both men had laughed.

Tom was happy a token of his youth was still there for everyone to see. Megan had known about his unusual upbringing, but Tom wondered at what point, if any, would he share it with his children; and, definitely, not while they might repeat it to his mother.

It was in the club Tom had learned the art of observation, the importance of keeping a secret and discretion. He had also learned compassion, humility and cruelty. Here he had made the contacts that would enable him to eventually get to Dartmouth and to Megan.

Tom put his hand on the door handle. The brass had started to tarnish from the years of sweaty and oily hands. He took in a deep breath and let it out as he opened the door and walked through.

And then, he took another deep breath in as he stood in the foyer and let the door shut behind him.

It was like a vacuum - everything looked the same, sounded the same and smelled the same. Tom took a deep breath in and his nostrils filled with the smells of polished wood, cigars, scotch, beer and sex.

"Well now, there's a pretty boy," Tom didn't quite recognize the woman who approached him. But then, that life style aged women in unusual ways. Tom grinned and as he had learned, removed his hat and nodded.

"Hello," as if he knew her.

"So, the prodigal son returns. How long has it been Thomas?"

The lilt in the way she said Thomas reminded him of many errands for opium from the Asians across F Street.

He looked her up and down. Time and occupational side effects had not treated the woman in front of him as harsh as he had seen it treat others. Her face did show her age, but in a distinguished way that Tom felt earned respect...as if she was Charlotte MacGregor, madam of The Agate Club herself. The hair was pulled up and back like Charlotte's but brown, as were the eyes.

Tom remembered Charlotte's bright green eyes vividly. These were not Charlotte's.

"It's been a long time, Evelyn."

"Yes, it has, young man. Here on business?"

Tom stuttered, "Uh..."

"I mean police business, Tom," she clarified, resting her hand on his arm.

He grinned, regaining his composure.

"In a way…I'm investigating a murder and wanted to ask some questions."

She leaned into him and moved her mouth up to his ear.

"You don't look that upset to be here."

"No, I…I…"

She laughed as she leaned back.

"I know…you had fun here. There's no shame in that, Thomas. Everybody comes here to have fun, and very rarely do they leave not having achieved that. You didn't turn out to be a degenerate for working here. If I remember correctly, though, it did take you quite a few years to figure out what was going on here."

"Yes, it did."

"I hope you're a better detective now…"

"I would like to think my skills have greatly improved."

"We shall see. Rufus is tending bar…"

"Rufus is still here," he said interrupting her.

"Not everyone received a golden ticket out of here, Tom," she said with a bite to her words. Tom realized his misstep and grimaced as he nodded.

"Of course," he said as an apology, dipping his head.

"I'm sure you can find your way to the bar," she said as she gestured towards the monstrous mahogany set up that took up a fourth of the main salon.

"Yes Ma'am," he said.

"You might want to take the silver spoon out of your ass before you talk to Rufus. Remember, no one is fooled here. We all know exactly who you are," she said as she caressed his cheek and indicated to the rest of the clientele.

As her hand left his face, it was like a veil had been moved and the lanterns had been turned up brighter.

And, then he saw.

It wasn't the docket of San Diego famous names he saw that shocked him. Rather, the time of day.

Tom looked at his watch again.

Yes, it was day…before lunch.

As Tom walked slowly to the bar, nodding at the prominent business men he recognized and let the atmosphere take him in and secretly take him back.

He didn't need to see where he was walking, he knew exactly where the bar was, even if the room had been pitch black and he took the opportunity to look into his mind's eye as he slowly maneuvered his way to Rufus by sight and smell.

Tom remembered being no taller than the bar when he first arrived at The Agate Club and his shoulders soon developed from having to heave mugs of beer up and over the lip of the bar and walk them over to the patrons who were too occupied with the women sitting on their laps to notice a boy had just served them. And, if they did notice, they usually tousled his hair, gave him an extra coin and sent him on his way.

The first couple of days, his forehead ached from where he had leveraged his head while blindly grabbing the mugs.

No doubt about it, he felt like he had been built like his mother's father and uncle short – but only for the time being.

Then there was the first time he saw Madam Charlotte MacGregor.

He had been waiting for Rufus to get a round of drinks together for a group of Channing Kimball's guests (the great man would never be seen there himself) when Tom felt the energy of the room shift.

Even though he had only been there for two weeks he knew where every piece of furniture and pathway was without looking.

That evening, he felt the shift of energy warm the side of his face so that he turned and looked to the main stairway that descended down the west side of the main salon.

His mouth gaped as he focused on the vision that glided slowly down the stairs.

He had never seen hair that bright before. Most of his family had the jet-black hair and some, like Tom Had brown, but nothing like the carrot red he saw pulled back, up high with a peacock feather tucked in the back to offset the color and make it even brighter.

Charlotte MacGregor stopped halfway down and moved closer to the railing and surveyed the lay of her land.

He had seen his father and uncles with this same look as they oversaw their heads of cattle and land atop their horses, but this was a woman, and one like young Tom Rubidoux had never seen.

She was holding court over the bustle and noise and music and (Tom was realizing) people.

He watched as she nodded at a girl and man in a three-piece suit who walked up the stairs past her and then returned her gaze back to the main floor.

It was then that it looked like something caught her eye and she slowly turned her head in his direction.

A smile widened across her face and she seemed to float down towards the bottom of the stairs…and caught Tom staring and smiled.

Tom was startled as a wet bar towel came over the top of his head and jolted him and made his ears ring.

"That's Miss Charlotte. She belongs to Judge Frost," he heard Rufus chastise him.

"Judge's Frost's," Tom questioned shaking his head. "She's his slave?'

"No dumb ass," Rufus said with another whack of the towel. "She is exclusive to him. Shit, I told her we shouldn't hire kids. She's your boss. Be respectful. For Christ's sake shut your mouth."

But, it wasn't Judge Frost whom Charlotte was looking at or walking toward when she reached the main floor.

"Shit," Rufus said under his breath as she closed in on Tom.

Tom had only seen such graceful movements before when he was back on the ranch as he watched a rattlesnake approach a bird's nest and suck up the eggs in the nest and slither away like it was a cloud moving along with the breeze.

Tom snapped his mouth shut, but, other than that, didn't change his expression.

And, like the snake, never broke eye contact.

She put her hand on his cheek.

"And, who are you," she asked, glancing at his hands on the bar.

He started to pull his hands off and she grabbed one of them and looked at it carefully, running her thumb over his crooked finger.

"Thomas S. Rubidoux."

"Thomas S., is it? And what does the 'S' stand for," she asked.

"Sebastian."

She let go of his hand and moved her hand until his chin was cradled by her index finger and thumb, studied him and leaned closer to him so that he could smell her.

"Well, Thomas S. Rubidoux, do you know how to keep a secret?"

"Yes, Ma'am, I do," he said slowly.

She smiled and slowly let her hand glide away from his chin as she straightened up.

"Yes, I believe you do."

She tousled his hair, walked away and he continued to watch her as she went about working the room, playing hostess.

She looked back once as he still observed and she winked at him.

And, then, Rufus smacked him with the wet towel again.

"Take those to the tables will you. You've gawked so long they're almost flat," the barkeep growled at him.

Tom jerked the mugs off the bar without spilling a drop and smiled to himself.

He knew.

Even then he knew he was protected from Rufus and all others, because Madam Charlotte MacGregor, of the mighty and indestructible Agate Club, mistress of Judge Charles Miller Frost, liked him.

Over time Tom became a favorite with all the women of The Agate Club and he even accepted the different roles he fulfilled for them: younger brother, pet, comforter and shoulder to lean on, first aid administrator, nurse, surgeons' assistant, bar back, waiter, host, horrible back up piano player and surrogate son.

They introduced him to the wealthy and to the "less than's". They taught him that he could get something from even those who appeared that they had nothing to give. The "girls" would send him out into the streets to run errands for them across to Chinatown to get opium, down to the fishing boats to get fish or even around town to be a messenger for them and their clients.

Lucky for him, Alonzo F. Horton had seen he could make more money on corner properties so every city block was shorter than the conventional city block. Literally, The Agate Club's book of business was on every corner….in a tall buildings.

The girls had pointed out to Tom to listen to the conversations, not just because they needed a spy, but because they knew what he could learn.

And, Charlotte had made it known to all, it was important for him to learn.

Vocabulary was learned from the businessmen and local officials and math from the financiers so that he could almost do compounding interest in his head.

Multiplication tables were practiced with clients by fees and by hours.

Charlotte's payroll.

With time, the women positioned Tom so that he became a favorite of the men of the club as well. Not in the way that they craved him sexually, but in the way that they appreciated and looked out for the young man and took him in as a son or younger brother, like the women had. He was smart, easy going, quick, charming and most importantly, he was discreet.

The men nodded back to him if Tom saw them on the streets – even if it was on a Sunday after church.

"He's one of the messenger boys," they would always tell their wives and families.

It was never a lie. They just didn't know what the content of the messages were.

After awhile the nods became a series of signals that Tom learned to read like a baseball player and he would pass the secret messages along when he returned to the club.

"Mr. Engleman won't be in tonight," he would report by indications that the shipping magnate's walking cane had touched the brim of his hat rather than his hand.

Sunday strolls in the city became part of Tom's weekly duties so he could get an idea of the business for the week.

It was Miss Charlotte's working relationship with one of the potato farmers that had brought Tom to her attention. She paid top dollar for the potatoes to only be delivered to her and one other club she shared an interest in – The Robin's Nest. Tom occasionally would make the deliveries with his uncle so, Miss Charlotte would also loan Tom out to help unload the sacks of potatoes to both establishments once he worked for her.

He liked going to the Robin's Nest and would volunteer to run errands there any time he could – much more than Madam MacGregor approved. The women fawned over him and catered to him. They stashed his favorite root beer, black licorice and horehound candy for when he came by.

And, very much like the women of The Agate Club, they doted on him like a favorite nephew.

It was on these excursions and outings that Tom started to see and hear other things.

The first incident that struck Tom as odd was when he was down in the alley behind The Agate Club unloading sacks of potatoes one afternoon during school hours. He was being lazy and was trying to open the back door without setting the sacks down. Suddenly, he was face to face with a girl a little younger than him.

She smiled at him.

Befuddled, he just stood there with a sack of potatoes on his shoulder, blocking her exit.

"Excuse me, but you're a little hard to walk around," she giggled.

"Uh, oh, sorry," he said and stepped so that she could walk out the door by him.

"Thank you."

Tom was still looking at her when he tried to walk through the door, but was stopped by a hand that planted firmly on his chest.

"Not so fast," a boy, about Tom's age said.

"Cabot," Tom heard Charlotte's voice come through behind the boy, "Don't be such a snot."

"Excuse us, Tom," she said.

"You, too," she said shoving another boy, about the girl's age, through the door.

"Come on Tom," she said pulling him through the door.

"I'm tempted to call your parents and let them know," Charlotte told the kids in the alley. "Consider this a warning. I don't ever want to see you here again. Do you understand?"

Tom had already set down the sack as he was looking through the doorway around Charlotte.

None of the kids heard her. They were in a silent conversation of their own. The older of the two boys, Cabot, was scowling, the girl was still smiling and the other boy looked like he was about to cry...but they were all looking at Tom.

It was a few months later when Tom saw Cabot after Sunday mass. Tom didn't see him at first. He was busy watching Judge Frost, and his wife, Beatrice. A fact he only knew from seeing the judge's wife's photo in the newspaper.

She was a striking woman and in many ways resembled Charlotte. Tom could easily imagine Charlotte walking arm and arm with Judge Frost. In fact, Tom often thought the Judge might look happier if he was.

Beatrice Frost looked like she had spent too much time sucking on a lemon. Tom would almost describe her as "too starchy" – a term he used for many of the society women he saw.

Rufus described it more as "silver spoons shoved up their sanctimonious asses."

"That's why they walk funny," he explained to Tom one afternoon while the boy hauled blocks of ice down the chute into the club basement. "You try walking around with something stuck up your butt."

Tom had grimaced at the thought and shuddered a little, but then giggled.

The Judge caught Tom's eye and Tom nodded to keep from being embarrassed that he had been caught staring.

He was quite familiar with Tom since he had spent many afternoons tutoring Tom in social studies, history, politics, horse racing and guns.

The Judge nodded.

Tom continued to watch the Judge as he walked on and it was after he passed that Tom noticed Cabot walking behind the Judge with another couple. He wouldn't have thought they were all together until the Judge slowed and turned to talk to the couple.

Further behind them were another woman and the younger boy from the alley. There was a man with them as well, but it was also hard to tell if they were all together.

"Miss MacGregor," Tom slowly asked a few days later when he was practicing his math by doing the books from the night before.

"Yes, Tom."

"What were those kids doing here?"

She pursed her lips and continued looking at the cigar order.

"I saw one of them on Sunday, walking with Judge Fros..."

She looked over at his work.

"Pay attention to what you're doing."

"Who were they," he said, not hearing her.

"I heard you," she said looking up at him and then back down. She flipped through a couple of pages. "I asked you once if you could keep a secret, Tom," she said without looking up, "and you said you could."

"Yes, ma'am, but..."

"I believed you."

He thought intensely about what she was saying.

"It's rude to stare, Tom."

"Yes, Ma'am, I'm sorry, I was just thinking," he said.

"Yes, you do that often."

"I..."

"Tom," she said looking up at him, "what happens here, all of this – is a secret. It doesn't exist beyond those doors," she said looking towards the front doors, "or through there," indicating the way to the alley.

She studied Tom's face as he processed what she was saying. She saw the look on his face change.

"Do you understand?"

She waited until his expression changed.

"Tom, you do know what we do here, don't you?"

He thought of the 'emergencies' he had to help with and the naked women and what was meant when the girls were told to 'be more careful next time.'

He suspected it was similar to spring on the ranch when they had calves being born. He had never seen so many failed pregnancies before and wondered what the girls were doing wrong.

He thought about the noises he heard behind closed doors and the funny smells. He thought about how everyone looked like they were getting dressed once room doors opened. He saw men give the girls money and thought it was their allowances.

"I think so," he hemmed and then, conceding as he shook his head, "no."

Charlotte smiled, "Well, maybe it's better that way for now. Trust me, by the time we send you away to college you will be the most popular man on campus," she said patting his arm.

5.

A Less Than Warm Reception

Tom ran his hands along the bar. As if he was still trying to absorb some memory through the wood.

"Well look who it is," Rufus said extending his hand out to Tom. Tom thought he looked like a greyer, heavier and woollier version of the man he had known before.

Tom grabbed the bear of a hand and shook it.

"I thought that was you there standing in the doorway, but then I thought, 'naw, that kid never come here again.'"

"How are you, Roof?"

"Can't complain, what can I get you to drink?"

"Sarsaparilla," Tom asked.

"Of course," Rufus said smiling. "Still haven't grown into long pants?"

"Nope."

Rufus set the mug down in front of Tom.

"I was sorry to hear about your uncle..."

"That was seven years ago, Rufus."

"Really?"

"Really - I guess it has been a while." Tom took a sip. "How many kids did I have the last time you saw me?

"You have kids?"

"That long, huh?"

"I think I remember hearing you got married."

A man at the end of the bar cleared his throat. Rufus looked down at him.

"Let me go tend to business."

Tom nodded and turned to look over the main floor.

Rufus came back down to pour the other man's drink. Tom turned and looked at him.

"Is today a holiday?"

Rufus looked at him puzzled, looked out at the clientele and smiled.

"No...the older they've gotten, the earlier their evenings start...and end in some instances."

Tom looked back.

"In fact," Rufus said from behind him, "your boss is in the far booth on the right."

"Judge Frost's old seat? Tom turned back around and leaned on the bar with his sarsaparilla. "I did wonder why I had a hard time finding him. I should have known. I just didn't think he was the type."

"Come on, Tom," Rufus chided him, "as long as you're a man – you're the type."

"Roof...do you remember seeing a girl around here, say...within the last couple of days or week."

Rufus stared at him and threw his hands out, "women all around, Boy."

"I...no, no...she would have seemed out of place. I don't think she would have been mistaken as one of the girls."

"Besides the Crusaders? No, no woman would be caught here...still...even if they didn't know any better."

Tom hemmed.

"Hey, did they suck out your brains at that expensive school of yours," Rufus said, "You've been spending too much time with that high society crowd of yours for too long. They've made you soft and stupid."

Tom proceeded slower.

"I just want to know – have you seen anything unusual?"

He realized how inane he must have sounded.

"That's what makes this so normal. Everything is unusual and out of the ordinary."

Tom was getting frustrated.

"I'm investigating the murder of a girl."

"The one found up on Torrey Pines?"

"Word travels fast. Yes, the one found up on Torrey Pines."

"Something that shocking spreads quickly. Yeah, I heard a couple of the men talking about that," Rufus said, nodding his head.

"She wasn't one of ours," Evelyn said as she came up behind Tom. "We're all accounted for."

"No, she was...no, I know she didn't work here."

Evelyn looked at him and then Rufus, who walked away to help someone else.

"There was," he reached over the bar where he knew the matches were kept, grabbed one of the small boxes and slid the cover off, "one of these stuck to her."

Evelyn looked a little surprised and then Rufus grunted.

"You've got to be joking. Do you know how many matches we go through a night?"

"As a matter of fact I do."

"There's nothing else we can help you with," Rufus said abruptly.

"Alright," Tom said as he set his glass down. "Thank you." He tossed a coin on the bar and he walked towards the front door. He caught the Captain's eye before reaching it.

"It was good to see you again," Evelyn said.

"Good to see you to Evelyn."

"I'd tell you not to be such a stranger," she said cheekily.

Tom smirked at her and walked out the front door.

Tom didn't remember much of his walk back to Dead Man's Point.

He was thinking about the case: the girl, The Agate Club and the murderer.

He was so engrossed in his own brain that he stepped off the curb without looking and almost straight into traffic. Luckily someone grabbed his arm and pulled him back before he the oncoming cars reached him.

Something in his gut was telling him that answers were at The Agate Club, but logic and the facts contradicted the feeling.

He left the potato sack out of his conversation with Evelyn and Rufus because he knew the basement of the club held piles of the empty sacks and with the Robin's Nest being in shambles that basement was the only place where those sacks should be, but he knew he would have to find out for sure.

Corey came by his desk as he was looking at the file.

"Where have you been," he asked trying to see what Tom was looking at.

"Hum, oh, uh, I was down at The Agate Club," he answered as he closed the file.

Corey leaned in more.

"Was the Captain there," he asked taking a bite of an apple.

Tom looked up at him quizzically, "as a matter of fact, he was."

Corey took another bite of the apple as a piece fell from his mouth onto Tom's desk. Annoyed, Tom flicked the piece with his finger and pushed Corey back.

"How did you know...," he started to ask.

"How did you not," Corey answered with his mouth full. Corey looked at him and Tom went back to the file.

"You know, for a man who is so persnickety about getting dirt in his car, I see that the sentiment doesn't go for other people's things," Tom said pointing at the apple.

"I hear it's not looking good for your cousins," ignoring him.

"What?"

"Well, the witness who called in."

"What witness? There's nothing in the report."

"That's why I was looking for you," he said and set an operator form on his desk. "Captain gave me this. It's the witnesses' statements claiming they drove by at 10 o'clock and saw your cousins' car parked."

Tom started reading the report as Corey continued.

"The cops pulled up as your cousins were about to leave."

"They didn't...well, I didn't," Tom said slowly.

"Well then, I guess you're not the top detective you think you are," Corey said sarcastically.

Tom scanned the paper. The witness' names were Paul and Faith Carpenter.

Their statements said they had been driving home to Del Mar when they came upon the Durant with the head lights on and they saw the passenger get out and walk towards the bluff.

They called the police and the police came to investigate.

"Hey, I'm going to go eat dinner," Corey announced.

"Huh?"

"Remember, I'm covering your shift tonight – you know for pay back for the night you took," he waved his hand over the desk, "the night all this happened. You were covering me so I could go on that date."

"Oh yeah, the one that didn't show," Tom said absentmindedly.

"Yeah, you didn't have to mention that."

"I'll see you tomorrow."

Corey slapped him on the shoulder.

"Don't stay too long. I don't want your wife calling."

As soon as Corey was out the door Tom put the paper in the file and left for home.

6.

DISTRACTED

"Yes Tia Lena," Tom said trying to get a word in on the kitchen phone. "No, Tia...Tia, I need...no, I don't think...yes, it has been...you see if Sylvestre and June...I'm trying...no, no please don't cry...yes...of course we'll come...Tia I need to speak with Sylvestre or Juneau..."

Meg laughed watching Tom get flustered and finally give up with the aunt on the end of the line.

"I take it we're going up there on Sunday," she said.

Tom nodded sheepishly.

"Hey Jay," Tom said back in the phone. "Huh, yeah, well...yes, I know...no, nothing...look, that night...did you see a car go by you and Sylvestre? Um mm, so it was just you? How long was it before the police arrived?"

Tom looked around for a pen and paper. Meg grabbed both for him.

"Really, ten minutes. How sure are you? It might, thanks. We're planning on it, but you can understand the circumstances. I can't really be there if you and Sylvestre are there. No, we'll figure something out. Don't tell your mom either way because then she'll call mine...exactly...thanks."

He hung up the phone.

Meg had her back towards him as she moved around the kitchen.

"There wasn't another car, was there," she asked.

"No," he said shaking his head.

"From what I remember, Juneau is the more reliable of the two."

Tom nodded his head, "Yes, he was the one everyone went to when I was 'missing'. I learned not to share anything with him."

"Really, he never struck me as being a snitch."

Tom laughed, "No, it was never anything like that. It was more naiveté. Sylvestre on the other hand was a weasel and was always getting us all in trouble."

Tom heard the kids squealing in the backyard.

"I don't wanna, Louie," he heard Alice yell. "Buce."

"Are they all out there," To asked.

"Yes."

"Even Joe?"

"He's holding his own."

"Do you need help?"

"No, I have it under control, but thanks."

"Okay," he said and turned to walk out of the kitchen.

Then everything happened at once.

He saw Meg look out the window.

He saw his desk drawer was open.

He heard Louis' voice, "Bang...bang, bang."

Meg's face go pale and the terror on her face.

Tom was out the back door before Meg could say anything.

Louis was holding Tom's revolver in both hands trying to point it at Bruce who had his hands up, but the gun was a little too heavy for the boy and it dangled at a weird angle.

Joe played near Bruce and Alice was near the door poking at a caterpillar.

"Alice," he said very slow and stern, "go inside."

There was something in Tom's tone that made her look at him and know immediately to obey and she ran past him to the top step. He heard Meg grab her and pull her inside.

Anger and terror gripped Tom. The boys looked at Tom concerned and he was trying not to scare them. Joe suddenly ran for Tom as fast as his unsteady legs would carry him.

"Louis, do not move," he said as he bent to scoop Joe up, turned and handed him to Meg, who had come back outside and stepped on the stoop. Tom had yet to look away from the older boys. Meg pulled him into the house as Tom took a few steps so that he was in arms length of Louis.

Tom knelt down and took the gun. He heard Meg breathe a sigh of relief. Then he grabbed Louis' arm.

"What were you thinking going into my desk drawer? How many times do I have to tell you this is not a toy?!"

Louis started to cry, terrified.

"Bruce," he said sternly, "Get over here. Meg do we still have that watermelon?"

"Yes," she said a little puzzled.

"Grab it for me."

He heard her walking toward the ice box.

"Since you don't seem to trust my word, respect what I tell you or believe me about how serious this is…I'm going to show you."

The screen door squeaked as Meg came out and walked down the steps to hand him the watermelon.

"They can watch from there," he told her indicating that Alice and Joe were standing outside on the top step. Meg walked back to them, kneeled between them and held them.

Tom stood and walked to the end of the yard, set the watermelon down and walked back.

"Maybe if you see what a gun does…"

"Tom…"

He ignored her as he lifted the gun, took aim and squeezed the trigger. The loud bang probably would have been enough to scare the children, but it was what they saw that became a memory that would forever stay with them.

The watermelon exploded in all directions with the red flesh splattering on plants, trees, the grass and the sidewalk. Chunks dangled from parts of the fence. There was only a small bit of the rind shaped like a small bowl lying sideways where it had fallen.

"Do you understand, now," he asked Louis and Bruce.

They both nodded their heads fervently. Tom felt a little bad when he noticed the wet stain going down Louis pant leg and into his sock. He heard the younger two whimpering behind him. Tom turned, walked into this house, to his desk and locked the gun up.

Later, after they had eaten dinner and the kids had bathed and gone to bed, Tom came out of the boys' room after reading them a story. Meg had just finished cleaning the kitchen and walked into the living room and sat in her favorite chair and curled her legs up. She pulled out a book and opened it. Tom sat at his desk and pulled out the file, but didn't open it just yet.

"That was quite a display this afternoon," Meg said sarcastically. "I don't think I'll ever touch your gun."

Tom smiled.

"I forgot watermelons were red."

"You know you need to be more careful when you're this much into a case. You're more distracted. You neglect a lot of things."

"I know," he said nodding his head, still frustrated with himself. "I could have sworn I locked it in my drawer. Apparently, I set it in there, but didn't shut and lock it."

He looked at her.

"Are you mad," he asked.

"Not anymore. Not that everything turned out okay. Just pay a little more attention when you're here."

He nodded.

"I felt bad for Lou," she said. "For once, I don't think he was worried about being embarrassed."

"It actually made me feel a little better…realizing they hadn't gone through the desk," Tom said.

"Okay, Detective, let's have it. My curiosity has been peaked since you were on the phone. Let's see if I can figure any of this out."

He stood up and went to pour himself a drink.

"First of all, I need to tell you something just in case someone saw me."

"I'm intrigued."

"I went to the club this afternoon."

"So," she said perplexed.

He stared at her.

"What?"

"I went to *the* club," he tried to clarify.

"Oh, ohhh...Tom, do you think that it's somehow tied in?"

"No, I actually went to the club to get sex," he said grinning.

"Smart ass."

"I think the girl had something to do with it, or her murderer. I come up with these bright ideas that sound dumb once I try to work them out."

He sat back down with his drink and opened the file.

"Tom, what's wrong."

"Something, I don't know, it has to do with the club, and not having a clue as to who this girl is."

"Do you think you might be a little upset that part of your childhood might be tarnished?"

"That's a little redundant under the circumstances, don't you think?"

"Was Charlotte there?"

"No, she retired from the day to day business of the club for a while. She has another woman in charge there now...although I know she still knows everything that goes on between those walls. I will need to go speak with her, but that will be another day."

Tom started to frown and Meg looked up from her book.

"This thing's really getting to you."

"You saw the photos...who does *that* to someone?"

He looked back at the file and the report he received that day.

"Tom...?"

"There are so many little things nagging me on this."

"It's not just that. There's something else. This is different. To be honest, I've never seen you wound up this tight."

"I know if I don't solve this thing the murderer is going to get away...if he hasn't already."

"I hate to point this out, but murderers have gotten away before."

He looked at her. She had never seen him look so frustrated.

"I know, but I also know that Sylvestre and Juneau will be convicted for it whether or not they're guilty."

"Are you sure? I mean what possible…"

He shook his head, "My gut tells me. That's why all these little details and unknowns are irritating."

"But if they're innocent…"

"I think they were just at the wrong place at the wrong time."

"It's not just because they're your cousins? I mean, you're not getting so twisted up because you have a personal tie to this case?"

He shook his head.

"No, trust me, there have been plenty of things that Sylvestre has done in the past I would have gladly choked him for."

"Tom, if they didn't do it how could they," she stopped.

He took a deep breath.

"That's why I think some way somehow there is something from the club involved. It wouldn't be the first time I'd seen a truth from that place buried. For Christ's sake – it is a brothel right smack in the center of downtown. The raids were supposed to have closed down all those establishments and there it is still cranking away…so to speak."

"Well, when you put it that way. What does the Captain say about all this?"

"I haven't told him. I was going to today until Corey gave me the witness report."

She didn't understand. He sighed.

"The report came from the Captain and I know it's a lie."

Over the next couple of days Meg and Tom went about their morning routines without saying much.

There were cases that Tom and Corey were called out on, but every time Corey brought up the girl in the burlap sack Tom answered in short answers. Tom also thought Corey might be happier not to be involved since the tiniest look at the photos made him queasy and uncooperative.

That's pretty much how the rest of their cases went as well. Corey was relegated to interviewing witnesses and left all the gritty, dirty and gruesome work to Tom.

The evenings were spent reviewing the little details and trying to put together a plan as to what direction Tom's focus needed to go.

Megan kept reminding him to keep to the simple questions and not to get carried away.

That was always Tom's weakness as a detective: He always made things more complicated when they were really simple and he had a tendency to look past the answer which was so obvious if he would just open his eyes and look in front of him.

7.

THE UNWANTED LEAF OF THE FAMILY TREE

The fly tried to climb up the glass. The condensation ran down the slick surface, pelting the small insect and pushing it further from the lip of the glass. It tried to escape by flying off the glass, but its wings became wet and it only slid further down until it was standing on the table, and then it walked away. The sun quickly dried its wings so it could fly away.

The only person who witnessed the whole endeavor was Tom, trying to ignore the incessant babble of his uneducated but gracious and loving family. He was trying to bide time and look for an opportunity to leave. Throughout his childhood he had felt like an outsider. Moving to the city made the feeling even worse even though Charlotte made sure he was driven up to the family's ranch whenever she could spare him.

His mother hugged him when he arrived and made sure to have his favorite things to eat, but besides the hug, she always moved around him like he had the Plague.

He knew his brother Aldo was the favorite, but Tom was the one they spent what precious little money they had to send to college.

Tom wondered why he couldn't just go locally, why had they sent him so far away?

He knew he could rely on them - for anything.

"More lemonade, Hijo," his mother asked. He nodded his head, his concentration on the fly broken. "I wish you would come visit more," she said very plainly without any emotion, which was typical for her.

He felt the sentence could easily have ended with, "but not really."

She filled his glass as he watched the lemonade pour over the ice, swirling around and raising the ice up to the top.

Family members were seated around several of the large tables under the trees. All the children were running in various groups, self-segregated by ages and likes.

"You mean, you wish I would come with the children so you could visit with them more," he said back.

"That's not true. If that were the case I wouldn't ask at all. Frank, Ysabel, Ignacio and Faustina have provided me with plenty of grandchildren."

Tom smiled.

"Iggy's kids tear up your garden and Frank's torment the life stock."

"I like the sound of children through the house and yard. Like when you were all small."

"At least...," he stopped himself. He looked over at Aldo as his brother's head listed to the side. No one had noticed or bothered to make a move to help him. Tom saw Meg out of the corner of her eye continue her conversation as she stood, gently put her hand on Aldo's hair and readjusted his head.

Frank and Iggy worked together in the railroad offices. Tom's mother knew what Frank had done and was disappointed that Ignacio had no problem following his lead. Aldo was her prince and she would have preferred to see him meet his demise with one of his cousins on the World War I battlefields or have been lynched by a mob rather than suffer the way he was. She knew he could still understand what was going on. She knew he could process everything and it was slowly driving him insane.

Meg had sat herself down next to Aldo with her hand on his arm as she continued listening to the conversation. Alice stood by her side and watched her.

"Is he sick," Alice leaned in and whispered, but loud enough that Tom could also hear.

"He hurt his head," Meg told her.

"How?"

"He was running away and someone shot him."

"Shot? With a gun?"

"Yes, shot with a gun."

"Like Daddy's?"

Meg hesitated realizing she was remembering the lesson with the watermelon.

"Yes, like Daddy's."

"But Daddy didn't do this."

"No, no he didn't. Uncle Aldo is his brother, like Bruce and Louis are your brothers."

"And Joe?"

"And Joe," Meg smiled.

Alice wrinkled her face as she thought.

"I thought only bad people got shot," she said.

"Well, all people can be shot, but mostly bad people," Meg said very carefully, looking up at Tom.

"Daddy has a bad brother," the little girl continued.

Meg thought about Frank and Iggy.

"No," she finally answered.

Alice thought really hard and then looked up at her mother.

"Will Bruce and Louis be shot?"

"No, no, no - they're not that bad."

"How would you like to come inside and help me," Tom's sister, Faustina asked Alice before her mother could overhear.

Meg turned around and then looked down at Alice.

"Okay," Alice answered.

Aldo's hand slumped off the arm of the chair as Meg turned to help Alice. Meg reached for it.

"Don't help him," Tom said.

Meg startled, looked at him. He smiled.

"He's flirting with you." He looked at Aldo. "Aren't you?"

Aldo started what sounded like humming, but not quite.

"Just as I thought," Tom smirked.

"Is he trying to talk," Meg asked as she set his hand back and sat next to him without removing hers.

"No, he's humming. He used to whistle."

"It sounds familiar."

Aldo's head jerked.

"I thought so," he looked at Meg. She was patting Aldo's arm and then picking up his hand in hers.

"Daddy liked that tune and whistled it, sang it, hummed it while he was working."

Meg looked at Aldo's hand, curiously.

"What is it," Tom asked.

"He doesn't have your crooked middle fingers."

Tom looked down at Aldo's hand and shook his head. "No, I'm the only one. I inherited them from somewhere down on my mother's side I think, but they skipped her and her siblings. Bruce is the only one of ours who has them."

"No, Joe has them too."

"He does?"

"Yes."

"Did I know that?"

"Yes, you did…Detective."

His mother, Alice and sister Ysabel walked out with a tray of steaks.

"Tom," Ysabel started, "will you do the honors."

He walked to her and grabbed the tray.

"You mean Mother's going to let me play with matches?"

"Just don't burn the field down."

"I wonder if smelling a bar-b-que bothers the cattle."

"That is really disturbed."

She touched Aldo's head and sat down next to Meg.

"So, the talk in the kitchen is that you are going to save Juneau and Sylvestre," Ysabel asked.

"Hmmm."

"Well, are you?"

He threw a match on the pile of kindle and paper but nothing happened.

"I'm working on it.," he said concentrating on the fire, bending down closer so that he could try and see why the flame wasn't catching.

"How's that fire coming along on," Meg chided.

"I'm working on that too."

Ysabel smirked and looked at Meg, who shook her head, stood up and walked over to Tom.

Ysabel continued her conversation as Meg reworked the kindling. Tom took a step back.

"You know they don't really understand. Things are still very simple up here. You either did something or you didn't. So you are punished or not."

Meg motioned to Tom that she wanted the matches. He reluctantly gave them to her.

"It's not that simple though, Ysabel" Tom said as he frowned.

"I know that," Ysabel said watching Meg light the match and then proceed to light the fire. "Most of us know that, but Tia Lena and Momma and the others do not and they have no doubt that you will save them, Tom," she hesitated before she said her next words, "Actually, Momma's insisting you do."

Meg stood, brushed her hands and marveled at her accomplishment and looked at Tom to gloat. He was looking down the driveway. She turned to follow his gaze.

A big dust cloud was moving up towards the house.

"Should I gather up the kids," she asked, assuming by Tom's sudden change in posture and demeanor indicated the Juneau and Sylvestre were in the car.

He waited until the car was all the way up the drive and parked.

"Yes," he said once he saw Sylvestre get out of the passenger side. Sylvestre saw Tom and waved. Tom nodded, handed the tray to Ysabel.

"Sorry, we have to go."

"Are you sure," she said when she saw Sylvestre and Juneau start walking towards them. "No one will know. It's not like anyone here is going to say anything or know anybody you work with."

"It's just for the best," Tom said.

She nodded and looked at Sylvestre.

"I wouldn't feel so bad about the whole thing if it had just been him in this mess. Why did Juneau have to be with him?"

"I know," Tom said, "I feel the same way."

Prison was hard, inmates were lost in paperwork and killed by fellow inmates; especially those that were considered soft or sensitive. Juneau was both and he shuddered at the thought. There was no question, Tom knew that Juneau would be violated in some way or fashion and he knew he had to find the murdered if for any only one reason – to save Juneau.

8.

Miss Charlotte MacGregor

"Rubidoux. Hayes."

Corey turned around. Tom was too engrossed in his thoughts and what he wanted to ask the coroner. Corey reached out and grabbed the back of his jacket. He turned around.

"What," he asked.

"Captain wants us," he said pointing over his shoulder.

They walked back to Captain Moran's office and shut the door behind them. They sat in the seats directly in front of the desk. Tom always speculated that the captain had his desk and seat especially made so they stood higher than the rest of the furniture in the offices of the detectives. He thought Moran always wanted a superior edge, to let everyone not only know, but feel that he was the one in charge and none of them could over ride what he said or thought or think independently of him.

Tom always thought there was an edge or tension with the conversations he had with he and Corey that he didn't have for the rest of the officers.

Tom felt it was especially reserved for them.

"So, what do you have for me?"

"We don't have a suspect yet," Corey blurted out.

Tom cocked his head a little perplexed. He could always rely on Corey to say the stupid thing that he wanted to say sarcastically.

"Well, uh, had we known," he stammered as Tom gritted his teeth, "had we known you wanted something to eat then we would have picked you up a bite."

In his mind, Tom corrected himself. Only Corey would say something dumber than he was thinking.

He took a deep breath. In any other circumstance Tom would be trying to keep from laughing.

The captain glared at Corey and opened his mouth to say something.

"Sir," Tom said, cutting him off, "could you be a little more specific. We've been working on several cases."

The captain moved his focus over to Tom. Corey looked like he was trying to mentally play catch up.

"The girl off Torrey Pines," the captain clarified and looked back at Corey, wanting to say something.

"We have lots of clues, but not enough to start trying to piece it all together or target a suspect," Tom added.

"What about the two who found the body?"

"No," Tom said shaking his head, "the time the coroner said she died is much earlier than when they found her."

"Even with the amount of time it took for them to report it and the witness report?"

Tom's shoulders tensed.

"Well, that's the other thing. It would have been very easy for them to leave without anyone ever knowing they found the body. Besides, I found another set of tire tracks up on the side of the road about a mile. And, there was a set of footprints."

"Yes, but they couldn't leave because they were caught."

"Yes Sir, but…"

"No…is your cousins' involvement why you've been harassing the people at The Agate Club?"

"No Sir…"

"I want this case wrapped up quickly. It looks pretty simple to me. A hooker from another town…she probably ran away…and those boys."

"There's no evidence against…"

"What do you think is going to work? We want this wrapped up quickly, Rubidoux. Sylvestre Rubidoux has a record of assault and battery, especially against women. This wouldn't be the first time...as you well know," Captain Moran barked back.

"But Juneau doesn't," Tom argued.

"Maybe he hasn't been caught. I'm sorry, Tom, but you have a list of relatives, including your older brothers, who we have files on."

He shot a look at Corey.

"For Christ sake's Hayes, do you have anything to say," the Captain barked.

Corey looked at Tom and then the captain.

"No."

"Look Tom, if you're family involvement is getting in the way I will assign it to someone else, but we are short-handed as it is. Can you handle this?"

Tom's teeth were clenched.

"This thing is messy and this town doesn't need to know there is some degenerate around town hacking up girls into little bits, stuffing them in bags and dangling them from trees for everyone to see."

Tom stared.

"Rubidoux!"

"Yes," the words slowly came out, "I will take care of it."

"And you," he said back at Corey, "stay out of the morgue and go do whatever it is that you do. Show me you earned that badge on something other than you're a veteran of the war and your relatives. I don't ever want to have to explain to the district attorney that he can't submit evidence because you vomited all over it."

Tom stood, opened the door and walked out followed by Corey.

"Wow," Corey said as he shut the door behind him.

"Um uh," was all Tom said as he walked back towards his desk. He stood over it looking down at the file. In a split second he picked it up and started walking out the door.

"Where are you going," Corey asked.

"I have a hunch."

"The captain just indicated that you were not supposed to go to the club."

"Yes, I know," Tom shot back, "they wouldn't like that."

Corey questioned back, "They?"

"Exactly," he said with a smirk.

"I missed something," Corey asked, perplexed.

"Who else besides the captain would want this thing closed quickly and can?"

Tom knocked on the door. He removed his hat and held it in his hand and then started to fidget with it.

He heard steps inside the house approach the door. His heartbeat quickened.

"God," he thought, "what if my mother sees me?"

That was ridiculous since she was three hours up in Vista and it had been a very long time since her opinion mattered. He laughed to himself for a quick second when he realized he was more concerned about being seen here than down at the club.

"What if anyone I know sees me?"

Quickly his mind raced through everything that could be, that would be thought or said.

The doorknob clicked.

Thoughts stopped.

The door slowly opened.

"Detective Rubidoux, this is a pleasant surprise."

"Hello Sophia," he said tipping his head.

"Please come in," she said pushing the screen door ajar so Tom could open it and let himself in.

Tom stepped in and looked around.

"May I get you something to drink," she offered to take his hat, but he shook his head. She looked up at him and eyed him wisely. "I suppose this is not a social call."

"No ma'am."

"Iced tea or lemonade then?"

"Lemonade, please."

"I will let Miss Charlotte know you are here."

"Thank you."

Tom had heard a lot about Charlotte's Banker Hill home. He had also heard the rumors of "Miss Charlotte" still running her side "business" out of this house.

It struck Tom as odd that it looked a lot like any other home. It strangely made him think what his own home would look like without all the toys strewn about. Odd water color and oil paintings were hung in a precise order which drew a visitor's attention to the divan and chairs. Tom looked at the family photos amassed on the credenza. On closer inspection he recognized that many of them were "friends". There was an old one of a man in his forties. Tom thought he looked familiar, but wasn't quite sure. He was surprised to see a photo of himself in his army uniform. He picked it up, looked at it and then placed it back. As he put it back a similar one caught his eye.

This young man was also in uniform, but it was British. He picked the photo up to look closer at the medals. The rifle the soldier held wasn't one that Tom had recognized from the standard British armies, but the face of the soldier was one he recognized from his youth.

"Thomas."

Tom spun around.

"Miss MacGregor."

She frowned a little, as if to scold him, "Tom…"

"Sorry, Miss Charlotte."

He turned back and set the photo down.

"Now you are making me sound like a madam."

Sophia entered and handed Tom his lemonade.

"Thank you," he said as he quickly tightened his grip as the glass almost slipped through his fingers.

"Oh Sophia, if I remember correctly there are several bottles of root beer outside. I believe the detective would prefer that."

"No, really, this is fine," Tom said.

"Suit yourself," Charlotte said nodding at Sophia to dismiss her.

Sophia left them and Charlotte started walking to the divan and gestured for Tom to take the chair next to her.

"Have a seat Tom."

Tom waited for her to sit first and then, obeying her, took the seat she had indicated. He took a sip of the lemonade as soon as he set his hat down and settled.

Charlotte had been right - he would have preferred the root beer…even warm.

It was too sour. He tried his best not to make a face.
Charlotte just smiled and acted as if she hadn't seen anything.

"What can I help you with today Tom?"

He was very uncomfortable and sheepish, which was
unnerving to him, an experienced investigator.

"Ma'am."

"We're now at Ma'am, are we?"

"Please," he said shifting in his seat. "I have some
questions..."

"...That you couldn't ask about at the club. Tom, you
know I cannot talk about my clientele."

"What if..."

"You should know that first hand."

"Yes ma'am, I'm sure you've heard..."

"You have questions about the girl."

He suspected before he had arrived that she knew or had
been told.

"I'm hoping you might know....I mean...there's nothing
you don't know about the club and who comes and goes." he said
ignoring her.

"The girl hadn't been there."

"Could it be possible that you just never saw her?"

"That's a very interesting statement, Tom."

"But isn't there a possibility...I mean even I know..."

"No," she almost snapped. He saw her jaw tighten and in
a blink of an eye it was relaxed again. Tom would have missed it
if he hadn't been looking for any small clue. "You know I am kept
informed of everyone that enters through those doors,"
Charlotte continued. "You were one of my moles Tom. Did you
ever keep anything or anyone from me? No, you kept everything
secret, even during the raids that tried to shut us down."

"You never left the building; we couldn't keep anything
from you," Tom said slightly incredulously. "You lived there."

"Thomas, if you insist on taking this tone of voice with
me..."

"I am no longer one of your boys."

They glared at each other. Charlotte felt herself losing the
edge.

"Why was one of your matchbooks found stuck to the inside of the bag the girl was found in," Tom pressed.

"Just because it was stuck to the inside of the bag doesn't mean it was hers."

"The bag had the stamp from the old potato farmer we used to buy from. Not one of the stamps from the docks. There were only two clubs who did business with him."

"The Robin's Nest is still standing, somewhat. Just because it's empty of people doesn't mean there isn't anything there."

Tom's thoughts stalled for just a second, *"The woman should have been an attorney,"* he thought. He quickly realized she had acquired a lot of experience with her line of work and establishment.

"Even if that were true," he said, sure that she knew he had been sifting through the Robin's Nest remains, "it means that someone involved had been at the club or the building and you own both...and I know how you protect what is yours."

Charlotte's expression slowly changed to one Tom had never seen before, but couldn't interpret. Her jaw tensed slightly again and she took a sip of her drink. Tom thought it was just a gesture so she could stall him.

Suddenly, everything about her softened.

"Where were you when my sister was killed," she asked quietly.

He started to feel himself relax as he remembered the times she had spoken about her sister, niece and lost nephew.

No, he would not let her play to his weaknesses.

"Which was it, Charlotte?!"

She tensed, thought for a second, took in a slow breath.

"I can honestly say, under oath if you prefer that whoever it was has never been a customer of mine. Thomas, if you choose to ask me any more questions you will need to go through my lawyer. You know him...he's usually found in the fourth booth at the club. Now, if you'll excuse me."

Tom stood as she stood.

"I have other matters to attend to. You can show yourself out."

She started to walk away.

"Be sure to tell your lovely wife hello."

Tom just watched her and was about to dump his lemonade into the nearby plant and stopped abruptly when she said something walking through the doorway."

"And, Tom," she said slowly, "you were *never* one of my boys."

The door closed behind her. Tom finished pouring the drink in the plant, set the glass down, walked towards the front door and reached for the knob. A flicker of light flashed out of the corner of his eye and he turned to see two glasses. He turned more to look at them more clearly. One had lipstick around the rim, the same shade Charlotte had been wearing and the other...nothing.

Business as usual.

Tom stepped out, walked down the steps of the porch and towards his car. He looked up and down the street, but it wasn't until he stepped around to the driver's side of his car that he saw it.

Model Ford, dark blue, mahogany interior and sitting very erect behind the steering wheel was Judge Frost's driver and butler, Paul, and leaning against the car was Captain Moran's son, Cabot – the British soldier from the photo.

Tom thought about approaching him, but then looked up the pathway to the house and then back at the car.

He got in his car and drove to the station.

9.

CABOT

Tom did not like Cabot Moran. He never had. It could have started from the simple looks they had exchanged that afternoon in the alley behind The Agate Club or it could have just been something that Tom saw in Cabot as he strolled behind Judge Frost and his wife on Sundays.

Tom did know that the intensity of his dislike came about the time Cabot joined his tutoring sessions with the Judge.

Tom would sit back as Cabot would interrupt him when he was trying to answer one of the Judge's questions. His blood boiled when Cabot would fawn over the Judge, lapping up any ounce of attention the Judge gave him but then reminded himself he knew Cabot was nothing more than a very large "kiss-ass".

For Tom, it all came to a head when Cabot passed off an idea of Tom's as his own...right in front of Tom.

Tom didn't say anything in front of the Judge at the time, but waited until the boys had been dismissed and were heading out the side door to the alley. Tom was right on Cabot's heels and was going to confront him outside when he was jerked back by his arm.

"Not so fast," Rufus said and pulled Tom back inside to the bar where Charlotte waited for him.

"Let it go Tom," she said as a command.

Tom didn't say anything and just continued to glare at nothing.

"Tom," she said more sternly.

Finally, he refocused his attention directly at Charlotte. "It was my idea. He..."

"I know."

He blinked.

For the first time he realized he wasn't the one who was protected.

"Tom, he's not doing it to you. You know that. Cabot would undermine anybody. He would screw himself if he thought it would help him get ahead. It's ridiculous, you know. All these rich and powerful men think they just came about their power. I bet if you go back to their childhoods they were all just as greedy and shrewd and callous."

"But that's not right. The Judge lets him..."

"Tom," she said in a way that made her sound tired, "the Judge knows. Sometimes you need to work around and with things that aren't right. Bad people get away with things as do good people who do bad things. The world goes on. Don't be so quick to judge others Tom. Maybe Cabot doesn't get any attention at home, maybe..."

"Home," Tom yelled, "at least he has a home!"

No one had ever heard him raise his voice.

"Thomas," he heard the Judge speak softly behind him.

He kept his gaze focused on Charlotte. Rufus stayed at the other end of the bar drying a glass, acting as if he heard nothing.

"Thomas," he said, "look at me."

Tom slowly turned around and looked at the Judge.

"You don't think I became a judge by being a fool, do you?"

"No, sir," he said feeling ashamed.

"You are better at this game than you think you are. It's a lot like poker. You allow someone to think that you have something that you really don't in order to see what they will do."

"A bluff."

"Yes, a bluff."

"Where I'm from," he hoped the words would sting, "we call it 'playing opossum'."

"Yes, you do."

Tom, ignoring that his barb didn't have the desired effect, wanted to tell them what Cabot was capable of. He had seen the boy tie firecrackers to dogs and cats and light them. He had seen him bully smaller weaker children and laugh over it.

"I know Cabot, Tom," the Judge said as if he was hearing his thoughts. "You will let it go though, won't you?"

Tom reluctantly nodded his head.

Another secret he would keep within the walls of The Agate Club.

Regardless, Tom continued to tally Cabot's indiscretions silently in his mental notebook as they occurred.

In his mind, he seriously thought someday the Judge or Charlotte or someone would pay him back.

He watched as Cabot continued to bully other children; including the other boy he had seen with Cabot that day in the alley:

Corey Hayes.

His future partner.

The younger and smaller boy seemed to be a favorite target of Cabot's wrath.

Everything Tom saw and allowed played against his nature of wanting to help those who were weaker; especially when they were being tormented in the way Cabot tormented Corey.

Cabot's demeanor was obviously the opposite. When he saw someone weaken it was like watching a shark that senses blood, creating a frenzy.

Tom started to watch Corey more and more. Every once and a while, he would see fresh bruises and cuts on the boy. He felt sorry for him because it seemed that his resolve seemed to get weaker and weaker with every new bruise or cut.

Tom, who never forgot the lashings from his parents, became less and less convinced that Cabot was the only one taking his rage out on the youngster.

He despised those that felt they became stronger by picking on the weak. It infuriated him when he thought or knew it was a larger man and he resolved he would do what he could for Corey.

One day Tom was unloading a shipment of ice down the chutes to the basement of the club when he heard a girl's voice somewhere else in the back alleys.

"Stop it Cab. Leave him alone."

Tom set the block of ice back on the truck bed and went down the alley and looked around the corner in time to see Cabot push Corey. Corey stumbled backwards and fell to the ground.

"Leave me alone," Corey cried.

Tom cringed, his muscles tensed.

"What," Cabot said as he kicked him.

The girl grabbed Cabot's arm. Blindly, he pushed her back, flinging her into the wall so that her head bounced off the brick as she fell to the ground.

That was Tom's limit.

"That's enough Cabot," he said walking towards them.

"Why don't you mind your own business," he glowered, "don't you have work to do?"

"This is my business and I'll make it the Judge's business. I don't think he thinks very much of a sniveling brat who picks on little girls and boys."

"How do you know what he thinks?"

"You're right. I don't know for sure, but we can go ask him. He's in the club right now."

"You don't have the nerve."

Tom thought for a second. He wasn't certain the Judge was in the club, but he did know that the Judge ranked snitches somewhere along the same level as bullies and those were ranked as "not fit to lick his boots."

"Maybe not, but only so I could give you a taste of your own medicine," Tom said confidently.

Cabot's expression changed, especially as Tom closed in on him. Although Cabot was a bit taller, Tom's experiences of fighting with his brothers and cousins and working at the club gave him the edge.

Cabot backed up until he was against one of the brick walls.

"You wouldn't dare," he said feebly as Tom's body started to tense, preparing to hit Cabot.

The girl went behind Tom and helped Corey up as Tom continued to close the gap between him and Cabot.

"You know I would," Tom challenged him.

Cabot tried to hold his ground. Tom waited until Corey and the girl were clear, but there was an exchange of looks that altered Cabot's resolve. He straightened his posture and Tom saw his jaw and shoulders tense.

Tom grinned.

That was all that was needed to send Cabot swinging.

Tom stepped to the side and aided Cabot's momentum by pushing him as he fell through his punch past him. Cabot stumbled and ran into the other wall.

Cabot turned around and lunged at Tom. Tom stepped forward and punched him in the face. Stunned, he teetered back onto his heels and as he rocked forward, Tom punched him twice more. Cabot fell forward to the ground on his knees and then keeled over on his side.

Tom turned to Corey and the girl.

"Are you okay," he asked them.

Corey nodded and then the expression on the girl's face changed to alarm.

Tom immediately knew the mistake he had made.

Never turn your back on an opponent unless you are far from arms reach or he is completely knocked out.

Cabot was neither.

Tom had just enough time to tense his muscles and step forward with one foot to brace himself before Cabot grabbed him from behind and locked his arms.

Since the move didn't quite work the way Cabot intended, he improvised and leveraged his height to take Tom down to the ground.

Before Tom could face Cabot or get up, Cabot sat on him and started punching him frantically.

Tom couldn't get a punch in and just tried to protect his face and deflect as many punches as he could. He hoped Cabot would tire, but it seemed as if his energy was limitless.

He realized the only way he was going to get a punch in was to take one in the face.

Taking a deep breath, he let his hands fall away and swung a punch at Cabot.

The momentum of both boys' fists abruptly stopped as they connected with the other's face.

Tom was seeing stars and felt Cabot list to one side. He ignored the pain he was feeling and shoved Cabot off him and then sat on him. With one hand he pulled Cabot up by the front of his shirt and with the other he punched him again.

Cabot managed to push Tom back, but Tom was able to jump to his feet. The bigger boy scrambled forward and tackled Tom at the waist causing both to tumble back to the ground.

Tom suddenly felt himself being pulled up. A man Tom didn't know, was holding Cabot back.

"That's enough boys," Rufus said.

He let Tom go and turned him around so he could look at him. He nodded, almost in approval of the blood, scrapes and bruising that was beginning to appear on Tom. He looked closer at Tom's face and put his thumbs on either side of his nose.

"Stay still," he said as he wriggled Tom's nose and with a quick "snap" had put his nose back into place.

Tom winced.

Rufus leaned back to admire his work.

"Good as new."

Tom's eyes watered and he heard Cabot scuffling behind him.

"He started it," he whined.

"I don't think so," Rufus said handing Tom the bar towel from his back pocket.

Tom hesitated for a second remembering the towel sometimes missed Rufus' back pocket and ended up being tucked in somewhere else.

As a precaution, or just to make himself feel a little better, he put the non-tucked end to his face as the blood from his nose started turning it crimson.

Tom turned so he could see Cabot.

"Ask them," Cabot said pointing to Corey and the girl who were at the end of the alley.

"Who do you think got us out here, you dumb git," Rufus let his mouth go unfiltered.

"When my father finds out..."

"Shut up. The Judge wants to see you," he said looking at Tom. Tom was looking down the alley at Corey and the girl. Tom quickly realized Rufus was looking at him when he was talking about the Judge's request. Out of the corner of his eye he saw Cabot gloating. Tom dropped his eyes, nodded and started to walk away, seething inside.

"Oh, not you," he grabbed Tom's shoulder, "No, you need to go finish unloading the ice shipment. Judge Frost wants to speak with you," he said turning to Cabot. The man holding him shoved him forward.

"What," Cabot said in disbelief.

Rufus who had let go of Tom, grabbed Cabot by the shoulder and pushed him towards the end of the alley.

"Thanks," Rufus nodded at the man.

He winked at Tom as he ushered Cabot down the alley.

Tom followed behind them still mopping his face, his nose throbbing and eyes beginning to swell.

Tom saw Charlotte come into the alley opening and put one hand on Corey's back and the other on the girl as she guided them out of sight.

He made it to the end of the alley and back to the ice truck in time to see Charlotte take the two children through the alley door of the club ahead of Cabot and Rufus.

Tom kept his head in his work for the rest of the afternoon – his one bit of fun was sliding down the ice chute once he slid all the blocks down to the basement.

By the time he made it back upstairs to the salon, Cabot and the other two were gone. Tom wanted to know what happened, but wasn't surprised they weren't there. Rufus reminded him of his appearance and he cleaned himself up and changed his shirt before continuing his work.

The night was uneventful, or may have just felt like that to Tom because of the afternoon's events. The biggest excitement came when he felt his stomach flip when Rufus told him Charlotte wanted to see him upstairs.

Nodding, he headed down the bar and up the staircase.

For some reason there seemed to be more steps and the staircase seemed steeper. Evelyn and a gentleman that Tom only knew at that time as Mr. Farnham were leaving her room. Tom nodded at both and Evelyn winked at him. Mr. Farnham kissed Evelyn and seemed a bit flustered exchanging nods with the boy.

Tom continued to walk down the hall until he came to the double doors of Charlotte's room. He ran his hands through his hair and tucked in his shirt before knocking on the door. He only heard music playing and knocked again.

"Come in," he heard her say from far away.

He stepped into the salon and turned to shut the doors behind him. He didn't step too far in, partly out of respect and partly because he wasn't sure he was supposed to.

This was the one room in the club he had never been. He had expected the room to be darker as the other rooms were; but, instead, it was bright from all the colors. There was a settee of lime green velvet towards one of the walls and behind it he could see the arm of the Victrola move up and down as the record he heard spun around on the turn table.

He took a couple of steps forward.

The curtains were a pattern of orange, green and purple and, oddly, matched the red carpet.

He wasn't quite sure what the color the walls were. He just knew that the mismatch of palette didn't hurt his eyes.

"I'm in here," he heard Charlotte say from a room off to the side.

Tom walked into the doorway and stood stiffly at the arch.

Charlotte's room was a continuation of the front room in subtler tones. She sat at her dressing table and saw him in the reflection of the large mirror.

"Good evening Tom," she smiled.

"Good evening, Ma'am."

He caught his reflection in the mirror and saw one of his eyes was already black and there were a couple of red scrapes as well as the cut across the bridge of his nose.

At that point the music stopped and he could hear the needle dragging along the inner part of the record.

"Would you mind starting that again please?"

"Yes, Ma'am."

He walked to the Victrola and looked down at it. His cheeks became flushed as embarrassment took over because he didn't know how it worked. He stared at it for a second trying to remember how the other girls had started one. Looking along the side he found the crank and gave it a few turns and then reached in to pick up the arm when he saw the black disk begin to spin. He started to gingerly set it down, but it slipped, landed on the record and skidded across with a screech. He cringed and quickly picked the arm up again and waited for Charlotte to say something. When she didn't, he leaned in so he could set the needle down more precisely. A large breath was released as he stood up in relief, satisfied that he couldn't do any more damage.

"Come here, Thomas," she said from where she still sat, getting ready for the end of business for the night. It was her practice to walk around the floors one last time before they "closed" for the evening. They never really closed, but it gave the married men a subconscious nudge that they might want to return to their homes. Most of the time they still stayed, but there was the occasional one who would leave.

Tom walked back into her room, but kept his distance and looked around. She watched him from the mirror with her back to him.

"You can come closer, Tom. No one is going to jump out at you from in here."

He moved so that he could touch her, scanning everything that was on the dresser. There were many containers of various shapes and sizes that held things like cream and talc. Towards the right edge there was another bottle that held an amber liquid that Tom thought was perfume.

A gift from Judge Frost, no doubt.

There were a lot of make-up containers holding colors that Tom imagined were the inspirations for many of the colors in the room.

All he knew was that none of the women up at the ranch had ever had a collection like it.

"About this afternoon," she started, but Tom's eye caught one of the two framed photographs that sat further back near the mirror. He knew the one of the man was the Judge. The other was of a woman he had never seen.

Charlotte had seen what he was looking at and stopped talking.

"You may pick it up if you wish," she said smiling at him through the mirror.

He looked at her and then leaned around her to pick the photo up.

Tom studied the face. The woman must have had light brown hair and it looked like her eyes might have also been light, but it was hard to tell from the black and white coloring. No matter what, Tom thought she was beautiful.

Charlotte studied him.

"Would you believe that was me when I was younger?"

Tom continued looking at the photo, partly because he didn't hear her and partly because he didn't know how to politely tell her "no."

His glance up at her told her his answer, "No, I wouldn't think you would, but you would lie to me and tell me you did as to not hurt my feelings."

He looked at her sheepishly.

"It's okay, you don't have to answer that," she said and was taken that he was so interested in the woman. She reached out and slowly took the photo from him.

"That's my sister, Ainsley."

Tom's breathing stopped for a second. The story was already familiar to him since he had heard it whispered or told out of earshot of Charlotte. He felt sorry for her.

"She was very pretty," Tom said.

Charlotte brushed her fingers over the woman's face.

"Yes, yes she was. You've heard what happened, of course."

He shook his head, "I might hear what's said, but I don't always listen."

She smiled, "Very diplomatic Tom. I see Judge Frost's tutoring is starting to take."

A small smile spread on his face.

"She was the madam of the Robin's Nest," she started.

"Where my uncle and I dropped shipments off," Tom added.

"Yes, that's right. One night her former lov...gentleman...well...I'm not sure what exactly happened. All I do know is a messenger arrived at 3:15 in the morning telling me that she had been beaten to death. The only witnesses or witness was her infant daughter. I couldn't get any more information."

"Not even Judge Frost or Officer Moran..."

"No," she said shaking her head and looking at the photo as she ran her hand across the image again. "We do not ask our men to do favors like that."

"Oh," he thought for a second, "what happened to the little girl."

She set the photograph back, ran her hand across Tom's cheek and stood up.

"Well, the Robin's Nest went to me to hold in trust," she continued moving to the front room. Tom followed. "My niece, she is actually being looked after by another family. I also have a nephew, but I believe his father took him that night...but it's..."

She shook her head and moved to the counter area where she stored alcohol and a bucket of ice.

"Why wasn't she taken too," Tom asked innocently.

She looked at him as she made a drink for herself, "like many children who are results of our profession...well, she had a different father. Rufus tells me you're fond of sarsaparilla or root beer," she said, changing the subject.

"Yes Ma'am."

She pulled a bottle from the bucket of ice popped the top and poured it into a glass.

"There you go," she said, handing the glass to him.

"Thank you," he said.

She picked up her drink walked to the settee and sat down.

"Sit down Tom."

He looked around and saw another arm chair adjacent to the settee. He took a step towards it.

"Tom," she said indicating that wasn't where he was supposed to sit. She motioned to the end of the settee.

He did as he was told and took a sip of his soda. Right away he knew he was going to have a hard time containing any burps.

Charlotte leaned back with one of her arms draped across the back of the settee and the other holding her drink.

"I want to talk to you about this afternoon."

Tom grimaced and looked her.

"I'm sorry about that Miss Charlotte."

"Let me finish, please," she said softly.

"Yes, Ma'am."

"How's your root beer?"

"Good, thank you."

"Cold enough?"

"Yes."

"You seem to act like you have to look out for the other children."

He thought about what she said. He had never been in a position where he was someone else's protector.

"It's more...well..."

"It's alright Tom. I won't be upset."

"Well, it's more that I hate what Cabot does and will do anything to ruin it...especially when he thinks he can get away with it."

She took a deep breath and exhaled.

"I would agree with you there, but are you sure that's all?"

"I feel sorry for Corey...and the girl. I still don't know who she is," he said with an edge to his tone.

Charlotte smiled.

Tom knew she wasn't going to tell him.

"You're protective...like you are with the girls here."

"Yes Ma'am."

She sighed, "Yes, I can see we are going to have to teach you not to be taken advantage of."

She ran her middle finger around the lip of her glass. It was something Tom had seen her do frequently when she was deep in thought.

"Cabot," she continued, "well, let's just say he doesn't behave as...we would like him to. He does tend to pick on those that he perceives are weaker. For some reason it makes him feel better. Actually, I suppose he has turned into some of our society boys and acts like them. Although, he's not really one of them, he seems to feel he's entitled."

Tom made a face.

She caught him out of the corner of her eye.

"What?"

"Officer Moran doesn't seem like…like he…how do you say it…fit in those circles."

"Travel in those circles," she said a little impressed. "You're absolutely correct. He doesn't, but he did marry well. He travels in his wife's circles. She's the one with the money."

He remembered that Sunday afternoon.

"She's the Judge's sister."

"Yes."

"Why isn't Officer Moran chief of police then?"

She knew he wasn't being cheeky…just observant, but still couldn't help laughing a little.

"Very good Tom, but be careful in whose company you say things like that. Money can hold you back as well as propel you. It just depends on who actually holds the money."

"Women," he said without thinking.

She laughed again, "as far as your world is concerned, that is correct."

She stood and held out her hand for his glass.

"Now, as far as Cabot is concerned – I ask that you do not go out of your way to antagonize him. Sadly, people like him will get their come-uppance. It just might not be in a way or as promptly as you would like. Continue what you're doing and you will be fine. And, I do appreciate you looking after the others."

She walked behind the settee to set their glasses down.

"The girl's name is Suzanne," she said unexpectedly.

"Suzanne," he repeated softly.

He felt as if he missed his signal to leave. He went ahead and stood up and walked to the door. He turned around as he opened it. She had walked to the Victrola and was putting on another record.

"She's your niece," he said.

Charlotte paused for a split second and took in a breath, leading Tom to think she was going to answer him…but no.

"I have your word. You will not go out of your way to antagonize Cabot?"

"Yes Ma'am, you have my word."

He stepped through the door and was about to close it.

"And Tom..."

"Yes, Miss Charlotte."

"You are right. She is my niece."

He stood thinking with his brow furrowed.

"What is it Tom?"

"Why...why didn't you get to raise her?"

She sighed.

"This isn't the type of place you can raise a child."

He thought again.

"But I'm a child."

He watched her as she carefully formulated her next sentence.

"Yes you are." She paused, "The world is different when it comes to boys."

She gave him a look he read as an ending to their conversation.

"Yes Ma'am," he said as he shut the door.

He didn't see much of Suzanne and Corey after that.

Both of their parents had shipped them off to boarding schools.

To Tom's chagrin, Cabot was not shipped off to boarding school. Tom hoped it was because all the schools had heard about his reputation and no amount of money could persuade anyone to take him.

Although that contributed to many schools' decisions, the truth of the matter was his poor grades just couldn't be overlooked and outside of San Diego the Frost name and relations meant nothing.

He wasn't a Whaley, a Horton or a Spreckles.

His last name was Moran, which...very often...was pronounced "moron".

So, for the time being, the tutoring sessions with the Judge and Tom continued.

Tom did as he had promised Charlotte and didn't antagonize Cabot any more than what was simple.

He aced all his tests and was in honor roll at the same school as Cabot. He was a better athlete – when time allowed.

Cabot drove his car around town way too fast and with girls he knew Tom liked. At times like that, Tom sought the refuge of the Club's women's beds and talked to them about what was going on as he held them, like a dysfunctional therapist-patient relationship.

It was a safe haven for him and he knew Cabot wasn't allowed even though sometimes Cabot would still try to force himself upon some of the girls.

Finally, came the day when Tom presented the Judge with his letter of acceptance to Dartmouth.

Tom knew it had been a long shot, but applied anyways on the Judge's suggestion. Judge Frost had helped him ask for and get letters of recommendation from some of the prominent men in town.

It didn't hurt that most of them frequented the club.

When the letter arrived, the girls had gathered by the bar and Charlotte was standing next to Tom who had been serving the Judge.

Tom opened and read the letter and by the look on his face they could all tell what the answer was. He handed it across the table to Judge Frost, partly because he wasn't sure he had read it correctly.

The Judge poured over the letter and looked over his glasses at Tom when he was satisfied what the letter said. Tom was standing in front of him.

"Well done Thomas," he nodded his head, "well done." He looked at Charlotte, "Rufus will be opening a bottle of champagne, of course."

"Yes, of course," she nodded.

She squeezed Tom's elbow and leaned up to whisper in his ear, "It's alright to gloat...a little."

Tom grinned and heard a cork pop from behind the bar.

And, there was Cabot to ruin the moment, sitting across from the Judge, but glaring at Tom. The Judge was folding up the letter when he looked over his glasses at Cabot.

"If only you would apply yourself," Judge Frost scolded.

Cabot couldn't hold his tongue.

"Why should I when I can just get my father to pay my way?!"

The Judge's hand came out of nowhere, reached across the table and slapped Cabot so hard across the face that it knocked him onto the floor.

Everyone gasped.

Cabot wasn't sure what hurt more: the man he respected the most didn't think anything of him or that Tom and the whores had witnessed his humiliation. He expected to look up to find Tom still gloating, but it was worse.

Tom pitied him.

Tom wasn't surprised when he heard that Cabot had enlisted in the British army before the United States was even in the war. For once he thought that Cabot may have found something he was well suited for: He could blow buildings up and hurt all the people he wanted...and get medals for it and paid for it.

He was so good he became one of the first sharpshooters of the war.

When he read the articles the girls and Rufus included in their letters to him, all Tom could think of was that he hoped Cabot's head wouldn't explode from the pressure of his ego.

As Tom's preoccupation with school and Meg progressed, his letters from home and the Club became more infrequent. Once he enlisted, the only other letters he received from America besides Megan's were from his sister, Ysabel, and the occasional care package...unlabeled, but Tom was always pretty sure where it came from...considering it usually included condoms.

He wasn't surprised that the rest of his family didn't write. His mother had seemed indifferent about the news and she didn't even flinch when he asked her about tuition which he knew would surely break the family. He knew that Charlotte had been putting some money away for him, but didn't think that it would cover everything. Charlotte had told him not to worry about it. Judge Frost would talk to the school and work with his mother to arrange everything.

Other than that, Tom's life was Cabot-free.

Once Tom and Meg moved to San Diego he only would hear about Cabot from time to time. He knew he'd been married, had a child and, sadly, his wife had died. Tom never found out what the circumstances were surrounding her death, but he thought he wouldn't be surprised to find Cabot had killed her.

Tom was sure Charlotte had something to do with his rapid promotion to detective and was still surprised that Officer Moran was now only Captain Moran and not Chief.

The other oddity was Corey's return to San Diego and position as a detective.

Tom had never figured out his role in everything or how he had found himself mixed up with Cabot.

Tom realized it was because he really didn't want to know. He was afraid to ask too many questions, which was dangerous for his profession, but he rationalized he just would ask within his own circle.

He wasn't surprised to find Cabot as one of the Judge's "men" nor that the Judge had become a state judge.

He occasionally would see Suzanne Phelps' name in the society pages, usually from some party item or European travels.

The correspondences between her and Cory were not a secret to Tom, but never knew what the intent between the two was. Corey's face would light up whenever her name was mentioned, but she was never in San Diego.

Tom wondered how he would take it when she eventually married and had thought maybe, just maybe, he had finally moved on that night Tom took his shift. But, it did nag at the edge of Tom's mind...

Who was Corey going to see that night and never did?

9.

BAD DECISIONS

Tom found himself at what remained of the Robin's Nest, poking through old and burnt beams and flooring. In some places, tattered pieces of curtain stuck to the stick Tom was using to sift through the rubble.

Tom only knew bits and pieces, but never asked Charlotte again about the location's tragic history after the night in her room; and, since tears filled her eyes every time someone mentioned the story he avoided it all together. Tom's heart hurt when he saw that pained expression on Charlotte's face; so, it was for his benefit as much as her that he never asked.

And, because the events were so scandalous there were no historical notes, just lore.

But even he remembered the structure had still been standing up until a few months after he had started high school. He remembered hearing the fire wagons and horses rattling through the streets to try to contain the fire that had suddenly started in the Robin's Nest and the ferociousness that ate it.

In his daydreams, he imagined it was Cabot's doing.

Charlotte had come out of her room and run into Tom in the upstairs hall of The Agate Club as she ran out and down the main stairs. Rufus had run up as Tom had tried to make his way down but was jerked back when Rufus pulled him back.

"No, you stay here," Rufus had told him, apparently on Charlotte's orders.

Tom had looked at the barkeep like he was crazy and didn't know that a fire and running horses were the most exciting things he had ever seen, but Rufus seemed to read his mind.

"You are the man of the house, you need to help look after the women," Rufus told him.

Tom suddenly felt important and could relate to what he was being told.

Tom woke up in his bed the next morning after falling asleep at the top of the stairs – and that was all he remembered, but he did piece together what had happened over the years. Even he knew it had to do with Charlotte's sister, Ainsley, and a man.

It wasn't until he was an adult that he really pieced the significance of it all.

Ainsley, the younger of the two, had gone against conventional practice and bore her two bastard children in the brothel and kept them, but only because Charlotte had done the same

The difference was that the oldest, a boy, had a different father than the girl and the boy's father had barged in one night to take him, but Ainsley wasn't going to let him.

There was yelling, and then screaming, bringing out some of the other girls and their customers into the halls.

Then there was a crash, sounds of a struggle and then other sounds that were later identified as the punching and bludgeoning of Ainsley.

Her bedroom door opened and the father stormed out with the screaming boy flung over his shoulder and he was grasping at the air for his sister.

Men scampered out, but in their hesitation to not be caught in a public scandal, they all hesitated and flew from the scene.

No one thought to follow the man, those that remained poured into the young madam's room to if she was okay.

They were greeted by a horrific sight – Ainsley's face was smashed in so far they started to turn her over before they realized it was actually her front they were looking at.

And the baby…

The baby sat on the floor in one of the pools of her mother's blood bawling.

The boy was never found.

When Charlotte took over the brothel as trustee the business slowly fell apart with most of the girls, including Evelyn, seeking refuge at The Agate Club.

By the time Tom was helping his uncle deliver potatoes for bootleg alcohol, the structure only had a few years left and then housed the extra potatoes and the brewed alcohol from The Agate Club.

The ghosts of the young murdered madam and that night were enough to keep Tom away, but tonight was different.

There was something about the place that drew him in and the ghosts he felt hung around over his shoulders were weaker than his resolve.

Tom poked through a pile causing the ash to rise up and some of the particles to stick to his pant leg.

"Freeze," he heard behind him. "Put your hands in the air," the voice commanded shakily although Tom knew exactly who the rookie was, he obliged.

"Now, turn around slowly…oh shit," the police officer said as Tom turned so the officer could see his face and confirming Tom's guess of the officer's identity.

"Detective Rubidoux, I'm sorry," Officer Lambert stammered.

"No, don't be, you're doing your job. You never know what people are up to. We can all be as guilty as the next person," he said nodding his head towards his arms that were still up in the air.

Lambert nodded and Tom lowered his arms.

"Yes sir," Lambert said.

"What brings you here Lambert," Tom asked as he turned back to digging around.

"We had a call," Lambert said as he encroached on Tom's space to see what the detective was doing.

"Someone concerned I was digging in their pile of rubbish," Tom said in a sarcastic tone that Lambert missed.

"I suppose," Lambert said absent-mindedly, "just what are you looking for sir?"

"Just checking if the fire might have left anything behind."

"It doesn't look like anyone has been here in years," Lambert said looking around.

"No," Tom sighed, standing up, "it doesn't. There doesn't seem to be anything at all."

The two of them started to gingerly walk out of the rubble and make their way back to the street.

"I'm sorry you didn't find what you were looking for Detective," Lambert said.

"But I did," Tom answered him and Lambert didn't want to look like he didn't know what he was doing, so he didn't ask what the detective meant.

Tom didn't know how long he had been sitting in the driveway in the car. Bruce and Louis had gone out to pick up their bikes and when Tom didn't move from his place behind the driver's wheel, they ran inside the house for reinforcements.

Meg stood in front of the car for a few moments before walking around to the driver's side and tapping on the window.

"Excuse me sir, you'll have to pull over."

"Huh," Tom snapped to, "what did you say?"

"Come inside, you're holding up the chow line," she yelled out behind her as she ushered the boys inside the house.

Tom blinked and gathered himself and then his stuff off the passenger seat. He looked up again.

Alice stood on the front porch waiting for him.

He jumped out of the car, forgetting to shut the driver's side, stepped onto the porch, scooped Alice up and ran into the house in one big swoop. He ran to the kitchen phone, dropped everything, shoved the phone between his shoulder and ear and frantically hit the receiver while still holding Alice.

The operator picked up.

"Dr. Hill, please."

"Would that be Dr. Hill the dentist or Dr. Hill the surgeon?"

"Dr. Hill, the coroner," Tom clarified, cutting the operator off.

"Oh…Please hold…connecting…," the operator said.

"Tom…," Dr. Hill asked, perplexed.

"Doc, I need some more photos of that corpse," Tom.

"Really...well..."

"Please, Doc," Tom pleaded.

"Well, it's not like I have her stuffed in the ice box here at home. Do you think you can wait for me to take the photos tomorrow?"

"Yes, of course. I need close ups of just the..."

"Leave a list of what you want in the morgue tomorrow. Goodnight Detective," he said and hung up.

"Oh," Tom said. He hung up the phone.

Tom sat in deep concentration not looking at the paperwork he had been flipping through, but not looking at. Meg looked up from her book several times, concerned.

"I need to break into the basement of the Club," Tom blurted out to himself.

"You're going to break in," Megan asked with a little too much enthusiasm for Tom.

"What?! Ah, yes," Tom answered, realizing he had said his thought out loud.

"When are you and Corey going?"

He paused since he was still in his own thoughts and not really paying attention to her.

"Uh, Corey will not be going with me."

"What? Why?"

He felt ashamed for what he was thinking.

"I can't trust him."

"Oh," she said and thought for a moment, "Ohhh."

Tom nodded his head. Then her eyes lit up.

"Great, when are we going?!"

"What...no, I'm going. You...are staying."

"No, I can help you."

"Megan, the children?"

"Tom, you have to be joking. We are talking about the same children who slept through the herd of cattle walking through the living room at your mother's house aren't we?"

He stared, slacked-jawed at her.

"It's much easier for me to talk myself out of the club," he said.

"How are you going to get in?"

Tom thought about it for a minute, "The ice chute."

She started to laugh.

"What?"

"When was the last time you went down the ice chute?"

"I don't know...12, 13..."

"Honey, I don't know if you've noticed, but I'm sure you've grown a bit since you were 12."

Tom stood in the alley shivering – partly from nerves and partly because he'd forgotten how cold the narrow space and bricks were at that time of the morning. He had finally convinced Megan that this was not an adventure. This was real. He regretted taking her with him, but knew that she shouldn't be involved in any of his police work. It could jeopardize his case and her life. The risk he chanced sharing his cases with her was bad enough. This was worse because he knew the people involved and they knew him...and his family.

But she had badgered him and came up with every reason why should come. As it turned out, he had forgotten how resourceful Meg could be. She had gone next door to the neighbors' and cooked up some story that the woman believed at the late hour. The woman had no problem coming next door to watch the kids. She had slept on their couch several times after a row with her husband.

At that point, there was nothing he could do but to relent and take her with him. It was the one thing about her that her loved, but also frustrated him at the same time.

Finally, he heard the creak of the basement window open.

He ran over and pulled it open all the way.

He stepped back and sized it up. Yeah, he could fit. He was sure of it.

He got on his knees and then belly and then put both hands through and started to shimmy.

The space became very tight very quickly as he reached his waist.

"And you thought you were going to fit down the ice chute," he heard Meg say from the darkness of the basement.

"Here," he said tossing his flashlight down to her.

He ignored Meg's quip about his size and started to press with his hand against the inside wall to move further.

He stopped suddenly.

"Honey," he whispered.

"Yes?"

"Just how did you get the window open?"

"With this stick," she waved in the dark. "What's the problem? Are you stuck?"

"No," he said, "I'm just wondering how I'm going to get to the ground."

"What do you mean?"

"Meg, I'm stuck in a hole that's seven...eight feet above the ground."

"Don't be such a baby."

"I'm telling you, it's at least a seven foot drop."

"Really," she said in disbelief.

"Meg, find something to break my fall."

She moved the flashlight and stopped at one of the far corners where the potato sacks were stacked.

"Those look like they could be cushy."

Tom looked up and saw what she was walking towards.

"No," he said in a loud whisper, "that's evidence. Come here – we can make this work."

"You're not going to use me to fall on," she said.

"I promise I won't...but come closer...no stand back just a little."

She stood where he was in arms lengthy. He reached up with one hand and found one of the pipes he knew should be running across the ceiling. He shimmied himself a little more and put his other hand on Meg's head.

Any other time he would have thought the whole scene was comical.

"What was that," she said and started to turn to point the flashlight in the direction of the sound.

Tom started to teeter and lose his grip.

"Meg, stay still," he gasped.

"Sorry, what's that sound though," she asked, still distracted.

"It's probably nothing," he said while regaining his grip on the pipe. "It's probably just a rat," he added without thinking

"A what," she shrieked and spun where the sound had come from, leaving Tom unsupported.

His grip came loose from the pipe and he fell, face first, out of the window and onto the floor.

"Ooof."

"Are you sure it's a rat," she tried to screech quietly, oblivious to the fact that Tom was lying in a heap on the ground.

Tom was still trying to catch his breath and make sure he hadn't hurt himself.

"I'm okay...in case you were concerned," he said.

"What," she turned the flashlight on him so that she was shining the light directly into his eyes. He threw his arm up to his face.

"Oh Tom," she said as she knelt down by him. "I'm sorry."

"Well...we're in," he said sarcastically.

She laughed a little.

"Yes, but how are we going to get out?"

"Had to bring that up, didn't you," he said, "I'm working on that. Let's look around first."

He fumbled in the dark until Meg finally shined her light where his flashlight was so he could grab it, but then he heard the club door handle creak.

"Come here. Turn out your light," he said grabbing his light and turning it off.

He wracked his brain trying to think what anyone would need from the basement at that time of night and he reached for Meg's hand. He pulled her to him as he turned down between two shelving units and threw his hand over her mouth, but still allowing her to breathe. He then positioned her so that she was standing behind him. She put her hand on his back.

After the person came into the basement, Tom heard the person, most likely Rufus, walk around...without any agenda. Now he could see that it was Rufus as he walked past the space where they were at and head back towards the door and up into the club. Rufus seemed to wait a second longer before shutting the door. Tom didn't move. Meg waited for him, leaning up against him.

"Tom," she whispered.

"Huh?"

"Do you think it's safe for us to move?"

"Yes, but I don't think we have that much time."

"What?!"

"You shouldn't have come," he said moving quickly out of the aisle, pulling her up from her arm. He knew the words would sting, and that it wasn't really her fault, but she had to understand the brevity of the situation they were in.

Scanning the room quickly he remembered the pile of potato sacks Meg had seen earlier and quickly went over to them, kneeled and picked one up.

It had the same logo as the one sitting in evidence as he knew it would.

He shined the flashlight back on the pile and the area around it on the ground. There were loose matches scattered and some of the matchboxes. Some were empty and some were separate tops and bottoms and Tom moved the flashlight so it was beaming up to the shelves. One of the boxes (that he had probably stocked years before) had collapsed and cracked open under the weight of the other boxes on top of it.

Meg had come up behind him and was shining her light directly behind him.

"What's that," she asked.

He glanced at the object and then back to the evidence in front of him.

"It's an old tub that was used for...many things, but mainly making bootleg alcohol."

He realized it as soon as he said it.

He stood up. There was a large piece of wood covering the top. He sat his light down so it was shining up and started to lift the piece of wood up.

"Tom, do you need help," Meg asked.

"No, stay there."

He leveraged the piece so that he could gingerly slide it down the side to the ground and then picked his light up and shined it around the tub.

Had the murderer been that arrogant?

"Tom...?"

"Stay there."

The tub, which had always been a grayish-white, now was almost pink.

Tom shined the light down at the ground around the tub and the potato sacks. There were puddles and drops of blood.

"What is that," Meg asked.

"It's blood. We need to get you out of here now!"

He walked to her, grabbed her arm again and quickly dragged her to the window. He held out his hands to boost her up.

"How are you going to get out?"

"I will figure that out as soon as I can."

"Tom..."

"Megan, don't argue with me," he snapped and then quickly thought of the one button of hers he could push, "Meg, the children."

She nodded and stuck her foot in his hands and he pushed her up so that she could reach the window and then stand on his shoulders to get the rest of the way through the window.

"Shut it," he told her.

Hesitantly, she closed the window.

Tom turned back to the tub. It was just a matter of time before Rufus returned. He took out a knife, grabbed one of the open containers of matches, shook out the matches and scraped some of the blood and put the flakes in the container. He wrapped that in his handkerchief and stuffed it in his pocket with the folded knife.

Then he put the wood back on the tub and thought about how he was going to get out. He looked around and thought...how did the murderer get out with the sack?

He walked over and looked at the ice chute again. The sack could have fit through the top opening. Tom didn't see anything at the bottom of the chute but as the flashlight beam moved up he started to see dark streaks. He moved the flashlight to the beam that hung directly over the opening. He wasn't sure, but he was pretty sure he could see rope fibers.

He heard the basement door latch click. He ran underneath the stairs and turned off the flashlight.

"Here I am a man...and I'm hiding like I'm nine," he thought to himself, but as the steps pounded off the steps above him, he didn't feel so juvenile.

The light from the club illuminated a good portion of the room. Tom didn't dare look around and the thud of feet down the stairs made his muscles tense more and more with every step. He thought by the sounds it had to be a man, probably Rufus again. The steps reached the floor and walked to the end of the basement in front of the tub. Then they turned and walked back, stopping at each aisle until they stopped where Tom had been seconds before.

Tom felt the sweat start to run down his face even though the room was cold and his breath could have been seen had he not been breathing into his shirt sleeve. He could hear his heart thumping and focused on his breathing so that it was completely silent to everyone, but Tom.

Slowly, the steps headed back up to the door, but stopped at the top again like the first time and it sounded like the person turned around to look one more time over the room. Then the light narrowed and the room was dark again as the door shut and Tom heard the lock engaged.

He slowly let his breath out and stepped out from his hiding place and looked around.

"Now what," he thought to himself.

He couldn't leave through the window without leaving evidence that he had been there. His only option seemed to be the basement door to the club where he could quickly get to the alley door from there. The ice chute door locked from the outside, so that option was out as well.

He would have to wait until the club was quiet and he could jimmy the lock and basically walk right on out into the alley.

It sure sounded like it would work in his mind, but the more he thought about it the dumber it sounded.

It would have to do until another thought came to mind. He sat down on the bottom steps and patiently waited and tried to piece everything he had together.

Cabot was the one he wanted to guilty, but there were two other men besides him and Cabot who knew about the tub and he couldn't rule them out.

Tom had caught Corey hiding from Cabot one afternoon before the fight in the alley and his recent actions, mixed with Tom's suspicions, made Tom wonder what role Corey might have in all of this. He was pretty sure Corey didn't have the stomach or strength to perform the grisly job and he had seen how Corey folded up into himself the more he was pushed.

There was the added fact that he knew Corey loved Suzanne, but he knew that he would not have done anything to jeopardize that. But he knew that Cabot could push him until he snapped and lashed out. Tom wondered what happened during those times where he was not there to diffuse the situation.

Rufus, on the other hand, would do anything to protect the club and Charlotte. Tom had seen him turn violent with both the patrons and the girls without provocation and it usually took several men and Charlotte's voice to cease the fury he would exhibit on these occasions.

Tom heard the window creak open and a rope end slither its way down the wall.

Curiously, he stood and walked to the window.

"Hurry up Tom," he heard Meg whisper.

He looked at the end of the rope.

"Not to question your ability or seem ungrateful," he said through the window, "but who's holding the other end?"

"The horse's ass – come on, hurry."

He pulled on the rope until it became taut and put his feet on the wall and started to climb up. He felt himself moving up quicker than he was climbing and made it through the window.

It wasn't quite the back end of the horse the rope had been tied to, but Tom was grateful none the less.

He untied the rope from the reins; shut the window and Meg turned the horse around and walked it back down to Tom as he rolled the rope up.

"Where'd you find him," Tom asked.

"The stable around the corner."

It was like listening to her speak a foreign language.

"Hurry with the rope, we have to take him back."

He looked at the reins as they walked back down the alley and noticed there was no saddle. He loved Meg; but, even though she was raised on an estate with horse stables, she didn't know how to dress a horse.

"Honey, who helped you put the reins on?"

"What makes you think I couldn't---oh, I can't even joke about this. I was waiting for you in the alley and a woman came up with the rope and brought me here and helped me. She said you would know how to put it all back."

"A woman," Tom said stunned, "What did she look like," he asked.

"She looked like she had brown hair, dark eyes…"

"Did she slur her words a little bit…did her speech almost sound like she had an accent," Tom asked.

"Yes."

Evelyn.

After they returned the horse, reins and rope, they went home.

As Meg predicted, the children hadn't moved, except Joe from kicking his blankets off. Meg woke the neighbor, apologized to her for the late hour and thanked her repeatedly. Tom didn't miss the looks the woman gave him making him wonder what story Meg had told her to get her to come watch the children.

Tom went into their bedroom and sat on the edge of the bed, deep in thought. Meg, already for bed, climbed up behind Tom and wrapped her arms around him.

"You know…it was wrong for me to go with you tonight," she confessed quietly.

His eyebrow arched, "What? Did I hear you correctly?"

"Yes, but in my defense, you let me come along," she defended.

"Sweetheart, I learned long ago that when you have your mind set on something you are just going to do whatever you want. You just would have followed me."

"Now what," she said, resting her head on the back of his. He could feel her smiling against his skin.

"I don't know," he sighed.

"What else do you need?"

"I'm missing quite a lot. I don't have a motive, I don't really have evidence, the murder weapon...who my victim is, who the murderer is...all I have is a body and two crime scenes that may or may not..."

"But probably are..."

"...yes, they probably are related."

She knew he was frustrated.

"Tom, what is it? There's something else, isn't there?"

"I'm not sure if I had it all that I could get a conviction."

"Why?"

"I don't think I'll be able to get all the warrants or support together to solve this." He took a deep breath and his shoulders slumped. "I really think my cousins are going to hang for this."

"You'll figure out something," she said as she ran her hands through his hair and gave him a kiss. "I know you will. You always do."

She went back into the bathroom, but he didn't turn. There was something else bothering him.

If the Captain and the Judge were controlling everything, his reckless, cavalier nature may have done more damage than he was willing to share with her. He didn't mind his own life being in danger, but he knew the stunt in the club basement had put the lives of Meg and the children at risk.

Tom didn't go to sleep that night.

In fact, that night he went back to his desk, and pulled out the file that he smuggled out from the station every night. He couldn't believe that he hadn't taken his gun with him to the club.

In reality, he couldn't believe that he was stupid enough not to make Meg return home, but part of him realized there was no way he would have been able to fit through the window without Megan or with his gun on; and, besides, who was he going to shoot?

In hindsight, he wished he would have had it.

No damage had really been done.

The lack of sleep caused his mind to wander again.

Evelyn.

Evelyn was loyal...to him. He was the one who had saved her from Rufus and Cabot when both men had tried to rape her on separate occasions.

It came with the territory, or so Evelyn had told him. He just nodded telling her that it didn't matter what they did for a living. At least they weren't living off of their rich husbands.

"Now, you tell me who the real whore is," he had said to her. Next to Charlotte, Evelyn was the one Tom had the most interaction with and the one he went to when he had a problem that he was too uncomfortable to talk to Charlotte about.

A creak in the floor startled him and woke him up. It was still dark outside, but he saw Bruce standing in the doorway.

He didn't say anything and motioned for the boy to come closer.

"How long have you been awake," he asked Bruce.

"I saw the light..."

"How long have you been awake, Golpe?"

Tom's grandmother had thought that Megan and Tom had named the boy "Bruise", so that all Spanish relatives called the boy "El Golpe".

His father was the only one he accepted it as a term of affection. He knew it meant something else from everyone else.

"Where did you and Mommy go," he asked as he came closer to see what Tom was looking at. Tom flipped the file closed.

"Mommy went to help me with something. I'm sorry we weren't here when you woke up," he said putting his arm around Bruce and kissing the top of his head. He smelled the boy as he pulled back and smiled as he thought of milk, dirt and child perspiration. "Did anyone else wake up?"

"No," he shook his head, "Alice was snoring."

"Really," Tom said, "She gets that from Mommy," he said smiling in his ear.

Bruce laughed.

"You should go back to bed."

Bruce nodded.

"Daddy?"

"Um."

"Were you out catching bad guys?"

"Not quite…," he didn't want Bruce to be afraid, "it's not that simple some times."

"But you're really good at it…?"

"Yes, I usually do catch the bad guy."

"Mommy says you have to think like the bad guy to catch 'em."

"Yes, you have to know how they think…Bruce, what is it you want to know?"

"Do you have to be bad to think and catch them?"

"No."

He looked up at Tom.

Tom watched as Bruce's expression looked thoughtful for a second and then relaxed with some sort of satisfaction.

"Okay," he asked him.

Bruce nodded.

"Off to bed with you then," he said after kissing him and patting him on the butt.

Bruce left the room and Tom heard the bedroom door shut. He reopened the file and shuffled through the photos he had and the paperwork without really looking at anything. Frustrated, he shut the file and sat back.

Looking at it wouldn't help him if he couldn't get the warrants to collect everything he needed.

He needed leverage.

He had to get some sort of foothold in order to put the right murderer in jail. He felt rushed and he was being sloppy and careless to try to get things resolved. The solution was to slow the case and himself down.

Taking a deep breath he refocused on the night's events.

The killer had to know about the basement and could move freely throughout the club without anyone questioning his or her appearance.

The girl had to be known there as well because although the killer could be known, anyone would question him toting a body through the club and someone would have heard because, from experience, he knew there was no way to open the basement door with just one hand.

He leaned forward and opened the file again and took out the photographs. He would have to wait for the other photographs from the coroner, but he was pretty sure who the victim was. His recent memories and the basement were the only pieces of evidence he had.

There was only one other girl he knew could come and go as she pleased and was not one of *the* girls.

He couldn't really tell from the corpse because it was so badly mutilated and swollen, but there were flickers of things he remembered: the hair, the shape of the jaw and the set of the eyes.

Suzanne.

He had to be sure before he could say anything, but for that moment moving forward he was looking at the case as if the murdered girl was her.

It wasn't the right way to do things and he knew it. Instead of finding the evidence and making it solve the case. He was going to look for the evidence that would only prove that he was right.

Now what could he do to force the Captain's hand?

He thought of Bruce.

Parents will do anything to protect their children.

10.

ANGELS & SAINTS

Tom parked the car near the station and made the long walk up the hills to the café at Balboa Park. He knew he was early, he planned it that way. Charlotte had taught him it was disrespectful to make a lady wait – even if she was a prostitute.

He was seated at one of the tables overlooking one of the gardens and canyon and waited for his guest to arrive.

He knew when she had arrived because the air shifted. Looking towards the doorway he smiled as he saw most of the people turn to watch her.

Charlotte strolled in like she was a movie star and nodded occasionally at some of the people...well, some of the men, who turned at being noticed, making Tom grin even more. She spotted Tom, who stood when she saw him and he waited for her to approach their table.

"Good afternoon, Tom," she said as she leaned in so he could kiss her cheek, causing some of the other patrons to gape and start whispering.

"Miss Charlotte."

He waited for her to sit before he sat down himself. The waiter asked if they wanted any drinks.

She ordered a mint julep and he followed suit.

The waiter walked away.

"Drinking in the middle of the day, Thomas?"

He grinned, "It's Saturday and I'm off duty."

"Ah, Corey is on duty then."

"Yes Ma'am," he said a little curiously.

"You're not on duty…yet, I suspect this, again, is not going to be a social call."

"No, Ma'am, not really."

"That is a bit dishonest of you Tom. Asking me here under false pretenses. Is this going to be a civilized conversation?"

"That is the plan and why I selected our venue."

"It's close to my house."

"And, it's close to your house," he repeated.

"That's very considerate of you. Tell me, does your wife mind watching the children so much?"

"Well, we've had the children for a while…so she's very capable and doesn't mind the occasional weekend morning without me."

In his mind, he imagined Meg cursing him because she was probably trying to sleep in from the previous night's activities. He imagined all four children running into the bedroom and, with them finding extra space from his vacancy, jumping on the bed…and probably Meg.

He had left cereal and a note out for them, hoping to buy her some time, confidant that either Bruce or Louis would step in and help with the little ones. At least they usually did.

The waiter returned with their drinks. Tom waited for her tip sip hers before he did his.

"You look tired Tom," she said after looking back into her drink.

"Four children will sometimes do that," he answered, knowing that she probably was already aware of his late night visit to the club if his suspicions of Evelyn were correct. "Did the Judge enjoy his visit the other day," he asked her.

She looked at her drink, smiled coyly and set it down.

"Tom, you always did better being direct."

"I had good teachers."

"Yes, lawyers, businessmen and politicians…"

"I wasn't referring to them."

He took another sip of his drink.

"I need to ask for your help with something you will not like," he said.

"She wasn't one of my girls…"

"I know she wasn't," he said confidently. She looked at him, "But I do believe you did know her."

"You know who she was?"

"I believe I do," he said knowing they both knew it was probably Suzanne.

Charlotte took a deep breath to regain her composure, but years of learning how to read people and watching for little physical "tells" told him that he had rattled her. It was another reason he had wanted her to meet him at a place that wasn't her home and where she wasn't so comfortable.

"What is it that you want me to do for you, Tom?"

"I need warrants."

She ran her finger along the rim of her glass, but there was something different in the move than Tom had seen in the past. She was definitely nervous – a trait Tom didn't even know existed in her make-up.

"Help me," he said.

"And, just what makes you think that I can help you with that? You don't know what you've gotten involved with."

"If it's what I think it is then I have put my wife and children in danger."

"Tom…"

"Your club is involved. Help me so I can minimize the damage."

The line of conversation was cut short by the waiter, who had returned to take their orders. Charlotte waved him off, took another sip of her drink and set it down.

"She was your niece."

"I can't help you Tom. Not with what you are asking. And," she added, "you are the one who made decisions that put your family in danger."

Ignoring the fact she had confirmed his fears he continued, "You can't help me or won't?"

Tom looked her in her eyes. It seemed she was pleading with him to drop the whole thing; yet, he knew she wanted to help him. She knew him well enough that he would chip away until she relented. Abruptly, she started to push her seat out and Tom stood to grab it for her, but she stood before he could help.

"Is the Judge really worth that much," he said in a desperate attempt.

He knew if they had not been in public she would have slapped him. She looked at him for a long time. Tom thought she was weighing what she would do next. Finally, he saw her swallow and set her jaw.

"Judge Frost and I have known each other for years, since before he was married, when he was just starting out as a trial lawyer. Tom, just remember, sometimes people don't see the truth because they don't want to...because it can mean everything they believe in is a lie."

She put her hand on the side of his face and kissed him on the cheek. Tom watched her walk down the steps and leave through the garden.

Tom found himself at city records on Monday morning. Charlotte had said just enough to peak his curiosity even though what she had said was fairly banal. But, that was probably the way she had intended it.

Tom strolled through the door of the archives room still trying to think of what he was going to ask for. He was a bit distracted since he had received a phone call earlier that morning from his mother saying that the police had picked up Juneau and Sylvestre from one of the ranches.

"It's just a precaution," he had lied.

"Well, as I live and breathe - Tom Rubidoux," a voice on the other side of the counter said.

"Hello, Meredith."

"It's been a long time. I think we were still in high school."

"Yes, I think it was right before I left for college."

"It has been a while. I understand you're a detective. What can I do for you?"

"Well, I'm looking for some old trial manuscripts or files."

"They must be really old for you to be here."

Tom tried to calculate the Judge's age and how old he would have been.

"They are. I want to say at least...oh, thirty years back. Just for five years...to start with."

"No problem, it is going to take me a while."

"If I give you a specific lawyer does that help?"

"It actually makes it worse because I have to sort through everything, but it can be done. Who's the lawyer?"

He took a deep breath before saying it.

"Charles Miller Frost."

"Judge Frost?"

"Yes."

"He's a state circuit judge or something like that now isn't he?"

"Something like that, yes."

"I will get those for you. It will give me something different to do for a change. Do you want all the court cases from those five years?"

"Please."

He was still standing at the counter and she looked at him and smiled.

"When I said it's going to take a while, Tom, I meant a few days."

"Oh...of course, I'm sorry."

"I'll have them sent to the station."

"Actually," he said grabbing a piece of paper and pulling out a pen, "have them sent here please." He handed her the paper after scribbling the address down. She looked at it and put it with his request.

"It was good to see you," she said.

"Like wise."

He turned and started to walk out the door, suddenly stopped and turned back around.

"Meredith," he said loudly.

She looked up.

"Yes."

"Instead of cases that were tried, can you just pull papers that were filed?"

"Of course, but you just tripled my work so it will take longer."

"Understood," he said nodding. "Thanks Meredith."

"You're welcome, Tom."

The next couple of weeks were nothing but a blur for Tom. He couldn't do anything but wait for Meredith to deliver what he hoped would force someone to give him the warrants he needed for the club and to check the Frost estates in Del Mar where Cabot and Corey displayed their knife and gun collections.

He was also waiting on the other photos from the coroner.

In the meantime, he avoided Captain Moran unless it was to discuss another case and he said very little to Corey...as a precaution. He tried to make it seem like he had given up on the case (since no one was asking about it), but it was the only thing that consumed his mind.

Meg had actually yelled at him because he was staring off into space at the dinner table and not paying attention when he was playing with the kids.

"Two times four is eight Tom," she interjected when he was helping Louis with a homework assignment.

"Huh," Tom said, "oh, that's right."

Louis and Bruce giggled.

"Tom, you might as well let me help them if you're not going to pay attention."

"Okay," he said as he got up from the kitchen table. She watched him leave the kitchen and go outside to the backyard and sat down in his place to help the boys.

After the boys had gone to bed, Meg went into the backyard to find Tom. She found him standing in the middle of the path with his hands in his pockets looking up and the stars. He didn't even move when she opened the screen door and in creaked.

"Have you been standing here the whole time," she asked as she walked up behind him and put her arm around him and pressed a kiss to his back.

"No," he said turning so he could hug her. "I was sitting over there for a while," he said indicating the chairs by the back steps.

"You're not going to tell me, are you," she asked.

He looked down into her face and shook his head.

"Well, Detective, you are going to have to do something because this case is starting to affect your home life."

"I'm sorry I don't mean to make you worry."

"Not worried, concerned," she clarified.

She flicked his nose leaned up and kissed him.

"I love you," he said, his voice almost cracking.

"I know you do," she said putting her hand on the side of his face. "Coming to bed," she asked as she started to walk away.

"Yeah, in a little bit."

She had reached the steps when he turned.

"Charlotte said something to me the other day…"

"What's that," Meg asked curiously.

"Sometimes people don't see the truth because they don't want to…because it can mean everything they believe in is a lie."

Meg took a step closer to him.

"Am I that oblivious…at times," he asked, concern covering the words.

She thought about it for a moment and slowly formulated her answer.

"Tom, whenever anyone asks you what you did as a kid, you always tell them you worked at The Agate Club."

"Yes."

"Tom, you worked at and lived in a whorehouse. I've never once heard you say that…ever."

He thought about it for a second, but when he went to answer…she was already gone. Leaning back in his chair he looked back up to the stars and scanned the sky as if it held the files of his memories and thought back.

He remembered one afternoon when he had been working behind the bar drying the glassware he had just washed for the evening and staring off into space. He was so deep in his thoughts he didn't see or hear Charlotte walk down the stairs and by the bar. She stopped and turned around when she saw the furrow in his brow.

Tom didn't hear her the first time she said his name. It wasn't until he heard the stern "Thomas" that he blinked.

"Yes, Ma'am."

"You look deep in thought Tom. Something on your mind," she asked.

He opened and closed his mouth, trying to figure the best way to ask his question, his scowl still creased.

"It's easier if you just say it...don't think about saying it," Charlotte said to gently encourage him. She was a little concerned because she had never seen him so...distraught.

It unnerved her even more as he looked her straight in the eye and didn't waiver.

"I was walking home from school," he started slowly.

That in itself was new to Tom. Charlotte had felt the need to give him some normalcy (and to keep the meddling society women and school board out of her hair). She knew if it had come down to brass tacks that Charles would have taken care of everything, but she didn't want to play that card. So Tom entered public school.

"There were some people talking," Tom continued, causing Charlotte to refocus on the boy.

She studied the seriousness in his face again and realized they had all put him in a position where eavesdropping was normal.

"They were saying that everyone who walks through the doors," he said nodding his head towards the front doors, "they would..." he paused trying to remember the exact words, "...fall into the fiery pits of hell and all their guardian angels and saints who watch over them were left behind the doors in the streets to rot."

Charlotte pursed her lips and thought about what she was going to say next. Tom's gaze hadn't left her face for a second and she knew he wanted an answer and he expected an honest one.

"Isn't that the same as being damned," he asked innocently before she had a chance to say anything.

"Well," she said after taking a deep breath, "it would depend upon what you believe in. I know your family is Catholic, but do you believe that your uncle is damned for doing business with us and the Robin's Nest?"

"No."

"I am in a business that many...frown upon, but I do not think that any of the girls who work here are damned and will end up in hell. However, I would say the chief characteristic of my clientele is hypocrisy. They wear their Sunday best to church and then turn right around and walk in here asking for the very things they admitted to in confession and were absolved of...at least enough to clear their consciences."

She studied him to see if he understood. She could see him mulling her words in his mind.

"Those very people you heard talking have done and well do bad things...just various degrees of it. We are considered 'bad people', but we do good things." She cocked her head so that she could capture Tom's eye since his gaze had moved to the counter of the bar. He looked up and she continued.

"What troubles you, Tom?"

There were many things that he was torn about now, but he asked the most obvious without speaking. Charlotte anticipated the question and spared him saying the words.

"You are not damned Tom. The thoughts you have right now prove that. You lack the one thing that many of those people have. You do not have a judgmental bone in your body. It's against your nature. It's for the rest of us that our guardian angels and saints are left behind."

11.

THE NOOSE TIGHTENS

The next morning came with Meg shoving Tom, but she wasn't in bed with him.

"Tom…phone."

He opened one eye and looked at the clock. He wasn't late and it was still really early so he got up and stumbled into the kitchen and picked up the receiver.

"Good morning," Corey said on the other end.

"Morning," Tom grumbled, "Who died?"

"What?"

"Obviously, there's a dead body somewhere. You would never call me otherwise."

"They just fished a woman…well, parts of a woman out of northwest end of the harbor."

Captain Moran was standing near the edge of the dock overlooking the water when Tom pulled up. The marine layer was still hovering over like a canopy protecting the bay from the sun that was already shining on the rest of the city.

"Where's Hayes," was all he said to Tom.

"At the station I assume," Tom answered.

The Captain glared at him.

"Well, you did tell him to stay out of anything related with the morgue," Tom reminded him.

"I told him to stay out of the morgue…a contained area where he could get sick. This is the open air," he said waving his arms around, "Shit, even my great Aunt Fanny could deal with a gutted whale in this."

"Yes Sir," he said looking at the officers and fisherman pulling more remains onto the marina. Tom didn't flinch, which didn't escape the captain's notice.

"You just don't give a rat's ass, do you, Rubidoux," the Captain said looking at him.

"No Sir."

"Umm," he grunted.

Tom looked thoughtfully at the rest of the action happening on the marina. Action he started thinking was just for him.

"Did you tell Corey to call me?"

"What?"

"You know Corey couldn't handle this. You would have been the first person he would have called."

"And, just what do you think this is?"

"I don't know," he said looking the Captain in the eye, "Let's go find out."

Tom started walking to the remains that were now lying on the dock. Captain Moran followed. Tom could see a torso, an arm and then two legs.

But there was no head.

He knelt down by the remains and tilted the torso so it was up on its side. He heard one of the officers throw up into the water. There were saw marks that resembled the ones from the girl in the burlap sack.

Captain Moran stood behind him.

"Well, without a head we can't identify her," he announced.

"Yes we can," Tom said as he laid the torso back down. He looked up at the Captain. "Actually, you can too." He grinned maliciously, although he was hiding how sick he felt inside.

"What do you mean by that," the Captain demanded.

Tom remembered seeing the tattoo on Evelyn's back hip as she had turned one night after giving Tom an order to give to Rufus. Beyond her on the bed had been Captain Moran when he was still "Officer Moran".

Tom turned the torso up one more time so the Captain could see. He watched as the color drained from his face and the man staggered back...almost into the water.

Tom grabbed his hand and pulled him forward. The rest of the officers stood around looking confused and not seeing Tom's satisfaction.

"Get the remains to Doc Hill," Tom ordered.

The officers scurried and helped put Evelyn's remains into the ambulance and sent the vehicle on its way.

"I want my cousins out of jail by the end of the week," Tom told Captain Moran, "I don't care how tight a grip Cabot has on your cluster."

Tom walked back to his car and got in. Captain Moran was still standing in the same spot he had left him. He looked like a man that had been beaten...and over time was submitting.

Tom just wasn't so sure Cabot was the man who was doing the beating and he wasn't sure if this would get him the warrants he needed. As he drove away he thought that this was a warning...for him...and the Captain.

Tom had always been smart. He knew that and never wanted to go through life like the way he thought most of his relatives had gone through life...with not so many smarts or options.

With each passing year and as he became a father he realized he was wrong about most of those relatives.

And now, they were relying on him to save Juneau and Sylvestre. He knew Juneau wouldn't survive in prison and he knew Sylvestre would fight to the end.

He felt like a man who was being squeezed...like a man who was about to go mad.

He should have been relieved to see the large envelop sitting on his desk when he returned from the marina, but he wasn't. Rubidoux was written in grease pen diagonally from bottom to top. He didn't even open it at first. He knew by the writing it was from the coroner.

Instead, he slumped in his seat wondering what the hell it was he was going to do next.

Who was he going to squeeze?

With every day...his thoughts of who the victim was and who the murderer was started to come true.

The thought of mentioning Suzanne's name frightened him. Everything was like a carefully placed crust that one sneeze, one tiny move of a crumb would bring everything down around into bits of dust.

The evidence was going to come to him, but was he going to be able to take it to court? The Frost family had their fingers into everything. He couldn't go to a city official. The local paper was controlled by the family.

It was all giving Tom a headache.

Then, he thought like an employee of The Agate Club.

If he let the murderer go...what could he get in return?

No, they knew he couldn't be bought...but he could be made to choose.

He looked at the cover of the file on his desk and ran his hands over it, hoping the sensation would tell him the answers like one of the gypsies he had seen as a boy.

Flipping the file open he became quickly disappointed that it didn't immediately tell him what he wanted to know. It had been years since he had seen her and he was trying to remember what she looked like. Then, he pulled out a newspaper clipping from the society pages that had a photo of the previous year's Charity Ball at the Hotel del Coronado. In the photo were Mr. and Mrs. Jack Phelps, their daughter Suzanne, Judge and Beatrice Frost and their nephew Cabot.

It confirmed what he already knew, but didn't want to.

He looked at the faded photo and then at the photos from the file.

The first photo was a close up of her head. He ran his thumb around the outline of her mouth and remembered what it looked like when she smiled.

And, she always smiled at him. It was like they had a secret that no one else knew about even though they had never said a word to each other.

As he outlined her eyes he remembered the color of them and what they looked like. He thought of Alice, who looked the same and smiled with her eyes like Suzanne used to.

Tom felt as if a part of his childhood had been crushed. He didn't need to see anymore of the photos. He closed the file and stuffed it in his top desk drawer and continued with is shift, which included a trip down to the morgue.

He knew by the expression on Dr. Hill's face that the doctor had been waiting to show Tom what he wanted to know.

Evelyn had been cut up by the same knife as Suzanne.

He took the photos home with him that night and was more determined than ever to solve the case. The murderer had infiltrated his past and was now encroaching on his future.

"I know Cabot Moran has something to do with this murder," he announced as Meg sat in her chair listening to the radio. The children had been asleep for several hours.

"Do you have any evidence," she asked, not surprised at his sudden declaration.

"No," he said shaking his head.

"So, out of the thousands of men in San Diego, you know it's Cabot?"

"Yes."

"Honey...that's really impressive," she said sarcastically, "not that I am doubting you but..."

Tom ignored her.

"...he is the captain's son," she reiterated trying to make sure Tom was getting her point.

"I know."

"And Judge Frost's nephew."

"I know," he said a little louder.

"Tom, I know you know how ridiculous you sound."

"Yes."

She stood up and walked over to his desk and saw the folder he had been staring at and picked it up.

"Those are the other photos I had the coroner take of the remains," Tom said watching her.

"You're no longer calling her a girl," she said opening the file.

"It's just...easier. She hasn't been a girl for a very long time. Meg, I wouldn't," he cautioned as she started to pull the photos out.

She ignored him and was saved any further warnings from Tom by the ringing of the phone.

"It's never for me at this time of the night," she said as she studied the first photo.

Tom stood and went to the kitchen. Meg pulled the photos out and gasped. She shifted through them and became more and more horrified.

Tom was right – she was no longer a girl. For that matter, she wasn't even an animal.

The butcher had turned her into pieces of meat.

Meg took a deep breath. She felt her upper lip begin to perspire.

Tom was still on the phone.

She went back through the photos – partly to help Tom, but also because of her morbid curiosity.

Why would someone do this to another human being?

There was the head (which she quickly shuffled out of view), half of the torso, one leg, the hands, the broken foot...

She stopped and shuffled the photos back and stopped again at the one that had caught her eye.

Had Tom seen it?

No, no...he would have said something, but there was the chance that he had not looked that closely yet.

Her decision was made in a split second.

She removed the photo as she heard Tom hang up the phone and start to walk back into the room. Scrambling for a place to hide it, she ran to her chair, lifted up the cushion, flopped it down and plopped down on it as he walked in. When Tom returned she was flipping through the remaining photos without really looking at them.

"You're right," she said, "these are really...gruesome."

He stopped in front of her and took the photos.

"I think you've seen enough...you're very flushed."

"Am I...I guess it is a bit much," she said a bit breathlessly.

"Uh, huh," he said suspecting her of something.

"Who was on the phone," she asked hurriedly.

"There's been another...another crime scene," he stammered, knowing she was trying to change the subject. "Two of the other officers are on it."

"Why did they call you then?"

"It might be related to mine."

"Which one?"

"Both."

"Tom," she said slowly, "Who was found in the marina this morning?"

He thought about whether or not he should tell her, but he had never kept anything from her before, but also thought she should know how serious this all was.

"Evelyn...from the club."

"Who's Evelyn? Do I know her?"

"She didn't introduce herself that night in the alley?"

No, of course she wouldn't.

"That night," she asked, horrified at the pieces that were starting to fall into place.

"She helped you with the horse."

"She helped me with the...oh my God," she said as she ran to the kitchen to throw up.

Tom followed her in, but kept his distance. She turned and looked at him. It was all too much and she started to cry.

"Tom?!"

"I'm sorry," was all he could say.

She collapsed to the floor and he ran over and put his arms around her trying to quell her shaking body.

"There are two ways for me to go with this. I have nothing to prove any of it, but I could keep you and the kids safe. I might be able to make a deal."

"And, what about you? Do they know you don't know for certain?"

"No, it's a little bit like playing poker at this point. I think those involved think I know. They don't know that I'm really just stumbling around with assumptions."

"You stink at poker," she said.

He pulled back to look at her. "Did you mean to be funny?"

"No, it was just the first thing that came to my mind."

"Oh, it was pretty funny...any other given time."

"What are you going to do," she asked.

It was the first time she hadn't said "we", causing his heart to sink a bit.

"I think you and the kids are long overdue at your parents' house for a visit. Just give me some time to figure all this out. It's so sticky right now...it's a bit like taffy."

"Are we going to the fair," they heard Louis ask from the kitchen door.

He walked around the kitchen table so they could see him.

"Why are you sitting on the floor," he wanted to know, dragging German by his leg along the floor.

"It was closer than the chairs," Tom told him.

He looked at the chairs and then at Tom and Meg. He walked over and sat down next to Meg, yawning a bit.

"We're going to the park on Sunday aren't we? You promised," he said and then looked at Tom.

"Yes, and then you and Mom and Bruce and Alice and Joe are going to go see Grandma and Grandpa," he said.

Louis wrinkled his nose.

"You're going on the train," Tom said trying to convince the boy it was going to be fun, "You like the train."

"You're not coming?"

"No, I have to stay here and work, but I will join you when I'm done," he said, but Louis was skeptical.

"I promise."

Tom had never broken a promise, so that was good enough for Louis. He stood up.

"May I have a glass of milk please," he asked.

"Of course," Meg said as she stood up and walked to the refrigerator.

"Five more days," Tom thought as he watched. "Five more days and I can get them out of harm's way."

12.

AN UNINVITED GUEST

Evelyn's head washed up on the rocks by the lighthouse a day later. Tom kept looking for some indication that the Captain was going to let Juneau and Sylvestre go, but there was no sign.

Corey had taken some kind of administrative leave, giving Tom the impression it might have been to hide him away and making Tom think his suspicions about Cabot were correct. His focus shifted to getting through the next couple of days and to get Meg and the children out of town. He knew she was going to make him promise not to put himself into harm's way, but they both knew that he would do whatever he could to solve the case regardless of what he promised. That was the only reason Meg didn't want to leave. She knew if she stayed he wouldn't risk everything so easily; but, there were the children. Tom knew on his word she would protect their safety over his.

He was surprised when he showed up home on Thursday and found Corey's car parked in front of the house and heard the kids run from the backyard through the house as he entered the front door.

"Daddy, Daddy, Daddy," he heard like the sounds of music echoing throughout.

"What's going on monkeys," he asked as he bent and scooped up Alice. Joe clamped on to one of his legs was yelling "up, up, up!"

"Daddy, I got an 'A' on my paper," Louis said.

"Daddy, can I ride over to the Gustafsons' after dinner," Bruce asked

"Daddy," was all Alice said, throwing her arms around his neck.

"Really, that's fantastic Louis! And yes, Bruce, you can as long as you finish your chores...and keep your bicycle out of the driveway. You won't be doing anything if I have to put it away for you again."

Bruce ran out the front door to see if he needed to remove the bike. Tom continued to walk towards the kitchen and smiled as he saw Meg and then saw Corey walk up behind her to fill the doorway.

"Hello," he said to Meg as he leaned down to kiss her. She and Corey backed up to let him through with the two smaller kids still attached to him. Alice grabbed Tom's face in between her hands and turned his face so he could look at her.

"Yes Sweetheart."

"Grandma sent me a new book. You'll read it to me please," she said in her little voice.

"Of course I will."

He set Alice down and pulled Joe off his leg, swung him up for a kiss and sent then them on their way.

"How is your vacation going Corey'" he asked as he went to the sink and washed his hands.

"Well, you can imagine...since I didn't have a chance to plan...it hasn't been exactly ideal. Luckily the weather has been nice. I've been spending a lot of time in Del Mar with the horses."

"Too bad they aren't running. Are you staying for dinner?"

"No..."

"He was asking about the case," Meg interjected, knowing Tom would be interested.

"Which case...why are you asking about any case if you're on leave?" Tom stared at him for a second, trying not to act suspicious. "You're going to resign, aren't you?"

Tom shot a glance at Meg. She nodded.

"Come on you two," she said herding Alice and Joe through the door. "Let's go outside with your brothers. Would you turn off the oven Tom?"

He nodded and did as she asked.

"What's going on Corey," he said turning the knob on the oven until her heard a click and the flame go out with a "woosh".

Corey didn't say anything and Tom gestured for him to sit. He was slow to react and Tom noticed he was pale.

"Would you like something to drink?"

Corey hesitated.

"We have beer."

"Scotch," he said quickly, but quietly.

Tom nodded, went into the next room, grabbed two glasses and the bottle and brought them into the kitchen and set them on the table next to Corey.

"Ice," Tom asked.

"No, Corey answered, shaking his head.

Tom grabbed himself some ice, dropped it in his glass and poured into both. He slid Corey's glass in front of him and he reached out with both hands and wrapped them around the glass. Tom thought it looked like he was strangling it.

Tom corked the bottle, walked behind Corey and sat at the head of the table next to him. He studied Corey's troubled expression.

"Are you resigning or are you being made to resign," he asked, hoping to reach that part of Corey that would remember that he had trusted Tom when they were boys. If for nothing else, that Tom had always looked out for him.

"Apparently a weak stomach is not acceptable for someone in the police force."

"You never wanted to be a police officer anyways."

"No, I didn't. I wanted to work for Marston or Spreckles, but my family had other plans and the Judge already had a favorite. It seems he couldn't divide his attention."

Tom thought about Beatrice Frost and Charlotte.

"I beg to differ on that."

Corey looked up at him and glared.

"What," Tom asked.

It seemed Corey was thinking about what he was going to say and changed his mind. All Tom could see was the weak little boy who was always being beat up on.

Meg popped her head in the door behind Corey and gave Tom a look.

"Say," Tom started, "stay for dinner. Meg always makes too much and we can finish talking after."

"Yes," Meg added, "please stay."

Corey turned around.

"Thanks."

There was just small talk at dinner, with the kids being more quiet than normal and studying the situation around them and Tom spending most of the meal studying Corey. He felt if he could watch him then he wasn't off reporting to the Captain. Tom wasn't completely sure if that was Corey's agenda, but he wanted to play it safe. He was planning on interrogating Corey where he had home field advantage and he could control Corey easier.

Over the last couple of weeks Tom had realized why Corey had been so sick in the morgue.

It hadn't been the gore.

It was because it was Suzanne.

Corey stepped outside as Meg cleaned up the kitchen and Tom grabbed the glasses and bottle of scotch. Tom poured...a little more into Corey's glass as they sat down.

"Did you hear who it was we pulled out of the marina this morning," Tom asked.

"Yes."

"Did you know before or after you called me," Tom asked as he took a sip.

Corey didn't answer and took a sip. Tom poured more into his own glass.

"I actually assumed you knew before...I mean, knowing how you are about seeing corpses you knew when they were alive."

"It was before," Corey confirmed.

"Huh," he said, "you know she was decapitated."

"I heard that."

Tom took another sip. He knew Corey had the answers to all his questions he had and he wanted them...now.

The path was going to be tricky and knew he had to be careful because whoever was involved would question Corey until he cracked and told them everything he and Tom had talked about and anything Tom had asked.

That's if Corey remembered it at all...

Tom filled Corey's glass again and leaned back to decide what to ask next and how.

Many men like Corey had been interrogated by Tom in his career. There was a fine line – if he pushed too hard they would shut down and go within themselves; too soft and they would only talk about superficial things. His quiet demeanor often caught people he was studying and talking to off guard, especially when the questions turned harsh and accusing. Suspects found they were telling him everything he wanted to know before they realized it.

Of course, in those instances, the men he usually interrogated were only offered water.

He felt he knew Corey well enough to manipulate him, but then he thought it could also be the scotch giving him that feeling.

"Aw, hell," he thought, "what do I have to lose?"

"Corey," he said as if he was preoccupied acting as if he was watching the ice swirl around in the scotch, "whatever happened to Suzanne."

Corey slowly swallowed the drink he had just taken, lowered his glass and stared into it. His expression looked like a combination of sadness, confusion and anger.

Tom found it to be the reaction he was hoping for without realizing it. This was his chance to open the wound more.

"I always thought you two would end up together."

Corey didn't move. He was still staring into his glass, thinking.

"Again," he said, "my family had other plans."

"Damn it," Tom thought gritting his teeth in frustration. That was all he was going to get. He was trying to think of what to do next when Corey grabbed the bottle and poured more into his glass.

"I always loved her. Cab – I don't think he liked that she was always taking my side. She never took his. We were only kids. We were all just kids."

"Corey," he said slowly, "was she the one you were meeting the night you had me cover your shift?"

"Yes," he nodded.

"Is it her body in the morgue?"

"Yes."

A panicked look came across Corey's face and he abruptly stood up.

"I...I really need to go."

He gulped what was left in his glass and set it down. Tom jumped up to try to slow him down.

"You don't have to go. We'll talk about something else."

Corey glared at him.

"That's okay," he said and headed for the steps, weaving. Meg stood in the doorway. Tom watched as she opened the screen door and blocked his way.

"You're not leaving yet are you Corey? I just finished getting the kids to bed and was coming out to join you."

Tom knew she was lying.

"Yes, I really have to get going," he said taking a step closer to Meg, trying to get her to move.

Meg looked at Tom. He nodded his head begrudgingly and she stepped out of Corey's way.

"Let me grab your jacket," Tom heard her say to Corey.

Tom sat back down. He'd had every intention of doing the polite thing and seeing Corey to the door but the scotch had started to affect him. He slouched back down in his chair with his thoughts crisscrossing unable to focus on just one. The screen door creaked open and closed shut as Meg walked down the steps and sat in the chair next to him. She looked at him and laughed as she grabbed the glass out of his hand.

"You have the silliest look on your face."

"I think I might be drunk. I was so concerned about getting Corey lit I think my plan back fired."

"Oh, I don't know," she said, finishing Tom's drink, "he sounded like he was saying a lot."

"How long were you standing there?"

"Long enough. Did you know from the back, the two of you look like you could be related."

"Don't let the kids see you. We don't want them thinking that eavesdropping is okay."

She took his glass from him and had a sip of his watered down drink, "He didn't do it, did he?"

"No," Tom said slightly shaking his head. "He didn't, but he knows who did and more importantly he knows why."

"Did he say so?"

"No, but..."

"...you just know," she finished, referring to their previous conversations.

"Yes."

"Like you know it's Cabot?"

"Yes."

"How's the gathering of that evidence?"

"I'll tell you what, when the Captain becomes chief of police I'll recommend you for his replacement," he joked.

They sat there for a while not saying anything: Partly because they could, partly because Tom's head was foggy and partly because Meg was hiding something from him and she was trying to figure out how to tell him about what she had seen in the photo that was still hiding under the seat cushion.

Suddenly, he stood up and started to walk to the back door. He stopped and put his hand on her shoulder.

"Are you coming to bed," he asked.

"No, I think I'll stay out here for a while."

"Okay, I'll see you in the morning," he said bending down to place a kiss just behind her ear.

She turned and looked at him, "Where are you going?"

"Nowhere," he said on the steps, "I just don't think I'll be waking up when you get into bed."

"Should I leave you in your clothes if you don't make it out of them?"

"Naw, I'll be good," he said pulling his shirt out of his pants and unbuttoning it as he walked into the house.

13.

A Desperate Plan

Tom was swimming in the ocean off the wash where the salt water mixed with the waters of Agua Hedionda in Carlsbad where he used to sneak off to when he was a boy. He was pretty far from shore and laid back in the water so he could float and stare up at the sky. Taking in a deep breath he could smell the warm salt air and watch seagulls fly by and remembered how life was like on the ranch...and how much he had missed it.

He heard a large exhaust behind him and recognized the sound immediately. The dolphins that had sprayed him were playing in the surf on their way south. Further out were some whales, that he noticed weren't swimming as fast as he thought they should be.

In fact they looked as if they were turning quickly and coming towards him and the passing dolphins.

But still, he wasn't afraid even though he felt his muscles tense as if he should be terrified.

As they came closer there were two larger whales and two smaller whales bumping into each other.

A scream from the beach made Tom turned around abruptly and start swimming closer so he could see. The screams had come from a little girl who was sitting in the sand covered in blood. Tom tried to swim closer to help her, but he seemed to be caught in a rip current. He started to swim parallel to the beach to get around it, but the whales wouldn't let him. Anger and frustration fueled his determination and he kept pushing the smaller whales enough until he felt he could cut around the rip current. When success relieved him, he looked up to see if the girl was still there, but he was shocked to see another figure standing over her. It was a man who was also covered in blood. The little girl was crying so loudly and Tom struggled to swim closer once again.

"Hold on, I'm coming," he yelled.

He swam with his head above water so his sights were on the girl like the lifeguards had taught him, but the sight he saw made him stop. The man turned and looked at him. He held a machete looking blade in his right hand and blood dripping down it onto the sand. But, it wasn't the little girl's blood, and that wasn't what stopped him from swimming in. He stopped because he recognized the man...he was staring back at himself. Before he knew what to do, the little girl crawled towards the waves and one of the whales swam onto the beach, scooped her up in its mouth and swam back out to the sea with the others following.

"No," Tom yelled and swam after them desperately. Something pulled at his leg and he tried to kick it free and then he felt it around his waist. He stopped swimming and tried to get untangled from what seemed to be kelp, but he didn't remember there being any kelp there before. Breathing became harder and he started gasping as the kelp wrapped itself around his neck and became tighter and tighter until...

...Tom woke up with a jolt. His suspenders had come loose from his pants and wrapped around his neck. He sat up, sweating profusely and unraveled himself as he sat up. Shaking his head a couple of times to try to wake up wasn't successful and only made his head pound.

Meg came walking in on her way to the bathroom, with Joe on one hip and Alice toddling behind.

"You're late."

"Hi, Daddy," Alice said smiling.

"What," he said.

Meg came back out of the bathroom.

"Late, I said you are late."

"You look funny Daddy," Alice added.

Joe laughed at him too, "Bunny," he gurgled.

"Yes, Daddy is funny," Meg confirmed.

"Did the station call," Tom wanted to know.

"No, I called them and blamed one of the kids. Since you've never been late, they said everything would be covered and get there when you could."

He nodded his head, which wasn't a good idea, "Good." He took in a deep breath and looked at her. She was looking at him like she was waiting for his next move.

"Have I told you I love you recently," he asked.

"Not as much as you should," she said setting Joe down to chase Alice and pulling a clean shirt from the closet, laying it on the bed for him.

"Remind me to make that up to you."

"Don't worry, I will," she said as she turned to walk out the door. Alice smiled at him and then turned to follow Meg. Tom watched them and saw Joe turn to look over her shoulder. What he didn't see was the grin on Meg's face as she took the two younger children back into the kitchen because she knew the look he had on his face having caught him with it many times before and she never tired of seeing it.

It didn't matter if it was just her or the children or both...he was in love.

After taking a shower and shaving, Tom walked towards the kitchen. He saw an envelope sitting on his desk and picked it up as he walked into the kitchen. Alice was playing with Joe on the floor and Meg, like a skilled choreographer, worked around them without ever stumbling. She sat Tom's breakfast plate at his spot.

"What's this," he said, holding up the envelope.

"I don't know, Corey brought it in last night. He said it was on the stoop when he walked in."

"Huh...he just walked in," he asked curiously.

She turned and looked at him, "Yes, it was a little creepy. He wanted to know where you were."

"Uh," set the folder down as he sat to eat his breakfast, "What would you say to going back east to see your folks with the kids a little sooner."

She turned and looked at him, a bit upset, "When?!"

"Tomorrow," he said shoveling a forkful of food into his mouth, trying to be nonchalant. He looked up and when he saw her glaring at him he shoveled more food into his mouth.

"We promised the kids to take them to the park this weekend!"

"Daddy," Alice piped in.

"Fine, Monday after the park," he said uncomfortably with his mouth full of food. He had to close it so he could take in a breath to continue chewing and swallow.

She stood there with the skillet in one hand and a spatula in the other.

He hated this part of a discussion when he knew she would start waving the spatula, especially since it still had food on it.

"Please don't wave the spatula."

She flicked it instead.

"What's going on Tom?"

He was going to have to change his shirt.

He stopped eating and set everything down. He looked at Joe and Alice, who was still looking at him, and back at her.

"Alice, Honey," she said, "Please do Mommy a big favor and take Joe out to the radio room."

"We will still be going to the park this weekend Sweetheart," he said to the little girl. "I promise."

That was good enough...he had never broken a promise to her. She stood up, grabbed Joe by the back of his pajama top and started to drag him to the doorway. Joe flailed like an upside down turtle.

Both Meg and Tom cringed.

"No, Sweetheart, let him follow you," Meg offered as a suggestion. Alice looked at them as if she wasn't happy that they questioned her idea. She released him.

"Come on Joe."

As promised he flipped himself around and toddled after her. She positioned them so they weren't that far from the kitchen door.

Tom turned and looked back at Meg.

"Put the skillet and spatula down."

She had never seen him like this before and it scared her. She did as he asked and sat down at her seat, opposite of him.

"No," he said touching the table in front of the space that Bruce usually sat, "Sit here."

She stood up and took her place where he had requested. She saw the look in his eye and her fear was increasing.

"Please, on Monday, take the kids back to see your folks."

"Please tell me what's going on," she quietly pleaded, "I already agreed that I would. I'm already scared, but now you're making me feel panicked."

They both knew Alice was probably straining to hear the conversation. She usually filled Bruce and Louis in on the happenings at the house when they returned from school...which is why he hadn't asked Meg to sit in Louis' spot, which was directly across from Bruce's.

"Tom," she whispered.

"I don't think Corey's sudden appearance last night was on a whim...or his idea."

"You think he was sent," Meg asked, terrified.

Tom nodded and then begrudgingly said, "So you remember me ever mentioning the little girl who played with Cabot and Corey every once and a while?"

"Vaguely," she answered, her curiosity peaking.

"Her name was Suzanne, she was Charlotte's niece," he continued.

A sudden gulp of air caught in her throat, but there was no way for Tom to know that it was because Megan had heard him mumble that name in his sleep, but always figured it was one of the girls from club.

"But...," she started to ask.

"She didn't live at the club and she was never supposed to be there, but found her way occasionally. She was adopted by the Phelpses."

"Suzanne Phelps was the little girl from the Robin's Nest," Meg said, her heart pounding.

She had to tell him.

He kept eye contact with her, and when he thought she might lose control he grabbed her head in his hands then dropped them down to her hands.

"Keep looking at me," he told her. The tears started to stream down her face. She had to tell him. "Tom…"

"I know," he said, cutting her off. "Focus Meg."

She nodded, straining against his hands.

"Until I can find the evidence…or work a deal…I have to get you and the kids out of here."

He hated the look in her eyes.

"Cabot has no boundaries," he said remembering the tub in Agate Club's basement, "And he's protected."

"He has no boundaries because he is protected," she stammered, angrily.

He looked over her shoulder to make sure the two younger children were still playing.

"I want and need you here…but we have them and one of us has to go with them."

She nodded in agreement. It was the first feeling of relief he had felt in weeks. He let his hands fall from her face and she grabbed one of them.

"Tom," she started to say, but she couldn't tell him about the photo she took, "I love you," was the only thing that came out more feebly than she would have ever said.

He nodded and let go of her hand. He didn't finish eating and stood up, grabbed the envelope and grabbed her shoulder as he walked out of the kitchen to leave for the station.

"Call your mother," was all he said before stopping to play with Alice and Joe for a quick second.

By the time she reached the phone, he was already gone. She stared at the chair where the photo was hidden and finally moved when Alice tugged at her dress.

"Why's Daddy so sad," she asked.

Meg knelt down and took her in her arms.

"Because a lot of people have lied to him and he's starting to feel like telling the truth won't matter," she said, not thinking.

Some how, Alice understood what her mother was saying.

14.

Putting Dux in a Row

Tom sat leaning back in his chair at his desk with his head propped up on his index and middle fingers and his elbow on the arm rest. The headache he had was partly because of the hangover and partly because he just really didn't know what to do...who to ask...where to look...who to trust...why this all happened...and how to prove how it all happened.

He looked at the envelope he had placed on his desk where it sat unopened. He pondered what contents it might hold. He leaned forward and rubbed his face with one hand, realizing he had missed a few spots while shaving as his fingers bristled against spots of stubble.

Before he opened the envelope, he pulled out a clean sheet of paper and the working file with the photos and reports. He drew a line down the center of the page.

On the left side the first word he wrote was "who".

Well, that was his most loaded question: who did it, who knew, who was involved.

He shook his head and decided to answer that last.

Okay..."what"?

What happened? What happened to the girl...no, he could write Suzanne? What happened to Evelyn? Where – the tub was obvious, but he would have to get in there to find out if that's where Evelyn had been separated from her head as well. And, why had Suzanne's body been left where it was? Evelyn's body…well, she wasn't the first body to be pulled up in the marina. But it was the first one that Tom could remember having the head appear several days later. How…Tom shuddered at that one, but he still didn't have the weapon. He would have to try to pressure Corey for that one. He knew there was a collection, but he didn't know where for sure.

Which left him with "why"?

Meg was right. All he had was his imagination.

Again, Evelyn he knew, but why Suzanne? Why would anyone want to cover it up?

He looked back at the unopened envelope.

He set the piece of paper inside the folder marked "Rubidoux" and opened the large envelope. He started shuffling through the papers trying to find what the judge may have been involved with.

Finding Meredith working in records had been a stroke of luck. She was more organized and anal than Tom could have imagined. Not only did she have everything he had asked for, but she had it alphabetized according to topic and had provided a table of contents that broke every subject down by case and date so that everything was also in chronological order.

It took Tom a minute to actually look at the files and contents because he was so in awe.

"Shit," he thought, "she should be working as a detective."

Then he laughed to himself, "maybe she should be Corey's replacement. I wonder how her stomach is."

He didn't think he was so funny a few minutes later when he heard Meredith's name being mentioned in conversation.

He heard the commotion of a few officers returning from the field.

"Well, look who's here," one of them shouted. "Hey, Dux, too bad you were late."

Tom acknowledged them, but he didn't listen to too many of them. He usually just nodded as they would talk and he would be thinking about something that he was currently working on. Today was no different.

"You should have seen this case we just came from. If I didn't know better I'd say that it was related to the ones you've been working on."

Slowly, Tom started to tune in.

"I've never seen so much blood," another one chimed in, "I don't think Hayes would have been able to stand it."

"Yeah, especially since there was so much mutilation. Shit, I didn't know human beings could do that sort of things to each other."

Now they had Tom's attention.

He turned in his seat.

"Was the head cut off," he asked.

They looked at him. It would have been an odd question under any normal circumstance.

"No, but it might as well have been. The sick fucker looked like he tried and then just decided to pop her eyes out. He sliced the hell out of her body as well."

"Her?"

The officers didn't hear him, "It looked like he was just swinging his arms about like a wild monkey," the officer said demonstrating with his own arms, "There was no rhyme or reason...it looked like he didn't know what to cut. But you can imagine with someone flailing like that he was flicking and flinging blood all over the place. It was all over the ceiling, walls, furniture. The worst part it looked like she was trying to crawl away, so the mess wasn't contained to one room."

Tom had stood and had slowly moved so he was almost standing next to the group of men. He didn't realize he was standing there with his mouth open staring at the officers describing everything. The sound of his heart thumbing steadily became louder in his ears.

"Do we know who 'She' was?"

"That's the worst part. I know I've seen her at lunch and some of the city Christmas parties. It was that woman from records..."

The words came out in slow motion.

"...Meredith," he confirmed looking at a small notebook.

Tom didn't move.

He felt his insides harden.

He had only felt this way once during the war. When he was out on his only patrol and he was separated from the soldiers he was with. There were two enemy soldiers that he came up on and Tom had startled them as much as they had startled him. The little bit of German he did know how to speak escaped him and he just stared and the men. On instinct he went to fire his rifle but it jammed. One of the soldiers was fumbling with his pistol and the other didn't move. Instead of running, Tom became angry and charged them both. He rammed his shoulder into the one and knocked him over as he bayoneted the other and then he swung his rifle down so that the force cracked the soldier's head open. He did the same to the other while the soldier had tried to grab his breath.

Tom told no one.

His resolve was just as strong at this moment, but there were no enemies directly in front of him to take his anger out on. More importantly, he couldn't just act out because he had to think about Meg and the kids.

"Are you okay Dux," one of the officers asked, "you look pissed."

"Huh, oh well this guy's getting away with...what, this would be the third body if it's the same man," he said.

"I guess that means your cousins are innocent if they are related...the cases, I mean."

"What do you mean?"

"Well, since they've been in custody."

"You're absolutely correct."

Tom felt it was safer that they were in custody at this point.

He turned and walked back to his desk and then looked back as he was about to sit down.

Captain Moran had been listening to the whole thing, but he was only watching Tom. Tom glared back, turned and sat down...

...and then let a little panic set in.

He was careful not to make any strange moves or change the expression on his face. He pulled an old file that was almost closed and opened it as if he was reviewing it. His fingers flipped through the pages without any engagement from him since he really didn't see it, but his fingers were still trying to sense something from them to help him.

Everything he had gathered from Meredith and the file was going to have to be kept safe from strangers' hands and eyes. It was too dangerous to leave it all at the house and too big for him to be toting it around with him (not to mention, frowned upon and against the rules.)

His fingers turned another page.

If was left it at work he was sure that someone would break into his desk to search the drawers. They would probably break into his car...at least, he thought, he would if it were him. It was all making him so frustrated! Without thinking he grabbed the front edge of the desk out and heaved up on it.

There was a little bit of give.

Stunned, he turned around to see what everyone was doing...to make sure they weren't looking at him. The Captain had returned to his office and shut the door and the other officers were busy putting together their reports. Satisfied Tom leaned over to get a better look.

He grinned.

There was still a way to hide the file in his desk and he wouldn't need a key.

He acted like he was going to the bathroom when he went to the maintenance department and borrowed a screw driver and waited for everyone to go to lunch...and for the Captain to go to the club.

Scouting the desk out earlier, he had already figured out the rear left corner of the desk would be the best because the file wouldn't interfere with any of the drawers.

Tom opened up the file from Meredith, threw out the subjects he really wasn't interested in and pulled the first section on adoptions then opened the other folder and placed the remaining papers in with the entire case notes, reports and both sets of photos.

Then he went to work on the desk top trying to find the weakest point. When he was satisfied that he had, he looked around and then wedged the screw up into the crack between the top and desk. Just to be safe, he looked around again before slamming his hand against the butt of the tool and then worked it until the blade went in further. He leveraged his weight against it until he felt the top give and the nails screech as the two pieces of wood strained to separate. He did it a couple more times and then moved onto the other corner. Every so often he would look around to make sure he was in the clear. Anyone just walking by could easily assume that he was doing one of his experiments.

He slid the file into the corner so that the edges were even on all sides with the top. When he was satisfied, he did one last look around, slammed the heel of his hand down on the corner and then the rest of the way around the desk. He reached under the lip until he could feel the folder and tried pulling it out. It didn't budge and he couldn't really detect it. Anyone grabbing the desk to move it wouldn't feel a thing.

Tom folded the papers he had taken out of the file and put them in his coat pocket, returned the screwdriver and left.

Tom made two stops before heading outside: one to his cousins and one to the coroner. He made the one to the coroner last because Dr. Hill had the disgusting habit of eating while conducting autopsies. It made Tom shudder when he wondered how many bodies had been buried with remnants of the doctor's lunch inside of them. It was one of those things he knew about...he just never wanted to see it himself.

Juneau was sitting on the edge of his cot with his arms on his knees, hands clasped and his head down as if he was praying.

Sylvestre was in his...asleep.

Juneau lifted his head as Tom stopped in front of his cell. There was a flicker of hope in his expression when he saw Tom. It made Tom's heart sink knowing that he didn't know what he was going to do get the two of them off. He also knew that freeing him and Sylvestre was secondary to trying to keep his family safe.

"Tom," he said relieved.

"June" he said trying to reassure him as Juneau grabbed his hands through the bars. "How are you doing?"

"They don't tell us anything. We didn't even get to speak in front of the judge."

"I know."

"Our lawyer didn't even say anything. Your brothers' reputations didn't help us."

"Oh, I completely forgot about that. I'll see if we can get you a different lawyer."

"We can't afford anyone. You know that."

"I have some favors due to me."

"Tom," Juneau's voice cracked, "Are you going to be able to get us out?"

"I'm working on it," he said with the most non-committal answer he could think of. "There's been some developments that may allow me to get you out, but there's a lot of paperwork I'm going to have to get through and the cooperation of a lot of people. It's just going to take some time."

Juneau nodded his head.

"Is there anything else you can tell me about that night? Has Sylvestre said anything else?"

"No," he said, "There wasn't much to see. And Sylvestre," he said looking back at him, "I'm surprised he was even able to see that sack. He was so drunk. You know how he gets."

Tom nodded.

"If you think of anything tell the guard to call me."

"I will. Please call our Mom and let her know we're all right?"

"Sure," he said as he turned to walk away. He took a few steps and then turned back. "And Juneau..."

"Um?"

"When Sylvestre wakes up you might want to tell him guilty people sleep."

"Is that body from earlier today here," Tom asked walking into the morgue.

Dr. Hill was cutting into a body and didn't even look up.

"I didn't think that was your case," he said, and then looked up smirking, "but I was expecting you."

"Thanks."

"She's over here," walking over to one of the other tables. Tom came over and was happy to see that there weren't any signs of the doctor's lunch.

He pulled the sheet back. Tom had to take a deep swallow and thought he might have felt a little of what Corey had experienced, but with Tom there was guilt. He thought Meredith might still be alive he hadn't asked for the files.

The corpse displayed signs of a crime of rage, very similar to Suzanne's murder and mutilation and Evelyn's.

"Go ahead," the doctor said, interrupting his thoughts, "ask me."

"It disturbs me how excited you get around on this gore, mortality and carnage."

Dr. Hill cocked his head one way and then the other.

"You should hear me when I talk to them," he quipped.

"They're not talking back to you are they?"

"No," he said, "that'd be crazy."

"Maybe you should get out more," Tom said as he looked closer at the wounds on the body. "Did you want me to ask you about the weapon?"

"Yes," the coroner said excitedly.

Tom looked at him and shook his head.

"It was the same blade, wasn't it," he said looking up.

Dr. Hill nodded his head.

"Used it more like a machete this time. Which..." he said walking to another table on the opposite side of the room, he pulled back the sheet and flipped the decapitated body onto its side, "...would explain these wounds on her."

Tom turned and looked from where he was at.

"She was running away from the ghoul," he said before turning his attention back to Meredith's body.

Dr. Hill came back to watch him.

"You still don't have a weapon, do you," he asked Tom.

Tom shook his head and waved his hands over the body, "Obviously."

He put the sheet back over her and went to the sink to wash his hands.

The coroner looked at Meredith's covered body and then he looked back at Evelyn's and then Meredith's again.

"Say, didn't you know these two," he asked.

"I did," Tom said matter-of-factly.

"That'd make you a suspect wouldn't it?"

"I hadn't thought about that, thanks," Tom said dryly.

He hung the towel after drying his hands.

"Has anyone else been down here," Tom asked.

"Besides you and Hayes...and the Captain."

"Yeah."

He thought for a second, "The D.A....Fordham...Farley..."

"Farnham, Bradley Farnham," Tom said.

"Yes, him."

"To look at her," Tom asked pointing towards Evelyn's body.

"Yes."

Tom nodded his head, not surprised.

"Charlotte MacGregor and her barkeep, Rufus came too and told us who she was."

Tom smiled a little. He was amused that the coroner didn't know the D.A., but knew the other two.

"Anyone else?"

"Yeah, that stuffed shirt that hangs on with Judge Frost."

"You mean the Captain's son?"

"Oh shit, I forgot he was Moran's son. You wouldn't think it to look at him. Pompus, pretentious shit. Maybe because he spends so much time with the Judge."

"When was he here," he asked interrupting Dr. Hill's rambling.

"A couple of days ago."

Tom looked up and down the room.

"Where's my body?"

"The first one?"

"Yes."

"We buried her after I took that other set of photos for you."

"She hadn't been identified yet."

"Well I can't just let them sit around here forever. They do start to smell after awhile. And when I have more than one..."

"Under what name did you bury her?"

"The same as we always do. We just add a number."

"Jane Doe...number three."

"Something like that, but sadly, it was closer to 221."

"Closer to that number or it was that number?"

"She was 221."

"I was never told she was being buried."

"The Captain knew. He signed the final papers."

Tom nodded, "thanks."

Tom felt like giving up, but he didn't want to because he was pissed off.

It reminded him of when he was younger and he'd watch the men at the club do and say things without any discretion because they could. Tom would grit his teeth and he would feel his muscles tense when he would see things happen right in front of the men who were supposed to be upholding and enforcing the law. He watched them go about their business and not even acknowledge what he knew to be wrong.

Since all these men knew things about one another, Tom would see the same things get overlooked outside the walls of the club in the streets of downtown.

Tom knew it was his fault it had all bled into the walls of his home. It was his fault there were two extra bodies in the morgue.

"No," he thought, "this is Cabot's doing."

Without thinking he stepped into traffic and was almost hit again. This time he flashed his badge when the driver started yelling at him and he continued to run in and out of traffic until he was on the other side and heading up 4th to Broadway where the U.S. Grant Hotel was…and Cabot.

15.

CHESS

Tom marched through the atrium of the Grant. It was the late afternoon so Tom knew where to find Cabot.

Dr. Hill had tipped Cabot's hand by letting Tom know he was in town and if Judge Frost was working, Cabot wouldn't stray far, but he also knew Cabot wouldn't be caught dead in the club. Cabot was always afraid the people who could give him more would find out.

At least that was the impression Tom had.

It had become truer since Cabot had been appointed as the Judge's aide and Cabot no longer frequented The Agate Club. Tom had heard the girls were relieved since he was a bit of a cad and had "strange tendencies" when it came to sex.

That wasn't anything new. Tom had heard that when they were teenagers.

Tom found him sitting exactly where he imagined he would - in the lounge reading the newspaper. He was dressed in his summer whites – pristine – not a spot of news ink anywhere on him.

Cabot set his cigar down and saw Tom as he turned the page of the paper and flicked it with both hands so it made a cracking sound.

"Cabot," Tom said casually.

"Tom," he said with a lecherous smirk itching at the corner of his lip.

A waiter came and set a drink down next to Cabot and then looked at Tom.

"May I get a beverage for you sir?"

"No, thank you."

"Oh, come on Tom," Cabot said, "I won't tell anyone. Bring him a scotch on the rocks."

Tom shook his head and the waiter left.

"You seem to be here in town a lot these days," Tom started.

"Don't be rude. At least sit down," Cabot said, gesturing to the other chair near him.

Tom sat as Cabot grabbed his cigar and put it in his mouth.

"Would you like one," he asked Tom and started to reach inside his coat pocket.

"No, thank you."

"Oh, please, they're not poisoned."

Tom didn't move a muscle. Cabot shrugged his shoulders and took another puff of his. "Suit yourself. You always were a bit of a goody-two shoes."

Tom smiled a little.

"It's all right, you can laugh. That was pretty funny."

Tom still didn't do any more than he already had.

"I remember you as having more of a sense of humor," Cabot said.

"I guess working from the time I was nine and mopping up the shit of those that didn't deserve it took its toll," Tom shot back.

"It has been awhile, hasn't it?"

"Yes it has."

"I have daughter about the same age as your youngest...what's his name...Joe?"

Tom's muscles tensed. He had to remind himself that Cabot knew how to get under his skin and was good at it. It did bother him that Cabot had been keeping tabs on him all those years and knew his family.

"How's your wife," Tom asked.

"I no longer have one."

"Divorced?"

"Widowed."

"Really, I'm sorry to hear that. How?"

"Natural causes."

"At our age?"

"It happens."

Cabot leaned back in his chair, his glass in one hand and the cigar in the other. Tom leaned back in his, studying every muscle twitch Cabot made, every subtle change in his expressions, body language and tenor of his voice.

"What do you want Tom?"

Tom looked at him like he remembered the Judge used to. "I think I will have that drink," he said as he motioned to the waiter.

"I understand you've been working a difficult case," Cabot said.

Tom nodded his head, "Yes, especially since it keeps growing."

"It must be getting a little sticky with your family...with your cousins being in jail and all."

"People keep pointing that out to me and seem a lot more interested in that than I am. Of course, your father would know about having family members in sticky situations wouldn't he?"

"My father, your boss."

"But then he and I have different ideas about handling situations like that. I believe in doing what's right. Did I hear you're running for the state house of representatives?"

"Senate," he corrected cautiously.

"I bet you've been campaigning a lot."

"Yes."

"I imagine you're being well received down here."

"Yes."

"Wow," Tom said almost genuinely, "something like that must take a lot of time. I suppose with the Judge's and your father's connections it's been a little easy. When did you start - last year at the horse track?"

"Not that long. I started the night I announced it at the Charity Ball."

It was always held in October.

"Never been," Tom said, "but you probably already know that."

The waiter brought his drink.

"My wife has always tried to get me to go. You know I've never been comfortable in a monkey suit," he said taking a sip.

"You should make the effort to go. Hell, if Corey can…"

"The Phelps' go every year, don't they," Tom interrupted.

"I believe so."

"Yes, I think I remember seeing a photo with them, you and your family and Suzanne."

"Perhaps…that night is always a bit of a blur. I take lots of photos at that event with a lot of different people. You seem to be stopping every ten seconds and having a flash go off in your eyes. I don't remember everybody."

"That's probably where Corey and Suzanne met…again," he thought for a second and chuckled, "she always hated you."

Cabot's cigar was dangling from his index and middle finger. He didn't realize that it had burned for so long that the tail of ash had grown so that it was about to break away and drop to the carpet below. Tom also noticed that Cabot's eyes were beginning to turn red. Just then the ash separated into a million tiny flakes and floated below, leaving a small grey cloud imprint into the fabric.

"Judge Frost always seemed to favor her," Tom continued, "I guess being Charlotte's niece and all…but you were never good enough for her. That goes to show you it doesn't really matter who your parents are."

He saw Cabot's jaw tighten.

"But then you were never interested in her were you?"

Cabot relaxed slightly.

"No, I wasn't."

"However, that would have been really emasculating to have her pick a weakling sap like Corey and not you."

"She deserved to die in the same type of place where she was born."

Tom sat for a moment very reserved. He nodded his head, stood and took a few bills out of his wallet and set them down by his glass.

"Well, looks like you're always being overlooked. Hopefully that won't happen in the election...but with your contacts I don't think you have anything to worry about. You can count on my vote."

"I'm sure I can," Cabot said seething. "Don't bother trying to catch up with Corey. He's staying at the Judge's estate in Del Mar."

"Cab..."

Cabot looked up at Tom who was grinning.

Tom quickly reached down and grabbed the area between Cabot's neck and shoulder and squeezed until Cabot gasped. Cabot tried not to wince, but couldn't help it. Tom, still grinning, leaned down to his ear.

"I know you killed Suzanne and you just confirmed where," he said slowly.

Cabot squirmed and Tom tightened his grip.

"I also know it was you who butchered Evelyn and Meredith."

"You'll never find anything," Cabot said through his teeth.

"You never knew when to shut up did you? I already have. And I will find something to force your father to help me get the warrants to search every inch and crevice of your life. After all that do you really think the Judge will want anything to do with you? It's going to get sticky and he will drop you and your ambitions will go down with you. I am going to take hold and squeeze and squeeze until every vessel inside your body ruptures."

Tom stood and relaxed his grip. He straightened Cabot's coat and patted it down. Cabot twitched trying to stretch the muscle.

"It was good seeing you again, Cab," Tom said as he left.

Tom responded to a couple of routine calls to help clear his mind and make the rest of the day go by. He went through the motions of taking down statements and asking questions, all the while thinking about what Cabot had said and unwittingly confessed.

Corey was off limits if he was up at the family's estate. It would not have taken a master of interrogation to force out of him what was said, but Tom had not told him about the tub in The Agate Club basement. He knew the boys knew it was there, and Suzanne for that matter, because that was where they always hid from Cabot.

He had to find the weapon. Cabot was arrogant enough to have it on display somewhere and Tom's bet was at the residence he also kept on the Judge's estate. If the knife was from Corey's collection, Cabot would have returned it.

Tom's money was on Cabot. No, it would have been beneath him to use something that belonged to Corey...unless...

It was then Tom remembered the article when Cabot they had returned from the war and Cabot had been awarded a medal. He had been the golden boy of the city for several months and one of the articles had an interview covering mementos taken during the war.

Tom stopped by the newspaper on the way home. The man in archives paid Tom the favor of staying late since Tom had helped him get out a jam with some belligerent public activities. Tom was never sure if people like this remembered him from the club or from some police duty so he always smiled and nodded and usually said, "It was no problem, just doing my job."

Tom took off his coat, threw it around the chair and rolled up his sleeves as the man brought the stack covering the time frame he had given and he started going through them. It took him about an hour to find the copy he needed. He turned the page and his heart leapt.

On the page was a photo of Cabot kneeling down and in front of him where items he had taken as tokens of his kills.

"That figures," Tom thought, "only Cabot would have the gumption and stupidity to go through a battle field to collect trophies."

There were rifles and helmets, but it was the centerpiece of the collection that was most impressive. Lined up in several rows were about 21 knives. No two were alike.

"Do you have a magnifying glass," Tom shouted to the clerk. The man nodded and disappeared.

As Tom was trying to look closer the clerk brought the magnifying glass. He took the magnifying glass and thanked the clerk and then scanned each of the knives in the photo until he saw the one he knew was it. Back in the third row, near Cabot's left knee was an unusual looking blade. It was about a foot long and the blade had a straight edge on one side and a serrated one on the other, but it was only on the upper half that the blade had a slight curve. The handle and bolsters looked very heavy. It looked like a cross between a hunting knife and a fisherman's knife or even something used on a farm or ranch.

This was not a knife that a soldier would be carrying.

Tom's imagination went into overdrive as he ran through so many scenarios as to who Cabot had taken the knife from and how. He wondered if these were the first women he had murdered or were there more in Europe where they could have been disguised as casualties of war.

"I'm sorry sir," the clerk timidly said, looking between the clock and Tom.

"No, I'm the one who's sorry. You would probably like to get home to your family."

"No," the clerk said a bit perplexed, "I don't have a family."

Tom remembered how he knew the man.

"I'm sorry that was callous of me. Let me help you clean up."

He handed him all of the papers, but the one he had been looking at. When the clerk turned to go into the back Tom coughed and ripped the page. Stuffed it into his pocket and folded the paper back up. He grabbed his coat and noticed he had black ink smudges all over his shirt and pants. He pulled out his handkerchief and wiped his hands after putting his coat on.

"Thank you for staying," he said as he handed the clerk the paper and some money as he left.

The mood was very somber at the house as soon he entered the door. Tom's dinner was sitting in front of his seat covered with a dish towel. He lifted it and pulled out the piece of chicken and took a bite. Meg was sitting in the back yard and she turned when she heard the squeak of the screen door.

This time she was the one with the bottle of scotch next to her.

He walked down to her and gestured for the glass. She handed it to him and he took a drink before sitting in the chair next to her. Even in the dark he could see she was worried.

"You're late."

"I know. I'm sorry."

"I got worried. I called the station and they said you had left hours ago. Actually Tom, worried is an understatement. I started to panic."

He reached out for her hand and pulled her out of her chair and into his lap and held her.

She started to cry.

"I'm sorry. I wasn't thinking," he said.

"No, you weren't," she blubbered. "I was so frazzled I sent Bruce and Louis to bed without eating. They didn't even do anything wrong...really."

"We just need to make it through this weekend...you called your folks, right?"

She nodded, "We leave Monday morning before lunch. I went to the school and talked to Bruce's and Louis' teachers and picked up homework for them. I didn't tell them anything," she added when she saw a look of concern pass across Tom's face.

Tom was relieved. Meg was still crying a little and pulled her head back to wipe her eyes and frowned when she looked at him.

"What is all over your shirt," she sniffed.

He looked, "Huh, oh...newspaper ink."

She frowned.

"How did you get so much ink on you?"

She leaned back and tried to getter a better look at his face.

"It's all over your face."

He wiped his face with his hand and decided to wait to clean it later.

"I was looking for a photo."

"A photo, haven't we seen enough photos?"

He reached down and pulled out the wrinkled photo out of his pocket. Meg took the photo and held it.

"Tom, although I can see black smudges all over you it's too dark to see a faded old newspaper clipping. What is it?"

"It's a photo of my murder weapon," he said smiling.

"You know where it is?"

"Well, not exactly. I know where it is...I just don't know where it is."

Tom heard something at the screen door.

"I think were being watched," he said.

Meg looked over Tom and saw Louis and Bruce standing at the screen door.

"What are you boys doing up," Tom asked without looking.

They opened the door and stood on the top step.

"We're really hungry," Louis said.

"And, really sorry," Bruce added.

Meg turned, feeling a bit guilty.

"You stay out here," Tom said, lifting her up out of his lap. "I'll feed them. I'm rather hungry myself."

She watched him walk into the house behind the boys.

He walked to the ice box and pulled out a plate of chicken and a bottle of milk.

"Grab some utensils and napkins and get in your seats," Tom told them. They both did as they were told and sat where they always did.

Seats had never been assigned, but over the years they always sat in the same ones.

Tom went back and pulled out the corn cobs thinking they might not be too bad cold and put one on each plate next to the chicken and placed a plate in front of each boy and then returned to give them each a glass of milk.

As Tom took his spot, they watched him as he acted like a magician, jerking the towel away from his plate.

"Wallah," he said, exposing his plate of food.

Bruce and Louis giggled.

He studied them as they ate. It never ceased to amaze him what miracles they were. Louis' hands were still too small to grab the milk glass with one and had to keep putting his food down and reaching up with both hands to drink. He was always very careful not to tilt it too quickly so he wouldn't spill.

Then he would repeat the action in reverse.

Tom and Meg always thought he was nothing if not methodical. Meg blamed Tom's genetics.

"Are you excited to go to the park tomorrow," he asked both boys, but directed the question at Louis since he had been the most excited.

"Yes," Louis said quietly.

"Yoamm," Bruce said, nodding his head enthusiastically.

"Don't talk with your mouth full," Tom said.

Bruce smiled apologetically.

"And then on Monday, you're going with Mom and Alice and Joe back to see Grandma and Grandpa."

Bruce looked at Louis. Louis shrugged his shoulders.

Tom thought the exchange indicated that they thought one or the other must have known.

Bruce looked at Tom, "You're not coming with us Daddy?"

"No, not right away; I have some things to take of first and then I'll come join you."

That wasn't really his plan, but it sounded like one he could keep. He was always truthful with the children. He always remembered the sting of being to be lied to as a child.

The answer was satisfactory for Louis, but Bruce didn't seem so convinced.

"What is it Bruce," he asked.

"Why are we going? No one asked us."

Apparently Louis felt this was a fair question because he stopped eating and waited for Tom's answer.

Tom put his elbows on the table and clasped his hands. He leaned forward and thought about what he was going to tell them.

"Moms and Dads have conversations all the time to make decisions that will help us to do what's best for our children...in this case you," he said to Bruce and turned to Louis, "and you and Alice and Joe."

They listened to him intently.

"People have conversations all the time involving other people who are elsewhere and decisions are made that will affect those people for the rest of their lives without them ever knowing. Mom and I will always do what is in your best interest. Some times that means we have to make decisions without you."

The boys stared at him.

"Do you believe me?"

Bruce looked at Louis who nodded his head.

"Yes, Daddy, we do," Bruce answered for both of them.

"I need to ask both of you to do something very, very important. It's also important to know that it's okay if you can't."

They sat very still. Bruce was clenching both ends of his corn cob, and didn't notice the juice starting to run over his fingers and down his small arms.

"Until I get there I need you two to help Mom take care of Alice and Joe. I am trusting you two to be on your best behavior and do whatever Mom asks you to. Can you do that?"

"Uh huh," Bruce said.

Louis yawned and nodded his head.

"Thank you. Why don't you guys finish your milk and go to bed. I'll clean up your plates."

When they were finished they slid off their chairs, came and kissed Tom and started to leave the kitchen.

"Bruce?"

"Yes Daddy."

"Leave the corn."

"Oh, I forgot."

He walked back and put it on his plate.

"Good nigh' Daddy."

"Good night Bruce."

"Wash your hands and faces before you go to bed," he yelled after them as he leaned back in his chair wondering how everything had come to this.

15.

A LOVELY FAMILY

Balboa Park was bustling with parents and children running in all directions.

"Louis, get off that railing," Tom shouted as Louis was scaling one the barriers between the main midway and covered arcade near El Prado.

He shifted Alice in his arms and finally moved her to his other arm. The poor girl was beginning to perspire, become uncomfortable and squirming.

"Do you have her," Meg looked up from under her parasol.

"I have her, I just feel like she's going to slip out of my arms."

Alice, if on cue, fussed and squirmed again.

"Shh, Alice, Honey it's okay," he said. "It's not right for such a little girl to sweat so much."

"It's the middle of July, Tom."

"I know I...Bruce, get over here RIGHT NOW!"

Bruce scampered out of the plants and stopped in front of Tom, suddenly realizing he was supposed to have been behaving.

"Yes Daddy?"

Tom raised an eyebrow as he looked down at Bruce's clothes, which were now streaked with green and brown from the plants, grass and dirt. One of his stockings had slid down and was a wrinkled pile above the shoe and had some leaves feathering out.

Bruce took a heavy breath and exhaled and looked up at Tom. A chunk of his hair was plastered over his brow.

"I know, I'm 'posed to stay on the walkway and not go in the bushes."

Tom felt Meg hold back a snicker. Tom changed his face as if he was pondering Bruce's explanation.

"I'm sorry Daddy. I don't know what happened. My brain must have escaped me."

"Urmph," Megan couldn't hold it in any longer. She tried to cover it with a small cough.

"Hmmm, do you think you could find your brain so it can help you behave the rest of the day?"

Bruce thought about it for a second and then nodded his head.

"I think so."

"Good, that means the ponds and fountains too."

"Yes Daddy."

Satisfied, Tom released him, "Good, move along then."

Bruce smiled, turned and ran off to catch up with Louis and some other children.

Tom looked at Meg. She didn't want to look at him. When she finally did she started laughing. Tom held his stoic expression, but that didn't last for long. He cracked and grinned.

"You sure seem very pleased with yourself."

"I just find it very amusing," Meg said back to him.

"What do you find amusing...that one son misbehaves?"

"No, that he is a smaller, younger version of you and you don't see it."

"I..."

"Now Tom, you cannot honestly say you never..."

"...not once, I was a perfectly behaved child."

She leaned into Alice.

"Don't listen to him, Sweetheart. Daddy's lying."

"Besides," he said to try to defend himself, "boys were meant to be dirty."

"Yes they are," she said as she tried to brush some dirt off of Tom's lapel.

"Why don't you walk with Mommy," he told Alice as he set her down. She reached up and took Meg's hand and Tom looked in at Joe who was still asleep in the pram.

"He could sleep through a stampede," he said looking up at Meg.

"That, they all got from me," Tom added.

They strolled through the park greeting other people, but all the while Meg was thinking of Monday and the photograph she had taken and hidden from Tom. Tom was thinking of the case and the papers he had stuffed in his pockets. He had not had a chance to take a look at them the night before and the morning had just run away from him. He kept wondering who had the Judge arranged adoptions for when it wasn't his specialty. He figured Suzanne's name would be on the papers. Maybe the Judge had done it as a favor. He did a lot of favors to keep himself and his nephew in position.

"Stop it Tom," Meg said.

"What?"

"You're thinking too much. We're supposed to be enjoying the day."

"I'm sorry."

"You've been saying that a lot lately."

"How'd you know I was thinking?"

"Your mouth was hanging open. It's not attractive."

He cleared his throat.

"I have a confession," he said.

"Is it about the papers you've been toting around in your pocket all weekend?"

He stopped walking and looked at her.

"It would disappoint me greatly me if you asked how I knew," she said smiling. "I know you Tom Rubidoux."

He leaned down and kissed her.

"I love you," he said.

"I know that too."

Louis came scampering over and interrupted them. His clothes were in disarray and there was blood running down his shin into his no-longer-white sock.

"What happened to you," Tom asked him.

"I fell," he said matter-of-factly.

Tom knelt down and started cleaning Louis knee with his handkerchief.

"Where's your brother?"

"He was talking with some lady."

"A lady," Tom said alarmed.

"Tom," he heard a slight panic in Meg's voice. He shook his head.

"What lady?"

"I don't know her name," Louis continued, "I've seen her before. She has pretty orange hair."

"Tom," Meg said again – the panic level rising in her voice.

He shook his head again as he looked past Louis to see if he could see Bruce and Charlotte.

"Did she tell you who she was?"

"No, but she knew our names."

"Why don't you stay with us? We're going to eat in a little bit before we go to the organ pavilion. Are you getting hungry?"

"Uh huh."

"Straighten yourself up then," he said as he stood up. "Charlotte won't let anything happen to him," he said softly to Meg.

"Are you so sure?"

"Absolutely," he said, confidently as he still tried to see down the parkway.

"I think you're missing one," Charlotte said from behind.

Tom and Meg turned around. Charlotte stood there and holding one of her hands was Bruce.

"Hello Charlotte."

"Hello Tom."

Before he could say anything else Charlotte let go of Bruce's hand and extended it to Meg.

"You must be his wife Megan."

Meg took her hand and shook it like ladies did. Tom stammered a little.

"It's alright Thomas, I know you're not rude."

"It's nice to meet you," Meg said sincerely.

"It's nice to finally meet you," Charlotte said. "Tom you really should teach your children that it's not safe to talk to strangers and just walk off with them."

"Your hair can be very mesmerizing."

"Yes, I suppose it can be," she said winking at Bruce. He smiled bashfully.

"I speak from experience, and it's also hard when you call them by name."

Charlotte put her hand on Bruce's head, ran it down his cheek and put her finger under his chin so she could see his face. Tom would have missed the next thing if it hadn't felt so familiar.

Her hand dropped down Bruce's arm and the grabbed his hand, squeezed it and then let it go. To most people, it would have seen an innocent gesture; but to Tom, it triggered something in his memory...because she looked at the little boy's hand before releasing it.

"Yes, but I'm not the only one who knows their names."

"He's here," Tom asked, broken from his train of thought.

"Of course he is," she said letting her hand fall and smiling. "He and the Judge wouldn't miss an opportunity to glad hand."

"Thank you," Meg said.

Tom realized why she was there.

"After all these years...you still have to watch from a far."

"After all these years," she said nodding her head in agreement, "It's just become my way of life."

"Thank you," Tom said.

"We should really get going. We need to get them all fed before the concert starts and possibly get a few naps in," Meg interrupted.

"Of course," she said, "It was nice meeting you, Megan and you two," she said smiling at Louis and Bruce. "You have a lovely family Tom."

"Thank you Charlotte."

He was looking down and admiring the children when he felt her hand on his cheek and he looked up.

"You were always my favorite."

She let her hand fall, "Enjoy the concert."

She walked away.

Meg looked at Tom.

"Just how many boys worked there?"

"Just me," Tom said perplexed, "I was and have always ever been the only one."

"You said Suzanne was her niece?"

"Yes, that's an odd thing to say, Meg. Are you okay, you've gone awfully pale?"

"I'm fine. I think I just need to eat. Let's go grab the picnic basket and find a place on the grass...in the shade preferably."

"Alright...come on boys," he said as they all walked back down the parkway together.

Tom lay on the blanket propped on an elbow and Meg sat across from him. They were watching the four children romp around. Tom appreciated how the older two always included the younger two without ever having to be asked. He didn't like having to ask them to look out for everyone because he was afraid it might scare them, but he wasn't sure how things were going to turn out. He knew that Cabot or Judge Frost might do everything possible to stop him.

And what was the situation with the Captain?

He felt the Captain was probably a weaker link than Corey, but he didn't know how to get to him.

Tom turned at looked at Meg, who was also lost in her thoughts.

"You know," Tom started, "it seems as though you have wanted to tell me something for the last few weeks."

"Um," she thought for a moment, "I suppose now I know what it must be like for you on a case."

"I'm sorry you feel that way."

"I asked for it."

"It's embarrassing, but you're much better at it than I am," he told her, "maybe I should have stayed home with the kids and let you go to work."

"No," she shook her head, "I could never shoot someone."

"Oh, I think under the right circumstances you could."

He looked back at the children.

"Let's herd them up. It's getting dark enough for everyone to be heading over to the pavilion."

After gathering their brood and putting everything away, they followed the rest of the people who were heading to the organ pavilion that had been donated by Mr. Spreckles years before for the Pan-Am Exposition.

Joe was already asleep in the pram again and Tom carried Alice on his shoulders. Meg walked holding Louis' hand. Tom had asked Bruce to "lead the parade" so they could keep an eye on him.

"Tom, we're late. All the seats are already taken up front."

"With four children we're perpetually late." He looked around at the back seats and nodded to them. "They don't need to see the band to hear it. Bruce and Louis can stand on the small wall."

She nodded and followed him as he used the pram to get through the crowd.

Tom helped Meg get Bruce and Louis situated, but, out of habit, he was scanning the crowd and area. In the far right atrium, he spotted Beatrice Frost. He looked to her right and left and saw the rest of the family: Cabot and his mother and father, another older woman, about the same age as Mrs. Moran, Corey and, of course, Judge Frost. Tom then scanned the rest of the crowd until he spotted Charlotte – watching the same group he was.

Louis shifted and without looking, Tom grabbed the back of his shirt and steadied him. Alice tugged on his pants since she had wanted down to go around with Bruce and Louis.

"Up Daddy...please," she pleaded.

He lifted her up and then put his foot up so that she could stand on his thigh.

Meg shook her head knowing that her little foot prints would be on his pants and that he didn't really care.

Then out of the corner of his eye his saw movement from the Frosts. There was another couple walking below them and watched as the Judge shook the man's hand. He watched them exchange pleasantries and then turn to walk towards the back.

Jack and Claire Phelps.

"I'll be right back," Tom said to Meg as he whisked Alice onto his hip and started walking quickly through the crowd.

"Daddy, slow down. I gonna get sick," Alice cried.

"Oh, I'm sorry Sweetheart," he said as he slowed down...slightly.

About the same time Tom saw a police officer walk up to Captain Moran and it looked like he excused himself and quickly followed the police officer. They were followed by a couple others.

Tom had to stop to see where the Phelpses had gone to, but quickly found them.

"Mr. Phelps," Tom yelled.

Mr. and Mrs. Phelps kept walking.

"Jack," Tom yelled.

Mr. and Mrs. Phelps both turned.

"Hello," Mr. Phelps said as Tom reached them.

"Hello, I wanted to know if I could ask you a couple of questions."

The Phelps looked at him confused.

"I'm Tom Rubidoux."

"Detective," Mr. Phelps clarified excitedly.

"Yes Sir."

"Suzanne has spoken of you many times."

"Really," Tom was surprised, "I...really. Uh."

"Daddy," Alice said impatiently.

"This is my daughter Alice."

Mrs. Phelps smiled at her, "It's nice to meet you. That's a very pretty dress you're wearing."

Alice smiled and then buried her face in Tom's neck.

"She's a little shy," he said impatiently. He wanted to get to his questions. "I know this is a public venue and all, but Suzanne had been helping with some research into a case and it involved an adoption. She thought maybe you could help."

They both looked surprised. He forgot that adoption was not as common in the rest of society as it had been in his.

"I'm sorry," Tom stammered.

"We didn't know she knew," Mr. Phelps said. Mrs. Phelps looked as if she was about to cry.

"She loved you. It didn't matter to her," Tom said, realizing he was stumbling since he really didn't know the truth.

"Judge Frost said they would never know. He knew we were looking for a child and he found Suzanne at an orph..."

"I'm sorry, did you say 'they'," he asked, suddenly feeling the papers burning in his coat pocket.

"Yes, there were three adoptions he...well, you know, his sisters couldn't have children," Mrs. Phelps said, "But that horrid man Hayes and what he did to that poor little boy. It was a blessing when that man died. There were three children and his sisters only wanted the boys."

Tom knew his mouth had to be open. He pinched Alice's leg.

"Ow, Daddy," she started crying.

"I'm sorry. I should get her back to her mother. Thank you and again I'm sorry. I need to get her back to her mother."

"Detective," Mr. Phelps yelled after Tom. He turned around and Mr. Phelps stepped away from his wife.

"By any chance, have you heard from Suzanne recently? We haven't received a letter from her or heard from her in awhile. We were expecting the Hayes boy to ask for permission to marry her, but we think it ended badly."

Tom cringed a little, "No sir, but I will let you know as soon as I find something...out or hear something."

"Thank you. We're very worried."

Tom shuffled back through the crowd.

"Why is she crying," Meg asked him when he reached them.

"I pinched her," he said as he handed put Alice in her arms. "You helped Daddy do something very important by letting me pinch you. Thank you."

"Welcome," she said through her sniffles.

Tom pulled the papers from his pocket and opened them and scanned it until he found the first case.

Suzanne's was not the first name.

Tom looked back up at the Frosts who were all still greeting people. Corey stood slightly behind Cabot and the Judge. He watched as the Judge put his arm on Cabot's back as he introduced him and then turned slightly to do the same to Corey and introduce him. Cabot turned and caught Tom staring at them.

They weren't his nephews.

They were his sons.

How had he not seen it before?

He knew Edna Gladney was having a law passed in Texas removing the word illegitimate from all birth certificates and he knew the Judge would become a crusader of the same bill and force it through the California court systems before Cabot would be elected.

He also realized he had what he needed to force the Captain's hand.

He tore the first couple of pages off and stuffed the rest under Joe in the pram.

"Tom, what are you doing," Meg demanded.

"I have to go."

"Tom, the concert is about to start."

"Great, they will be entertained until a get back. Just in case, though, here's the key to the car."

"Tom, you don't have to do this right now."

"Yes, I do."

He quickly kissed Louis and patted Bruce on the head. Then he kissed Alice and Meg.

"I love you."

"Tom," she yelled after him, "Be careful."

He waved his hand as he ran off.

"And, I love you," she shouted.

He never heard her.

16.

IN THE SPIDER'S PARLOR

Tom went frantically through the crowd looking for the Captain, but ran into another officer who told him that Bradley Farnham had gone berserk down at The Agate Club and the Captain had gone down to minimize the damage and possible scandal.

Tom guessed it had to do with Evelyn.

He tore the top sheet off, held it in his hand and put the remainder back in his coat pocket.

He hopped in one of the police cars with another officer who was also headed down to the old Stingeree.

"Did he light the place on fire," Tom asked.

"Just about," the officer replied.

Tom jumped out of the car before it stopped moving.

There was a bit of a mayhem going on in front of the club. Tom was scanning the streets for the Captain. He finally spotted him as they were dragging Bradley Farnham out through the front doors of the club.

Tom knew he must have done something really bad to have about fifteen officers with guns drawn circling him. He watched as they shoved him into one of the cars and drove off to the station. He saw some of the officers walk away from the Captain. He walked towards him.

"Rubidoux."

Tom looked around, "Captain. I guess Mr. Farnham was a bit upset over Evelyn's murder."

"Excuse me? Well, yes and he's not going to be able to get out of this one...I don't care who he knows."

"Almost like he knew who did it, don't you think...or maybe he knows he'll be contributing to the execution of two innocent men."

"Watch it Tom or you'll end up just like him."

"Oh, I don't think so," he said as the Captain started to walk away, "Why is it that the Judge never made sure you were Chief."

The Captain stopped and turned around.

"I used to think it was because you were a just a good guy and understood that the Judge had bigger pawns to position."

The Captain took a step so he was face to face with Tom.

"Watch yourself Detective. I am no one's pawn."

"You've always sidled up to him. Even as a boy I could see that. You did everything he asked you to. Covered up every indiscretion...including those of his *nephews,*" Tom studied him, "or was taking in his illegitimate son as your own part of the bargain. You thought he would repay you some day."

Even at night, Tom could see the Captain's face turning red. He held up the page.

"But Cabot was a double-edged sword. He used it against you didn't he?"

"You don't understand. You never did. You never did! Do you think that all your merit badges and medals on your uniform got you to where you're at?"

"That doesn't matter. My cousins are innocent, you know it!"

"Tom, this is not the time or place."

"You are going to let two innocent men hang..."

"No, you are."

Tom waved the piece of paper in front of him.

"Your son," he screamed as the crowds started to get louder and the fireworks began, "your adopted son, the Judge's son, who has done nothing for you, is going to go free."

"Tom it could have been anyone you knew. Besides, that part of your family has never meant anything to you."

Was he really that callous?

"It was time you knew, Tom. I'm sorry."

"Knew what?"

"You can't thumb your nose up at those who have helped you, Tom. Everything comes with a price. Even I know that."

"My family…"

"Be thankful…"

"I don't know what you are talking about. I never asked…"

"Didn't you?! You naïve little shit. My brother-in-law's pet…his whore's favorite cause. He made me clean up his mess, take in his bastard…wrapped him up as a gift for his sister and gave me nothing. He kept me under his thumb while he got to climb higher and higher. He promised me I would be Chief. She gave you a ticket to escape, but you came back. Charlotte paid for you to go to school. There was no scholarship. And the Judge made a huge donation, called in favors for you to get in…for you to get a desk job during the war. After all he took from her you were all he could give. It's time to pay for your stupidity, Tom. The boys have to be protected at any cost…and who better to pay than an ungrateful asshole like you?"

The anger Tom felt welled up in him to the point he felt every muscle tense and an undecipherable amount of words run through his brain.

"No," he yelled as he grabbed John's shirt and for a split second he thought of Megan, the kids and what might happen. "I don't care Cabot has to hang for this and for the murders of Evelyn and the records clerk."

"Cabot," John asked completely bewildered, "What about Corey? Did you ever stop to wonder what his role was in all of this?"

"Help me get the warrants and get you out of this."

"I can't. I love my wife. Oh, son, you really don't know. You haven't read the entire file," he said pointing at the paper. "We couldn't let Suzanne marry Corey…she would have told everyone."

"Told everyone what," he yelled over the commotion.

"She's their cousin."

"What?"

"But then so are…"

Tom felt the nick before he heard the shot. It wasn't the look of disbelief on John's face that suddenly made him aware of what was happening or the sudden stop of John's conversation. It was the tiny, dark spot on John's white shirt suddenly become darker and then blossom like a crimson flood across his chest to reach out to meet the other pink sprinkles across John's shirt. John swung his hand out to grab Tom at the point that Tom realized the pink sprinkles were tiny pieces of him.

Tom felt the second shot stab through his shoulder and dive down towards the inside of his chest.

It was then he realized the shooter was somewhere on the roof tops.

He went to take in a breath but couldn't.

People scattered in all directions as Tom reached in towards John. He had no idea of what he was going to do. So many things ran through his mind:

- Get the people off the street.
- Plug John's bleeding.
- Turn and look up to where the shots came from.
- Tell someone what he knew.
- What he knew.

The third shot sounded like a deadened "pop". John's head snapped back and then slumped forward. Tom felt the fourth one hit him in the back of the head before the next popped. John slipped out of his grasp and crumpled to the street. He moved his hand to the last shot as if he were trying to smash a mosquito that had bitten him, even though, he knew it wasn't going to help.

The last caught him in the neck and spun him around as if he were a puppet on strings.

Tom Rubidoux had never been a heavy drinker, but he thought that this must be what it was like – feeling disjointed, unable to control his movements and stumbling around.

He dropped to his knees and had spun back around so that he could see John lying in the growing pool of blood and saw his eyes glaze over.

The crowd sounded as if it were miles away.

He started to sway.

He tried to keep his mind focused on seeing where the shots came from, but something else took over.

Meg...oh, how he loved Meg. He saw her look up from the table in the library, he saw her turn from the sink in the kitchen...and there was Bruce – running down the driveway to greet him ... and Louis – always patiently waiting ... and Alice and Joe.

"I know...," was all he could say.

Heavily, he slumped over and then down on the ground.

"I know...I know," he said as moments of his life quickly passed through his mind.

"I know," as he thought of his cousins in jail. He tightened his grip around the Cabot's paperwork.

"I know," he said as he thought of the killer...of his and John's killer.

Cabot.

"I know," he said weaker as a crowd gathered closer and people were running here and there.

"I know."

As his head slowly hit the ground he saw a familiar face, but then it became so blurry. He couldn't make the words form together to pass on what he wanted everyone to know...things he wanted Meg to know. The shadow of a person kneeling over him made things darker than he was ready for. He felt the paper being torn out of his hand which had turned into a fist from the pain, but still he held on to what he could.

"Oh," he garbled with his last breath, "I know."

"Yes...you do," a familiar voice said with new-found confidence as he stuffed the torn bloody paper in his back pocket and watched Detective Tom Rubidoux die.

BRUCE
JULY 1948

17.

AN ABSENTMINDED LAD

There was an early morning haze over the meadow that crept through the surrounding trees. Everything was silent except for the whimpering of the soldier slumped over on the ground.

He wasn't injured.

He was petrified.

"What are we going to do Cap'n," another soldier asked the brooding officer. "He'll slow us down and give away our position and if we leave him here the Germ…"

"Sergeant, take the patrol on ahead. The private and I are going to have a conversation."

The sergeant nodded his head hesitantly concerned about the captain's tone, "Yes sir."

The captain never took his eyes off the cowering soldier. He could smell the distinct odor of urine on the young man as he felt the rest of his patrol leave and move on ahead and over one of the knolls.

Then raised his service revolver brought it to the private's head and shot the boy.

The sound cut through the air and sent a small flock of birds into the sky, but the officer didn't notice.

He holstered his weapon, bent and jerked the boy's dog tags from the chain. He stuffed them in his pocket and the private's personal belongings as he stood and grabbed his rifle.

He looked in the direction the patrol had gone and started walking when a figure in the meadow caught his eye.

It wasn't a soldier. He was a civilian, but there was something familiar. The captain started walking towards him as he approached and he saw the man was wearing a white shirt, but there was something wrong with it.

As he got closer he saw the shirt was littered with bullet holes and blood.

The captain looked into the man's face and into his eyes. They were sad and full of worry. Captain Bruce Andon Rubidoux suddenly felt ashamed.

"Daddy?"

Tom shook his head in disappointment...or was it despair?

Bruce woke with a start and rolled to the edge of the bed, letting his bent legs flop over onto the floor. He pressed down so that he could raise his slumped shoulders, stretch up and back so his 6'3" frame was almost recognizable from sitting on the edge of the bed. He braced both hands on either side and pushed to try to get more of a stretch and then he slumped his shoulders again.

He took in a couple of deep breaths and let the perspiration caused by his dream run down his face and drop on the floor.

He had been home nine months. He had been with the San Diego Police as Detective B.A. Rubidoux 115 days.

Lazily, he stared out the window, reliving another scene from the war and letting it wash over him like the waves that used to off the rocks in Children's Cove in La Jolla. He felt the force but relaxed and let it take him in and out and then release him back to himself.

"Bruce", he heard his mother yell up at him from downstairs.

He didn't answer. It was too early to answer. It took less time for him to get moving these days, but it still took time.

War gave him the opportunity to become someone else and he had taken advantage of it. He didn't want to be known as "The Bruise" or El Golpe, as his father's family had called him and the rest of the city (being small) called him.

It had come so naturally to him to sign his name as "B. Andon Rubidoux, PFC" when he enlisted. Sure, his cousins still called him Golpe. This only lent an air of mystery as to who he was and what his background had been. No one ever thought to put two and two together, nor would anyone think that his brown hair, green eyes and light skin would have come from the black-haired, dark-eyed, olive-skinned San Diego enlistees from the rancheros.

They all thought he was French.

"Ignoramuses," he would think, secretly smiling at them, knowing he was getting away with – away from his heritage. It was their fault, their stupidity. The French didn't even spell it that way...or did they? He didn't even remember. Later, he would secretly scowl and cringe in his bunk, ashamed and wondering if his brothers were doing the same.

He was the oldest and was supposed to lead by example. What would Louis and Joe think if they knew?

Did they already know?

He often wondered if this was what his father had gone through.

There were times when he didn't remember his father at all. Then, the memories would come back at odd times. He remembered finding his father's gun. Now it made him cringe to think Louis could have killed him.

Maybe that would have been better than knowing Louis lost his life at the "Bulge".

Louis had always hated the cold and filth. Bruce hated the thought that his brother had died in a place like that.

Louis never remembered their father after he died. Neither did Joe. Joe was asleep in his stroller when their father had been killed. Louis should have remembered.

Had he chose not to?

Louis had always been the one to play Guinea Pig. Louis was the one who was always handcuffed. He always was the one to play the bad guy so Bruce ... no El Golpe ... could be the hero.

So, Bruce had returned from war bitter, broken and lost. Going to college at Brown had only engrained the negativity more. The East Coast had belonged to his father and it only reminded him of what he had missed out on.

He missed his father.

He missed Tom Rubidoux and he didn't want to be his father, but he wanted his father's guidance and approval. He remembered the easy going nature his father had, even in the midst of crisis.

He drank what his father drank and smoked his brand of cigars because for a brief second he could smell his father and imagine hearing what he would say.

He also missed the something about his father that he could never put a finger on. Had it been a sadness or loss of his own? Had it been a struggle between who he wanted to be and who he thought he was supposed to be?

"Bruce," he heard his mother shout again.

"Coming," he shouted down.

His thoughts would have to wait.

As he stood up the floor creaked and his feet cracked as all adjusted under his weight. He opened the door and walked down the hall to the bathroom. He still swayed with sleepiness as he peed in the toilet trying not to drip on the porcelain or floor.

One of his mother's, and now sister's, pet peeves.

He ran the water in the sink and stared at it. Everything still seemed like such a process. None of it moved quickly. He would find his mind wandering off to the war. He knew that a few of his buddies that were willing to talk suffered the same thing, even though the war had been over for three years.

He broke his own trance when he drove his hands through the running water, cupping his hands and splashing his face.

Staring at himself in the mirror for a while he wondered, well wondered about nothing, then lathered his face and started shaving.

Megan was busy in the kitchen cooking breakfast. She enjoyed having Bruce home because she could sometimes pretend, if only for a little while, that it was Tom.

But Bruce didn't hum or whistle when he was thinking or puttering around the house. Bruce was always more serious, or had there been something very innocent and blissful about Tom?

She turned to place Bruce's breakfast plate on the table. Sometimes she would absentmindedly place it where Tom used to sit and Bruce would sit in his same spot and move the plate without thinking.

Bruce, like Tom, was about order.

Tom's seat had always remained empty, waiting for him to walk through the door.

Bruce bounded into the kitchen with his coat in his hand and he draped it around the back of the chair. He plopped himself down in his seat and started to dig into his pancakes and eggs.

This was a day that he would not have to move the plate.

Alice was already there and looked at him in disgust.

"Why do you bother wearing white shirts or dressing before breakfast at all. You're only going to have to change because you're going to be wearing most of your breakfast Bruce."

He had given up correcting his sister or mother about his preferred name; especially since Alice was respectful enough to call him "Andon" when they were out at night.

"Bruce, slow down," Megan said as she touched his shoulder in passing. "You're not late and you're not in the Army anymore."

He nodded and slowed his chewing down. Three years of being in the war had ruined a lifetime of table manners.

"And, take your arms off the table," she added just as he was sliding his arms off.

Alice smirked at him.

"Can you drop me off on the way to work," she asked him.

"Sure, but I don't know what time I'll be able to pick you up."

"That's okay, Ryan's picking me up."

Bruce frowned. He didn't like the idea of anyone going out with his sister. It always took him awhile with any new boyfriend to realize she could take care of herself and would ask him for his help if needed.

Ryan was someone new. The week before it was Robert and the week before was Ted. The more he thought about it the more he realized that none of them ever stayed around for very long. Although Ted had been around a few times.

He went back to finishing his breakfast. Alice set her fork in her plate, stood from the table and took her plate to the sink where Megan was already cleaning up and washing the dishes. Alice kissed her on the cheek.

"Thanks Mom."

"Should I assume that you won't be home for dinner then?"

"No, not tonight."

Bruce shoved a big bite in his mouth and got up from the table and also dropped the plate in the sink. Megan leaned in and he kissed her, even though he had syrup around his mouth.

"Catch lots of bad guys."

"Ummm hrum," he agreed while still chewing and swallowing.

"And, Bruce," she said, as he was putting his coat on.

"Um?"

"Don't forget your gun."

"I don't understand how you can forget that you don't have that thing on," Alice said pointing in the direction of his holster and service revolver, which he had dropped in the back seat.

"I just do."

"Maybe you wouldn't so often if Mom would just let you wear the thing at the table. It doesn't bother me."

He looked at her. "But, it bothers her. I think it reminds her of Dad."

She looked ahead at the street and watched the people walk in front of them when they stopped at the red light.

"Do you think she'll ever get over it?"

"Would you," he asked.

"I don't know. I mean, she's gotten over Louis and Joe."

"She knows who killed them and why," he said dryly.

She looked at him.

"Have you?"

"Have I what?"

"Gotten over it?"

"No."

"I'm talking about Dad."

"I know what you're talking about."

They sat silently for a second and he felt her start to ask another question.

"No, I haven't gotten over the war yet either, but it has been a little bit easier than Dad."

"You know, sometimes I'm jealous."

"I know."

He waited a second and smiled at her.

"You really would have loved him," he thought for a moment, turning his attention back to the road. "We always felt really safe around him and you could tell how much he and Mom loved each other. I mean, you could feel it. Do you know what I mean?"

He looked at her again and realized by her expression that she did not. She smiled at him at touched his knee.

"I think I know. Sometimes I see Mom staring off like something caught her eye. I think she is thinking of him at those times. I only know by how you talk about him."

She looked ahead again. "I never told you this, but, when I was little I used to imagine him in my room at night talking to me...reading to me. I would do the same thing when I would walk to school. I would hear him talk to me, feel him next to me...it was comforting, even though he really wasn't there at all."

He stopped in front of Allen's Pharmacy, where she worked and she opened the door, leaned in and kissed his cheek and got out of the car. She shut the door and then leaned back into the open window.

"It's okay to miss him, Bruce, but you can't bring him back. Living in that sadness is only going to keep you in your memories of the war and keep you from going on. It's not fair to Mom or who he was. Let it go." She smiled, "I'll see you tonight."

She walked away and into the store.

Bruce pulled into the police department on Market Street. It had moved up to Dead Man's Hill in the years between his father's death and the war. He got out and shut the door, took a few steps, walked back, reached into the back seat of the car and grabbed his revolver and holster. He took off his coat, slid the holster and gun on, shut the door again and walked away towards the front door.

A few minutes later he had to return to get his coat off the roof of the car.

Once he settled in, Bruce went about sorting out his day which he was meticulous about. He felt he could handle the unexpected case that sometimes dropped in his lap much easier. Although he knew he was confident that he was the best at his job, comments like the ones Alice had made this morning rattled his hidden insecurity that he was just filling his father's position and that it was not his own.

It was irrational of course - none of the officers in his division, except his captain, had known his father. In fact, in the retelling of the Stingeree Shooting it was always Captain Moran and another officer that were murdered in the street, with his father being "another officer".

Bruce still remembered the non-stop flow of officers and their wives parading through their house in the time after Tom's death. He remembered "Uncle" Corey trying to console his mother and how his shoulders had tensed at the sight. He still remembered the man-to-man talk Corey had so ineptly tried to give Bruce and how uncomfortable he had felt when he saw him take Louis outside with his arm around his shoulder.

Bruce went outside after Corey had come back into the house and slowly sat down next to Louis on the steps of the porch. Somehow he suddenly felt older. Louis had sat very still, looking out at the traffic going back and forth on the street as he looked down at his feet.

"He said someone shot Daddy and he died," Louis had said in a half question tone then looked at Bruce.

Bruce could see the deep concern and sadness in his brother's eyes, the tears gathering along the rims.

"Was it like the watermelon?"

Bruce looked back out to the street.

"I think so," was all he said.

Joe and Alice had been too young to remember everything that had happened in the days and weeks afterward. Only once did Joe ever mention Tom again. Bruce and Louis were sitting in front of the radio listening to Lil Annie, Alice and Joe were both supposed to be in bed and Megan decided she had wanted a drink. She came out to the living room and poured some of Tom's scotch in the glass, but knocked the decanter on the lip of the glass as she tilted it upright, making a very distinct "clinking" sound.

Joe appeared in the doorway in a happy, excited state. Bruce and Louis turned to look at him as he frantically looked around.

"What are you looking for Joe," Louis asked him.

"Daddy, I heard Daddy," he said, almost pleading.

Megan, Bruce and Louis all knew why he thought Tom was home.

Megan stood frozen, unable to think of the words that would hurt him the least.

Bruce spoke up in a cold, unfeeling tone, "No Joe, Daddy's dead. He's never coming home."

Bruce had settled at his desk flipping through files that needed final paperwork, those that needed leads and those that just needed to be looked at. He liked being a detective because he didn't have to wear a uniform and he could look through and handle some of the older cases. He had already established a reputation as an officer who was able to see the important clue in a pile of clues that everyone else missed. More and more he seemed to find unsolved cases hit his desk and the opportunity to work alone. Most of the officers were those who were trying to relive their glory moments from the war and those that were trying to make up for not having any or never having served. The latter always started off their conversations with veterans with some sort of explanation as to why they hadn't served.

"Well, if it weren't for my bum leg," one started off. The real reason was the guy had five kids and only one nut. As if that would prevent him from shooting a gun. "Maybe they thought he would fertilize the countryside and make more Germans," Bruce thought.

"Old shoulder injury." They guy couldn't see to hit the side of a barn.

"Bad back."

Couldn't read

"Bum leg."

Too old.

"Bum leg."

Too young.

After a while Bruce thought it was miraculous that any of these guys were on the police force with all their physical ailments. Heaven forbid they should have to chase a suspect. The ones who acted holier than thou were those that had already served. Bruce got the sense they felt they were entitled to bond with him.

The only one he liked and got along with was Kurt Brummel a behemoth of a man who loved local history and lore.

Bruce waited to hear his excuse for not being in the war and Brummel was just as candid as he could be.

"Too fat," he said bluntly, "they couldn't find any uniform to fit me."

Bruce had nodded his head in agreement.

"Could you see me on a ship or on a plane? I wouldn't fit in the galley of the one and shit...the material for the parachute alone would take up the majority of the army surplus."

Bruce just nodded again.

Frankly, he wanted to be left alone to work and didn't want to bond with any of them. It was a struggle for him and something his mother and sister worked with him on because he knew he needed to be social to move up.

And, part of him felt the need because Tom had been so social and easy going. Bruce knew he would run into people that could help him and they seemed to have known his father and had some story to tell him about Tom.

He had learned more about Tom over the last few months in the police department than all the years before.

Bruce continued to go about his day. He went on a call for a domestic abuse. Of course when he arrived the only one willing to say there was abuse was the neighbor who had called it in. Bruce did what he did best and scared the crap out of the drunk husband by threatening to rearrange his genitals.

He knew being a big guy helped make his job easier, but he also knew that guys like this husband would only behave for a little while and it was just a matter of time before an officer would be here again – with or without the coroner was the only question.

After that, he went to investigate a shooting down by the marina.

Crime seemed to be up in San Diego.

There were still too many young veteran's with demons and way too much time on their hands that seemed to be spent drinking. The drinking inevitably led to mischief or, more so than not, some sort of crime.

This shooting was no different.

One of the senior officers, Lambert, greeted Bruce.

"It's a mess I tell you," Lambert started.

Bruce looked at the two bodies and at all the blood and tissue splatter. He knelt down to take a closer look at the shooter, a soldier.

The officer continued to babble.

"I'm telling you. It's not like when soldiers came home after the Great War."

Bruce tilted his head so he could look at the officer. He looked him up and down and then looked back down and shook his head.

He knew enough about the officer to know he was a kid when World War I ended and when the soldiers returned.

"They just had more time to...um...reacclimatize," Bruce said looking closer at the body and the uniform. The man had been a lieutenant. He noticed a hole on the side of his face.

Lambert looked at him quizzically.

"It took them longer to get home...the ships and trains were slower."

Bruce started searching his pockets, but couldn't find what he was looking for.

"Hey," he said to the officer, "do you have a spare pen or handkerchief?"

Lambert reached into his pant pocket and pulled out a wad of cloth and handed it down to Bruce. Bruce looked at it and grimaced.

"You didn't blow your nose in this today did you," he asked.

"No," he said shaking his head, "not today."

"Not today huh," Bruce said grabbing a corner and shaking it out, wondering if it was clean at all.

He put it between his finger and thumb and then grabbed the dead soldier's nose and turned the head towards him. Flies scattered as some of the brains spilled out the gaping hole and plopped onto the dock.

"Ew, God," he heard Lambert say over him and felt the officer lean in over him. Bruce looked up at him and gave him a look that he hoped Lambert would take as a "back up" signal. Bruce quickly realized again why this man was only an officer and had never been promoted.

Bruce leaned back against Lambert's leg forcing the officer to take a step back.

"That's pretty bad. I haven't seen anything like that down here since that madam's body was pulled out of the water...and I really mean it was just the body. We didn't find the head for days."

"Um hmm," was all Bruce said as he continued to investigate the body and started on the victim who was a few feet away and missing a good portion of his face. Then Lambert said the magic words.

"That was one of the first cases I responded to. Your daddy was the detective on that one. For some reason it was a big hoo-ha because that Captain that was shot in the Stingeree was down here too."

Bruce stopped what he was doing.

"Really?"

"Yep," Lambert nodded, "I know your dad didn't get to close the case himself, but they caught the guy none the less. Let's see...it was...um...Bradley Farnham...that's right, Bradley Farnham. He was the one who was arrested and found guilty of her murder...and if I remember correctly, he also killed the records clerk...God what was her name?"

"Wasn't Farnham the D.A.," Bruce asked.

"Yeah he was."

Bruce stood up as the ambulance and coroners came. They looked at Bruce to see if they could start their jobs. He signaled for them to come closer.

Lambert continued talking. Bruce thought it might have been an attempt to forget about the gruesome scene at their feet.

"I think he would have been convicted of your dad's and Captain Moran's murders if he hadn't been in the police car on the way to jail."

"Do one of you have a tape measure or string," Bruce asked the coroners.

One of them shook his head, "No, but these are all fishing boats. I'm sure one of them has some rope or line. What do you need it for?"

"I need a measurement on the distance between these two," he said, indicating the bodies. "Would one of you go see so I can wrap this up and you can get started?"

One of them nodded and went in the direction of the closer boats.

Bruce turned back to older officer, "I'd forgotten about that. Oh, here," he said handing the handkerchief back, more as a joke, but was mortified as Lambert took it and stuffed it back into his pocket.

"Whatever happened to him," Bruce asked trying to ignore what he had just seen.

"Whatever happened to whom?"

"Farnham."

"Ended up in County Hospital I think. I don't know where he's at or even if he's still alive. Those mental wards changed so frequently over the years."

"County was over near Mission Valley wasn't it," Bruce asked.

The one coroner who had gone in search of line returned and handed Bruce some twine. He went about measuring while he continued talking. He handed one end to the coroner and pointed for him to go stand by the victim.

"Wasn't Farnham at one time the Frost family attorney," he asked.

The coroner holding the other end of the twine spoke up.

"He was, before he became D.A. and somewhere along the lines the nephew...well, I guess he's still considered a Frost...anyways, Corey Hayes took over the family accounts and legal matters."

"I didn't know he was a Frost," Bruce said as he knelt down with the twine and measured out the distance and then stood up again. He nodded at the coroner to let go of his end.

"Yeah, his mother was a Frost. I hear his dad used to beat the shit out of him. I think his mom died of alcoholism. I don't know...that family seems to be able to bury anything they want to. I actually think Judge Frost had George Hayes taken care of...if you know what I mean."

"Corey was your dad's partner...of sorts," the officer added.

"That, I remember," Bruce said cutting the twine and rolling it up.

The part that Bruce remembered of Corey being his father's partner was one day shortly before he was killed. He and Louis had been playing out front, secretly waiting for Tom to come home, like they often did. Bruce had something to ask Tom and Louis had a test grade he wanted to show off and rub Bruce's nose in.

The car that turned the street corner and slowed as it approached was not Tom's, rather it was a burgundy Ford Roadster. The two boys could clearly see who was sitting in the front seat.

"Hey boys," Corey said as he got out of the car.

"Hello," Bruce said cautiously.

"Hi," Louis said following Bruce's lead, inching his way closer to his brother's side.

"Daddy's not home," Bruce said.

"Yes, I see that, but your mother is, isn't she," he asked walking across the lawn and to the front door.

Bruce had always felt that Megan could take care of them and probably herself if she had to, but like Tom, he would rather not have to see her in that situation.

Corey seemed to dismiss the boys and bent down to pick up a large manila envelope that was left on the porch.

"That's for Daddy," Louis said.

Corey read the front of the envelope.

"I see that," he said to the boys.

"It's not yours. You should leave it where it was for our dad," Bruce piped up.

"And, you should learn to respect your elders," Corey said as he entered the house with the envelope.

Bruce and Louis followed Corey into the house. Alice had been playing in front of the radio and Joe was asleep on the rug next to her. Alice watched the boys as they stood near the doorway to the kitchen, then stood up, walked behind the boys and reached to hold Bruce's hand. Bruce wanted to hear. Louis just often did what Bruce did without thinking.

"You're his partner. Don't you know," he heard Meg say.

"Um, hum...he left some time after lunch and never returned."

"Well, I haven't heard from him," she said. Bruce thought she looked like she was wondering where he might be.

Corey walked closer to the counter where Megan was standing

"He talks to you about the cases he's working on, doesn't he?"

It was an innocent enough question under usual circumstances, but Bruce could tell by Megan's expression that it was strange.

"Daddy," Bruce heard Alice and Louis say. Joe woke up and chimed in just as Alice dropped Bruce's hand. Bruce saw the manila envelope sitting on Tom's desk as he turned to follow his siblings. The four of them stampeded out through the screen door in a chorus of "Daddy, Daddy, Daddy."

Tom bent and scooped up Alice and Joe clamped onto one of Tom's legs, yelling, "Up, up, up!"

Louis told Tom about the "A" on his paper and Bruce tried to talk over them all. Tom greeted them all and reminded Bruce to put his bike away.

That was the only time Bruce remembered seeing Corey at their dinner table. He didn't like it. There was something dead and vacant in Detective Hayes' eyes. He reminded Bruce of a sick calf like he had seen on his grandmother's ranch before it was slaughtered.

After his shift, Bruce met Alice at the night club. She was waiting there with Ryan at a table for six which meant some other couple was also meeting them all. Bruce hoped that the sixth chair would remain empty, but Alice had a habit of trying to set him up with someone.

"Don't worry, it's empty," she said noticing he had frowned at the number of seats. A look of relief crossed his face and he grinned having been caught. "Jenny and Pete are meeting us too," Alice added, "I ordered one of those margarita things you like."

"Don't say you're ordering it just for me. I've seen you take sips of mine before...don't lie," he winked at her.

Bruce stood by their table and looked around the dance floor and surrounding tables. He always wanted to see what the "playing field" looked like. It was a habit he had acquired from playing sports as well as the battlefield during war.

"Andon," Alice called after him, "Andon...Bruce," she finally yelled.

He turned around.

"I don't know why you just don't go by your first name," she said annoyed, "Everybody here knows you as 'Bruce' and you don't even answer to 'Andon'. We would probably have a better chance at you answering to 'Golpe' than 'Andon'."

She wrinkled her nose at him and he did the same back to her.

"What did you want," he asked.

"Kathlyn Moran's here."

"What," he said looking around, "Where?"

"Over there with Bill Kirby."

"With who?"

"Have you called her since you've been back?"

He shook his head.

"No...but you know I haven't you little sneak."

"She asked about you at Joe's funeral."

"Really?!"

"Mom didn't tell you?"

"She never seemed to like Kathlyn dating any of us."

"Neither did her dad from what I remember, but you know Joe. He could always find a way around things he was told not to do."

Bruce watched Kathlyn cross the dance floor, greeting people as if she was the belle of the ball.

He knew she was well practiced in that area since she was the only child of Senator Cabot Moran. Bruce had seen her photograph in many of the newspapers Alice and his mother had sent him during college and the war.

His mother had sent them to him to keep up on the events at home. So had Alice, but he knew she had different events in mind. She had a habit of only sending the society section to him.

There would be photos of Kathlyn with her father at some opening, at some ball or dinner, with her family in their box seat at opening day of the racing season, dressed in her nurses uniform, with a Navy officer or Marine at some benefit.

He did notice it was always an officer.

It was just like her not to be seen or date anyone that was an NCO.

Lucky for Joe he had been a first lieutenant. Bruce would have been in there as a Captain. Louis only made it to sergeant.

Bruce watched the guy Kathlyn was with and guessed he would have also been a captain, maybe a major. He saw them reach their table for two. He grabbed Alice's arm and started pulling her away from her conversation with her date.

"Dance with me," he said.

"What," she said looking for what he was watching. "No, that's a firecracker you can light on your own."

"Come on, you would do it for Louis and Joe."

"Louie and Joe would have let me talk to my date."

"Fine."

"B, there are a lot of girls here that would love to dance with you. Go ask one of them."

She scanned the room.

"There, over there," she said indicating a table with three girls, "all those girls are dateless and have been eyeing you."

"Huh, oh," he said looking in the direction she was. "Okay." And, without thinking he was headed to the table.

Alice just shook her head

It wasn't unusual for her brother just to wander off without thinking...well, it was usually because he was focused on something else and that's what would lead him to saying or doing something that was grossly inappropriate. He always dealt with it in his oblivious state, seemingly unscathed physically, emotionally or socially.

He brazenly walked right up to the table.

"Alright ladies who's ready to dance? And, sorry, it's just me. I don't have any single friends with me this evening."

Hell, the only friends he even had were the ones who became his friends after dating Alice.

Two of them giggled. Finally the third who didn't seem as inhibited took a sip of her drink. "I am," she said and looked at Bruce, waiting for him to hold her chair for her. He was distracted watching Kathlyn.

The girl cleared her throat.

"Sorry," he said grabbing the back of her chair and pulling it out so she could stand. He focused long enough to extend his hand out to her so he could lead her to the dance floor.

"I somehow think it's not really me your interested in dancing with," the girl said as he spun her around.

"Excuse me," Bruce said, distracted.

"Honestly, Andon Rubidoux are you always on duty, detecting?"

He looked at her curiously.

"I have no pretenses that you are out here to get closer to that girl," she said nodding towards Kathlyn. "You helped one of my friends over there with a drunken husband once."

He didn't understand what she was saying.

"He hit her..."

"Oh...ohhhh," he said vaguely remembering.

"You are Detective Rubidoux, aren't you?"

"Yes, I am."

He still hadn't really taken his eyes off Kathlyn.

"It doesn't take a detective to know you're watching that girl."

She waited for some sort of recognition.

"Besides, I've seen pictures of her with your brother, Joe."

Bruce looked at her.

"At least I assumed it was your brother, considering the papers always listed his last name as Rubidoux. Am I wrong?"

The song slowed and so did their dancing.

"No and yes, he was my brother."

"Ah, was," she said, but was used to this faux pas. "I'm sorry...another one lost."

Bruce pursed his lips and nodded.

"Your other brother," she asked hesitantly.

Bruce nodded again and she nodded back, "I see. Well, let's see what I can do to help you."

He saw her look around his shoulder.

Even though he was leading he felt her lean so that he had to dance backwards.

"Why would you help me," he wanted to know.

"I have my reasons."

Bruce steeled his gaze.

"Care to share what they are?"

"You helped my friend get out of a horrible situation. I'd like to repay you...in some way, no matter how small it may be. Besides you seem nice."

"You're a little odd," he accidentally said out loud.

"And you're a little rude."

She pressured his hand so that he turned again.

"Your conquest has hit the dance floor...move!"

He wasn't quite sure exactly what she was up to but felt he suddenly had a kindred spirit and let her take the lead as she shoved him closer to the middle of the floor.

He questioned that decision when his body abruptly came to a halt and he heard an "ow" behind him.

"Watch where you're going," Bruce heard a man's voice say. He turned around and was face to face with Kathlyn's date.

"I'd love to switch partners," Bruce's cohort squealed grabbing Kathlyn's date, jitter bugging, leaving Kathlyn and Bruce facing each other.

"Hello Kathlyn," Bruce said sheepishly.

"Bruce," she said.

"Care to," he asked extending his hand.

"Give it up Brew," she said taking his hand, "You and I both know we've been watching each other tonight."

About that time the song ended. They let go of each other to clap and then the next song began. It was a little slower than the two of them would have liked, but they immediately fell into a natural rhythm like two people who had known each other for years.

He studied her trying to figure out what he should say.

"Stop trying to figure me out, Bruce...or is it Andon, I hear you like to be called that now."

He looked up, scanned the floor and saw his dance partner had maneuvered her and Kathlyn's date so they had at least another song.

"I seem to remember you had a few other choice names for me," he answered.

"And as you remember they are not suitable for a lady to repeat...in public."

"Lady..."

"Bruce..."

He saw Alice on the edge of the dance floor looking at him as if he were crazy. He quickly refocused on the task at hand.

"How have you been?"

"Fine, thank you," she said as he spun her out and brought her back in. "How long have you been home?"

"Home in the States or home in San Diego?"

"You know exactly what I'm talking about."

Bruce felt he could use another margarita to keep up.

"Long enough," he cringed as soon as the words came out of his mouth.

"Long enough to call?"

"You know I have," he seethed, "Besides, if I remember correctly, I wasn't the Rubidoux boy you were interested in," he added almost losing his grip as he spun her around again.

The song stopped and the band started to play another slow one.

She had started to step away and loosen her grip, but he grabbed her hand, put his hand on her waist and brought her closer.

She bit him just under his shoulder.

He flinched slightly and kept dancing.

"I'm sorry about Joe. Thank you for giving your support at his services. My mother appreciated it"

"I'm sorry about Joe...and Louie."

Bruce saw his original dance partner and kidnapped victim making their way back towards them. He stopped dancing as they came right up to them.

"Just for the record Bruce," she said as he watched her date shaking his dance partner loose frantically to get back to Kathlyn, "Joe was never the Rubidoux I was interested in."

His head jerked to look at her as her date grabbed her. She was scowling as he asked her if she was okay and whisked her back to their table.

Bruce stood there with his mouth open. His dance partner grabbed his arm.

"Did you find out what you wanted to," she asked.

"I'm not sure," he said and looked down at her, "I may have found out more than I wanted to."

"My fee is for you to actually dance with me," she said pulling him deeper into the dance floor.

"I thought you were repaying me," he asked.

"It turned out to cost more than I was anticipating," she replied.

He obliged, shaking off the conversation with Kathlyn.

They continued to dance and for the first time in a long time Bruce was actually having fun. He walked his partner in crime back to her table, where her friends were waiting.

"Thank you," she said, "that was actually the most fun I have had in a while."

"Me too," he said as he held her chair out for her. "Have a nice evening," he added as he took a few steps towards his table. Alice caught his eye and gave him a look that he was forgetting something and then he turned around.

"May I call you...," he started to say as she handed him a cocktail napkin with her number on it.

"Yes," she answered.

He took the napkin and folded it before sticking it into his pocket.

"Tell me one thing though," she said before he walked away. He turned around.

"Is it Andon or Bruce?"

He paused for a moment.

"It's Bruce."

18.

THE MAN OF THE HOUSE

Bruce sat outside...sobering up and also, subconsciously, waiting to make sure Alice made it home.

He knew she could take care of herself, but he just wanted to be there...just in case.

The evening had shaken him up a bit. Kathlyn had always been in his thoughts in one form or another and he hated admitting it.

From the time they first met as children she got under his skin...and the more he tried to be mean to her the sharper her witticisms became until he could actually feel the steam blow out of his ears.

It was worse when she would fawn over his brothers. Louis always looked befuddled, but Joe ate it up, not realizing how much it burned Bruce.

Bruce thought he let it go and tried burying his feelings when he was accepted to Brown.

He packed up as quickly as he could dismissing Megan's offers to help him get settled in. If she knew what he was feeling, she didn't let on.

But Alice did.

Even at fifteen she could read him.

"Why are you running away," she asked, lying on his bed, watching him pack.

He ignored her as he threw items in his suitcase.

"She's just a girl Bruce," was all she said as she hopped off his bed and left his room.

He enlisted in the Army in the middle of his second year and when he was discharged he returned to pick up where he left.

He just wrote a note to Megan saying he would be home when he was done.

It was Alice who thwarted his plans of returning home right after his final exam.

"Mom's planning on attending your graduation, B. Frankly, I am too, so there's no sense in being an ass," she said.

She knew on his end of the phone he was making a face and was about to sound disgruntled.

"Bruce, it's just the two of us now. Do this for Mom."

Kathlyn may have always gotten under his skin, but Alice knew how to push his buttons.

There were fifteen people there for his graduation.

He had forgotten that he and Alice were only two of three grandchildren remaining on Megan's side of the family and he was the only boy and male heir.

They were all given an invitation to stay at the family estates that Bruce had managed to avoid throughout his entire education.

"One day this will all be yours," Megan's father had announced as he and Bruce walked around the grounds with his arm around Bruce's shoulders.

"Thanks," Bruce answered a little sharply. "You know, I'm sure Alice or Sara would like…"

"Oh, don't you worry about the girls. They'll be taken care of."

"Uh huh," Bruce muttered as he took a step forward away from his grandfather's arm. He looked out over the grounds, the acres of grass, the beautiful horses…the lake.

Bruce hated horses.

"Sara loves the place…and the horses," he said, trying to make a point.

"Trust me," his grandfather continued, "after you've gone home for a while you can come back here and work for me until you've learned the ropes and then you can take over."

Bruce thought that there was an obvious flaw to the old man's plans and he had not consulted Megan, his daughter. Bruce still had to ask and turned and looked at his grandfather, "Did you talk to my mom about this?"

He knew not telling Megan more about what he was doing was about to bite him in the ass as usual.

"Well, no I didn't," the old man stammered.

"Typical man," Bruce thought.

That was an area he strived to be more like Tom.

"I just thought…"

"You just thought you would leave your daughter essentially alone on the west coast…take her only son…or was it your hope that she would follow me?"

"I mean, you haven't been home in so long and you chose to come to school back here…and with your degree; well, I just assumed."

"My father attended school here…Grandpa, what do you think my degrees are in?"

"Degrees," he said slightly confused, "well, business of course."

It wasn't that he didn't like his grandparents he just wasn't particularly close to them. Even though he was going to school on the east coast where they lived, they never invited him down to their home for the holidays or even just a visit.

They were always traveling.

"No, sorry Grandfather, I majored in Psychology…"

"Well you can make that work with a master's degree in business…"

"…and my other is in cognitive science. You see, I plan on being a detective."

"Even though we weren't paying for your schooling I thought the plan was for you to come work for me and take over the family business," his grandfather stammered.

"The family business <u>has</u> always been my plan - to return to San Diego and follow in Dad's footsteps. You would have known that if you would have ever asked me."

That was the last time he and his grandfather ever spoke about his future.

It was the first time that Bruce learned that someone other than his grandparents had helped him financially.

And, he wondered...who it had been?

He and his siblings were never in want of anything. Megan never had to work. The house was expanded.

He just never gave it any thought.

What child would?

Bruce thought it had all been on Megan's parents' dime. He knew Tom's family didn't have anything.

Bruce woke up late the next morning, his face feeling like a glazed donut. He was faced down and his mouth stuck to the pillow as he raised his head up. He sat at the edge of the bed and tried to get his bearings. The only thing he was wearing were his pants from the night before. They were unbuttoned and zipped down, but his belt was missing. He looked and saw it draped over the back of his chair.

Alice.

He rubbed his face and squinted at the clock.

It was late.

He went to the bathroom, came back and put on some swim trunks and a shirt and went downstairs.

Megan and Alice were already gone.

He stumbled into the kitchen opened the refrigerator, opened it and grabbed a bottle of milk. Studying the bottle, he thought for a split second about getting a glass, shrugged his shoulders and drank from the bottle instead.

He got in his car, returned to the house to grab his surfboard he had forgotten and then headed to the stretch of beach that was north of the bluffs on Torrey Pines Road and south of Del Mar.

"Well if it isn't the Great Dux," Bruce heard behind him as he paddled out through the waves. He felt his shoulders and arms strain as he dug deep and pulled through the water. When he saw a wave coming towards him he grabbed the board and flipped over and went under the wave so the water washed over him, then rolled his body and the board back over and continued to paddle in such a fluid motion that he didn't lose any momentum. He didn't stop until he was past the break and then he looked around. Another surfer was close behind him and Bruce recognized him as soon as the surfer lifted his head.

"Jesus," the guy said, "you still cut through the water like a dolphin."

"Jesus actually walked on water," Bruce quipped, "How's it goin', Mike?"

Mike paddled close so he could shake Bruce's hand.

"Not bad…good to see you in the water again. Sorry to hear about your brothers."

They were all still playing roll call.

"I was sorry to hear about yours too," Bruce said to him.

"How's your sister," Mike asked, a little too eagerly for Bruce.

"Yeah, you know Alice. She's still not interested in you."

"And, you're still a dick."

"Pretty much," Bruce said grinning.

Bruce just sat on his board and rode the waves up and down almost letting them lull him to sleep. He inhaled a deep breath and looked up and down the shore and surrounding area. He felt the sun start to bake his back and shoulders and the reflection of the sun off the water was also starting to bake his face.

As far as he had been concerned there had been no sun like it in Europe. There were times when it had been out that he closed his eyes and imagined that he had been it this very spot…and then a gun would go off or the rancid smell of the battle field would waft into his nostrils ruining his daydream.

It was at that time he looked up towards the bluffs. Mike caught him looking in that direction as well.

"I wonder how many people have stumbled off getting to close to the edge. I know I almost did once or twice," Mike said.

"Me too," Bruce added.

"You know who I see up there sometimes late during the day," Mike said.

"Um mmm," Bruce said.

"Corey Hayes."

"Really," Bruce said curiously.

"Yeah, it's really weird too. He wanders around and sometimes he just stands there for hours. From this far out it's really hard to tell what he's looking at. I mean there's nothing up there but the pine trees and dirt."

"The sunset...it's not far from the Frost estate," Bruce said nodding north towards Del Mar, "Oh hey," he said as he saw a swell and set coming towards them. He paddled as hard as he could, trying to time it just right, popped up and caught the wave and rode it in almost to shore. He bailed and paddled back out. Mike had been unsuccessful and was already on the other side of the break.

Bruce secretly gloated.

He and Mike started a quiet competition for the next couple of hours with Bruce out surfing Mike in the end. Although Bruce did have to admit in the end that Mike had improved greatly in the years since he had seen him last.

"Where were you stationed," he asked Mike as they walked back up to their cars.

"Pearl Harbor."

"What'd you do? Take lessons from King Kamehameha?"

"One of his descendants," he said bluntly.

"Ah, no wonder you've improved."

"We should get together," Mike said.

"Sure," Bruce said, "But my sister still won't like you."

Bruce drove up the hill to the bluff, parked the car and got out. He looked around and tried to see what the fascination would have been for Corey Hayes considering the family estate had a gorgeous view of the ocean, including the guest house he knew Corey had on the property.

He looked south down the road and saw where there was ground being broken for the proposed university, but there was something about the ground he stood on that bothered him.

Squatting down he picked up a handful of dirt and rubbed it between his hands until it was gone. He looked around at all the pines and could see how, in the dark, they would be very creepy and foreboding, but there was nothing about the view of the ocean that looked compelling.

He finally gave up, got back in his car and left without knowing he had been looking in the wrong direction.

It was in the middle of the next week that Bruce's mother received a phone call from his father's sister to tell her that Tom's mother had died. Bruce drove Alice and Megan up to San Luis Rey Mission for the services and burial. The older family members seemed a bit annoyed that they had not been up two days before for the viewing or the rosary.

"Do we even own a rosary," Alice leaned over and asked him.

Bruce shook his head. "The only rosary I remember seeing was Dad's black onyx one and the last time I remember seeing it was when Mom was yanking it from my hands because I was using it as a leash for the dog."

Alice looked at him.

"You didn't?!"

"I didn't know what it was," he said shrugging his shoulders.

Bruce went through the motions of the Catholic ceremony, not feeling any particular sense of fulfillment.

It had been a long time since he had seen his father's family. He visited Nana once since he had been back from the war. He was no dummy and knew that if she had favored any of his father's children, Louis was the one. The ranch house had always felt cold and vacant to him, even though every room was filled. The German shepherd, Sergeant, exuded more life force than any human there.

That was except for Aunt Ysabel, who finally moved her family in with her mother once the old woman had become too ill.

Bruce always liked her because she was good to all the kids and didn't differentiate between any of the nieces and nephews or her own. Bruce remembered she was the one who comforted Megan after Tom had died. Nana had seemed almost relieved when Tom was gone, yet at the same time annoyed that he had...what was it that Bruce had heard...no seen...no felt...his father had failed at something. It seemed as though she thought Tom had owed her something. He remembered seeing Megan waving a paper or photograph at her some time after the funeral, and then they hardly ever saw them after that.

Bruce looked around at the small pews. Most of the men seemed as though they had been stuffed in between the benches and the backs of the pews in front. From experience, Bruce knew that the padding for kneeling hit below the knees...into the gap just below the patella...and he saw many cousins fidget, including himself, as they tried to get comfortable.

"These pews were made for midgets," he grimaced to Alice. She elbowed him and he grunted before Megan cleared her throat and glared at him.

After the services were done, they followed the rest of the family out the side door to the cemetery. Everyone stood around very somberly as Nana was put to rest. Family members cried, but Bruce couldn't help but catch the occasional glance towards him and his small family. He knew his mother was crying a bit, but not Alice...or him.

They hadn't known their grandmother that well.

Bruce, respectfully, kept his head down, but he couldn't help but catch the glimpse of a person standing far away...but definitely paying her respects.

Bruce cocked his head ever so slightly so he could get a better look.

He had seen her before...he wasn't quite sure who she was, but he was pretty sure who she was.

He had seen her at a distance at his father's funeral...

...and there was the occasional glance across the street from his school...

...football practice...

...and, if he didn't know any better, his college graduation.

And, there were the history books and photographs at the historical society.

There were things Bruce never asked his mother about; especially if he thought it might remind her of Tom...and he knew this woman had something to do with him.

He knew Tom had worked for her as a child and he remembered seeing her the night Tom was murdered. There was something more grandmotherly in her touch than Nana's. He remembered her soothing voice and how her fingers felt when she had cupped his chin. He knew he trusted her more too, but it unnerved him that he didn't know why.

"You're staring," Alice whispered to him.

"What...oh," he said as he started to look back down at the ground, but then glanced over at Megan. She was staring as well. He quickly tried to get another look at the woman, but she was gone.

Once the services and the burial were completed Bruce started walking around on the brick paths that wove through the cemetery, segregating and separating family members. The cemetery was full of relatives...Bruce's relatives. In fact, he knew he was related in one way or another to every tombstone that was there. He started to walk down towards where Tom was buried and slowed when he felt Alice walking behind him.

There were husbands and wives buried together, parents and children...and siblings. There were multiple Juan's, Ramon's, Sylvestre's, Leo's and Maria's. There was one set of brothers...Rubidouxs...buried at the intersection of the path to Tom's grave. Another group of relatives stood around one grave that Bruce was familiar with. He only ever remembered it because the tombstone read "Two innocent boys" and it was dated the same year as Tom's death. One of them had been named Sylvestre and the other Bruce could never pronounce.

They had to be some distant cousins of his.

Alice reached out for Bruce's hand as they approached where Tom was buried and he took it gently as they walked the rest of the way together.

He felt her grip tighten like she used to do when they were little and she was upset. They stopped at Tom's grave. She let Bruce's hand fall and she walked to the tombstone and ran her hand over the top.

"I do remember him," she said.

Bruce noticed there was a blank spot to the right of Tom's name and it bothered him knowing it was meant for Megan.

"I remember him being really tall."

"You were little," he said, noticing the flowers lying in front of the tombstone, "everyone looked tall."

She frowned at him.

"But," he said smiling at her, "he was really tall. I don't remember seeing Mom with any flowers," he said pointing at the bunch.

Alice looked down and shook her head.

"She didn't bring any. Maybe," she looked around, "never mind."

"What?"

"Nothing...I was going to say that maybe the church provided them, but then they would be on all the graves."

Bruce looked around the cemetery. Many family members were already leaving through one of the small gates to the parking lot. There were still a few visiting other relatives graves like he and Alice were.

"I don't see Mom," he said.

Alice looked around.

"She's probably visiting Joe or Louis."

Bruce shook his head, "no, their graves are that way at the far wall. She's not there."

"I don't know Bruce...you're the detective...and quit acting like there's always a mystery. Sometimes things are what they are. Nothing more. You're like the doctor who starts exhibiting the symptoms he's researching."

He knew she was right.

She stood and squeezed his arm as she walked behind him, "She's probably out in the parking lot talking with some of the relations," she said as she continued down the path towards Louis' and Joe's graves.

Bruce stood there for a few more minutes, then he squatted low to the ground, picked at a blade of grass missed by the gardeners and stared at the stone's engraving.

Tom had only been thirty-two when he was killed. Bruce could never understand why someone would want to kill his father.

Captain Moran he could believe. From the stories he heard, he thought the man had been a colossal prick.

But not his father.

It had to have been a mistake.

He played the last moments he had with Tom often, always trying to find something more.

His very last memory was seeing Tom's back as he pushed through the crowd at the Organ Pavilion. It seemed to Bruce as though the crowd swallowed him up.

"Where's Daddy going," he had asked Megan.

She didn't answer him, but there was something in her eyes that prevented him from repeating his question. He knew something was wrong by how she clutched Alice and kissed her.

He looked back in the direction Tom had disappeared.

It was then he knew he would never see Tom again.

Louis tugged at him.

"What's going on Bruce?"

Bruce grabbed him and pushed him until they were out of earshot from Megan. They never kept secrets from each other, but he didn't want to scare Louis and he knew the night at the kitchen table with just them and Tom and frightened the younger boy.

"Daddy was right," he started, but Louis interrupted him.

"Someone decided something without him," he asked a little panicked.

Bruce nodded his head, but then tried to comfort Louis, "But Daddy will take care of it."

A look of relief spread across Louis face. He trusted Bruce so easily. There was just one thing...Bruce felt he had just told a lie he wouldn't be able to explain.

"Are you ready to go B," Megan said, waking Bruce from his daydream.

"Uh, yeah," he said standing, "I mean, yes."

"Where's Alice," she said looking around.

"With the boys," he said nodding towards their graves.

"Would you go get her please?"

"Sure," he said knowing that she still hadn't recovered from their loss and avoided having to be confronted by it, "are we going to the ranch?"

"Yes," she said distracted, "I'll meet you in the parking lot."

She walked towards the nearest gate and Bruce watched her as he walked down the path where Alice was. Alice met him halfway and they walked to the gate without speaking.

He was holding the gate open for her when he looked out into the parking lot and saw a quick exchange between Megan and the woman from the cemetery. The woman walked away.

"Who was that talking to Mom," Alice asked.

"Charlotte MacGregor."

"Who?!"

"Charlotte MacGregor."

"The madam?"

"Yeah...yes."

"What's Mom...I didn't know she knew her" Alice said sounding appalled.

"Dad worked for her when he was a kid," he said directly.

"Doing what?"

"I'm not quite sure. I never asked. I know he worked in her club in the Stingeree."

Bruce watched Charlotte as she walked to a car, got in and drove off. He opened the car doors for Megan and Alice and was walking around to the driver's side when he heard Alice.

"Mom, what did Daddy do for Charlotte MacGregor," she asked Megan.

Megan paused long enough for Bruce to get into the car.

"He was a pet."

Alice didn't say another word.

There was a line of cars backed up to turn onto the long dirt driveway to the ranch. The drivers were trying to space the cars far enough apart and go as slow as possible so less dust was scattered and blown into the cars.

Bruce remembered going down this driveway many times as a boy, but it always seemed like it was in the middle of summer with him, Louis and Alice sitting in the back seat sweating and the dust sticking to their little bodies and get in their teeth and hair.

"Tom," Meg would say with a blanket covering Joe on her lap.

"I'm trying," he would say.

"Go faster Daddy," Louis and or Alice would say because the bouncing made them laugh and feel like they were on one of the big draft horses.

And so the banter would repeat itself over and over again until they arrived at the house.

Now it repeated itself without the laughing and without Tom.

"Bruce," Megan said.

"I'm trying," he said, slowing the car down even more.

"Mom, if he slows down anymore we'll be stopped," Alice said from the back seat.

"Your father used to fly down this road."

Both Alice and Bruce looked at her and started laughing.

"Mom, we had a Model A it didn't go more than five miles per hour," Bruce said sarcastically.

"Well, it felt like we were going really fast...and it went faster than five miles per hour because it was a Durant."

"Oh, that makes a difference," Bruce quipped sarcastically.

"Maybe downhill," Alice said under her breath.

"Shush you two," Megan said, trying to hide a smile.

They pulled up to the house and Bruce got out and opened the doors for Megan and Alice.

They went in through the back door and kitchen. Bruce never remembered ever using the front door except to chase each other as kids. The kitchen, as always, was bustling with activity. It was almost as if every movement was choreographed with pots and pans being shuffled from the sink to the stove top and oven and others grabbing things from the ice box and taking it to the counter or adding to a mixing bowl.

Megan and Alice had disappeared, but reappeared as Bruce squeezed his way through all the women out to the dining room. He had his hand slapped as he stuck his finger in a bowl of frosting. Megan and Alice were jumping right in as the kitchen door swung back.

The rest of the men were out in the backyard. Bruce looked around and started walking through the house. The only room he had ever really spent time in was the kitchen, but now he felt he could roam through the other rooms and spaces without being interrupted and shooshed outside by an older relative.

He couldn't imagine how his grandparents had lived in such a small home with five children.

He went into the room at the one end of the hall. There was a single bed that Bruce's legs would have dangled off of, a nightstand, a small bookcase and in the far corner was a very old wheelchair.

He knew that had to belong to his Uncle Aldo who had died a few years after Tom. Bruce looked down at the books and read the titles on the spines and smiled as he reached and pulled one out.

It was a collection of boys' detective stories.

Bruce opened the cover and in the upper corner of the title page in a child's writing was scrawled Tom Rubidoux.

Bruce ran his fingers over the writing, closed the book and returned it to its spot.

Then he walked out of the room and into the next. It was smaller and still had little girl things on the shelves and bed.

Ysabel and Faustina's room.

Bruce realized the four boys must have shared the other, slightly larger room with the wheelchair.

He walked back out into the hallway and proceeded to look at the photos on the walls and on the credenza. He picked up one with all six children sitting atop one of the ranch's draft horses.

Tom was easy to spot between Ysabel and Aldo. He had the same dark hair as the others, but he was paler which made Bruce wonder how much times his father had spent hiding and reading for his skin not to darken.

Bruce held the photo and took a small step back. He looked up and down at all the photos and realized the one in his hand was the only one that included Tom. There were several others with Ysabel, her sister and the other three boys at various ages and there were individual pictures from the war, school and infancy.

In fact, besides the book, there was nothing indicating his father ever existed.

"That one was always my favorite," Ysabel said over Bruce's arm at the photo.

He looked at her with his mouth gaped open – still thinking.

"This is the only one with Dad."

Ysabel looked at all the photos. Bruce picked up another one that had the children when they were small – Aldo was a baby – no Tom.

"Dad was older than Aldo so why isn't he in the photo," he asked her.

"Photographs were expensive back then. He may have been taking a nap or hiding in the barn reading."

"You were dressed up for this. I hardly think Nana would have left him out."

"I don't know. I don't remember," she said taking the photo from him and placing it back. "I remember Momma removing photos of him when...well after our cousins died. I think she blamed him for them dying. Tia Lena didn't speak with Momma again. I think they all blamed him."

"I've never heard about this."

"Your father was trying to get them freed. They had been accused of a horrendous crime...a girl had been cut to bits...we never talk about it. Tom was killed before anything could be done."

"Well, there's no reason to hold a grudge, it's not like he could do anything when he was dead."

"The problem was no one could ever find what he did with the case file...at least that's what we were told. Momma never talked about him again."

"Is that why she never talked to us?"

"Yes."

"Louis thought he had done something wrong."

"No, I told her I thought what she did to you kids was cruel."

Bruce looked back at the photos.

"That's why Daddy's not buried with the rest of the family."

She nodded her head.

"Momma and the red-haired lady where he used to work..."

"Charlotte," Bruce asked.

"...yes, that was her name...I heard them arguing in the kitchen over it. I didn't hear all of it but I remember Charlotte saying something about he had to be buried up here and Momma really didn't have a choice in the matter since the plot was already purchased."

Bruce looked at her curiously.

"But the reason I came looking for you is your mother was looking for you. She left something in the car and wanted you to get it for her."

"Okay," he said, realizing the conversation was over.

"And Golpe," she said as he was walking away. He cringed slightly at the name and saw her reach for the photograph. She looked down at it for a second and then handed it out to him.

"You can have this."

"But..."

"I know you don't have any photos of your dad when he was little."

"I couldn't."

"You or Alice should have it. If you don't want it, give it to her."

"Thank you," he said taking it and then he took it to the car, wrapped it in a towel and put it in the trunk.

19.

AN OVERDUE PACKAGE

Moving the offices had not been the biggest problem for the police department. The replacement of all the antiquated furniture had been. It had been a challenge to find a company willing to deliver all the new desks and dispose of the old ones; so, the police department settled for everything in stages and had lived with both the new and old furniture for a decade.

The first to go were the old desks that were either broken, had handles missing or drawers that wouldn't open.

Of course these all couldn't have been stored on the first floor.

No, they were all on the second floor of the fancy new police station where no one had been assigned offices yet.

Finally, one of the local moving companies had decided it would "volunteer" its time (at a reduced rate) if the desks would be donated to one of the schools south of the border.

"Big desks for a bunch of little wet backs," one of the city officials thought, "but as long as we get rid of them it will work."

He didn't realize that any desk was better than no desk.

So a crew was brought in to remove and haul the 33 desks out of the building and down to San Ysidro.

It was an all day event. Most of the officers and detectives chose to go out in the field rather than listen to all the noise from desks dropping and workmen cursing, including Bruce.

Late in the day, as some were returning to fill out reports, two workers had just left carrying one of the old desks down and another two were staring at the ten remaining ones.

"Nine more after this one," one said to the other.

"Thank God, my back's killing me."

"Come on, let's go. Let's get this over with."

One grabbed a desk and shoved it around so the other could get a better grip. They shoved and heaved it towards the door by the top. They worked like a machine and knew exactly when to tilt the desk and twist so it fit though the door.

This was the fifteenth one that the two of them had moved.

They got closer to the stairs and switched places when they were at the top steps since they had agreed on taking turns as to who would have to go backwards down the stairs.

Both of their forearms ached and were weakening.

It all came down to one slip.

The one whose turn it was to go backwards got in position and started to lift the desk, but his hands had also become numb from all the lifting. He had it up above his waist and was about to step down when it slipped. He was quick enough to catch it by the lip of the top, jolting the bottom half.

A gap that had been started years before by a screwdriver and enlarged through the twisting and shoving opened up from the jolt.

As the desk was guided down the stairs the worker twisted to the side, allowing a long forgotten file to fall out and down the stairs.

The workers thought about stopping for a split second to pick it up.

"No way, we'll get it on the way back up."

As they continued to labor to get the desk down the stairs and out the front door, a young police officer came around the corner and headed up the stairs. He saw the file and picked it up.

"Rubidoux" was written across the stained and browning file. He thought it was odd the file was there, but thought maybe Detective Rubidoux had dropped it.

He knew who Detective Rubidoux was and thought he'd make some brownie points with the detective if he took him the file.

He was disappointed when Bruce wasn't at his desk and just left it so Bruce would find it and walked out.

Bruce returned and was removing his jacket when he saw the file sitting on his desk. He sat down, picked it up and looked at it curiously.

It had his name on it, but the paper and ink looked older and he didn't recognize the writing.

He opened the file and pulled out the contents. His heart beat started turning into heavy, irregular thumping as he began to flip through the pages and photos.

The photos were...were ghastly and made his heart lurch in his chest.

They reminded him of the war and seeing pieces of soldiers lying all around him. He felt perspiration start to bead up on his upper lip as the taste of vomit crept up into his mouth.

He swallowed.

He put the photos down, and then something made him pick them up and look again.

Frantically, he shuffled through them until he came back to the one that showed a burlap sack that was opened up towards the camera, sharing its gruesome contents with the viewer.

It wasn't the pieces of the body that had Bruce fixated though.

He took the magnifying glass from his desk drawer and looked closer at one of the hands that held the sack open. Bruce moved the magnifying glass to the watch on the wrist and then looked at his own wrist and back to the photo.

It was the same.

Bruce set the photos and the magnifying glass down and frantically started rifling through the paperwork.

The handwriting – the swoops in the g's, the little hole in the e's and always the r's were capitalized – confirmed what the watch already told him

"Did you see who left this file here," he asked one of the other detectives who was walking by.

The officer looked down at it.

"No, but it looks like it belongs to you."

Bruce looked at the envelope with his last name scribbled across the top.

"Yes it does, doesn't it," he said, feeling a little like a dolt.

The officer went about his business and Bruce returned to the file, shut it and stared at it for a second.

He had never talked about Tom's death or anything surrounding it with anyone. It was always a topic that was talked around, but as he stared at the file he started to remember things in disjointed pieces. Everything that had happened over the last few weeks also made everything fresh:

There were the names he hadn't heard in years.

The people he hadn't seen in a long time.

He opened the file quickly again and flipped to one of the pages he had briefly seen. There was a name he recognized that he was sure he could talk to immediately.

Once he confirmed he was right, he closed the file and headed downstairs to the morgue.

Bruce thought Doc Hill was an interesting person, and if it hadn't been for his profession or where he worked, Bruce might have chatted with him more. Most of the officers were leery of him and even more so at Halloween. Bruce had seen almost everyone go to wipe their hands on their trousers or handkerchiefs after shaking the coroner's hand. Bruce had caught himself going to do it a few times himself.

He knew that Tom had spoken about the doctor before so he knew that he couldn't be that bad. But, then again, Tom never seemed to judge anybody and treated almost everyone equally.

Bruce hovered around the door and peeked in.

There were three bodies laid out in various stages of autopsy. Bruce thought they might be the three bodies that had been picked up from a robbery the night before.

He looked around and spotted the coroner at the furthest end of the room leaning over open abdominal cavity of one of the victims. Bruce could see a couple of internal organs on a table near the dead man's head.

Dr. Hill lifted his head slightly and peered over the rim of his glasses at Bruce and then back down to his work.

"Hello, Andon, what brings you down here," he said as he stood up and lifted the forceps he was using, moved them over a metal container and dropped what appeared to be a bullet inside.

Bruce started walking forward. He always thought dead people looked so much smaller then when they were alive and walking around. Dr. Hill picked up the file, scanned it and set it back down.

"None of these are yours."

"No, they're not," Bruce answered.

The coroner studied him.

"What's on your mind, Andon?"

Bruce looked around at the room. Dr. Hill leaned over the corpse to him.

"Don't worry none of them will repeat anything we say."

Bruce turned and smiled.

"I want to ask you about an old case," Bruce started.

Dr. Hill cocked his head so he could see the file that Bruce held. Bruce lifted it and was about to set it on the body when the coroner held up his hand for him to wait. Bruce held the file up as the coroner flopped the flaps from the y-incision back into place. They sunk slightly since the coroner hadn't returned all the organs.

"There you go."

"Thanks," Bruce said as he set the file down.

"Unflappable like your dad with this dead stuff."

"I'll take that as a compliment," he said and was about to open the file when the coroner slapped his hand on the top.

"Where did you find this," he said, almost demanded.

"On my desk."

The look Dr. Hill made Bruce think the man thought there might be something more to it.

"There was no note...I have no idea who left it."

"That's creepy."

Bruce nodded his head and thought it was odd that the coroner would think that, but then thought if anyone would know about weird and creepy it was him.

"I wondered where it had disappeared to. In fact, many people have wondered over the years where it went."

"So, it's not the first time you've seen it."

Dr. Hill took a deep breath took the file from Bruce and opened it. He flipped through it very quickly and then took the papers out and sorted them into three piles with the smallest one lying on the corpse to the coroner's right and the largest, with photographs, to his left.

"You don't think Dad's cousins killed the girl found in that sack," he said pointing to the photograph on top of the largest pile.

"No, they didn't...and Bradley Farnham didn't kill Evelyn...oh, what was her name," he said grabbing the second pile.

"Bradley Farnham?"

"Just how far in the file have you gone, Andon?"

"I didn't look that close. I thought it was all the same case," he said looking down at the three piles.

"It is," Dr. Hill said bluntly.

He turned and walked to his office in the back. Bruce heard some shuffling and then drawers open and close and the coroner returned with a file of his own.

"Your dad wasn't the only one who kept files on things that seemed a little fishy."

He opened the file and pulled out more photographs that he sorted in the appropriate files. Bruce grabbed the photographs from the second pile and started looking through them. He was mortified at what he saw.

"The papers are just duplicates of what you already have."

Bruce looked at him, "Where's the head?"

"Uh," the coroner looked, "oh, those photos are further on the bottom. They're somewhat gruesome...even for my standards."

Bruce shuffled through them until he saw what the coroner was talking about. He felt himself vomit a little in his mouth again and a little bit of perspiration started on his lip.

"How could someone do this to another human being...not once, but three..."

"Probably more," Dr. Hill interjected. "It's not that hard to comprehend, Andon. You were in the war. Weren't you one of the soldiers who helped liberate the Buchenwald concentration camp?"

Bruce remembered the rotting bodies that were piled on top of each other...alive and dead.

This was something different.

Bruce picked up the last pile.

"Who was falsely convicted of this one," he asked.

"No one," Dr. Hill answered as he picked up the empty file with Bruce's last name written across it, "but I suspect she was killed because of this."

Bruce looked at him curiously. The coroner held it as he looked at each pile and moved the papers a little.

"This is her writing. She worked in records. I know that all of this didn't come in here so your dad must have put this all in here. It would seem that you are missing some paperwork." He set the file down and picked up the photographs from the first pile.

"As a matter of fact," he said as he shifted through them, "Yep, you're missing a photo."

He handed the pile to Bruce who looked through them.

"I remember because Tom had me take a second set."

"Do you know which one is missing?"

He thought for a moment and then shook his head.

"Vaguely, I mean it was a long time ago."

He took the photographs back and looked through them again.

"I don't know...there was one I remembered thinking how manicured her hands were."

"Her hands?"

"Yes, her hands. She had clawed at whoever attacked her. There was a nail missing. I don't think your dad ever caught that. I didn't tell him."

"Maybe that's why he pulled the photo," Bruce said.

A couple of other detectives entered.

"Hey Doc...Dux," one of them said.

Bruce turned and acknowledged them with a nod and turned back to the file.

"Just a second Andon," the coroner said as he went to talk to the detectives.

Bruce just stared at each pile.

He remembered the file sitting on the front stoop. He remembered waking up one night and seeing that there was a light on so he got out of bed and walked to the family room and stood in the doorway trying to be as quiet as possible and watching Tom. His father had looked very sad and (knowing what he knew now) how very tired and almost panicked he had looked. The floor boards had creaked when Bruce shifted his weight, alerting Tom to his presence.

Tom had looked up, didn't say anything and motioned for Bruce to come closer.

"I saw the light," Bruce started.

"How long have you been awake, Golpe?"

His nickname sounded so warm coming from Tom. Everyone else made it sound like a disease.

"Where did you and Mommy go," he asked as he came closer to see what Tom was looking at. Tom had flipped the file closed.

Now he knew why.

Tom explained where he and his mother had been. Bruce told him no one else had woken up because Alice was snoring and they were all used to sleeping through that.

Tom had brought him closer and said Alice had inherited that trait from Megan and that had made him laugh.

Tom had started to send him back to bed when he asked Tom a question.

"Daddy?"

"Um."

"Were you out catching bad guys?"

"Not quite...it's not that simple some times."

"But you're really good at it...?"

"Yes, I usually do catch the bad guy."

"Mommy says you have to think like the bad guy to catch 'em."

"Yes, you have to know how they think...Bruce, what is it you want to know?"

He hesitated.

"Do you have to be bad to think and catch them?"

"No."

Bruce thought about his answer for a second.

"Okay," Tom had said reassuringly.

Bruce nodded.

"Off to bed with you," he said after kissing him and patting him on the butt.

Bruce left the room, jumped in bed and watched the light until he fell asleep.

That was when the file only had one pile.

"Who was she," Bruce said, pointing at the center pile when Dr. Hill returned to him. "You said Bradley Farnham didn't kill her."

"She was the madam of The Agate Club. She also knew your dad."

"I thought Charlotte MacGregor was the madam."

"Oh, she was, but Evelyn took over in that capacity when Miss Charlotte retired. It was still her business, Evelyn just managed it."

Bruce saw the coroner look up at the clock on the wall.

"I'm sorry you're busy," he said looking at the corpses lying in the room.

He started to shuffle the three piles together then stopped and looked at the coroner.

"Go ahead, take them. I wasn't doing anything with them."

Bruce stacked the piles together and stuffed them back into the file while the coroner went to the sink and started washing his hands. Bruce thought he had should do the same and joined him.

"What was the girl's name...the first one," Bruce asked.

"Don't know," Dr. Hill said drying his hands, "we buried her as a Jane Doe."

"Does that happen often?"

"More so back then, but as you can tell, a lot of things happened more often back then."

"Thank you, you've helped a lot," Bruce said.

"Are you going to reinvestigate it?"

"Perhaps...more than likely...absolutely."

"Let me know if there's anything else I can help you with. To tell you the truth it's much more exciting than this," he said waving at the corpses.

Bruce washed his hands and started to leave as Dr. Hill went back to his autopsy. He was opening the y-incision again when he looked up at Bruce.

"You know there was something else I remember."

"What?"

"Your dad's partner, Hayes, Corey Hayes...this was the case that was his undoing."

"What do you mean?"

"I've never seen anybody throw up in a morgue more...not even a woman. His uncle removed him from the force right after I told him how sick he had been from seeing the body."

"His uncle?"

"Yeah, Captain Moran was Corey Hayes' uncle. I forgot about that; otherwise, I wouldn't have said anything. They all answered to Judge Frost."

"Senator Moran and Corey Hayes are cousins?"

"Yes and the nephews of Charles Miller Frost. You've been to their estate – I'm sure the boys were there. Did you just think they were all friends?"

"No, Bruce shook his head, "I never gave them any thought."

Bruce walked back upstairs and to his desk. He didn't seem to hear or see anybody, but he did have the sensation he was being watched and something was slithering its way towards him. "Hey," he shouted out to one of the nearby detectives, "do you have a phone book?"

The detective nodded and handed the battered copy to Bruce. He thumbed through it until he reached the "H's". He was pretty sure retired Detective Hayes still lived in the city.

"Hanks...Harper...Hawkins...Hayes." He scanned the register up and down with his finger. There was no Corey Hayes or C. Hayes, but there was a C.F. Hayes.

It was worth a shot.

Bruce grabbed the phone and dialed.

He picked up the file again and looked at some of the pages as he listened to the ringing on the other end. He only knew Cabot Moran, mainly because of his daughter Kathlyn, but never spoke to Corey Hayes after Tom's funeral.

The phone continued to ring and just as he was about to hang up, he heard the click on the other end as someone picked up.

"Hello," a deep gravelly voice answered.

"Yes," Bruce said, "I was looking for Mr...for Detective Corey Hayes."

There was a long pause.

"Yes."

"Detective Hayes?"

"Yes, who am I speaking to?"

"I'm sorry, Detective And...Bruce Rubidoux."

"Bruce Rubidoux?"

"Yes, you were my father's partner, Tom Rubidoux."

"Bruce?"

He sighed. "Yes sir, Bruce."

"Good Lord, I haven't spoken to you since you were a kid."

"No sir."

"How are you, well what can I do for you? A detective, you say."

"Yes sir."

"I was wondering if I could come by and talk to you."

"Sure, what's this pertaining to?"

"Something my dad was working on before he died literally landed on my...well, an old file I found."

"Really, uh, sure...not today though...I'll tell you what I'm going to be down at the track tomorrow. Why don't you come on up and we'll talk then."

"Okay, any particular time?"

"No, I usually go down first thing before the races start and stroll up and down the paddocks. After that, you'll find me in the grandstands in the Frost family box. You know the Frosts."

"Yes sir, I know the Frosts."

"I'm sure they will be delighted to see you again."

Delighted was not exactly the word that Bruce thought would come to mind. He expected Kathlyn would be there.

"Yes sir."

"See you there then. And, Bruce, tell your mother hello for me."

"I will sir, good bye."

He hung up the phone.

His mother.

Did he dare mention this to her? He knew how his mother felt about hearing stories about his dad. She avoided a lot of social circles and events because of it. She wasn't thrilled when Bruce became a police officer and then detective, but she went along with it because she knew it was what he wanted.

He knew Tom confided a lot in Megan, probably much more than he should have; especially for the day and age. Bruce remembered seeing on several occasions, her sitting in his lap as he held open one of the manila case folders he snuck home. Both of them would be poring over its contents with Meg always asking "what about this" or "what about that" and "did you think maybe".

His mother probably knew more about all Tom's cases than the police department.

Looking back at the file he shuddered to think his mother had probably seen it and its contents. Had she envisioned that the girl could have been her or Alice? Any time he saw cases involving young woman Bruce immediately would think of his sister.

What would his father have done?

His mother would have silently known and let him do whatever it was he had to do to put the criminals away.

That was one thing Bruce was sure they didn't talk about – the lengths Detective Tom Rubidoux would go to. Although his father was known as a quiet and peaceful man, there were stories of the brutality he had inflicted on criminals when he passed a point.

Bruce knew his father had been in the war and he'd seen on more than one occasion Tom come home with blood on his shirt or coat.

Above all, he remembered the damn lesson he gave the kids about what a gun could do. Tom hadn't even flinched. It was like he had gone somewhere else in his mind when he shot the gun.

Bruce was the opposite. Oh, he never flinched, but when he shot a gun the person knew he wanted to hurt or kill him.

Or was a risk to his safety.

Tom had a name for that.

Murder.

Bruce thought about what he was going to do and in a flash, reached across his desk and picked up the phone. When the operator picked up he gave her the extension he wanted.

His home number.

The phone rang for awhile, Bruce looked at the clock and figured she was probably reading in the front room like she did frequently at this time of the day.

"Hell...," he heard her start to say. He was too anxious right now for formalities, even if it was his mother.

"Mom."

"What is it Bruce," he heard her say slowly on the other end.

"I found an old file of Dad's on my desk...there are photos of a ...well, not to be gruesome and insensitive, but there are pieces of a body."

He couldn't hear anything on the other end of the line.

"Mom?"

"I'm still here."

"I was just wondering about...there are two people with the last name of Rubidoux named in the file."

"One was named Sylvestre and the other Judah...Juma...Yuma..."

"Juneau, his name was Juneau."

"That's it, like at the cemetery. So, it's true?"

"We've never spent much time with your father's family," she said.

"The file says they were suspected of murder," he blurted out.

He heard her take a deep breath and quietly exhale.

"Mom, is this the same case Daddy was working on that night in the par...Mom, I have to go," he said as a couple of other officers started to hover around his desk.

"We'll talk later and Bruce?"

"Yes Mom."

"Be safe," she said and he knew she was already worried.

"I love you."

"I love you too. Bye," he said abruptly and hung up the phone.

There was only one person he really trusted to talk to about this.

Bruce grabbed the file and headed out the door and then returned to grab his coat.

He walked quickly up the fifteen blocks to the pharmacy and bounded in through the door. He saw Alice helping a customer. She looked up and gave him a look that told him she wondered what he was doing there. The frantic look in his eyes and the way his body twitched anxiously was familiar to her. She took a deep breath and smiled at the customer and absentmindedly went through the motions of helping the person.

He walked to the end of the counter and waited for her and played with the items on the counter without thinking, almost breaking a perfume bottle.

One of the other girls approached him to see if he needed any help and then recognized who he was and just stayed so she could flirt with him. Alice smirked when the girl seemed annoyed that he really didn't pay any attention to her. The girl just had no idea that Bruce was oblivious to what she was doing. The girl seemed even more annoyed when Alice came up to him.

"What are yo..."

"Come with me," he interrupted her.

"What, why?"

"Come on...I'll buy you lunch...my treat."

"We really need to find you a girlfriend. Besides, it's almost time for dinner."

He didn't know what else to say, but she could see he was desperate. Something had unnerved him.

"I'll tell you what. I'll let you take me to dinner. Go down to the Grant and wait for me. I should be there in an hour or so. Okay."

He nodded his head. She kissed him on the cheek and went back to work. He sat there for a minute before getting up and walking to the Grant.

As promised, Alice arrived a little after an hour. Even though she hadn't told him where to meet, she knew exactly where to find him.

He was hunkered at the bar with his head propped on a fist and the other hand was playing with his glass of scotch. It looked like he was watching the melting ice cubes spin around in the glass.

She put her hand on his back as the bartender came up.

"I'd like a martini please...the kind with the olives," she asked, smiling.

"You mean vodka," the bartender clarified.

"Please."

He slid off his stool and held the one beside him for her. She sat and he slid back onto his...and didn't say a word.

The bartender arrived and she started to swirl the drink with the toothpick that held the olives.

"You know I cancelled a date for this. You could at least speak to me."

"Huh," he said, finally looking at her. "I'm sorry, I shouldn't have let you walk over by yourself," he said thinking of the photos in the file.

"I took a taxi. Bruce, what is it? You have me a little worried."

"Do you...you know after we were talking that day...do you ever wonder...I mean...does it ever bother you that someone killed Dad?"

She took a sip of her drink and looked over at the file he had sitting to the far side of him. She remembered that file. She remembered seeing it on the front porch the day Corey Hayes came to the house and stayed for dinner. Although she really couldn't read at that time she now recognized what it was she had been looking at.

Bruce took another sip of his drink and signaled for the bartender to get him another.

"Have you ever noticed that things happen all at once sometimes," he asked her.

"Bruce, you've been a little off ever since that case down at the embarcadero."

"Bradley Farnham."

"What?"

"Bradley Farnham's name was mentioned that day. He's in a nut house you know."

She quietly took a deep breath. Bruce and Joe would get this way some times when they were wound up really tight – their thoughts all disjointed. It happened with Bruce more often than Joe, but she liked that they thought she was the only one who could help them.

She nodded to herself.

"Who is he," she asked.

"He was there the night Dad was killed. It was because of him Dad left us at the park." He looked at her. "I know you were little, but do you remember any of those last few months?"

"He pinched me," she said suddenly.

"What?"

"He pinched me - he was talking to an older couple and he pinched me. I started to cry and he ran me back to Mom." She looked at him. "My last memory of Daddy is that he pinched me."

He could see her eyes well up. He looked back at his drink.

"Mine is of the back of his head."

"I remember that file Bruce. Where did you get it?"

He picked it up and held it in front of him.

"What if Captain Moran wasn't the target, what if the target was actually Dad," he asked not hearing her.

"It doesn't matter Bruce. It's not going to bring him back."

"But wouldn't you want to know?"

"No Bruce...I wouldn't."

"What if it was because he was trying to catch the bad guy?"

"Whether or not he caught the bad guy doesn't change who he was Bruce. And catching who killed him isn't going to change who he was."

Bruce thought for a minute.

"What if that person was still getting away with the murder of others?"

"Then Dad would want them to pay for what they have...for what they are doing."

She slid off her chair and grabbed his arm.

"If you do this, you do it on your own...you don't tell Mom."

He looked at the file and remembered Megan those last months with their dad.

"What if she already knows?"

"Then I don't want to know."

He set the file down on the bar.

"I'm going to go call Ryan and see if we still have time to go out. I'll let you buy me dinner another time."

He sat there for a quick second and then quickly turned around.

"Who would want to kill our dad," he said to her.

She stopped, turned around and walked back to him. She put her hand on his knee and looked at him, shaking her head.

"I don't know...but something tells me...somewhere in your mind...you do," she said concerned.

She hugged him and kissed him on the cheek.

"Don't let him drink too much," she said to the bartender and left.

The bartender looked at Bruce. Bruce looked at his empty glass and back at the bartender.

"Yes, I would like another."

The bartender nodded and grabbed the bottle.

Bruce sat outside in the backyard thinking about what had happened. He had continued his drinking binge, hoping to silence the voices or put the memories and thoughts to sleep in his mind.

He looked up at the night sky and wondered what Tom had thought about all the times he would sneak down and see him sitting outside late at night.

Frustrated, he stood up and went back inside taking the scotch bottle and glass with him. He walked through the family room where Tom's desk (which was now his) stood and he glanced at the folder he set there when he came home.

He walked up the steps with each one creaking under his weight.

He stopped in the middle and thought about how the steps didn't make nearly as much noise with Megan and Alice.

In his room, he set the bottle and glass down on his night stand and took off his clothes. He sat on his bed in just his boxers and rubbed his thigh where he had been shot by a German. He was lucky – that and the wound in his shoulder were the only war injuries he had sustained.

Well, the only ones that could be seen.

He laid down and stared up at the ceiling in the dark, but he couldn't get his brain to stop and let him sleep.

By the lack of any sound he knew Megan was asleep and heard Alice at the top of the stairs and go into the bathroom. He heard the toilet flush and then waited for her to go to her bedroom, back to the bathroom and then back to her bedroom.

Her second trip to the bathroom always seemed to last forever. Bruce didn't understand what could ever take so long.

If his mother only knew that there were a few times he had become so impatient that he had just walked out to the backyard to pee.

He didn't understand why they hadn't added more bathrooms when they had expanded the house. He thought Megan was more concerned with having enough rooms for all the kids than whether or not they would end up having some sort of infection from not being able to go in time.

Alice needed her own, at least that's what he thought; especially now with just the two of them.

Whenever he opened any of the cabinets they shared he was always overwhelmed at the endless amounts of jars and bottles of lotions and make-up.

One time he started reading the labels and finally gave up when they all started to say the same things.

After he heard her make her final trip back to her bedroom he threw on his bathrobe and walked down the hall to the stairs. Alice's light shone under her door lighting his path a little as he went down.

He stopped in front of his desk and pondered what he was going to do next. It felt as if the file were alive and staring at him. He stared at it and cocked his head. Hesitantly, he reached for it to open it. Alice's words played back in his head. If she had her way she wouldn't want him digging into it - she had already said as much - but he also knew she would be the first one he would catch flipping through it if he left it out in the open.

Besides, he had already made his decision – he had called Corey Hayes.

He pulled the chair out, sat down and took a deep breath then pulled the contents out and sorted them; separating the photos by what he could perceive was first, second and third dates and then piled them together. He tried not to let their contents distract him.

Next, he pulled out the notes and separated them by content. Some held notes for the suspects, the crime scene...no scenes (as he discovered there was more than one), witnesses and weapons.

There were old newspaper articles that were hard to read; and, in Bruce's state, he thought they might actually break from his handling.

One of the articles had a photo of Kathlyn's father after World War I kneeling behind an extensive blade collection, many that Bruce remembered from one of the trophy cabinets in Judge Frost's den in the Del Mar estate.

He put it aside and started reading the notes and reports from the beginning. Right away he recognized the name of the two suspects/witnesses.

They were the same as the two brothers buried together in the San Luis Rey Mission's cemetery.

They were relatives.

From what he could compile – a young female had been found by the two Rubidoux men in the early hours of the morning when it was still dark. She had been cut up into pieces and the pieces were stuffed in a sack that was hanging from a tree on the bluffs of Torrey Pines on Highway 101.

The Rubidoux's were arrested and put in jail.

There was nothing else – nothing about what happened afterwards, their convictions or executions.

Bruce wrote on a pad of paper, "Where is the rest of the report?"

Next he started going through his father's notes.

Scribbled in the margins were words (wrong person, why, adoptions and secrets) but more telling were names: Suzanne, Meredith, Evelyn, Agate Club basement, Frost, Phelps, JD221…Charlotte.

There was only one Charlotte and only one Frost family.

Bruce ran his hand down his face.

It suddenly felt much colder than it really was as he continued reading all the paperwork, including the coroner's report.

He felt himself go pale a he read Dr. Hill's report.

He had seen horrific mutilations and dismemberments during the war and, as Dr. Hill had reminded him, had been one of the soldiers that were there for the liberation of the Buchenwald concentration camp. He knew the unfortunate truths of what human beings could and would do to each other.

This…this was something entirely different.

This had been personal.

He saw the notes his father had made in the margins of the coroner's report describing the weapon. He quickly shuffled through the papers and found the browned article and photograph of Kathlyn's father and realized what may have happened.

Tom Rubidoux had suspected Senator Cabot Miller Moran of murder.

Bruce looked closer at the photograph and the truth tore at him.

His father hadn't suspected…his father had known.

Bruce leaned back in the chair.

He replayed every memory he had of the Frost family, every touch, every word and innuendo.

It was Judge Frost whom he had heard say keep your enemies close and he felt the creepy old arm and hand of the judge around his shoulder and weakly grab his shoulder when he was a teen. He cringed remembering it felt like a spider landing on his hand.

"Come into my parlor said they spider to the fly," he remembered from a nursery rhyme.

And, into the Frost's parlor he was about to enter.

20.

THE SON PLAYS CHESS

"What is all of this," Alice said as she stood over Bruce the next morning. She went to grab the photos and he slammed his hand down on top of them before she could pick them up.

"Don't," was all he said. His tone made her pull her hand back.

"Okay...that bad huh?"

"That bad," he said.

He thought for a minute as she started to apply pressure to his fingers.

"Battlefield hospital bad," he said grimly, appealing to her experience as a volunteer at the naval hospital.

She pulled her hand back and made a face.

"Oh."

"Besides, you said you didn't want to know."

"Ohh."

She walked behind him and into the kitchen.

"Have you been up all night," she asked.

"I guess so," he said looking at the grayness of morning through the windows. "I lost track of time."

He rubbed his face with his hands and went back to looking at the papers.

"Were you awake when I got home last night?"

"No...yes," he stopped to think why she would be asking the question. "I didn't hear anything...if that's why you were asking..."

She laughed.

"No, that's not why I was asking."

"Oh," he said perplexed and then went back to his work.

"I was going to make some breakfast. Would you like me to make you some?"

"Sure…please…where's Mom?"

"It's almost six Bruce. She's in bed."

He looked out the window again.

"It's that early?"

"Yes," she said.

"Huh."

"What's this box doing here," she asked.

"I don't know, it's not mine," he said.

She walked out from the kitchen with the box and walked to the hallway. Bruce heard the hallway closet door open and then shut. She returned to the kitchen and he heard her start pulling skillets out.

He could hear something frying so he stood up and walked into the kitchen, to the refrigerator, pulled on the latch and pulled out the milk bottle. He started bringing the bottle to his mouth and without looking Alice reached for the cabinet and started taking out a glass.

"Bruce, use a glass," she said handing out the glass to him without looking.

He took the glass and poured his milk.

"Why are you up so early," he asked her.

"I'm working early so I can get off early," she said as she loaded his plate and set it down in front of his seat. He sat down with his glass of milk. She giggled.

"You look like you're four years old," she said tapping to above her lip.

"Huh, oh," he said and wiped his mouth with the sleeve of his robe before she could hand him a napkin.

"Here, I'll get you a grown-up drink," she said grabbing a cup and pouring coffee into it for him.

"Thanks…say I'm not taking you to work, am I?"

"No, Ryan is."

"Ryan," he said thinking if it was the Ryan he already knew, "Okay, for a second there I thought I had forgotten."

She set her plate down, sat down and started to eat.

"I know better than to ask you to do anything when you've been drinking...although, even then, you usually do remember...or did you forget," she said grinning as she put the fork full of food in her mouth.

"Very funny," he said.

"Where are you off to today?"

"I am off to the races...literally."

"With who?"

"With no one. I'm meeting someone there," he said yawning.

"Kathlyn!?"

"God, I hope not, but I have a feeling I might not be able to avoid her."

"That girl from the club," she asked excitedly.

"Who...no..."

"You should have called her..."

"Yeah...no, I'm..."

"You should...you still can..."

"Eh...mayb...I'm meeting Corey Hayes."

"You should call her."

"So, I imagine Kathlyn will be there with the rest of the family," he said continuing to ignore her.

"If you get invited to the family's box."

He scooped the rest of his food in his mouth and took a gulp of his coffee.

"You already know they will," she said.

"For one reason or another they will," he said nodding. He stood and took his plate to the sink, then back and he kissed her on the cheek. "Thanks for breakfast." He headed out the door and up the stairs. Alice still sat there eating. As she thought, he came back. She picked up the coffee cup and handed it to him.

"You should call her."

"Thanks," he said, taking the cup and walking back out to get himself ready for the Frosts.

Bruce parked in the last row in the small lot just outside the main gate. He walked up a few aisles before he had to walk back for his hat.

The sound of the gravel under his steps reminded him of the drive up to his grandmother's house. It also reminded him of the sound of fire.

There wasn't a very large crowd at the front gate since he was early. He mentioned Corey's name and flashed his badge so he was let through without any fuss or ticket. He wandered until he was headed down to the paddocks.

It was an odd mix of smells for Bruce – wet hay, sweaty horses and men, leather oil, the ocean and dirt. He watched one of the trainers (or that's who he thought the man was) walking by with a bucket of new horse shoes. Others were getting the horses ready for the starting gates and strapping on the saddle and putting on their silks so they could be matched up with their jockeys.

Bruce looked down and saw his shoes and bottom of his trousers were already covered in muck. He shrugged his shoulders and looked over as a horse neighed from its stable. Bruce smiled and walked over. He looked around before he extended his hand out for the horse to nuzzle it. He scratched the animal along its jaw and then up around its ears. It dropped its head and then flung it up so that it pushed Bruce back and almost knocked his hat off. He adjusted his hat and took a step forward towards the horse again.

For someone who didn't like horses, he had a way with them.

"I hope you weren't planning on placing a bet on her," Bruce heard behind him. He turned around and saw Corey Hayes standing in a light colored suit, white shirt and a hat...not a speck of dirt on him or his shoes.

"Figures," Bruce thought to himself. He looked back at the horse and continued to scratch the horse behind its ears.

"No, I couldn't pick one from the other. I didn't even know this was a girl."

"Well, you're not at the best angle to tell...I'm sure," he pointed at a colt being led down the path, "you would know that was a guy."

Bruce cocked his head, looked and laughed.

"Yes, sir," he said turning and extending his hand out, "Mr. Hayes."

He looked at his hand and sheepishly shrugged his shoulders knowing the horse had just slobbered all over it. Corey didn't think anything of it and took his hand and shook it. The horse leaned out and shoved Bruce. He turned around.

"She likes you," Corey said.

"Eh, I have an amazing affect on women like that. I should have known she was female."

"Come," Corey said extending his arm out, "it's almost time for the races to start. Walk with me."

Bruce gave the horse one more scratch and walked with Corey.

"I bet your better at picking a winner than you think."

"Really, I know nothing."

Corey pointed out a horse, jockey and trainer that were walking ahead.

"What about that one."

"I don't know. Who's she...he racing against," he said after checking the back of the horse.

Corey looked at him and smiled.

"Well, you always have to know what the competition looks like," Bruce told him.

"I've just never heard of anyone take that approach before."

"Oh...really?"

Corey looked ahead.

"He's racing against those four," he looked behind them, "and those two."

Bruce looked at the parade behind them and then turned to look at the ones in front.

"What do you think," Corey asked him, "is ours going to win?"

Bruce looked at him and shook his head.

"No," he looked again at the others. "I think that one," he said pointing to one further ahead, "will beat yours."

"Really, any particular reason why?"

"No," he said coyly, realizing the other belonged to the Frosts.

Corey made a note in his catalog

"You didn't come here to talk to me about horses though, did you," he asked as they walked closer to the grandstand.

"No, I didn't."

They approached the seating area and Corey put his arm up and waved. A young man came over and Corey whispered in his ear as he handed him several bills that Bruce could not tell what denomination they were.

They walked a little further and then Corey turned and leaned against the railing, almost blocking Bruce from moving in any direction. He pulled out what looked like an old rifle scope and looked back out over the track. Bruce studied him for a second and planned his strategy on the spot. Then the starting bell went off and he couldn't hear anything as the horses ran by.

"What happened with my dad," he asked after the crowd had died down.

Corey looked down, thought...and then nodded his head.

"Yes, I knew this day would come eventually. I'm sorry Bruce, but I don't know much. I had left the force shortly before all that happened."

"But, why did you leave," he asked to see what Corey's answer would be.

"It was personal...I'd had a death in the family and at the time...I wasn't going to recover."

"But you still heard things...you knew things. I remember you at the house before and after."

"I was so distraught with what had happened to me...I'm sorry...I really don't remember that much from then."

"Who was Bradley Farnham...besides the D.A.?"

"That was all."

Bruce didn't believe him.

"But he was there that night," Bruce said. "Why did he end up in county?"

"He was in a relationship with one of the whores from The Agate Club and killed her out of jealousy. Hacked her head off, he did..."

Bruce noticed his body tense and saw his eyes start to flicker behind him.

"Does he know something?"

"Not that I'm aware...especially not in his state," he said very quickly and then stopped, "it seems we're being hailed."

Bruce turned around as Corey walked back by him and touched his shoulder. Corey waved and Bruce looked in that direction.

As he expected, part of the extended Frost family was flagging Corey down and wanted him to bring Bruce to them.

"Come on", Corey said grabbing his shoulder and pushing him forward, "The Judge is in town. The drinks will be free."

Bruce walked up the steps and watched Corey nod at some of the Hollywood set that were down for the day. Bruce kept moving as Corey stopped to chat with Robert Taylor and Barbara Stanwyck. He wasn't interested in being introduced - not when he could make Kathlyn squirm.

He strolled into the seating area focused on her. She couldn't look at him.

"Bruce...or is it Andon...Rubidoux," Judge Frost said looking over at Kathlyn and extending out his hand.

Bruce shook it, "Even San Diego is too still too small...too many people know me as Bruce or Golpe. Nice to see you again Judge."

He turned to Cabot, "Senator Moran," he said extending out his hand.

Cabot took it and gripped it a little tighter than needed. "Bruce."

"How is your lovely sister," Judge Frost asked.

"Very much like my mother...who is also well."

Cabot turned to look at Kathlyn.

"You of course know my daughter..."

"Hello Kathlyn."

"Bruce."

"What brings you here," Judge Frost asked him.

"Mr. Hayes invited me up."

At that point Corey ran up the stairs to catch up.

"Sorry about that...it doesn't seem that you needed my help with introductions," he said looking at everyone.

The Judge turned to the woman sitting next to him.

"I don't think you've had the pleasure of meeting my wife, Beatrice though."

"No, I remember you from when I was little and we visited your home. I remember sneaking cookies from the kitchen. It's nice to meet you again," Bruce said.

"Nice to meet you again, Bruce. I was sorry to read about your brothers."

"Thank you," he said politely...and practiced.

He wondered how it might feel to live in a bubble like her.

"May we get you a libation, Son," Judge Frost asked him as a waiter walked up.

The word "Son" made him bridle and his jaw tense.

"Yes, please," he answered coolly, "I would love a rum and Coke."

They seemed surprised by his request. Then he realized they were probably used to his father who never drank in public. Everyone else ordered and the waiter disappeared to the club house.

"I'm sorry we haven't seen more of you..."

"You used to see Joe all the time. I guess one of us at a time wasn't enough," Bruce said.

"No," Cabot said coldly, "Kathlyn didn't let us know about Joe."

"He was a wily bloke."

"It looks like the race is about to start, Daddy," Kathlyn said looking out over the track – changing the subject.

"You put your money on our boy there didn't you," Judge Frost asked, trying to confirm with Corey that Bruce had. Corey shook his head.

"No, he picked another."

"And who did you pick, Corey," Cabot asked him as the boy Corey had given money to returned and handed Corey a piece of paper.

"Hopefully the winner."

"Have a seat Bruce," The Judge said, gesturing to the seat in front of him. He heard Corey make a sound and assumed that the Judge must have offered his seat to him. He sat down and the Judge patted him on the shoulder, but he didn't look.

The bell for the race went off and like a fire alarm there was an instant fervor of movement and yelling as people stood to see their horses run around the track. The volume of the grandstand grew as the yelling increased as if the people's shouts could propel their picks faster around the track and to the wire.

Bruce found himself caught up in the moment and he jumped in his seat and also started yelling at the one he remembered picking.

The noise and fervor increased as the horses rounded the last turn and headed for the finish line.

Once the horses crossed the line there was a mix of cheers and moans and a few tiny pieces of tickets floating in the air from the losers.

Even though his horse didn't win, Bruce was still quite pleased with the performance. He looked around to see only he, Corey and Cabot were the only one in the box standing. The Judge didn't look like he had moved at all. Kathlyn was smirking at him.

He saw the Judge look at Corey and Cabot and smiled crookedly then looked at Bruce. Bruce felt he should sit – and did.

"I'm sorry we haven't ever had a chance to really talk before," the Judge said. "I was very fond of your father, Bruce."

Bruce could feel the stares of Corey and Cabot boring through his back. He also saw Beatrice shift uncomfortably in her seat.

"I know many were. His death was a tragedy," the Judge continued.

At that point the waiter arrived and served then all their drinks.

"I remember you at our house that night and the funeral," Bruce said, taking a sip of his drink.

"Yes, I'm sorry I couldn't go to the gathering afterwards...under the circumstances."

"It was okay. You weren't the only one if I remember...Charlotte MacGreg..."

"Yes, we're famil...," Corey started to say, but something or someone cut him off.

Beatrice stiffened slightly.

"She gave your father his first job if I recall," Beatrice said.

"Yes, I have heard that," he said slowly and looked at the Judge who stared at him. Bruce realized the Judge had to have been a patron of the club.

"Well, you know, there wasn't much out there for boys with his background and a family in need," Bruce continued.

"Yes, but how many others from that family did something else," Beatrice said.

Judge Frost put his hand on her knee and she seemed to back down.

"No, but at least he tried to make good...considering what his upbringing was," he turned to look at Cabot and Corey, "and the obstacles he must have had to overcome or get around. You two knew him."

Cabot slapped him on the shoulder causing him to almost spill his drink.

"You're quick," he said and then looked over at Kathlyn, "why didn't you ever go out with him," Cabot said snidely.

Bruce saved her, "Because you told her she couldn't. I remember when we were kids you were always separating us."

Cabot conceded.

"What was it about your brother Joe then?"

Bruce laughed.

"He never listened to what my mother would tell him...you certainly weren't going to be any different."

Bruce took another sip of his drink.

"I'm curious, how do your jobs work. I mean, don't you both work out of Sacramento," Bruce asked the Judge and Cabot.

They both smiled.

"Yes," Judge Frost started, "However, it's not like a regular nine to five job. We do take breaks and vacations...and Cabot is in the Senate. Senators are not required to be present to vote on everything."

"Really," he looked at Cabot and said with a slight cheek, "But isn't that what the people vote you in to do?"

"Sometimes I take off to come back down here to get back with the people and understand what they want."

"Huh," Bruce said matter-of-factly.

"I need to do that since I am voted in," he motioned to the Judge, "Uncle Charles here is appointed for a twelve year term."

"Wow, here I am a servant of the people and I know so little. I'm a little ashamed. Twelve years a Head Judge…

"It's Chief Justice," Corey corrected him.

"Chief Justice," Bruce nodded in fake gratitude then he looked back at the Judge.

"I am only an Associate Justice," Judge Frost corrected.

"For twelve years," he asked.

"It depends, I can be voted in to stay another twelve."

"How do you get to be 'Chief Justice'?"

"Well you're appointed."

"Can the old one just be ousted?"

"He either has to step down or retire or," he stopped.

"Or?"

"You were in the war. I'm sure you know about battlefield promotions."

"So, he has to die?"

The Judge nodded.

"I don't see them stepping down that often. It's a little bit like being a cardinal and waiting for the Pope to die isn't it? Some of those guys in red die waiting around for the Pope to kick it."

He heard Cabot clear his throat."

"I would imagine that would be really frustrating."

"It can be," the Judge agreed.

"I have an idea of what you do," he said to Cabot then he looked at Cory, "Not so sure about you, but what do you do…exactly," he asked the Judge.

"We are split up into two different departments. I oversee a lot of different cases and as a whole we also get to ratify the State bar."

Bruce cocked his head.

This was about to go in a direction he was not expecting.

He took another sip.

"I did not know that," he said wagging his finger, "There's been something interesting that has come up at work recently…tell me, if you had a lawyer…more specifically a D.A.

that was committed to a mental institute...would you disbar him?"

Bruce felt the air around him tense.

"It would depend upon why he had been committed. Alone, it would bring any case he tried or document he filed into question."

"What if it was murder?"

"We should save this for another time," Cabot said nodding towards Beatrice and Kathlyn.

"It's a good mystery. Hell...sorry...I know it interests Kathlyn. She was always reading Nancy Drew and Detective Comics."

"I don..."

"In fact, I think you know who I'm talking about," Bruce continued belligerently, "You were a judge down here when Bradley Farnham was district attorney. He was even a clerk in your law offices wasn't he?"

By the direction the Judge was looking, Bruce knew he was looking at Corey.

"That was a tragedy."

"Yes it was," he said and looked into his glass, "but what if he didn't do it?"

"What," both Cabot and Charles Miller Frost said.

"Honestly, what if he didn't do it. Her death was really similar to the one my dad was investigating. From what I've heard, the hacking," he considered the ladies in the group...well more Beatrice since he knew Kathlyn's curiosity, "Let's just say it looked like the same weapon could have been used for both."

The Judge looked towards his wife, who sat straight in her seat. None of them noticed that the races continued below them.

"And," Bruce continued, "I don't know where else to go from here. There are a lot of interesting things about this; especially, from a psychological point of view. Apparently he loved this woman... in spite of what she was...and the crime, even one of passion, might fit the brutality of how she was found, but never where and in the state she was found. You knew him," he said looking at the Judge, "and you seem to be a very astute and intelligent man..."

The Judge said nothing, but Cabot interjected.

"What's your point, Bruce?"

"Did you know...did he say anything...ever to you about this?"

The Judge seemed as though he was studying Bruce and slowly gave him his answer.

"No, he was a very private man. I couldn't even tell you what kind of car he drove."

Bruce leaned back in his seat.

"Well, I guess that's another mystery that won't be solved...like my dad's murder."

"Why is that," Kathlyn asked.

"Well, I went to go look up Bradley Farnham at the county mental hospital. He's no longer there. He's no longer anywhere. They have no record of where he went. He seems to have vanished into thin air."

Bruce slowly finished his drink, feeling the air about him and stood up.

"I apologize. I've been a bit of a bore and spoken out of turn. I should go. Thank you very much for your hospitality."

"We'll make sure you receive an invite for the Charity Ball. We'll send one for your mother and sister as well," Beatrice said as he leaned forward and shook her hand and then the Judge's.

"Thank you, I'll see if I can get them out of the house for a change," he said, thinking more of Megan than Alice.

He shook Cabot's hand as he made his way out of the box.

"Thank you for the drink," he said to all of them as he started to pass Corey and shake his hand.

"You're right," Corey said, "You're not very good at picking winners."

"Oh," Bruce said grinning, "my horse did exactly what I said it was going to. It beat yours."

He walked down the steps back in the direction he had come. He turned to take one more look at the family. Judge Frost and Cabot stared at him, Beatrice was expressionless, Corey looked nervous and Kathlyn looked...concerned.

There was another important piece that Bruce had gathered. There was something the Judge had told him without saying anything.

Where to look for Bradley Farnham.

21.

FINDING A OPOSSUM

It was a couple of weeks before Bruce could get the time and appointment to visit with Bradley Farnham, who had been committed to the city's hospital several months after his arrest and Tom's murder. It took Bruce awhile to hunt him down though. Farnham had been relocated to the Rabbit Grove Sanitarium some time in 1941.

Bruce landed early in the morning and rented a car and headed out to the facility.

On the drive up to Rabbit Grove Bruce could understand the allure of having a mental facility there. It was peaceful and calming and green. He imagined there was probably a small lake or fountain for the patients to sit around and "be soothed" like he had read in novels and seen in movies.

Bruce thought the driveway, building and surrounding grounds looked more like a vacation destination than a mental facility. It was a slightly different feeling once he opened the main door. The foyer was completely empty. There were some seats and couches that must have been the reception or waiting area. All the walls were white and very pristine and the tile floors were brown. As he let the front door close it echoed so loudly it sounded like a cannon going off. The whole thing had a very sterile feeling about it.

Bruce stood still in the same place, afraid of what his footsteps would sound like. He looked around for any sign of life, but there wasn't anyone one around.

He didn't have to wait for long for someone to appear...well a little while.

From somewhere far he heard the methodical rhythm of footsteps. The problem was he couldn't decipher from which of the three directions the person was coming.

And then his mind got the better of him...what if it was one of the patients?

The footsteps started to get closer. It made Bruce think of the times he had put his ear to the hose and turned the water on and waited for the water to come out.

It always seemed like it took the water forever.

A man in slacks, shirt, tie and white jacket appeared at the end of the main hall and walked closer to Bruce. Bruce thought he looked like he was one of the doctors, but Bruce was still leery about the security and had a thought that this could still be a "loose" patient impersonating a doctor. He looked around as he approached Bruce and extended his hand, making Bruce even more hesitant.

"Detective Rubi...," he asked as they shook hands and he looked at a note, "...docks."

"Close enough," Bruce said relaxing, "It's dough...Rubi-dough."

"I'm sorry."

"It's no problem, it happens all the time."

The doctor also looked around.

"I'm also sorry no one was here at the receptionist desk."

He looked in the direction of a small window with a grate in front of it.

"I hadn't made it that far," Bruce said looking at the grate. He wondered how anyone could even tell if anyone was even sitting behind the grate.

"This way," the doctor said heading back in the direction he had just come. Bruce followed.

"Mr. Farnham doesn't get many visitors," the doctor said.

"But he does get visitors," Bruce asked curiously.

"Yes, every so often."

The doctor laughed a little bit.

"What's so funny," Bruce wanted to know.

"I was just thinking back on the visits I've seen. Mr. Farnham never looks happy to see these people. He always looks like he's trying to avoid them. I've actually seen him get up from his bench and walk away in the opposite direction from them as soon as he knows they've arrived."

"Are they men or women?"

"Two men; although, I've seen a woman here every once in a while. Usually about once a year...and before you ask me...I don't know their names. I thought you might ask me and I went back through the sign-in sheets. It seems they've never signed in."

Bruce wasn't that surprised, he'd already seen the lack of security, but he still asked.

"Isn't that a little disconcerting? What person could just walk in?"

"Well," the doctor, "not that many. You'll see."

Bruce saw immediately what the doctor was talking about as soon as they turned the corner. There was only one way outside and blocking it was a locked gate. There was a very large uniformed security guard on the other side.

"Hello Doctor," the guard greeted them.

The big man waited and didn't move until the doctor produced and showed him his credentials. He nodded and then took out a set of keys and the doctor also removed a set from his pocket. A door unlocked and opened to the side and an attendant came out and unlocked the lock from their side and then Bruce could see there was one more lock slightly higher that the guard put a key in and turned. The metal door opened. Both men repeated the procedure as Bruce and the doctor continued through the hall and out the door to the garden.

"Down there," the doctor pointed down to a bench sitting in front of a small lake.

Bruce laughed to himself.

"Thanks," he said and headed down the lawn to the bench. He looked around at some of the other patients and thought how catatonic they all seemed. They moved as if they were in slow motion and all their limbs were limited with how far they could move.

He thought it was very eerie to watch and felt that was probably why there wasn't a lot of security. He stopped to look around for more security and heard the faint hum of an electric fence. He looked at the shrubs and realized where the fence was hidden. He turned back around and continued to stroll down the hill.

There was a lone figure on one the benches and as Bruce got closer he noticed the man just stared off towards the lake but didn't seem aware. He started to doubt that this was such a good idea. If Bradley Farnham was also medicated, or worse, he might not be coherent enough to talk to Bruce about anything.

The man didn't move as Bruce approached. He was dressed in modified prison pants and shirt and a robe. He had slippers on for footwear. He looked as if he didn't have a care in the world. If it wasn't for how he was dressed, he could have been a man on vacation simply enjoying the view.

Bruce thought he must have been older than Tom, but not as old as Judge Frost. He had the thinness of someone who was institutionalized, but didn't show the strain or wear that many did.

"Mr. Farnham," Bruce said, moving more in line with Bradley's line of vision.

Bradley continued to stare out over the lake. Bruce continued to stand there unsure of what he should do or say next.

Bradley slowly turned and looked up at Bruce.

"Tom," he asked.

"No sir, I'm his son, Bruce."

I smile spread across Bradley's face.

"Of course you are. For a minute there I thought I'd seen a ghost. You look like him a bit."

"I don't get that very often."

"Really?"

"No," he said shaking his head.

Bradley stared at him for a minute.

"Would you like to sit," he said offering Bruce the empty space next to him. "It's very rare I have someone sit with me."

He looked back to the lake and then laughed to himself.

"Well someone I've wanted to sit next to me."

"Thank you," Bruce said as he sat.

Bruce looked at him a little puzzled.

"You don't seem as...well...sedate as some of your co...bunk mates," Bruce said.

"I learned very early how not to take any medication. Contrary to what they all think and what they were told and what my file says...I am not crazy."

"Don't they check your mouths," Bruce asked.

"There are other places to hide small pills. After the first week they figure they have you under control and they don't bother wasting their time. The other ones that seem harmless have had the front of their brains scrambled."

"I believe the procedure is a frontal lobotomy," Bruce said.

The lake reminded Bruce of the lakes in Europe he had seen during the war. He never took the chance to enjoy them or never could.

"When I was just out of college I traveled through Europe. I stayed in this little town called Vevey in Switzerland. It was on Lake Geneva."

"Does this one remind you of it...on a smaller scale?"

"No, not really."

"Oh."

"It makes me think of that time though...before I returned home and sold my soul to Satan himself...Judge Charles Miller Frost."

He turned and studied Bruce and then back at the lake.

"That is why you're here, is it not?"

"You're not crazy," Bruce said as a half-question.

"No, but then a crazy man might tell you that to try to persuade you."

"But you've been interred for almost...twenty years."

"It was either this or be killed."

Bruce looked at him in disbelief.

"Come on Bruce. You should know better than most."

Bruce let what Bradley had said sink in. Bradley looked at him again.

"Just exactly what do you do," he said studying Bruce, "It's not like the white coats to let anybody; especially a likely stranger."

"I showed them my badge."

"Of course," Bradley said.

"You didn't kill, the hooker..."

"Well, that's a difference between you and your father."

"Excuse me?"

"Her name was Evelyn."

"You loved her," Bruce said bluntly.

Bradley didn't answer and turned back out to look at the lake.

"It was a long time ago," he said.

"You've been in here a long time," Bruce said thinking for a second. "You were also accused of killing the records clerk. How did they build a case against you for that?"

"The said I had lost my mind and was so distraught I killed a woman who looked like Evelyn."

He snorted.

"She didn't look anything like my Evelyn."

Bruce looked down at his shoes.

"It all seems very feeble to me."

"It was a different time...a few men with all the power and money. I imagine it's a little similar now. I did lose my mind that night, but there was nothing I could do. I went there looking for Charles. I forgot he was at the concert in the park. Hell, the whole town was there...of course he would have been there playing his part. Captain Moran himself came down to see what the ruckus was."

"And my father followed him..."

Bradley looked at him.

"I'm sorry about that. They were scared of him. They thought he might ruin Cabot's future."

"Did Cabot Moran kill my father?"

"I'm not sure...I'm pretty sure, but Rufus was an excellent marksman as well...so was Corey. I could never tell what Rufus thought about your father. Then again, I don't think Charlotte would have let him."

"My father," he hesitated, "thought Cabot was the killer."

Bradley smirked at him

"*That* is like Tom. Very shrewdly played Bruce."

Bruce didn't say anything.

"Don't you mean he knew?"

"What do you know?"

Bradley looked around to make sure no one was watching them.

"Cabot was definitely capable of...something that brutal time and time again. He was a sick little boy. I'd seen what he had done to animals. He beat up on little children and even adults he felt were weaker than him. He used to beat up on Corey...like that poor kid needed any more abuse. His father used to beat him...and then to have your only playmate torture you. Charles had me cover more stuff up than I would like to remember. I'm ashamed of some of the things I did for that family."

"You were the D.A.," Bruce said.

"Exactly," he said, "But there was something even more sinister about Cabot when he returned from the war. He had this confidence...no, cockiness that I've only seen people have when they've gotten away with something. He did something during the war and I have a feeling he was given medals for it."

"Whatever happened to his wife?"

"Kathlyn's mother? I don't know. They went on a trip and she supposedly died, but there was never a funeral."

"He killed her."

"More than likely, at least that's what I think."

"If you knew, why didn't you ever do anything," Bruce asked.

"I told you, I sold my soul to the devil. The one time I tried to do something I was paid back in kind. When everything you have and love is taken away you will do anything out of being beaten from the inside and out."

Bruce thought for a minute.

"Evelyn."

Bradley nodded, "Although she contributed to her own death. She made the mistake of doing the right thing by helping your father."

Bruce looked out over the lake and tried to process everything.

"I loved Evelyn, but a man in my position and Charles'...they couldn't be a part of our world...at least that's what I thought. I was wrong."

"There's something missing...a tiny piece," he thought aloud.

"No, not so tiny."

Bradley smirked at him. Bruce knew that he was not going to tell him.

"I cannot tell you. I've already told you enough."

"You knew the girl, the one my father's cousins were convicted of killing," Bruce said.

"I knew who she was."

"Did you help cover up the murders?"

"No...well not directly, I think...I wouldn't be here if I had."

"What...why are you still covering for them?"

Bradley stood up, looked around and then looked at Bruce.

"I've already done enough damage. Whoever they have watching me here will have already told them that you were here and that I actually talked to you. If I tell you, you won't dig deep enough to get them all," he looked around again, "Do you know who Charlotte MacGregor is?"

Bruce almost started laughing.

"Yes, I know who she is."

"Start with her."

"What do I ask her?"

"You're a smart man. You'll figure it out"

Bradley turned and walked towards the lake. Bruce stood up and started walking back to the main building understanding that the conversation was over. Out of the corner of his eye he saw some of the attendants walk from the side of the building and down towards Bradley's direction.

Bruce continued walking into the building, through the guards and gates and down through the halls and out the front door.

22.

AN ALLY

Bruce arrived back home in the early evening. He dropped his bag by his desk and walked into the kitchen. Taking a cue from his grumbling stomach, he opened the refrigerator and found a note on top of a plate of cold chicken and mashed potatoes.

He read the note as he took the chicken off the plate and took a bite.

> *B-*
> *Out with Tim*

Tim – who was Tim?

> *Mom is playing bridge at the Callahan's.*
> *Kathlyn stopped by.*
> *Call Terry and come meet us.*
> *A*

He smirked.

She was determined to find somebody for him.

Right now he was feeling a little guilty about leaving Bradley Farnham to certain ramifications for speaking to him.

He went back to the front room opened his bag and took out the file. He started to drop it on his desk and saw the piece of paper with Terry's phone number.

Alice must have left it for him.

He dropped the file on top of it and flipped it open.

Bradley Farnham had basically told him nothing except that he knew a whole lot of something that he wasn't going to share with Bruce. Bruce did know he was going to take Bradley's suggestion and pay a visit to Charlotte MacGregor: partly because Bradley said so and partly because he was curious.

Bruce sat down and pulled out a pad of paper, turned it around so it was horizontal and drew lines down to create four columns. At the top he wrote Suzanne (Phelps?), Evelyn, Records clerk, Dad, JD221. He stared at it a while and crumbled up the paper and repeated the process but instead of writing "Dad" he wrote "Tom".

On the left side he wrote "who was convicted", who probably really did it (he resisted the temptation to write Cabot's initials under all four), what the weapon was and any evidence there might have been. He flipped through the file and pulled out the information he needed. He had to go off of memory and things he heard when it came to Tom's column.

He realized that Evelyn and Tom's columns were more closely related because of The Agate Club. He couldn't see how the other two could have been tied to it. He could have kicked himself when he realized he didn't ask Bradley how Evelyn had helped Tom...but Bradley knew that she had. She must have told him.

Oh well, there wasn't anything he could do about it right at that minute.

There wasn't much else to add under the "Record's Clerk" which he crossed out and put "Meredith".

There was much more under Suzanne.

She was the only one with evidence.

Quickly, Bruce jotted down "matchbook" and "potato sack".

He hoped that they were still stored in the evidence locker, but he knew a lot of evidence had gone "missing" (as he liked to say) in the move.

He stared at everything again hoping something would tell him what he needed. All he could hope for was if he solved Suzanne's murder that it would solve the rest as well.

San Diego's crime had Bruce exceptionally busy over the next several weeks. He didn't have time to go down to evidence storage and the only communication he had with Megan and Alice was through the notes they left on his cold meals.

He found himself working more and more with the M.P.'s from the sub base, docks and the Marines north at Camp Pendleton.

He was filling out his most recent report involving a shooting of a young sailor who was armed with a knife. For some reason the young man thought it was in his best interest to flail his arms around with it with a good number of police aall aiming their guns at him..

Bruce thought it was in the young man's best interest and everyone around for him to shoot him.

He only injured the man, shooting him in the leg.

That had been one of the hardest adjustments Bruce had to make from the war…

Shoot to disarm, not to kill.

Although, in his mind it always played back to him as "shoot to kill…not disarm."

"Do you have a minute Andon," he heard the Captain over him. Bruce looked up. "Let's take a walk."

Bruce recapped his pen, stood and followed the Captain. He followed him outside and Bruce waited for the Captain to start talking.

When they stopped at the door to the local pub, he cringed and opened the door, remembering he had left his wallet in his desk drawer at the precinct.

The Captain walked to a table in the back.

Bruce looked around and realized not too many people could see them there.

"Have a seat Dux," the Captain said.

He started to talk as he took his seat and the waitress walked up.

"Sir, I was expecting a walk...not a stop. I left my wallet back at the office."

The Captain looked at him and grinned, "Of course you did. My usual," he said to the waitress.

He nodded at Bruce and when she looked at him he said, "Scotch on the rocks, please."

"Two scotches: one on the rocks and one neat," the waitress said as she left.

Bruce didn't have to wait long for the Captain to start talking, although it wasn't what had brought him there.

"Tell me," the Captain started, "how did you get through the war without forgetting your gun?"

"Everything was strapped to us in one way or another."

"Nevertheless, if you weren't so good at what you do I might have to put a disciplinary action in your file. One of these days you're going to forget your gun going to the wrong call and you're going to get yourself shot...or killed. And that would make for a lot of paperwork for me."

"I'm sure my safety isn't what concerns you enough to bring me here."

"I received an interesting phone call today."

"Really?"

"Yes...would you like to tell me what you're working on that would cause Senator Moran to call me and...well, bribe and threaten me?"

"What," Bruce said feeling the urge to laugh.

"Don't worry – I think he is a colossal prick and I told him to go fuck himself," the Captain said seeming proud of his self. "Hell, I didn't vote for him."

Bruce thought about what he could tell the Captain.

"Just to let you know," he started to tell Bruce, "I come here for 'unofficial' business."

Bruce smirked and nodded his head.

"You were on the force when Dad was alive," Bruce asked.

"Yes, I was a rookie. You're not looking into his murder are you?"

Bruce looked at him quizzically.

"Not directly, but why do *you* think that would make Moran...shall we say 'interested'?"

Bruce thought that the Captain knew he had slipped somewhat.

"Let's say there was talk...amongst the ranks when I first joined the force."

"Okay."

"It was more in regards to Captain Moran and his son..."

"Cabot, the Senator."

"Yes, since that was his only child."

"Good point."

"There were rumors that Cabot was the one who killed the Captain and inadvertently your dad...maybe."

Bruce pondered that for a moment.

"Cabot was overheard arguing with the Captain a few days before everything went down. The only part of the conversation I heard was remembered was that Cabot told the Captain 'If you can't handle him, I'll have my father take care of it.'"

"What?!"

"Exactly."

"And?"

"Files from records were missing and they didn't make copies back then."

"The woman from records..."

"Meredith."

Bruce didn't continue.

"She was murdered," the Captain said for him, "your father had gone down there a week or so before his murder and requested something. She wrote his name down in the log, but never wrote down what it was he asked for."

The Captain looked at him as if he was hoping Bruce had the missing information.

"I haven't seen *that* file," Bruce said.

"Exactly what file have you seen," the Captain asked.

"Apparently," he said slowly, "the missing one. The one my dad was working on when he was killed, but there isn't anything...there's photos and reports from Meredith's death, but nothing in regards to Cabot Moran."

"Are you sure?"

"Very."

The Captain thought for a moment.

"The Jane Doe case your father was working on," he asked.

"Yes."

The Captain studied him.

"It's more than that...isn't it."

Bruce didn't move.

"How deep into this are you?"

Bruce thought for a second. He had basically already handed everything over to the Captain there wasn't anything really left to hide if he needed more help.

And he was going to need help to get warrants to gather the proof he needed.

"I've been to see Bradley Farnham and I also believe there may be connection to a girl named Suzanne and the Jane Doe. There's lots of entries on the Jane Doe and my dad wrote the name 'Suzanne' in one of the margins on the JD paperwork."

"Suzanne Phelps...shit...you're up to your ears then aren't you?"

Bruce thought for a moment.

"I really have no idea."

23.

UNCOMFORTABLE

Bruce thought about his conversation with the Captain as he dressed for the Charity Ball. He had disregarded the Frosts' casual invite at the races and had actually completely forgotten about it until the tickets arrived on his desk via messenger.

There were four: one for him, Alice, Megan (?) and a date...but for whom?

Alice counted out differently.

"Me, you, my date and your date," she said matter-of-factly.

Bruce stared at her as he looked at the tickets in his hand, perplexed.

"Fine," she amended, rolling her eyes, "Me, you, my date and Mom."

Bruce frowned at her.

"You do remember I was the one who got the tickets?"

"Yes," she nodded.

Who was he trying to fool? Of course he was going to give two to Alice...and the other to Megan.

Alice was disappointed with his final decision.

"I'm telling you B, you should find a date."

"Mom will be my date; besides, I don't think Kathlyn would appreciate me showing up with someone other than her."

"What makes you so certain she won't be there with anyone?"

"Just a gut feeling."

"Uh huh," Alice said skeptically, "if I recall, your 'gut feelings' are usually way off."

"Do I hear a wager...say five dollars."

She glared at him.

"You're on," she said enthusiastically.

He read the tickets again to see the date and time.

"Suit yourself then. A date would be very entertaining," she said smirking at him.

"What would be entertaining," Megan asked as she came in from the backyard. She went to the sink to wash her hands.

There was another reason Bruce wanted Megan to go. Over the last few months, since he called her about the file, she had seemed distant and she seemed to look confused, like she wanted to talk to him about it, but didn't dare.

"Bruce received tickets from the Frosts for the Charity Ball...four of them."

Megan looked at Bruce as if she wanted to know how this had come about.

"So, I get two and Bruce is giving you the fourth. I was trying to get him to ask someone else...."

"And you would go unescorted," Megan asked.

Alice ignored the insinuation.

"...so he can make Kathlyn jealous."

"You should ask someone else," Megan said coldly, "You have no business associating with Kathlyn Moran. I didn't like you boys ever being around her and never forgave Joe for dating her after I asked him not to."

Alice was taken aback, but Bruce was used to this reaction from her when it came to conversations involving Kathlyn and any of the Frosts...but Kathlyn in particular.

"You will come, won't you," Bruce asked her.

"Please Mom," Alice added, "we haven't done anything like this since...well it's been a really long time."

Megan looked at the two of them and finally surrendered by nodding her head.

"Yes, I will go."

Alice and Bruce smiled, making her decision worth it.

"We haven't been shopping together in a long time Mom. This will be fun."

Bruce had sent a "thank you" note addressed to Justice and Mrs. Frost. He had to rewrite the whole thing when he realized he had only put "Judge". This, he figured, would tip his hand and let Kathlyn know he was planning on attending.

He wasn't sure how he felt about that.

He went back into the bathroom to check is bow tie. Not surprisingly, it was crooked. Tugging on one side and then the other didn't seem to work; so, he untied it and tried a few more times before he got it to where he thought it was acceptable and walked downstairs.

Megan and Alice turned to look at him and Alice started giggling.

"What," Bruce asked.

"Usually tuxedos are supposed to make men look more attractive."

"Alice," Megan scolded her.

"Mom, have you ever seen someone who looked more miserable?"

Bruce frowned and Megan let out a sigh.

"Son, she has a point. Come here," she said reaching out to him. He took a step and stood in front of her and she undid his tie and retied it. "Your father always had a problem with these as well."

Bruce's mind had wandered.

"There," Megan said stepping back to look at her work.

"Better," Alice said, nodding in approval, "But he still looks miserable."

Megan reached forward and put her hand on his cheek and he looked at her.

"You look very handsome," she said and then looked at Alice, "besides, haven't you read...brooding movie stars are in."

Bruce realized she knew something was on his mind; but, like always, she didn't prod, she didn't ask...she never asked.

"Shall we wait for your date to arrive," Bruce turned and asked Alice.

She looked at him, taken off guard by his terseness. She looked at Megan for guidance; but again, like usual, she left Alice to make her own decisions.

"No," she said slowly, "I'll meet you there."

He nodded and turned to Megan, "Ready?"

Megan nodded, walked towards the door and stopped to give Alice a kiss on her forehead.

"You look beautiful, Sweetheart."

"Thank you Mom," she beamed.

Bruce absent-mindedly started to walk out the door behind Megan. He hadn't even held the door for her, which caused a look of suspicion from both women. Megan turned and glared at him. He stop in his tracks and took in what she was trying to say and he turned around as Megan walked to his car.

"You really are breathtaking tonight," he said in all sincerity to Alice.

She believed him, but knew better.

"What's going on Bubba?" She studied him. "This is more than a fun night out, isn't it?"

He looked down at the seat that Megan usually read in and then slowly looked up. He knew she was concerned by the name she called him. It was her morphing of "brother" from when she was little, which also made remember painfully there had been two other "Bubbas". He also remembered what he was getting into and their conversation months before at the Grant.

"You don't want to know," he said sternly.

"This has to do with that file..."

"Alice, you are beautiful," he smiled and shut the door.

Bruce stood in the foyer of the Hotel Del Coronado taking in all the ornate, mahogany banisters and archways. A mixed smell of ocean air, orange oil and wood permeated his senses and added to the scene. He walked to the railing of the main staircase and raised his hand up and ran it down the banister as if he was trying to sense a memory or a feeling through the wood.

What was he doing here?

There was a mix of emotions he thought he felt; but, being so out of tune with who he was made it hard for him to decipher what it was he was thinking…and feeling. It wasn't like him to think about emotions, but he was trying to focus on the file and what he needed to do and Kathlyn.

And finally the obvious struck him.

"Bruce," Megan said, startling him. She took his arm. "It's in the main ballroom."

He nodded his head and they started walking. He kept replaying in his mind what questions he needed answered and how could he get them answered…

…and who would answer them.

Corey.

He was the weak link.

Bruce already knew that.

As did the Frosts.

But Bruce had a skill very much like his father had…he had a way with older women.

Beatrice Frost.

I slight smirk tugged at the corner of his mouth when he thought about this, and his mother must have caught on to something.

"Bruce, I don't know the real reason you accepted the invitation. I would, begrudgingly, like to think it was for Kathlyn, but I saw that look too many times in your father's eyes. You're up to something…don't embarrass us. I've sacrificed too much to get us where we are."

Bruce scowled and looked at her as they approached the ballroom door.

"And just where is that," he said, regretting the sarcasm as soon as it left his mouth.

"Don't be smart. I will trust that you know what you are doing," she added as she nodded at someone she knew. "Have fun…and don't forget, don't drink too much I'm expecting you to remember I'm planning on driving home with you."

They stopped at the table just outside the door.

"Bruce and Megan Rubidoux," he said to the woman checking guests in.

"Thank you, have a lovely evening," she said.

Megan let go of his arm as they walked through the doorway.

And then she gave him one more parting comment. "Behave yourself."

He nodded his head with a small smirk playing on his lips.

"I mean it," she said before walking to a couple and greeted them as if she was one of the chairpersons.

He stood in the doorway for a minute surveying the room.

Immediately he spotted the bar, but disregarded it since he knew he had to keep his wits about him.

To the far right of the room he saw most of the old guard and to the left were some of the "new money" society members. In between the two were the Frosts holding court...including Kathlyn.

Bruce watched her and she greeted everyone with a sincere smile and shook their hands very delicately and pleasantly.

As soon as they stepped away it was another story.

Bruce couldn't put his finger on it, but she looked bored and even...frustrated.

He saw Cabot put his hand on the small of her back and leaned forward into the next guest.

Bruce wasn't sure if he had caught what just happened.

She had stiffened against Cabot's touch.

Bruce cut his way around towards the Frosts, greeting people he knew and taking introductions where he didn't.

Most only knew him because of Tom and it seemed Tom knew everybody.

Bruce's hand was beginning to cramp by the time he reached the Frosts.

"Bruce," Judge Frost said extending his hand out, "Good evening. I'm glad you could make it."

"Good evening sir," he said returning the hand shake, "I'm glad we could make it. Thank you again."

"You look lovely tonight Mrs. Frost," he said taking Beatrice's hand and flirting slightly.

"Well thank you very much Bruce. You look very handsome tonight as well."

"I'd like to take all the credit for that, but my sister and mother helped me."

"Yes, well sometimes it takes a woman's touch."

"Senator...Corey," he said shaking their hands.

"Your mother came as your date, did she not," Beatrice asked.

"Yes she did."

She exchanged a look with Corey.

"She's somewhere near the door. I don't think she moved very far. She seems to know a lot of people."

"We've tried to get her to come for years," the Judge said.

"Really, I did not know that."

"You know Kathlyn does not have an escort this evening Bruce," Beatrice said.

"Is that a fact?"

Kathlyn looked at his chest.

"And, to be honest with you I think she's a bit bored," she added leaning towards Bruce. "I think she'd have more fun on the dance floor. Would you mind giving her a break?"

"Not at all."

He took a step towards Kathlyn and held his hand out.

"Would you like to dance?"

Reluctantly, she took his hand and they walked to the dance floor.

He spun her around before taking her in his arms, causing the hint of a smile start to form at the corners of her mouth.

She looked up at him.

"Don't look so pleased with yourself," she said.

He couldn't stop grinning. He felt like he was going to win the battle.

Turning them a bit he looked over her head so he could assess everyone's reactions, especially the Frost men.

Corey's looked slightly pale, the Judge's apprehensive and Cabot....well, Cabot's face was a deep, reddish purple.

"I do believe your father just might explode," he whispered in her ear.

He turned so she could see. She looked and then turned her heard and smiled.

"You're bad," she said to him.

"Admit it, you missed me," he teased her.

"I never said I didn't. I was just accustomed to missing you in the same room."

"You made your choice."

"And, you made yours. You never had the balls to go against my father or uncle. What did they promise you?"

"Excuse me?"

"For your future...their offer must have been too juicy for you to decline."

"I'm not sure I understand."

"Your college fund..."

"What? You have your facts all twisted around."

Bruce saw Megan walk over to an elderly couple and sat down next to the wife. He saw her take the woman's hand in hers and it looked like she was comforting her. Then he caught Corey out of the corner of his eye start walking to the couple.

"Daddy and Uncle offered to pay for your education and you took it."

"Is that what they told you?"

"Not in so many words."

"I stayed away because after your father caught us he threatened my life and my mother screamed...I mean screamed at me. She never so much as raised her voice to me until that night. I stayed away for fear of bodily harm...and in two weeks you were with Joe."

He blinked.

"What do you mean 'not in so many words'?"

The song stopped they parted and clapped and then started dancing again.

"I overheard them one morning at breakfast. They were discussing all of you. They said something along the lines of your education being taken care of and you could go anywhere you wanted. Then they said something about a deal."

"They never talked to me."

He saw Megan stand and it looked like she was now talking to Corey.

She didn't look happy.

Bruce felt a tug on his arm.

"B...sorry Kat," Alice said.

"Hello Alice," Kathlyn greeted.

Alice looked at him urgently and her date looked very confused.

"What…oh, hey I'm Alice's brother Bru…"

Alice cut him off.

"That's them," she said nodding towards Megan.

Bruce leaned down so she could talk softer. She leaned up.

"That's the couple Daddy was talking to that night."

Bruce stood up and looked in Megan's direction again.

It wasn't clicking.

"When Daddy pinched me," Alice said impatiently.

It clicked.

"Excuse me," he said as he let go of Kathlyn and walked towards Megan. As he got closer he saw Corey had a grip on her arm, but she was being very calm, even though the grip looked tight.

"Mother…"

"Bruce," she said surprised and relieved. "You remember Mr. Hayes."

"I'm very acquainted with Mr. Hayes."

Corey let go of Megan's arm.

"And, these are the Phelpses," she said indicating the older couple. "This is my oldest son, Bruce."

Alice, her date and Kathlyn were now standing behind Bruce.

"Nice to meet you."

"This is my daughter, Alice."

Alice smiled and nodded her head, "Nice to meet you," she said softly.

"But we've met before," Mrs. Phelps said, "Your father was holding you and, if I remember correctly, he had to leave because you were crying."

"Yes, I remember that," Alice said.

"This is Corey Hayes, Alice," Megan said looking at Alice curiously.

Alice held out her hand and Corey took and squeezed it.

"You look very much like your grandmother."

"Thank you."

Bruce looked at her.

He'd never heard that one before.

No way did Alice look like the Wicked Witch of the North.

Megan cleared her throat.

Bruce stopped his train of thought and realized the rest of the Frosts had joined them.

"Hello Cabot...Judge, Beatrice," Megan rattled off.

Beatrice stepped forward and gave Megan a hug.

Bruce knew he looked confused.

"It's so good to see you again," Beatrice said.

"We told Bruce we've been trying to get you to come to this event for years," the Judge added.

Meanwhile, the Phelpses had just sat there and watched everything as if they had been watching a tennis match.

"I'm sorry to say, but our reunion will have to wait for another time. We were just leaving," Megan said.

"What," Bruce said out loud and surprised.

"But thank you. I appreciate the invitation and the opportunity to get out and socialize again," Megan added.

She turned to look at her driver.

"Bruce?"

He looked at her, then everyone else.

"Thank you very much."

"We hope to see you again Bruce."

"Yes, me too." He looked at his sister. "Alice...and..."

"Doug," Alice's date answered.

"Yes, thank you," Alice said and they left.

Bruce turned just as they were walking out the doorway. Beatrice and Kathlyn were talking and the men were glaring at Bruce and his exiting party.

"Who are the Phelpses," Bruce broke the silence in the car.

"It's a shame Alice and her date had to leave," Megan said, ignoring Bruce.

"They didn't have to; besides, Alice goes out enough. It's not going to kill her. Now, please answer my question."

Megan continued to look out the side window.

"If you don't tell me then I will tell you what I know."

She still didn't say anything.

"Daddy talked them that night he was killed...right before he left us."

Silence.

"Whatever they said upset him enough that he felt he had to use Alice as an excuse to get away from them and leave us."

He was about to continue – with what he didn't know since he was out of facts – when he heard Megan take a deep breath.

"Their daughter disappeared a few months before your father died. She was never found."

Bruce listened intently.

"She was adopted."

"Did Dad know her?"

"As children...yes."

"But..."

"No 'buts'...it's presumed she was murdered because she wasn't the type of girl to just walk away and not tell a soul."

"Daddy knew it was her in the burlap sack."

He felt her turn and look at him.

"Yes."

"Do the Phelpses know?"

"No."

"You held her hand like you were comforting her."

"I was, Bruce."

Bruce frowned, thinking.

"I know what it's like to lose a loved one...and a child. Sometimes just knowing makes a difference."

"Why don't you tell them what you know?"

"It's not my place. Besides, I really don't know for sure."

"Is that really your decision to make?"

They pulled into the driveway and Megan didn't wait for Bruce to open her door. He was still waiting for an answer.

She went inside the house and never answered him.

24.

A DIFFERENT MAN

Bruce sat in his car staring at the old house. The years hadn't been too terribly harsh to the house. Surrounding neighborhoods had become a little questionable, but Bruce could still envision what it must have been like some twenty odd years before.

The lawn and yard was still very well manicured and the roof sagged a little bit in areas as did the porch and it might have needed a fresh coat of paint. The bricks in the pathway were rounded and grooved in some areas from all the foot traffic that had walked up and down it. Knowing whose house it was made Bruce question the amount of "gentlemen callers" there had been over the years to create such wear.

When Bruce stepped onto the porch he looked around. He could see the tower of the old California Building at Balboa Park through the eucalyptus on the other side of the gorge.

He still didn't like going there.

He was so entrenched in his thoughts that he didn't hear the door creak behind him.

"Thomas?"

Bruce turned around. What met him was not what he had imagined.

The woman standing before him was very striking and looked as though she had just stepped out of the society pages. Her hair was neatly pulled back and was still red, but there was a grayish tint to it. Her eyes were a deep green and there were very faint lines around them. In fact, there were hardly any wrinkles or creases at all. It was as if her skin had never a spent a single day in the sun. Bruce thought she could have passed for her fifties if it wasn't for the grey hair and the fact that he knew her real age, or so he thought he did. He quickly realized why she had been so popular and was starting to feel a little embarrassed that he was staring much more than he should be.

"No, ma'am," he started to correct her.

"Oh, of course…Bruce," Charlotte corrected herself.

"Yes, Ma'am."

"Please, come in," she said as she pushed the screen door open for him to open and step in.

She looked him up and down.

"You're not as fidgety as your father was," she said in a tone that almost sounded lovingly.

He looked around the front room while she continued to size him up.

"Would you like something to drink? Iced tea, water…scotch…root beer."

He looked back down at her.

"Scotch would be great, thank you."

"Neat or on the rocks or…"

"Rocks, please."

"I'll be right back."

Bruce nodded and proceeded to walk around the room. Odd water color and oil paintings were hung in a precise order on the walls which drew a visitor's attention to the divan and chairs. Bruce walked to one of the chairs and ran his hand over the back of the seat. It reminded him of the furniture his parents used to have. Something caught his eye across the room. On the credenza, that also held the scotch decanter were what seemed to be an arrangement of family photos.

Charlotte entered with an ice bucket, walked across the room and set the bucket down at the end of the credenza.

"You'll have to excuse my lack of…well, let's just say I'm sorry I'm not more prepared."

"I'm the one who's sorry; it was rude of me not to call first."

"No, no," her head shook, "I just don't receive many callers these days," she smirked at her witticism as she dropped a few cubes in his glass.

Bruce also grinned a little at the joke as he walked up beside her and picked up one of the framed photographs. It was the photo of the young man dressed in an army uniform. The uniform reminded him of one his father might have worn in the war, but not exactly. The photo was a little faded, but Bruce could still make out the medals.

"Sharpshooter?"

"Yes, "she said as she handed him his drink. She took the photo from him and gingerly set it back down.

"Son," he asked.

"Most of these are just friends, or were friends. Many of them are gone now."

There was another one that caught Bruce's eye. The photo was about the same age as the soldier's, but there was something very familiar. He lifted it up carefully, so as not to knock over the surrounding frames.

"He looks very familiar," he said turning it towards Charlotte so that she could get a better look. She tilted her head back a little so she could focus her eyes better. Even then, she still lifted her glasses, which had been hanging around her neck up to her eyes.

"Ah, yes, he should look familiar."

Bruce looked at the photo again curiously.

"You know him very well, although that is a much younger and thinner version."

Bruce frowned trying to place the face in the present.

"You don't see it."

"No."

"From what I hear, I believe you are well acquainted with him from the track."

Bruce felt her claws slowly begin to appear and try to play with him like a cat with a mouse.

"I also understand you know his great niece, Kathlyn."

He knew exactly whose photo it was.

"Associate Justice Charles Miller Frost," Charlotte said.

"Ah, yes," he said, refusing to be caught off-guard. "Now I see it."

He smiled as he placed the photo exactly where he had taken it from. He took a sip of his drink. Charlotte had not taken her eyes off him and Bruce knew it.

"What are you trying to see," he asked her as he continued looking at the photographs. He picked up another one.

It also looked slightly familiar.

"You," he asked, showing her the photograph.

She shook her head without looking at it.

"My sister."

He carefully set it back.

"You haven't taken your eyes off me...what are you trying to see?"

She ignored his questions, turned and walked to the divan and sat down. Bruce watched her.

"Please have a seat," she said motioning to the chair to her left.

"No, thank you. I just have a few questions," he said as he looked down at his glass and ran his fingers around the bottom. He thought about how he should start his line of questioning, but something inside told him that nothing he asked would surprise her.

"I've started investigating an old case of my father's," he began. He looked up at her.

He could catch her off guard. Her expression was one of discomfort, but quickly faded.

"The one about the girl," even though he knew he probably really didn't have to continue, but also knowing she would ask the hollow question of 'which one?'

She didn't give him any acknowledgement.

"The girl was chopped up into pieces, stuffed in a sack and hung from a tree by the side of the old 101....a little north of where the new university is being built."

She slowly adjusted her dress over her knee.

"You were one of the last people my father...shall we use a more polite term, say spoke to...about the case before he was killed."

"That girl again?"

There was a hollow curtness to her tone.

She stood up and walked next to him to pour herself another drink.

"I was very fond of your father. I'd known him since he was a boy. I thought of him many times as a son, enough that I set up the scholarship to send him to Dartmouth."

She took a sip.

"You set up the scholarship," he said puzzled.

"I never saw anyone who tried so hard to make up for something they thought they had done wrong."

She looked at Bruce.

"You don't know what I'm talking about."

Bruce shook his head.

"Your father was a boy when he came to work in my whorehouse. And, yes, that's what it was. I saw how he watched all those powerful men come through those doors and saw them in their personal lives with everything they had, saw the opportunities they had, where they lived, what they were able to do. He was willing to throw his family away for all of that...except for the whores. He'd seen the ugly side as well, what the diseases could do, the botched abortions, the suicides of girls who realized these men just wanted their bodies, not them. Your father wanted to be more than how he saw his family. He always had his nose in a book. Some of my customers started talking to him about what they did, but he was always polite and never talked unless they started the conversation with him. I'd get angry with them, protective of him because they filled his head and heart with dreams he was never going to be able to achieve without..."

"...without whoring himself."

"Yes," she smiled.

She picked up the Judge's photo and looked at it.

"Judge Frost took him in, tutored him. Like the snake taking in the mouse. We were all so proud of Tom."

She set the photo back down.

"Your grandmother was much smarter than he gave her credit. That goes for most parent child relations though. She found out who it was who paid for him to go to school. She cursed me and knew if he ever found out it would tear him apart.

That's where she was naïve. However, once I reminded her of her deal…well she backed down and realized she had no claim on him."

She finished her drink and poured another.

"I saw her a few years after he had been killed. She was sitting in the passenger seat of a car, waiting for the driver to return. Your Uncle Aldo had died the year before. I wanted to offer my condolences, but, well someone like me…you can understand. So I maneuvered so I could walk by instead. All she said as I passed was, 'see what your fine education brought my family'?"

"He never knew."

"No, but somehow he did. Your father wanted something better than who he thought he was, but spent the rest of his life trying to make up for it. That included being a better father than his was."

"I saw all of you that last day and night at Balboa Park. I watched how he acted with all of you. He loved you all very much. I felt guilty for the way I had treated him that afternoon he had come by. He was just trying to help someone who could no longer help herself. He was just trying to right a wrong."

"As am I. Two innocent men have died…and a girl, whose mother and father will probably die without knowing what happened to their daughter. And, there's a broken man committed to a mental facility."

"There were things I thought I couldn't afford to lose when I was younger. Now it all seems so silly and trite," she said.

"Help me, then."

She finished her drink, set the glass down, looked at Bruce and touched his arm.

"Not tonight. I wasn't prepared for this. Please come back. I'm very tired."

Bruce started to show himself, stopped and turned to make sure she was okay. She was looking at the photos.

"Three boys I've lost…and so many others have gone," she said as she picked up one of the photos.

Bruce turned and opened the door.

"And Tom," she said as he was stepping though the door.

"Yes, Ma'am."

"Don't forget to leave your glass."

He looked at the glass he still held in his hand and set it down on a table near the door. As he walked down the steps of the porch and the brick path towards his car, he realized she never answered any of his questions and would have thought her extremely manipulative if he hadn't seen the look on her face when she held the photograph.

He couldn't help himself and tried to get in one last dig. Miss MacGregor?"

"Yes?"

"You know my grandmother was very controlling."

"Yes."

"Then you would know that the only time she would ever get into a car is when she is driving and, frankly, I just don't see you ever having a reason to go north to Vista or Oceanside; unless you were the one who always put flowers on my father's grave."

He saw her tighten her grip ever so slightly on the frame.

"Bruce," she said as he started to step through the door.

"Yes."

"Do you know how to keep a secret?"

He thought for second...then shook his head

"No, I don't. Secrets are for people who have something to hide and it always eventually leads to lying."

He didn't wait for her to look up. He felt that she had as he walked through the door and walked down the steps and brick path to his car.

Bruce went down to the evidence locker and was pleasantly surprised to find the evidence box was still "alive".

He signed for it and took it to the only place he knew he could without anybody peering over his shoulder.

The morgue.

He went marching into the cold room.

"Hello," he shouted out.

He heard the wheels of a chair slide across the floor and Dr. Hill's head appeared from around the corner.

"Well, hello Bruce."

"Hey Doc."

"What do you have there," the doctor asked cocking his head. A grin spread across his face. "That wouldn't be an evidence box would it."

"Yes it would," Bruce answered, also grinning.

Dr. Hill stood up.

"Pick a table, as you can see it's a slow corpse day."

Bruce strode over to the table he had used the first day. He set the box down and lifted the top. He peered in and started pulling out its contents.

He found the match book and the potato sack. He also pulled out the evidence that the coroner had taken off the body – hairs, skin samples. There was a finger print. Bruce held it up looking inquisitively at the coroner.

"There was never a suspect to compare to...and before you think or say it...no, we didn't have anything on the people your father suspected."

Bruce nodded his head and set the fingerprint card down.

He picked up the matchbook and flipped it back and forth.

"Did anyone ever check The Agate Club?"

"Not that I'm aware of," Dr. Hill answered.

Dr. Hill picked up the sack that was now brittle from the dried blood and time. He tried to flatten it out.

"What's this," he said as Bruce saw him squeeze the bottom of the sack.

He pried the opening loose and looked inside.

"I'll be damned...and ashamed."

Bruce watched as he reached inside and struggled just a bit with what was at the bottom. The coroner pulled his hand out. He opened his palm and Bruce looked closer. In the center, encrusted with blood were a necklace and a charm.

The coroner took it to the autopsy sink and grabbed a bottle and rinsed it with something that looked like distilled water. He brought it back and spread it over the table. The two men leaned over it at and looked closer.

"How did you miss this," Bruce asked.

"The sack was so full of blood and I could rinse it...it was evidence. I don't know. Do you recognize it?"

"It looks familiar," Bruce said looking closer at the charm. "This is Celtic..."

"Then it can't be Suzanne Phelps."

Bruce looked up at him.

"Phelps is English, but not Celtic."

"Okay, do I want to know how you know that?"

The coroner shrugged his shoulders.

"There's lots of things to study when you're bored and all by yourself."

"It still could be her though," Bruce said, "She was adopted."

"It probably fell of when he cut off her head," Dr. Hill said bluntly.

Bruce rolled his eyes then stood up and surveyed everything.

"This should be enough to get my warrant...a little weak, but enough."

"A warrant for what?"

"To get into the basement of The Agate Club."

25.

DISCOVERY

·

The police had overtaken The Agate Club and marched straight to the old door that led to the basement, but when they quickly determined that there was nothing there but dead space they funneled right back out of the basement, up the steps and out into the restaurant leaving Bruce standing in the room alone. He was frustrated, angry, embarrassed and unsure.

He had been so sure.

He knew his father had been sure as well; and, although Bruce knew he was often wrong, Tom seldom was.

The frustration he felt had him pacing around, trying to see if there was something he missed. He walked over to the window on the side. It was at street level and he wanted just to rest his arms on the sill, look out and take a deep breath even though he knew the alley air wouldn't be that fresh.

But it would be cool.

When he got to the window he was surprised to realize that he couldn't lean on the window because his shoulders fell in the middle of it.

That was odd.

He knew he wasn't super tall…he was about average.

He never did carpentry…but it didn't make sense that someone would set a window at that height.

He took a step back, cocked his head and looked. Then he looked up at the ceiling.

Brummel walked back down the steps...each one straining against his weight.

"Whatcha lookin' at," he asked Bruce. He stumbled on the last step as Bruce had. The floor gave under his massive frame.

Bruce's head was still whipping around and up and down.

"How tall do you think this room is," he asked without looking at Brummel.

Brummel looked up and down and repeated the motion and then pursed his lips.

"Ahh, I don't know...seven feet...maybe a little more," he guessed.

Bruce stopped and turned to look at Brummel.

"What were these types of rooms used for," he asked.

He watched as Brummel went back into his historical memory bank. If Brummel was only good for one thing...this was it.

"Well, they were mainly for storage...of things that needed to be colder...and then ice...they would store ice." He thought a few more seconds before cocking his head and blurting out an addendum. "With as old as this building is...they probably would have made their liquor down here during the prohibition...and probably other times too. You know, to keep costs down."

"You know there was a potato sack as part of the evidence," Bruce asked.

Nodding his head, Brummel moved his flashlight along the wall that hugged the alley.

"You definitely can make alcohol from potatoes. There," he said as he stopped the beam in the corner. There was a black door...about the height of the window in the far corner.

"Gimme your light," he said reaching out to Brummel and taking the flashlight.

He ran the light along the old brick, "There should be a marking for the chute," Brummel said as Bruce scanned the light beam down the wall.

"Right there," Brummel said as the light unveiled the scar in the brick, but Bruce continued down the wall at the same angle as the marking...then stopped when he got to the floor. He moved the light across the floor.

There wasn't a mark.

Bruce squatted to get a better look then turned so he was on one knee.

He flipped the light over to the bottom stairs where everyone seemed to have problems throughout the day.

Then he saw the mark...there had been another step that was removed.

"Go grab an axe...from the fire house if you have to..."

Brummel looked at him perplexed. Bruce answered without seeing the expression.

"Didn't you feel it give as you moved," he asked grinning.

"What do you mean," he asked Bruce.

"The floor...you weigh...what...350?"

Brummel glared at him.

"Oh come on, I'm not going to report you to the Captain you oaf."

"Two...352."

"It's a false floor," Bruce said as he jumped up and started thumping his foot door on the floor listening for a hollow sound.

Brummel moved as fast as he could up the steps and out of the basement. Now he was grinning.

The owner came back down and stood in the middle of the steps.

"When are you lea..."

"How long has *this* floor been here," Bruce asked the owner.

"What?"

"You heard me. When was this floor put in?"

He walked further into the room and turned to look at the owner.

"You know...over the existing one...making the room smaller. You pulled out the chute," he said waving the flashlight over to where the chute had been."

The owner looked around dumbfounded.

"Why would anyone create dead space...unless..."

"I swear it was like that when I moved into the place," the owner said defensively.

Bruce slowly looked at the man. Brummel came in huffing and puffing with the axe. He rambled down the steps, knocking the owner out of the way and stumbling down the last step again.

"Did you buy it…or are you leasing it," Bruce wanted to know.

"Renting."

"From Charlotte MacGregor?"

"Yes."

Bruce took the axe from Brummel.

"A couple of the other guys are coming back," Brummel said as Bruce started to walk down the center of the room thumping the head of the axe along the floor as he went. Brummel thought he looked like a safe cracker of sorts; especially when he stopped about twenty feet from the wall.

He swung the axe back in a giant arc and the head was sweeping behind and up and over as the restaurant owner gasped.

"You can't!"

The axe swung up and around and Bruce pulled it with all his might land the blade square in the middle of the floor.

"My warrant says I can," Bruce said wriggling the blade out and then starting the process over again.

This time the floor cracked.

"I'm going to call the landlord."

"Great," Bruce said continuing the process and making the hole larger and letting some stale air gust out, "tell her Bruce is taking care of some unfinished business for Detective Tom Rubidoux."

And more wood gave way under the damage of the axe. Bruce knocked more of the wood away until he felt it was large enough for him to drop down. He lay on his belly, stuck his head down a little ways and the flashlight so he could look around to see how far down the actual floor was. He sat back up and swung his legs down into the hole handing Brummel the flashlight.

He dropped down with shoulders and head poking through the hole. Then he gestured for Brummel to give him the flashlight. He squatted down and shuffled along the floor, waving the light back and forth as he went. He heard Brummel talking to someone above him and assumed some of the officers had returned.

He inched forward trying not to kick up too much of the dust from the floor, but enough did forcing him to try to generate more saliva to swallow. He moved a little further, but something looked odd to him.

This space was not as long as the one above him. He was stopped short by a brick wall. He turned around slightly and sat down, leaning against the brick.

Then it occurred to him.

"Hey Brum," he yelled.

"Yeah," he heard muffled from above.

"Tell me how far am I from the wall," he asked as he started banging the butt of the flashing light on the wood above him.

He questioned this decision as dust started to fall on him causing him to cough.

"Ah, I don't know...what do you guys say...five feet."

Bruce heard mumbling above.

"Yeah, about five feet, give or take."

"Take the axe and knock a hole into the floor a few feet from the wall," he yelled to Brummel.

He heard Brummel walk across the floor and felt it give a little when he came directly over head. A little prayer passed his lips hoping to prevent Brummel from stepping through the floor on top of him. There was a pause and then the sound of wood being hit and splintered. Brummel had put a hole through the floor with his first swing

"Wooh," he said as Bruce came back up through the hole and climbed up. "That's more than just stale air."

One of the other officers helped Bruce to his feet and he walked over to the hole. He smelled what caused Brummel to scrunch his face up.

He had experienced that smell before.

It smelled stale like the battlefield hospitals after the medical staff had tried to clean all the blood up...unsuccessfully.

"Make the hole bigger," he instructed Brummel.

Brummel nodded and knocked more wood away until there was a very large oval...the size of a tub. And, when Bruce and the other officers lit up the area with their flashlights they could see it was exactly that.

A tub.

Even more, Bruce's memories served him well.

Someone unsuccessfully had tried to clean up blood which accentuated the scratches and flaws covering the surface.

"Why the hell, didn't they just remove the tub," one of the other officers asked.

"Brummel," Bruce said inspecting the area closer.

"If I'm not mistaken it's solid cast iron...most were back in the day when this was the Stingeree and probably, somehow, it's attached to this wall," he put his hand on the wall, "which has to be load bearing..."

Something caught Bruce's eye.

"...the room was probably built around it," Brummel finished as Bruce jumped in the tub and looked closer at the tiny glint that sparked his interest.

"Do any of you have any forceps or tweezers?"

"I have a pocket knife," one of them said.

Bruce thought for a second and nodded his head since his options were limited. Carefully, he opened the blade and started to work it down the drain. He felt the group starting to close in to see what he was doing, including the owner who had rejoined them.

He maneuvered the knife up and then flicked it ever so gently. The small artifact flew up and landed on the surface of the tub. Bruce stared at it and thought he felt tears start to well up in his eyes.

"What is it," the owner asked.

"A fingernail," Brummel said. "It looks like there's blood on it too. Are you going to tell us that you didn't know..."

"We've already been through that Brum," Bruce said very quietly. He stared at the knife and his heart started to race with excitement.

There was something else the knife had pulled up from the drain.

On the tip of the blade were three blonde hairs.

And they were bound together by blood.

26.

IMPATIENT

"Please tell me it's good," Bruce said leaning over Dr. Hill, who was trying to look at the hairs Bruce had brought. The coroner turned and looked at him.

"I find it very hard to concentrate with you huffing and puffing in my ear."

Bruce stepped back.

"Sorry."

Dr. Hill went back to the microscope.

"What exactly are you hoping to accomplish," he asked Bruce while focusing the microscope.

"I need to know if this was Suzanne Phelps?"

"It's a fingernail and hair...that hardly makes up a body."

"But the blood type..."

"We still need a body to match it to. Even if we match it to the blood type on the inside of that bag," he added interrupting Bruce before he could ask.

Then he saw the wheels in Bruce's mind turn and knew what Bruce wanted.

Bruce cocked his head and sheepishly shrugged his shoulder trying to hint at what he wanted.

"You know better than that Bruce. We just can't go digging up every Jane Doe just because you have an itch."

"But, you know it's her."

"No...I *suspect* it's her."

"But no one is going to care about digging up someone that they don't know," Bruce argued. "Besides, I'm only asking to dig up one."

"The city cares because the city has to pay."

Bruce slumped down against the table. He thought for a moment then looked up.

"What exactly happened to Sylvestre and Juneau Rubidoux," he asked. "I know they were executed."

The coroner stored the evidence and handed it back to Bruce. Bruce looked at it in his hands. Dr. Hill walked to the sink to wash his hands.

"No, not executed...exactly." He tried to remember. "Juneau...sweet kid...well, he was beaten to death by some of the other inmates. And, Sylvestre, he hung himself in his cell."

Bruce looked back down at the evidence.

No wonder his grandmother and the rest of the family were so mad.

"I'll tell you what," Dr. Hill said, "You get me the knife...and I'll get you what you need for the warrant to exhume."

Bruce started to shuffle out the door when Dr. Hill turned around.

"And, not to put any more pressure on you, but you may want to secure that evidence as best as possible. I heard Senator Moran is on his way down from Sacramento."

Bruce turned and looked around the room.

"You by any chance wouldn't have any space in your 'secret' file, would you?"

The coroner thought for a second and took a few steps towards Bruce.

"Go check it in. I'll go down later and check it out and tell the officer that I have some tests to run."

Bruce grinned and left.

"I know you're going to get me fired or killed," Dr. Hill shouted out after him.

Bruce didn't think that was very prudent of the coroner to say.

Bruce had to run out on another case when he returned to his desk. His mind was on what he needed to do during the call. Luckily he had gone with Brummel and Brummel knew his mind wasn't quite in the game, so the big man did all the questioning.

While Brummel jotted down notes for his report Bruce looked around the inside of the home. The photos on the wall caught his eye.

There were family photos and individual photos, including some men in uniforms.

Bruce wondered how many of them had made it home; especially since he didn't see any recent photos of the men.

There was a large bookcase with paned doors and Bruce bent forward and looked at the shelves and saw mementos from the Pacific Arena.

"Your husband served in the Pacific," he turned and asked.

"My youngest brother," she said, wincing a bit.

"I'm sorry I..."

"Oh no, he's alive...it's just that I don't like that he puts his trophies on display like that."

"Like how," Bruce asked.

"Well...we lost so many relatives...I would rather just forget the whole thing...especially when those items are from a man he killed."

"Is he arrogant," Bruce blurted out without thinking.

"Did you say ignorant," she asked as if she were insulted.

"No," he stammered, "maybe, he was just really proud about what he did...I mean surviving," he threw in to try to get him out the pickle. He looked to Brummel to help him.

The big guy just smirked at him.

"Anyways, about the car," Brummel interjected, relieving some of the awkwardness.

Bruce didn't say another word and continued to stare at the items on the shelves without seeing them.

Cabot Moran was arrogant enough to flaunt anything he had gotten away with in plain view.

Bruce knew all he had to do was look in the right place and he would find everything he needed to. It was like looking for the keystone that would make an arch collapse once removed.

He decided he would start at the Frost estate.

That meant involving Kathlyn. He felt smarmy at the idea because he realized after the night of the ball he still loved her.

Now he knew he would use her to get what he needed.

There was also the tiny nagging at the back of his mind...

How much did she really know?

"I never saw you as one with super human laser eyes," Brummel said behind him.

"What," he said a little startled.

"If you stare at that glass any harder I think you might just shatter it," Brummel joked. "Come on, let's go. We're done here."

Bruce walked out of the house still thinking. He started to get in the passenger side, forgetting he had driven. Brummel stood outside the passenger door staring at him.

"Ahem."

Bruce turned slowly.

Brummel held out his hand.

"Can I at least have the keys so I can drive us back to the station?"

"Oh," Bruce said reaching into his pocket, "here."

Brummel was busy adjusting the mirrors and put the key in the ignition.

"You do realize you're letting me drive *your* car."

"Sure...great," Bruce answered.

He didn't say another word and missed Brummel's entire diatribe back to the station. The fact that Brummel handed him his keys or that he sat back down behind his desk was all a blur.

The next thing he remembered was staring at the phone.

He went to reach for it several times before pulling his hand back. He had even taken off the cradle a couple of times before dropping the handset back down.

His hands were sweaty.

"This is ridiculous," he thought.

Finally, he grabbed the phone. The operator clicked through.

"How may I help you," he heard her say on the other end.

"Carnegie 2-800," he said.

"I'm sorry sir, but that's a restricted number."

"It can't be that private if I know it," he said.

"Sir, you don't have to be rude."

"I'm calling from the police station."

"Yes, I know that sir."

Bruce took a deep breath.

"Ma'am, what do I need to get the call through? Do I need a secret word," he tried to say as politely as possible, "'Please' perhaps?"

There was a long pause on the other end.

"Please hold," he finally heard her say.

She clicked back in.

"What is your name and who are you calling for, please?"

"And...Bruce Rubidoux. I'm calling for Kathlyn Moran."

"Please hold."

Bruce scowled.

"Here you are sir," he heard her say.

"Thank you."

"Hello," he heard a man on the other end say.

Bruce thought for a minute.

"Good afternoon, Paul. It's Bruce Rubidoux. I was hoping Kathlyn was available."

"Just one second Mr. Rubidoux."

He heard the phone set down and wondered one thing.

Did Joe have to go through all this?

Off in the distance, he heard heels on the floor that Bruce knew was in the entranceway of the main house.

"Hello," Kathlyn said.

"Hey, it's me Bruce."

"Oh, really."

"Say, I was leaving work early today and was going surfing up there and wanted to see if you might want to grab dinner afterwards."

"Are you asking me out on a date?"

"Wha..," he said.

"Because it sounds like you're asking me out on a date."

"We can call it a date...I suppose."

"You suppose? You used to be a lot more assertive. Isn't that something they teach you at the academy or OCS?"

"We're dealing with people pointing guns at us…not women…although I did have a German woman try to shoot me."

"You probably deserved it," she said laughing.

He thought back for a moment.

"Yeah…I did actually."

"Won't you need to shower?"

"I'll be in the water already…I believe there are showers down there."

"Okay. What time do you think you'll be at the house?"

"Five."

"Won't it be a little dark to surf?"

"Not if I leave now. I'll see you at five."

"Bruce…"

"Um?"

"You do realize my father won't approve."

He smirked.

"I really don't care what your father thinks."

Bruce hung up the phone and put his things together and stood up. He turned around to find Brummel looking at him holding a file open in his hands.

"I wish I could work on the types of cases you do."

Bruce chuckled and left.

Bruce was remembering how good it felt to get in the water as he drove up the coast to the Frost estate. It had taken him a little while to get used to the cold, but soon recovered once he started paddling.

He turned and started weaving up the road.

It had been years since he had been to the house that over looked the bluff and part of the race track. He remembered attending a few times as a child, but looking back could never remember what business his mother and siblings had there.

He turned again and drove down the long driveway, curving as the main house came into view. Across the green expanse of the back yard, Bruce could see the bungalow he knew belonged to Corey and clear across in the opposite direction the larger bungalow that belonged to Cabot.

Bruce figured that these two buildings were just for privacy because the main house was large enough to accommodate five families.

He knew Cabot and his family spent most of their time in the main house. Every time he had seen Corey there he looked uncomfortable, as if he was a guest rather than part of the family.

Bruce stopped the car in the turnabout and got out which allowed him to walk on the gravel path. The sound of it under his shoes was something he found very soothing and it conjured up memories for him. The front garden to the main door was as beautiful and well manicured as he remembered and pulled back on the massive brass knocker and rapped it a couple of times. Paul's slow methodical steps on the floor on the other side of the door were very distinct.

"Good evening, Paul."

"Good evening, Mr. Rubidoux," he greeted stepping back to allow Bruce in. Bruce stepped inside and looked up at the large entryway with the vaulted ceiling.

"Kathlyn asked that you wait in the study," Paul said motioning for Bruce to follow him.

Bruce knew exactly where the study was. He remembered playing hide-and-seek behind the massive furniture and trying to steal a kiss from Kathlyn on her twelfth birthday.

"It's alright Paul, I remember the way."

Paul threw an arm up as Bruce tried to walk ahead of him. Paul glared at him and Bruce felt like he was studying him.

"Or," Bruce said, "I could let you show me the way."

"Thank you," Paul said, "I would appreciate that."

"I guess you don't get to…," he couldn't think of the word, "buttle, butlering, butler much with Justice…"

"…Associate Justice…"

"…Associate Justice Frost and Senator Moran away so much."

Paul stopped in front of the study door and opened the double doors for Bruce.

"They're home enough."

"Thank you Paul," Bruce said.

"You're welcome."

Paul started to shut the doors then opened them slightly and leaned forward.

"It's nice to see you again sir," he said as Bruce turned back around and saw the doors close and latch.

Bruce grinned as he turned back around and took the room in. The studies in all three houses were set up exactly the same – everything in the main house was just twice as large as in the other two.

The desk was set up towards the back of the room, facing the front doors and the French doors (in this case framing each side of the fireplace behind the desk) went out to the sprawling back yard and gardens that overlooked the ocean.

He suspected, with a strong enough telescope, that Kathlyn could have seen him get out of the ocean.

As he stood in front of Judge Frost's desk and looked at the large portrait of the man that hung behind the desk Bruce could see the transition of the man in this painting from the man he knew now and then one he had seen in the photograph at Charlotte's.

Bruce turned and looked at the door. He imagined Judge Frost looked very opposing sitting behind his desk for anyone who walked in and thought it probably resembled the way it would look going to stand before him in court.

It could be why he wasn't afraid of the man.

As kids, they always came in through the French doors...and he always had a smile for them as well as candy in the middle drawer.

Bruce walked around the desk and pulled on the drawer. No candy.

He shut the drawer and continued to look around the office sifting through memories and looking for evidence.

Along one side of the room was a book case. Bruce ran his hand along the bindings...most of them were leather. He squatted down to the shelf he knew held the ones he used to like to read. He ran his fingers along them as if he could read the titles by Braille. He stopped in front of a very old one that seemed stuck as he tilted and gingerly pulled it out. It left a stain where the oils from the cover had sat for too long. He smiled as he read the title "Mathematic Fundamentals". He put the book to his nose and smelled it.

When he was younger he used to just hold it to his chest...almost hugging it.

He remembered when Judge Frost had pointed it out to him.

"I used to tutor your father from that book. It was his."

Bruce had looked up at the man. He wanted to touch it hoping he could feel Tom somehow.

Judge Frost had seen what he wanted and nodded.

Bruce's small hands had pulled it out and he had lifted it to his nose to smell. He sat down with the book in his lap. The binding crackled as he opened the cover. In the upper hand corner, written in a child's handwriting was *Thomas S. Rubidoux*. It looked a little different than the signature in the book at his grandmother's house.

He remembered smiling and feeling tears well up in his eyes as they started to do now. He ran his finger across the indentations his father's pen had made writing his name. Like the book up at the ranch, he almost felt he was touching Tom's arm or he could sense him through the ink.

Returning the book to the shelf, he replayed sounds and voices from his youth as he walked across the room to the other cabinet.

This held something much different.

Bruce looked at all the different guns and rifles that Judge Frost had collected over the years. He stared at one of the shot guns.

The one the Judge had taught him to shoot.

Bruce remembered that day too.

The judge had been shooting at crows or rabbits in the backyard as Bruce and the rest of his family arrived.

Bruce and his brothers ran into the study looking for the Judge and candy. Louis had seen one set of the French doors ajar and pointed it out to Bruce. He walked forward and opened the doors wider so they could walk through. Bruce walked out the doors, across the lawn and through the garden to where the Judge was overlooking the bluff with the gun tucked between his arm and body and balanced over his other arm.

The Judge turned and smiled.

"Hello boys," he said as Louis and Joe had joined Bruce.

"Hello Judge," they all chimed in unison.

Bruce knew the Judge saw him eyeing the gun. The big man looked down at the firearm and then up at Bruce.

"Do you know how to fire one of these," the Judge asked him.

Joe and Louis hung back...actually Louis stood back and held Joe back.

"No, sir...I've seen that type used on my nana's ranch and Daddy only had revolvers."

"Well, you're old enough that you should know."

The Judge reached into his pocket and reloaded the gun.

Bruce heard Louis make a noise. He turned around.

Louis shook his head vigorously. His eyes were pleading not to proceed.

Bruce ignored him and turned back to the Judge who had finished loading the shot gun.

"Do you know how to hold it," he asked Bruce as he held the gun out to him.

Bruce slowly nodded as he took the gun and mimicked how he had seen his relatives on the ranch hold it. He moved it up to his chin and then slowly brought it down and looked at for a second.

"That's right, you've got it. Keep it firm against your shoulder," the Judge encourage him.

Bruce took a deep breath.

"What is it son," Judge Frost asked him.

Bruce thought for a moment and looked up.

"What does it do to watermelons?"

The Judge looked at him quizzically, when they heard a woman's voice, "Charles."

The all turned up the path to find Beatrice Frost and Megan glaring at them.

Judge Frost took the gun as Megan marched up the path to gather them.

"He's old enough to know. He's going to have to learn sometime," the Judge said to her.

She grabbed Bruce's arm. He saw the disappointment in her eyes, but a thought ran through is mind.

If he was now the man of the family, damn it, he was going to be a man.

"He is a Rubidoux...not a Frost," Megan said between clenched teeth as she pulled Bruce away with Joe and Louis scampering behind.

"He will find out, Megan," Judge Frost assured her.

Bruce turned around and looked at the Judge as he nodded at him.

All he knew was that he didn't like the Judge talking to his mother in that tone.

The last thing Bruce remembered was the look on Beatrice Frost's face as Megan pulled him away.

He couldn't identify the look as a child, but in reflection he could.

She looked like a woman who had caught her husband cheating.

He shook himself from the memory and stepped down to the credenza that held all the smaller photographs. He scanned across all of them as he had at Charlotte MacGregor's.

There were pictures of The Judge and Beatrice Frost, Cabot and his parents, Cabot from World War one, Cabot and his wife (or so Bruce assumed), Kathlyn's baby photo (Bruce smiled at), Corey, Corey and his parents, Corey during the war, Corey and Cabot when they were little and older, Cabot and Corey and a blonde haired girl when they were little...and older.

She was standing in between the two of them.

In the first photo they all had their arms around each other...but in the older one...

Bruce picked up the photo and stared.

...Only Corey's arm wrapped around her waist and hers was around his...

...not Cabot's.

He looked closer to the both photos and then back and back and forth between each one and then picked up the one of Cabot and his wife.

The two women looked eerily similar. In fact, at a glance, they could have been mistaken as the same person. When he stopped to think about it, Bruce wondered if Corey had beaten Cabot out of his prize.

Bruce brought the picture of the girl between Cabot and Corey closer as he saw a glint of an object and then picked up the other picture of her.

Around the girl's neck in both of them she was wearing the charm Bruce and Dr. Hill had found stuck at the bottom of the burlap sack.

He didn't want to get too excited, but he knew this would be enough to get Jane Doe 221 exhumed.

He put the photos back with his shaky hands and looked on for more.

There was another photo of a couple. It looked like the same blonde girl and possibly Corey, but Bruce felt something burning into him as he stared back at the photo in his hand. He took his focus off it for a second to look back at the others.

He recognized Cabot's war photo as the same one he'd seen at Charlotte's. His eyes scanned back over to Corey's.

He set the one with the three young vibrant people down and picked up both army photos then looked from the one in his left and then the one in his right and back again.

Both sharpshooters.

He looked back at the gun case.

Only one gun had a scope, but he had seen Corey use an old scope at the track.

He kept going back and forth and finally set the photo down and picked up the one of Cabot and Corey when they were young.

The photo was in black and white, but he didn't need the color of the boys' hair to tell him what he needed to know.

Bruce had a thing for eyes. His were a hazel blue. He had inherited the hazel from Tom, the blue from Megan.

The Frosts had brown...except for Cabot and Corey...their eyes (and Kathlyn's) were green.

...as were Charlotte MacGregor's.

Cabot and Corey weren't cousins.

He jumped as she rested her hand on his shoulder.

"I'm sorry," Kathlyn giggled.

She rubbed her hand down his arm.

"Wow, you were really were deep in thought."

He took a deep breath to compose himself.

"You're sweating," she said.

He turned and set the photos back down and wiped his upper lip and mouth with his hand.

"Yes, I was. I was just strolling down memory lane as they say."

Kathlyn looked at him and put her hand on his cheek.

No, he couldn't get involved...not now.

"I was remembering my 'shooting' lesson I received from the Judge."

"Oh, I remember that," she said, "Aunt Beatrice was furious with Uncle Charles about that."

"Yes, my mother wasn't very happy with him either," he chuckled.

She smiled.

"I remember her yelling at Uncle Charles too."

He gulped and refocused.

"If I remember correctly," he said waving at all the guns, "your dad had a weapons collection of his own."

She stepped away from him and moved in front of the case and looked in.

"That one's Daddy's rifle from the war," she said pointing to one of the guns that held a scope attached to it. "The other one belongs to Cousin Corey."

Of course it did.

"But, I remember your dad had a shit...had a lot of knives."

"Yes," she nodded and looked at him, "Mother made him donate those."

"Donate them?"

"Yes, it took him a very long time, but he and Cousin Corey donated them to the historical society... last time Daddy was down here they unveiled the collection at Balboa Park."

Bruce couldn't help but stare.

Arrogant bastard.

"Bruce, what's wrong," she asked.

He didn't want her to touch him. He knew he was wound so tight that she would figure everything out or he would unravel if she touched him.

"It's nothing...it's a case I'm working on...makes me a little jumpy."

Then he had a thought.

"Kat, do you remember what happened to your mother?"

She smiled and looked at him.

"I haven't heard you call me 'Kat' in a very long time. I think the other night when your sister called me that was the first time."

Bruce didn't say anything, making the space between them suddenly feel awkward.

Kathlyn took a step back from him.

"No, I don't really remember and no has ever really talked about it."

"Weren't you ever curious?"

"I never really gave it much thought. I mean, she was dead...she was gone...nothing was ever going to bring her back. I remember Daddy sitting on the edge of my bed and told me something had happened to her, but he was going to take care of everything."

"But you never wondered how?"

"No Bruce," she said curtly, "I'm not like you. I don't always need to know how tragedy hits people...how people die."

Bruce studied her.

"Do you know who this girl is," he said pointing at the photo of Cabot, Corey and the girl.

"I'd like to talk about something else or even better – go to dinner."

He nodded his head and they left.

Dinner was a disaster.

Bruce sat across from Kathlyn at the Marine Room in La Jolla, feebly trying to hold a conversation but was so distracted by his internal warring that he failed. Most of the time he and Kathlyn looked out the window as the waves brushed up against it.

As he stared at his food the waves sounded like a few of the evenings he had spent on the battlefield with the guns shooting off in the distant and breaking through trees.

He would absent-mindedly look up at her.

If they happened to look at each other it was brief and as if they were embarrassed.

At one point he leaned forward and sea water spilled out of his nose onto his meal. He threw his hand up in a feeble attempt to catch the water.

He looked up at Kathlyn.

She smirked and went back down to her meal.

"Sorry," he said.

"Hazards of surfing," she said.

She smiled at him.

When he just looked at her, the smile disappeared and she looked out the window.

Bruce never knew Kathlyn to be like this. She was usually shrewd and always in control...and manipulating.

He remembered manipulating.

"Why do you stay down here rather than in Sacramento," he asked her.

"Have you been to Sacramento?"

"No," he shook his head.

"Trust me, this is much better. You have to drive a ways to get to the ocean up there."

"There's snow..."

She laughed.

"Really Bruce? We grew up in one of the sunniest places on earth and ran around in swimsuits and sandals. Why would I want to run around like Nanook of the North?"

"It's just something different to do."

He took a sip of his drink.

"Plus, I'm trying to find something to talk about."

"Oh."

She seemed to think for a moment.

"Since when have we ever not been able to talk to each other?"

Bruce nodded and took a sip of his drink.

"Since no one is around to buffer us...since we grew up," he answered.

The waiter came and asked them about dessert and coffee. They declined. Bruce paid and was polite and courteous as they left the restaurant.

They slowly started to walk to his car and she turned.

"Can we take a walk," she asked.

Bruce nodded his head and they started down the path to the beach, but stopped as soon as they saw the high tide covering the way down.

"Come on, we'll go along the cove," he said escorting her to the car.

He drove the winding road and found a place to park over looking Children's Pool. He remembered many days spent there as a child...days with his family...days when Kathlyn and her nanny would show.

He left the car and walked around to Kathlyn's side and opened the door for her. He held his hand out and she took it as she stepped out, then he shut the door and she walked to the hood of the car, removed her shoes and carried them with her fingers through the straps.

They started down the steps to walk down to the retaining wall that reached out into the cove and ocean. Bruce could see the dark shadows of seals playing in the night surf. Out of insecurity, he started to walk with his hands in his pockets, but held one hand out for her as they started down along the uneven surface. When she looked steady enough he put his hand back in his pocket and she looped her arm through his.

He thought about saying something and changed his mind.

Some of the water sprayed up onto the path, causing Kathlyn to scream. He had made sure he was walking to take the brunt of the water so she was only getting a little.

She stopped during one of the waves and looked at him.

"Why did you become a detective?"

Bruce looked down and pondered.

"I mean, I remember how morbid you were as a kid," she added.

"My dad," he said quietly.

She looked at him.

"You wanted to follow in his footsteps," she tried to clarify.

"No," he shook his head, "my dad was a good man. I thought...I thought...I thought I could be a better person if I found out what happened to him and helped people like he did."

Bruce's mind flashed back to the photos at Kathlyn's home.

The bookcase.

The gun rack.

Kathlyn suddenly tugged on his arm to walk back towards the street.

"You are also a good man, Bruce."

"I always hoped that they had named me for Bruce Wayne...that maybe, secretly, I was Batman."

She looked at him.

"But, he came after me...much later."

He waited until they were up along the bluff...walking in the direction of the Shores.

His mind had not stopped replaying everything he thought of...everything he had seen...everything.

"Why Joe," he blurted out.

She had taken a few steps ahead of him and turned around. She looked up into his face.

His jaw was clenched.

She walked towards the edge and looked over the cliff below.

He watched her and could feel the mist of the water as it smashed against the rocks and sprayed up.

She took a deep breath.

"I thought it was you," she said, turning and looking at him. "I was walking along the beach where you all surfed and swam. I called after you and he turned. He must have been used it...you two looked so much alike."

She turned back to look at the ocean he knew she couldn't see in the dark.

"It wasn't until he got closer and I looked at his hands that I realized it wasn't you."

Bruce just watched her.

"I thought he was you," she whispered again.

Bruce felt his chest tighten.

He took a step closer.

"We should go," he said softly, extending his hand out to her.

She nodded and took his arm.

He positioned himself in between her and the cliff as they walked back to the car.

"I'd like it if you came back to the house for a nightcap," she offered.

"I'd like that too," he answered.

"Bruce," she asked as he started to open the car door for her.

"Um?"

"Do you think you'll ever figure out who killed your dad," she said as she slid into the car.

"Yes...yes I do," he said as he shut the door and an image of Cabot and Corey flashed through his mind.

27.

DISCRETION

Bruce remained tight-lipped with his revelation. He knew his mom and Alice were concerned, but he also knew they would keep their distances and not pry if they though he was working on a case.

Especially since he knew he was working on *that* case.

He would catch his mother looking at him with same expression she had looked at his father with.

And, now he knew why.

He decided to go back to the one person who would confirm his suspicions...without saying anything.

Anxiety filled him as he drove back up to the sanitarium. When he pulled on the front doors they didn't seem as heavy.

He went to the grated window nodded his head and flashed his badge and I.D.

The nurse nodded and said he knew where Mr. Farnham went in the yard.

Bruce strolled down the hall, turned the corner, greeted the guards at the gate, walked through and outside to the fountain.

He looked up to the sky and marveled at the brilliant blue and the birds that flew by. He took in a deep breath and looked towards the lake and saw the back of Bradley Farnham's head as he walked down the hill feeling ten feet tall.

Something made him stop just slightly passed the bench with his back to Bradley. He looked over the lake. This time it looked inviting...not a scar on his memory.

"You were right," he said, assuming Bradley would have been expecting him, "Some of the answers have been in front of me the whole time, like they were for my dad. I'm hoping you can help me with the paperwork I need since I'm sure you knew about the boys' adoptions."

He turned around.

A sickening feeling filled him as his heart stuck in his throat and he immediately tried to erase his face of any expression.

The urge to throw his hands to his mouth was almost more than he could control. He fought the impulse to ball them up in fists...to look for the person who he knew would be watching him.

He forced any tension that might have been in his upper body down to his legs and stood up as tall as he could.

There was a section of Bradley's head that had been shaved and a pink, raised scar running its length to his forehead.

Bruce stared, composing himself, as he watched a string of drool pour out of the side of Bradley's mouth and dangle...then finally drop to a spot already saturated on his robe.

Bruce gritted his teeth and looked up with his eyes to look around.

He walked around to the other side and put his hand on Bradley's shoulder.

"I'm so sorry," he said and turned and walked back up to the main building through the door. He thought one of the guards smirked as they let him trough and locked the gate behind him. He started out the front door and stopped at the entrance plaque and scanned the board of directors and benefactors.

He should have known.

Charles Miller Frost

Someone walked up to him as he stared at the name and he turned his head to see who it was.

The girl from the reception window nervously approached him.

"I'm sorry, I couldn't hand this to you before when you checked in. It took me a minute to register who you were."

She held out an envelope to him. He took it.

"He knew you'd be back. He wrote this right after your last visit and gave it to me to give to you."

She ran off down one of the other halls.

Bruce took the envelope and left.

Bruce,

Your visit here today made me realize how much I have missed. I thought by being alive I would be living.

When I realized you weren't Tom I realized that wasn't the case.

If you are reading this then you have found something –
– The tub down in the basement of The Agate Club.
– The secret of the Robin's Nest
– That Cabot Moran and Corey Hayes are actually the sons of Charles Frost and his mistress, Charlotte MacGregor

If you know any one of those, then there's not much left for me to hide.

The last thing I can share without disclosing too much is that the youngest is the favorite, but they didn't pay any attention to him because the oldest needed all the help and he had someone to look after him.

Two people for that matter:
Suzanne Phelps and Tom Rubidoux.
My one regret was trusting in their words.
You don't seem the type to trust anyone.
Good. Don't.
That was your father's mistake.
B. F.

Bruce folded the letter back up and put it in his coat pocket on the plane.

It was too cryptic for him to figure out.

Why couldn't he just have said what he needed to plainly?

He leaned against the window and watched the landscape pass beneath him and the clouds by his window.

The more he became involved in the case the clearer the memory of his father became...and his own childhood.

He remembered the late nights he'd peek out and see his father with his hand in his hair looking like he was on the verge of tears.

He would catch his parents taking secret glances at each other while the other one didn't know.

And there were others with his mother in his father's lap teasing him and making him laugh...and other looks that he didn't understand until he was an adult.

He remembered more and more the last conversation Tom had with him and Louis around the kitchen table.

It was if he had known.

He remembered lights pulling up into the driveway and hearing Megan walking to answer the front door. He slipped out of bed and walked across the wood floor and opened his door and snuck to the doorway that looked to the front door.

Megan backed up like a wounded animal and threw her hands to her mouth.

"No," she shook her head as if she had been furious, but he could see she was about to start crying. "No," she repeated as two officers stepped inside their home. Judge Frost walked in with his hat in his hand.

Megan continued to walk, no stagger, backwards until her back hit the door jamb to the kitchen. Just before she fell forward, Bruce saw *her* walk in and clutch Megan to her and fall to the ground with her.

Bruce had watched as Charlotte rocked his mother back and forth and cried.

And now, as he remembered, he understood part of her anguish.

She had loved Tom as her own...and one of her own had killed him.

He remembered his vision was suddenly blocked and he looked up to see the Judge looking down at him.

The big man was holding out a handkerchief.

It was then that Bruce realized he had been crying.

He took it and looked up at the Judge.

"Go to bed. We'll take care of her."

Bruce looked back down and passed him. Charlotte's eyes and his connected.

It was then he knew for certain his father was dead.

He turned and went back to the room he shared with Louis.

Who would murder his father?

The man who always listened to every story they had to tell, who taught them how to ride bikes and catch, laughed at every joke, who never raised his voice and caught bad people.

He would catch whoever would take his father from them...no matter it took.

28.

THE LIGHT THROUGH THE FOG

Bruce had coaxed Brummel into going to Balboa Park and looking for the knives. He figured he wouldn't be able to get very far and he didn't want to run the risk that Kathlyn had told her father about her slip about the donation to the museum.

Brummel was a member of the historical society and used that and his position in the department when he asked to have special privileges with some of the artifacts in the various museums at the park.

Bruce took the opportunity to take some time off to get his head together and relax.

He parked where he normally did and changed into his trunks. He knew the water would be freezing, but he didn't care and thought the shock might invigorate him. He looked up at the bluff as he slipped his pants off from beneath his towel and shimmied his trunks on.

He thought of Suzanne...how innocent she looked in the photos. There was something about her that reminded him of Alice.

You could tell by her smile just how nice she was.

He wondered what Cabot had said to lure her down into The Agate Club basement. How she probably would have gone without thinking anything of it.

And the terror she must have felt when she knew it was all about to end terribly.

How did she know about the club in the first place?

It wasn't the place a lady like Suzanne would be accustomed to.

He shook his head to move onto happier things.

Bruce dove in the water and cut through the water to catch a few waves before going home to the big dinner.

His heart jolted as the cold waves lapped up against his back.

It was almost too cold.

He smirked as he sat on the end of the board and spun it around.

Alice had finally made her decision and accepted one of her suitors request to marry.

But that's not why he was smirking.

He suddenly thought of a scene from "Gone With The Wind" with Scarlett O'Hara surrounded by all her beaus.

He thought of how they all vied for her attentions and of how so many of them were probably jealou...

He stopped and looked up at the bluff.

Of course, why hadn't he seen it before?

He paddled back in as hard as he could without waiting for any waves. He threw everything in the car and didn't bother getting dressed and drove up to the bluff. His badge was thrown onto the dashboard and parked wherever he could.

He jumped out of the car and ran out to where he thought the girl...where Suzanne had been found.

Then he ran out and stopped at the bluff overlooking the ocean.

Bruce took a deep breath and closed his eyes and turned back around.

He watched all the people out for a Sunday walk stepping where his father must have...where the murderer walked...where a nameless girl had hung for someone to find.

The road had changed over the twenty years, but some things hadn't.

How often had he and his brothers fought over petty things...over toys, their parents' affections...over girls.

Finally, he had the biggest piece his father never thought of.

Motive.

His stomach lurched

He remembered the story of the Robin's Nest. How a little blonde-haired girl had been found by police officers in a pool of her mother's blood.

She had been taken to her aunt's establishment.

The Agate Club.

Suzanne was their cousin.

They would never have let Corey marry her.

He looked north over the bluff towards the Frost Estate.

Cabot was in town and they had already started to squeeze in on Bruce.

He also remembered from the report who had made the call about the body.

He ran back to the car and peeled out in the direction of the Frosts.

Bruce tore up the driveway and gravel kicked up as he slammed on the brakes.

He ran into the main house.

Paul tried to stop him and he mowed right by the elderly man and headed for the study.

He peeked out into the yard and could hear raised voices in the direction of Corey's bungalow.

He looked down and realized he was still in a shirt and his swim shorts.

No gun.

Turning, he looked at the place he knew he could grab a gun and felt as if the distance seemed further than the three feet it took him to reach the gun cabinet. It didn't matter to him which one he had so he picked up the only weapon he was familiar with.

The shotgun.

"Bruce, what's going on," Kathlyn said panicked. Bruce knew that his presence and the yelling from the other side of the grounds had alarmed her.

He was scrambling for shells.

"Bruce...?"

"Did you ever look at these," he said grabbing the photo of Cabot, Suzanne and Corey.

She looked confused. She didn't know what he was talking about.

"Why are you dressed like that," she asked.

He pushed the photo into her hands and went back to pulling open drawers for the shells.

She looked down at the faces looking back at her.

"It's not your mother…you thought that was her the whole time didn't you," he ran to the desk and started pulling out more drawers.

She looked closer…and finally saw.

"Oh my God."

"Didn't you ever wonder," he said loudly.

It didn't surprise him that she had tried to reach through her clothes at the charm that tangled from the chain around her neck.

His memory kicked in and he remembered where the Judge hid the shells and ran over to the book case. Books came flying off the shelves as he searched until he found the box he was looking for and loaded the gun and stuffed as many as shells as he could into his pockets.

He set the gun down and grabbed the photo of Cabot and his wife.

"Your father killed her," he said waving the picture of her parents in front of her and pointed at her mother, "Because she wasn't her."

"No," she creaked in disbelief.

"Didn't you ever wonder why only you, your father and Corey have green eyes…and no one else in this family does. And, why do you all have reddish hair?"

Kathlyn started to sob and looked up at him.

"No," she said between her gritted teeth.

"Why was Charlotte MacGregor always…always in the background?"

She looked back at the photographs.

"You never wondered…because you never wanted to know."

He stormed out through the door and almost ran into Paul.

"Did you know what you were covering up when you made that phone call and served as a false witness," he asked the butler.

Paul took a measured breath stepped back for Bruce to get through.

"That," he said dryly, "was not what I agreed to."

Bruce ran as fast as he could across the grounds, leaving Kathlyn to trail.

He could hear a commotion in the back and slowed for a second to confirm it was Corey he could hear shouting.

He decided quickly that his best move was through the cottage.

The front door was unlocked and could see through the rear windows that Corey was standing and yelling at someone, but he couldn't see who. Bruce approached slowly and leaned left and right so he could confirm his suspicions.

Corey was brandishing a gun.

The other person had to be Cabot or Judge Frost.

He went down the small hallway that led to the study. He peeked around the door jamb and saw the French doors to the backyard were open.

He heard the Judge's voice...almost pleading.

"Corey."

"You knew and did nothing," Corey yelled.

As he entered the room, Bruce heard Kathlyn enter and come up behind him. She entered the room and stared at him and then started to walk by him when she heard the argument, but he quickly grabbed her just as she passed him and pulled her back. He put his finger up to her lips and she nodded her head. She looked through the doors, but Bruce knew she couldn't see anything from where she was standing.

"You covered up for him," they heard Corey yell.

Bruce could hear the anguish in his voice as he slowly made his way to the doors.

"We're both your sons and yet you gave him everything and gave me nothing and you let him take everything from me!"

Bruce turned and looked at Kathlyn.

The look on her face answered any doubts he may have had about her knowledge of the family.

She had no idea.

Bruce felt like he was back in the war leaning left and then right so he could get a better view of what was going on. Suddenly, something in the way Corey moved made him step out with the gun aimed and pointed at Corey.

"Drop the gun Corey. It's over."

Corey stood to Bruce's right and to his left, behind him was Judge Frost – slumped and terrified on the ground. A few feet further stood Cabot.

Even in the sun, at a quick glance, Bruce could tell he was pale. Bruce could also tell that he had pissed himself which would have given Bruce some satisfaction if he wasn't concerned about the situation at hand.

"And you," he hissed at Bruce, "She wouldn't let us near you. You don't know," Corey started to argue.

"I do know," Bruce stated.

Kathlyn stepped out.

"Daddy," she screamed as she started to run towards Cabot.

"Kat," Bruce yelled, keeping his aim on Corey.

"Kathlyn," he heard the Judge say and he heard Kathlyn stop by him.

"Uncle Charles," she said bewildered.

Corey snickered.

"Corey, drop the gun," Bruce said again.

"You don't understand. You don't know."

"But I do...I do understand...and I do know. I know. I know what he's done...just like my father knew."

Cabot hadn't moved.

He saw the Judge try to move and he waved him and Kathlyn to stay.

"I know," Bruce repeated.

"I loved her," Corey cried.

"I know."

Corey's resolve started to waver.

"But she was your cousin. They weren't going to let you marry."

"We didn't care."

"But people would have figured out eventually...and they would have talked."

"I never asked for anything...just this one tiny thing after everything he covered up for him...he wouldn't do this one thing for me."

Cabot started to hyperventilate.

"I was supposed to be on duty. I was supposed to find her. He wanted me to see what he had done," he said refocusing his aim at Cabot.

"She never wanted you," he screamed at Cabot.

"Corey, I know...that's why you got sick in the morgue...that's why you came to our house...my father knew," Bruce said trying to bring him to reason and it seemed to work as he saw the tension in Corey's shoulders ease.

"He let him," Corey said suddenly waving his gun in the direction of Judge Frost and Kathlyn. Bruce stepped between them.

"She loved you, not him. Is this how she would want to see you," Bruce asked him.

"You gave him everything...and you left me...you left me with that man who beat me and you did nothing," Corey blubbered at no one, but Bruce knew who he was talking to.

"Corey, I know," Bruce said. "It's over," he tried to reason with Corey. "Do you really think he is going to let Cabot ruin his name...take everything he's worked for become a joke? He'll throw him to the sharks in a heartbeat...just like he did to you."

"It'll never be over."

His eyes glazed over.

"Corey, he won't get Cabot out of this one. I'm not the only one who knows about this. The tub in The Agate Club's basement has been found. Her blood, fingernails and hair were stuck to the drain. I have proof that the girl was Suzanne. People will remember and start to talk."

He had said too much.

Corey smiled.

He slowly looked at Bruce.

"I'm sorry," he said quietly, "I will still have nothing...but I do know how I can win."

Bruce knew what was going to happen before he could react.

"NO," he yelled and lunged for Corey.

In one smooth and quick motion Corey raised the gun to his head and squeezed the trigger. The bang resonated over the cliff as Corey's body crumbled to the ground.

"No, no, no," the Judge said as he crawled to Corey. "No, my boy...my poor sweet boy."

It was the first time Bruce had ever seen the Judge emotional.

Judge Frost picked up Corey's upper body, cradled it and rocked back and forth. Bruce noticed that the man didn't care that his son's brains and blood were getting over his pristine white shirt.

It was probably the first time the man had ever held Corey.

"Shhh, Daddy will make it better," he said into Corey's hair, "I'm so sorry."

"Daddy," Bruce heard Kathlyn say.

Bruce walked towards father and son and knelt down.

"Daddy," Kathlyn said again.

Bruce could feel someone walking closer to him as he put his hand on Judge Frost's shoulder.

"Judge."

The Judge turned and looked at him.

"I couldn't...," was all he could say.

"I know."

"With their mother who she was...I wanted a future for them."

"I know," and then he took a deep breath. "When did the boys know?"

"Cabot followed John to the club when he was little. He heard us talking. He told Corey. That's why he resented your father – he was someone Charlotte and I could treat as a son where we could be together."

"Suzanne."

"I don't think she ever knew. She just went wherever the boys did, but she knew they all belonged together."

The Judge tried to run his fingers through Corey's bloody hair.

"I wanted everything for him. He was the one who was good, and you," he said with distain at Cabot, "I had to clean up every one of your messes. You thought it was for you...it was for him. Everything I ever did was for him. I would have taken Tom over you if she would have let me. You fucking good for nothing..."

"Father," Cabot croaked in disbelief.

Bruce went to reach for Corey's gun.

He had forgotten about the gun.

Click.

"Cabot," Judge Frost said.

"Corey's right – you will make me pay for having a whore as a mother. You're going to make me pay for all of this while you get to go back to your cozy lifestyle untouched. I refuse to be left paying for your mistakes."

His gaze was fixated on the Judge and then he slowly turned to Bruce.

"She should have been mine," Cabot seethed.

He raised the gun.

"Daddy," Kathlyn screamed.

There was a loud bang...

...and a scream...

...and then nothing.

Bruce walked outside and sat down on the steps of Corey's bungalow with the shotgun waiting for the police to arrive.

He knew Paul would have called them.

Exhausted, he sat there and thought.

His father had never favored any one of his siblings or self over the others.

He treated Bruce differently, because he was the oldest; Joe, because he was the youngest; Louis...because he had been sensitive; and, Alice...well, because she was the girl. Bruce never once felt that Tom would have ever sacrificed one over the other and he had always made it clear that they were to follow their own paths.

He was remembering that last night with Tom as he and Louis had sat across from each other and Tom explained how things could be set in motion without them having any knowledge, but those decisions would affect the rest of their lives.

Years before Charlotte MacGregor and her sister came to America in search of a dream and became two of the most prominent business women in San Diego.

But that wasn't enough to squelch their maternal needs.

So, they made the decision to keep any children.

Charlotte made a deal with her sons' father and the boys were taken as soon as they were born.

And one night changed it all and her niece was thrown in the bargain and her nephew to the wind. She would have taken care of her son, Bruce was sure of it, had she known what had happened to him.

All of that led him to this moment.

He heard the sirens blaring as they approached the main house.

Officers got out of their vehicles, but didn't draw their weapons...hell, it seemed as if they didn't know what to do at all.

Bruce handed the shotgun to the first officer to reach him and walked to one of the squad cars.

He gave them two things:

His statement and his badge.

They were surprised to find him in nothing but his board shorts and a t-shirt.

He also asked them to collect the vintage sniper rifles from the main house and to compare the ballistics against the ones from the murder of Captain John Moran and that "other" officer – his father and the photographs by the gun cabinet.

29.

THE LOST SON

Charles "Corey" Frost Hayes was laid to rest in a private ceremony on a Tuesday. The Frost family said it was just for respect for the family and it wasn't any one else's business to see, as his 'uncle', Charles Miller Frost, told the press.

There was no reason for the press to doubt him. He was an Associate Justice.

His "cousin" Senator Cabot Miller Moran was buried three days later.

Bruce attended both in support of Kathlyn, although she seemed not to notice or care.

He watched as the Judge mourned his sons, with Beatrice by his sides.

Charlotte was forced to mourn from the fringe, unable to say goodbye like a mother should.

Bruce glared at the Judge throughout the services until his sister elbowed him in the ribs.

His mother had chosen not to attend.

The Judge was very interested in Bruce and Alice though.

Like the creepy old spider, he walked up to them and put his arm around Bruce once the crowd started to dissipate.

"I'll meet you at the car," Bruce told Alice and nodded at her to move along.

"What are your plans now, Bruce?" The Judge asked.

Bruce looked around for Paul.

"I'm not sure...what are yours?"

"You know you can't prove anything," the old man whispered.

"Oh, but I can," Bruce said very calmly. "You see, besides all the new evidence, I have something that my father didn't have."

"And, what is that," the Judge said, calling his bluff.

He turned and looked the Judge in the eye.

"A police Captain and Chief that are not under your thumb."

The old man stumbled a little and regained his step.

"Cabot's and Corey's fingerprints were taken while they were in the morgue. They will be matched up to the prints that were found on Suzanne and the tub. You know which tub I'm talking about."

"It will destroy Kathlyn. Are you willing to do that?"

Bruce looked up and over at Kathlyn. He wasn't so sure he was that tenacious.

"Don't be so quick to spill the truth when it won't get you anywhere, Bruce. You're libel to nick a vein and spill your own blood in the process."

"Suzanne's body is being exhumed as we speak. The charm will tie one of the boys to her crime. But you're right, at this point what does it matter. Your legacy is dead...well," he said gesturing to the Judge himself, "Bradley Farnham will never recover and Kathlyn's fantasy has been destroyed...already."

The Judge just listened.

"I see at the museum they already have added to Cabot's knife collection. They pulled the blade in question, but added a note that it is being put into evidence for a suspected serial murder from the late twenties. That should pull in some more patrons."

The Judge nodded at Paul who came to help him.

"Ask your lovely mother what it means to sacrifice to protect the ones you love and to give them everything," he said before Paul reached them.

Bruce and Alice entered the house. Alice went into the kitchen and he heard her go out the screen door and start talking to Megan. He took off his coat and went to the closet to hang it up. As he took a small step in its doorway and his foot hit something. He looked down and saw a box he had never noticed and bent down and picked it up, took it into the kitchen and set it on the table.

He remembered it had been sitting on the table months before.

He grabbed himself a bottle of beer and went to the sink to open it. The sound of Alice laughing caused him to look out the window and saw his mother on her knees, fussing with some flowers while Alice stood next to her telling her something about the funeral. At least that's what Bruce thought she was saying. He turned and looked at the box.

It was a curious thing that drew him in and he walked around to the side of the table it was at, set the beer down and removed the lid.

He didn't have to pick up or look closely at the pages on top. He immediately knew exactly what they were...because he had the remaining ones in his father's folder.

They were the rest of the adoption papers that had been in Tom's possession the night he was killed. His blood still covered some of the words that Bruce already knew.

Cabot and Corey were the sons of Charlotte and Judge Frost.

The murdered girl had been their cousin Suzanne.

She had been adopted by the Phelps'.

He took a second and ran his fingers over the dark splatter before setting them aside.

Another, cleaner set of documents caught his eye. They seemed to be the deed to some property downtown.

Bruce was about to put the papers back, return the lid and save the contents for later when he saw the corner of a photograph. He pulled it out and recognized it belonged to the photos he had from his father's file.

It was the picture of Suzanne's hands.

What was it doing here?

And, he remembered the folder sitting on his father's desk that night he talked to him.

He looked at the photo…and then looked again…and then closer…and then saw what Megan must have seen all those years before.

He looked at his own hands.

Only he and Joe had inherited Tom's family trait…a trait Tom had inherited from his mother.

Behind the photo the rest of the paperwork Tom had received from the record's clerk was there.

Papers Tom never saw.

Bruce looked around where he stood and realized where his mother had received the money to support them.

He grabbed the property deed again and looked at the address.

Of course it would be passed on to him and Alice.

He suddenly felt light-headed and vomited a bit in his mouth. He clenched his fist and with it the photograph and court documents.

Slowly he walked through the kitchen and pieces of conversations ran through his mind, the weight of his feet seeming to gain with every step.

He flung the screen door open and trod down the steps outside towards Megan and Alice with each foot step feeling heavier as he got closer.

"Bruce what is it," Alice asked, "What's happened, you look horrible."

Meg turned and Bruce saw the color drain from her face as she saw the photo and papers crumpled in his hand. She slumped back and the tears immediately started to well up in her eyes.

"Did he know," he croaked. "Did Daddy know?"

She shook her head, "No."

"Mom," Alice said, confused.

"I wanted to tell him, but I didn't know how."

"Bruce, what's going on," Alice wanted to know.

"Tell her," he said to Megan.

Megan started to sob and Alice bent down to comfort her.

"Tell her," he yelled.

She shook her head violently.

"Bruce, stop it! What do you want her to tell me? Mom, what is it?"

Megan looked up at him. She looked so tired. He now knew what the Judges' parting words had been about.

"The case I've been working on...the one Daddy had been working on..."

"No," Megan pleaded.

Alice nodded.

Megan couldn't look at him.

"The victim, Suzanne Phelps, she was his sister."

"What?!"

"Charlotte MacGregor didn't just hide her children in plain sight she hid her sister's as well...didn't she Mother?"

Megan slumped over with Alice's arm around her and slowly began to nod.

"That's where all the money came from, that's why the Judge always took such an interest and why Charlotte was always in the background."

"Stop it," Megan demanded.

"Everything...has been a lie!"

"Bruce!"

"Charlotte had to know you knew...the whole family did."

He shook the contents of his fists at her.

"You blackmailed them!"

"Bruce what are you saying," Alice was now demanding to know.

She couldn't talk.

"That's why there are no photos of him at the ranch. That's why Nana beat him. He was Poppa's son...by another woman...not because he was lazy. And Judge Frost struck a deal with her. Oh, she was always a shrewd woman. That's why she thought that Daddy owed it to the family to save Juneau and Sylvestre...because they had kept his secret. Daddy was all he could give back to her...to Charlotte. The Frosts paid for everything, didn't they? That's what grandfather meant that they hadn't paid for our educations Alice...because the Frosts and Charlotte MacGregor had. I always wondered why you never had to work."

Alice had leaned back away from Megan.

"Mom?"

"Kathlyn's our cousin. That's why you all tried to keep her away from us."

"Mom," Alice demanded and started to cry.

She looked up at Bruce.

"Bruce," she sobbed.

"Daddy was the missing boy from the Robin's Nest," he knelt down to Megan, "wasn't he?"

Across the city in her Banker's Hill home, Charlotte MacGregor stood in her living room, sipping the drink she had made, staring at her photographs, waiting...for Bruce.

She had just cranked the old Victorola and put on an old clay record...the one that played the night she summoned Tom after he and Cabot had fought in the alley.

She knew it wouldn't take Bruce long to put the pieces into place.

And, she knew what pieces would need to be filled - pieces she would have to dig out from where she had buried them in her mind.

She ran her fingers over Tom's photo as if she could still run her finger along his jaw line and lift his head as she had so many times before.

She would tell Bruce that as a three-year-old boy his father sat in his mother's room playing with his little sister when his father returned to the Robin's Nest drunk and belligerent to claim what was "his". Tom watched as his father beat his mother to death, scooped the toddler up and forced his way down the hall and out the front doors.

The only other thing Charlotte knew from the Robin's Nest girls was the little boy had screamed for his sister who was found sitting on the floor by their mother bawling in her mother's blood.

Suzanne.

She ran her fingers over the frames of the others...and then stopped at the photograph Tom had so intently looked at that night in her room.

She picked up the photo, held it to her chest, walked to her chair and sat down and stared into the face of her sister.

It had taken her years to get the courage to ask Charlie to find him. After all, he had taken their sons from her and her niece.

He at least owed her this one request.

As she sat there her mind started to drift back...and she remembered.

She remembered standing at the top of the staircase looking over the floor of The Agate Club one night, surveying her domain. She caught Charlie's eye. He smiled and nodded towards the bar and she turned and looked down towards the bar and saw him staring with his mouth gaped open.

Her heart skipped and she smiled to herself as his mouth snapped shut.

Even if he had not been the only boy there she would have known him immediately. He had her sister's eyes, her chin...her nose. And, there was something in the eyes. Her heart began to race as she walked down the stairs and closer to him. He never broke eye contact.

She reached out and put her hand on his cheek.

"And, who are you," she asked, trying to be casual and glancing at his hands on the bar.

And, she saw it.

He started to pull his hands off and she grabbed one of them and ran her thumb over his crooked finger.

A family trait neither of her boys inherited, but both of her sister's children had. She almost started to cry, but kept her composure.

"Thomas S. Rubidoux."

"Thomas S., is it?" She smiled even more, "And what does the 'S' stand for?"

"Sebastian."

Her father's name.

She let go of his hand and moved her hand until his chin was cradled by her index finger and thumb, studied him and leaned.

"Well, Thomas S. Rubidoux, do you know how to keep a secret?"

"Yes, Ma'am, I do," he had said slowly.

She smiled and slowly had let her hand glide away from his chin as she straightened up and tried not to cry.

"Yes, I believe you do."

www.ingramcontent.com/pod-product-compliance
Lightning Source LLC
Chambersburg PA
CBHW020331180626
46812CB00001B/143